AN URGENT MURDER

AN URGENT MURDER

ALEX WINCHESTER

Matador
9 Priory Business Park,
Wistow Road, Kibworth Beauchamp,
Leicestershire. LE8 0RX
Tel: 0116 279 2299
Email: books@troubador.co.uk
Web: www.troubador.co.uk/matador
Twitter: @matadorbooks

ISBN 978 1789014 969

British Library Cataloguing in Publication Data.
A catalogue record for this book is available from the British Library.

Printed and bound by CPI Group (UK) Ltd, Croydon, CR0 4YY
Typeset in 11pt Adobe Garamond Pro by Troubador Publishing Ltd, Leicester, UK

Matador is an imprint of Troubador Publishing Ltd

This book is dedicated to all the Police personnel who still believe in and strive to abide by the principles as laid down by the founder of the Police himself, Sir Robert PEEL.

The primary object of an efficient Police is the prevention of crime: the next that of detection and punishment of offenders if crime is committed. To these ends all the efforts of Police must be directed. The protection of life and property, the preservation of public tranquillity, and the absence of crime, will alone prove whether those efforts have been successful, and whether the objects for which the Police were appointed have been attained.

Prologue
The End?

He had planned to die peacefully and painlessly in his own bed at a time of his choosing. Not lying face down in front of his fireplace in agony with the sole of a shoe resting on the nape of his neck gently holding him in place as his convulsions grew. The pain was coursing through his body and he felt the throbbing in his head growing stronger. His pupils were dilated, his eyes wide open, watery and staring unseeingly at the fireplace. Slowly they closed as the excruciating pain shut everything down and he drifted into a merciful unconsciousness.

It was to be a short respite. He came to and was immediately aware of the torture being inflicted upon his body by the small amount of ingested poison. A groan escaped his throat. No one heard. The foot had left his neck some minutes earlier. His hazy eyes alighted on a small pocket diary covered in dust from years gone by that was lodged under the electric fire that stood on the hearth. An arm appeared in his eye line reaching for it. A Herculean effort considering his discomfort.

They had to pay for the torment he was going through. They had to pay. Fighting the pain, his hand slowly inched towards the diary. Latching onto it with his little finger he watched, as if an outsider, as he dragged it back towards his face. He pulled the small pencil from the diary freeing its pages which flipped open spraying dust into the air. Focusing hard on the page from about 6 inches, he attempted to write. A short black squiggle appeared on the virgin page. Too much exertion! The pain was growing and starting to rack his body with intensifying impulses. Twisting his torso, he lifted his arm and dropped it onto a flat stone slab breaking the pencil in half.

His body started to jerk in uncontrollable spasms. As he lay there, the pain seemed to envelop him. Thoughts flew through his mind of how it had come to this. Not much longer. It had been a good life. Ups and downs like everyone else. Would he be remembered? He passed willingly into unconsciousness for the second time.

Liberation!

1

The Beginning

George was very slightly built. Those who had passed him by in the street and noted the hang of his clothes often thought he looked emaciated, but they were unkind. The previous war with its lack of food had taken a toll on all it touched, especially the pregnant. Some war babies were taking longer to thrive than others. 'A great war to end all wars' was how it had been promoted. Even the most uneducated realised they may have been conned. As the second war loomed, and rationing was on the horizon, it was even harder to build up weight. Accepted, his facial features were drawn and collected shadows in some lighting, but it was more the norm to be thin than fat.

George had suffered dreadfully from asthma since birth and had often collapsed when under acute stress. His parents had blamed the constant smog that had enveloped London as industries and transport had begun to burgeon without consideration for the inhabitants. Then again, health issues were not a priority when profit and progress were the order of the day. As he had grown, he had managed most of the time to keep it under control.

Charity was the supplier of most of George's clothes, and his objective was always to grow into them. He had tried. His parents had done all they could putting as much food on the table as they could afford. They were proud of their son who in turn was immensely proud of his parents, and would do anything for them. When he began teaching, his Mother took great pride in letting all and sundry know that he was not a manual worker, but someone who used his brain for the benefit of others. Then she would fold her arms and her chest would puff out like a preening pigeon awaiting a cooing response. Woe betide anyone who did not comply!

England had lost many of its prime young men to the ravages of the first world war. Yet most who returned were fiercely loyal to the throne, as they had seen the righteousness of their course rewarded whatever their commanders had said or done. Those left at home had remained patriotic and supportive as the war had ebbed and flowed. The older survivors now watched with trepidation as the second world war seemed to become an inevitability as would the deaths of millions more young men. The majority of the young watched with impending fear that it was their turn to step forward and stand up to tyranny. Some with unrestrained bravado relished the fact that they would acquit themselves valiantly on the field of battle and others saw it as a point of duty. George was amongst them. All believed sincerely that whatever happened, they would survive.

At the outbreak of war, George, against his Mother's wishes, had immediately responded to the call to arms and had gone to the recruiting office with the honest intention of signing up. Cyril had served with distinction during the first war and was now the sergeant recruiting officer. Some questions posed by potential recruits he answered straightforwardly as if their surrogate Father, but mainly he embellished his replies in order not to put anyone off. He watched George enter from the street. No one had been rejected at his office, and he could see that George was going to be a challenge.

He appeared skeletal with a deathly sallow complexion and his short mousey hair looked lank and lifeless against his sunken features. Shaking visibly because of his nerves, he tried to enlist for what he believed was his patriotic duty to serve his country in a just cause. He collapsed. A medic who was present soon realised it was no pretence, and that was George, out of the war.

2

Saturday 14th December 1940

There are days in everyone's lives that people seem unable or unwilling to forget, whether they want to or not. They can remember detail in minutiae. George seemed to know this more than most even though it is different for everyone. It could be a religious occurrence depending on one's faith, a challenge overcome, a birth or death, or even some pointless minor event. He had had a few of these days already. Trying to put them out of his mind was futile. They were there and going to stay there forever. One such day was just prior to Christmas, in December of 1940. George remembered it as though it were yesterday. Saturday 14th. He could recall everything he had done and said from the time he heard the first birds chirruping in the morning to: well when he fainted.

During an air raid on the docks of East London, a large mine had landed at the entrance to the purpose-built shelter he and his parents had constructed at the bottom of their garden. It was their retreat from the little terraced house they had lived in for some 18 years prior to the outbreak of war. His Father, a Docker for his entire working life knew that any stray bomb aimed at the docks was likely to hit one of the hundreds of similar homes that were scattered around the East End and Essex. So, with George's occasional indifferent help, he had spent the first months of the war reluctantly digging into his prized vegetable patch and laying the concrete foundations on which he put an Anderson shelter. Then he laboured alone feverishly covering it with sandbags and tons of earth. He thought his family would be safe. Technically he was right. Even if a bomb had landed right on top of it, those inside would have probably been shielded from the resultant explosion. But it didn't land on top of it, it landed at the entrance.

The first wailing of the air raid siren had sent his Father and Mother scurrying from the back door of the house. Quickly traversing the winding garden path that led between some hoary, but productive fruit bushes they descended into the shelter. They had made it as comfortable as possible. Two worn out old fireside chairs and several threadbare blankets that George's Mother had no other use for. A single Tilly lamp swung from some twine that had been affixed to the arched roof and a rickety upturned box, which had been purloined from the dockside, supported an old primus stove in one corner. This was essential in order that they could make a pot of tea and wait for the all clear: which this day they would never hear.

George was at the market making some small purchases for the minimal preparations he and his family could afford for Christmas under war conditions. Like all those about him, he had run for cover at the sound of the first siren. The same one that had sent his parents scuttling to their shelter. George knew, like most people in the area where the safest place was. He soon plunged into the entrance of the underground station surrounded by several hundred others all with the same intention of reaching the lowest point which was the station's platform. A giant air raid shelter in all but name.

Although he had lived in the area for such a long time, George had no real friends, nor for that matter, many acquaintances. His parents' friends became people he knew, but that really was as far as it went. As he looked about the platform, he recognised several people, but didn't have the confidence to speak to them or even give a polite nod. He found a small space by the wall at the rear of the platform near the mouth of the tunnel furthest from the entrance stairs. Sitting down with his back against it, he let thoughts of the future drift into his head. His eyes slowly glazed over shutting out the movement of everyone around him, and his ears closed to the hubbub that several hundred people caused when they were crammed so tightly together.

The parachute mine didn't detonate as it should have done at about 40 feet from the ground. Nor did it immediately explode on impact. It's 25 second delay failsafe detonation kicked in. It bounced on the concrete path into the sunken entrance of the shelter slamming into the door before coming to rest. Hearing the loud noise, and believing George had arrived home and wanted to get into the shelter swiftly, his Father unlatched the door just as the mine exploded. Both his parents were dead in the blink of an eye. They didn't suffer or even know they were going to die. One minute they were happily chatting over the kettle which had yet to boil, and then they were no more: incinerated by the mine.

George didn't actually hear the all clear, but was brought out of his musings by the people about him all moving off in one direction. Rising from the safety of the seat he had by the wall, he brushed imaginary dust from the back of his trousers and sauntered slowly towards the exit. Joining the rear of the horde, he queued patiently awaiting his turn to climb the stairs to leave the underground in order to resume his hindered activities. He had most of what his Mother had asked him to get, but was desperate to see if he could find some fruit. Nothing. No one had any. Dawdling slowly, he made his way down the street towards the terraced house he had called home for the last 18 of his 20-year life.

Both his parents, he knew, would have got to the shelter at the first drone of the siren. He wasn't unduly worried as he had spent time in the shelter himself and liked to believe he had helped his Father construct it. That's what he wanted to believe although he knew his Father had done at least 95% of the actual work. He knew it was as safe as possible as they had dug it deep and covered it well. As he sauntered towards his house he could see a few of the neighbours standing huddled on the pavement outside the front door. One of them, who was looking in his direction, saw him coming, and within seconds, all the others turned to watch him approach. George began to worry. The house was still standing there between other identical terraced houses; no sign of any destruction that he could see.

Still, he quickened his pace anyhow, and reached his front door as a neighbour uttered the dreaded words, "I am so sorry".

Within seconds, George had been told his parents were dead and that there was a worry he had been with them in the shelter. The lights went out for George as he collapsed on the threshold of his little home.

3

Friday 4th April 1941

George had never been late for anything in his whole life. Even arriving in the world a day before the prescribed time to his happy Mother in the house that his parents had shared with his widowed Grandmother in Stratford. He wasn't going to be late or miss the train either. The early, and final departure from his parent's small council house to reach the station on time was not delayed even by the incessant wailing of air raid sirens. Wistfully, he looked back twice as he left the house he had called home. In the distance, he saw the tops of the dockyard cranes that often appeared to him to be dancing, albeit to sundry tunes. They were still now. The sirens ensured that. Barrage balloons appeared to be drifting aimlessly amongst the frothy white clouds in the tranquil sky. Not a plane in sight!

George stood on the platform with his two battered suitcases standing upright on the floor, one either side of him, together containing all his worldly goods. There was at least another 20 minutes to wait. After the death of his parents, George had decided to give up his job teaching infants in the East End and seek employment a long way off where he could start life afresh. Littlehampton, which his parents had once taken him to as a child, was on the coast and seemed the perfect place. The air would do him good and the war, he hoped, would be a long way off.

The train steamed backwards into the station slowly pushing its four carriages towards its allotted platform. As it reached the shelter of the vaulted station roof, the steam it was emitting started to pervade the platform's length. Large sections at a time were obscured as it puffed effortlessly at regular intervals. One of the clouds of steam obliterated George's view of the locomotive itself, leaving just the four coaches eerily moving slowly as if by themselves. George had been the first to arrive on the platform, but it was busy now with people saying their farewells to friends and relatives – not knowing if they were to ever see them again.

'Where are they all going?' thought George.

As it was the only train that week, everyone who needed to travel had only the one choice and they were unquestionably going to be on that train. They had their tickets and travel documents for wherever they were going. It could have been any one of the stations the train was due to pass as it wended its way around the southern countryside of England on its journey to Portsmouth.

George clambered into the last but one carriage, struggling with his two suitcases in the process, and moved down the corridor past the second-class, and into a third-class compartment with six empty seats. It was probable, he realised, that others would come in after him, so he didn't bother closing the sliding door to the corridor running the full length of the carriage. As he struggled to lift his suitcases one at a time onto the overhead luggage racks, he found his booked seat which was by the window.

When he had booked it, he had stipulated to the rather belligerent woman in the ticket booth that he wanted to sit by the window facing the way of travel so if he saw anything interesting he could turn to watch it passing.

Before he had settled, a tall, well-proportioned man stepped into the compartment. George glanced at him before turning quickly to look out of the window. He didn't want to make eye contact as he often felt embarrassed if he thought he would be caught looking. The reflection in the window revealed the newcomer to be with a small child who had followed quickly behind him into the compartment. George got the impression straight away that he seemed to be irritated by the presence of the child accompanying him. Taking another sly peek at the man, George saw he was only in his very early twenties wearing a nice three-piece suit and matching tie. He was carrying a small attaché case in one hand with a coat over the same arm and a suitcase similar to George's in his other hand. He had neat, short, smart black hair and a very slightly tanned skin. His eyes were blue and George thought that he saw them twinkle and everything he observed about him exuded confidence.

"How do you do?" the man said, "I am sorry about Jean, she will be quiet so you don't have to worry."

"Oh" said George, starting to turn a very slight shade of crimson, embarrassed now that he had been spoken to. "Alright thank you, yourself?"

"Truthfully, I could be better if I didn't have to act as escort for her" as he nodded in Jean's direction. "I have important work in Portsmouth and did not want to be saddled with her."

"Oh" said George again.

If he had actually been truthful, he may have said that he was going to stay with a woman he was having a casual affair with when he went to Portsmouth on regular business for the war office. He had only got the job after managing to avoid the draft by claiming and feigning some unknown illness. His wife had insisted that he took their only child to stay with a relative of hers outside Fishbourne where she thought Jean would be safest. Living in such close proximity to the aerodrome at Hendon was getting too dangerous as it was becoming a regular target for the Luftwaffe. On several occasions they had missed with their bombs and hit homes in the area. They had to drop their bombs from a greater height than they wanted due to the barrage balloons that enveloped London.

"The name's Archie" and he put out his hand.

"George" and he took it and gave it a couple of flaccid shakes before releasing it as though he may have caught something.

For some reason, George also now seemed to ignore the child which, had he thought about it, was very unusual for a teacher of infants. Jean who was probably only about 4 or 5 was very quiet and sat opposite George looking out of the window at the steam rolling around the platform. George felt obliged to tell Archie he was going to teach Mathematics at Littlehampton Boys' School.

"Say no more George, remember the poster, Walls have ears" and then Archie tapped his nose with his left index finger a couple of times.

George started to return to his crimson shade of embarrassment. He began to stutter and said, "Oh I don't think it's a secret or anything" but realised immediately that Archie probably did not care and did not want to know.

In fact, Archie pulled a newspaper out of his maltreated looking attaché case before swinging it onto the luggage rack after his suitcase and coat. George observed as Archie unfolded the paper, that it had not yet been opened or read and the creases were as though ironed in with starch they were so sharp. Accepting that the formalities had been complied with, George realised that Archie was now no longer to be engaged in conversation.

4

Friday 4th April 1941

As the station clock struck a muted seven the train's whistle sounded as the guard, now installed in the last carriage, waved his green flag vigorously out of an open window. The sleek black locomotive puffed a few extra times as it took up the slack of the four carriages. Then it strained a little more as it started slowly to pull them behind it as it moved off and away from the shelter of the station. Jean saw the steam which had at times obscured the platform suddenly become free and climb into the open sky as the train gathered speed. She didn't understand why she was on the train nor did she care because it was a new experience for her.

One thing though had confused her earlier when she was ready and waiting to leave home was why her Mother had hugged her and hung onto her for such a long time crying convulsively. It was something that she wasn't used to. If she was lucky, she would normally have got a quick peck on the cheek as her Mother always seemed to have very little time for such frivolities. Her Father who appeared desperate to leave and was gradually getting more and more aggravated by the delay, finally prized them apart.

Pushing a small brown artificial leather bag into Jeans hands saying, "Don't lose it" he ushered her out of the front door.

Jean knew better than to do something her Father told her not to do. She may have been very young, but it hadn't stopped him using his belt on her in the past.

Her hands clutched the bag's handles which she held on her lap not daring to let go of for a second. The train gathered its momentum and the sound of the carriage's wheels on the rails settled into a pleasant rhythm. Jean was glued to the window watching the conurbation surrendering to the countryside. Blue sky above with white billowing clouds that grew thicker the further South the train travelled cast large galloping shadows across the landscape. Occasionally, hefty plumes of steam would hurtle past the window in ghostly forms.

Other passengers with tickets for the same compartment seeking peace and quiet had approached, but on seeing the young child and fearing a disruptive journey, had moved on past seeking solace and an empty seat in an all adult compartment. Archie slid the door to, and settled down to read the Daily Sketch which he had purchased from the old man seated in the dilapidated and depleted bookstall on the platform.

George started to panic fearing he may have lost some of his important papers from within his securely buttoned up inside jacket pocket. He knew in his heart that he hadn't, but he felt compelled to look. Quickly unbuttoning the pocket, he removed his Identity card, travel permit and the item he treasured most; the letter confirming his position as a teacher at the Littlehampton Boys' School with full responsibility for the mathematics department. He didn't know he had been the only qualified Mathematics teacher available who had applied for the post and was therefore guaranteed a successful outcome. Archie let his eyes drift slightly from his newspaper and saw all the documents held in George's bony hands as he studiously checked each of them before returning them to their sanctuary inside his jacket pocket. Of course, he could not resist the urge to re-read the letter for the umpteenth time prior to replacing it in his pocket.

George was happier today than he had been since that fateful day the previous year.

The train plodded slowly around the countryside from one station to the next sporadically disgorging passengers who all appeared to have someone waiting for them. A few people got on, but still avoided the compartment believing the young child was going to be a disruptive element should they want a peaceful journey. Archie had soon read the paper, or as much as he was going to, and returned it to his small bag. He knew his papers were in his pocket and did not need to check or confirm the fact. From the same small attaché case, he took a little square lacquered wooden box which he opened to reveal a chess board and pieces. George could not help but admire its simplicity and beauty.

"Do you play?" said the confident baritone voice of Archie as he set the pieces on their correct squares.

"Yes, but I am not too good," lied George.

"Well nor am I but it will help pass the time if you fancy a game?"

George loved chess and was a keen amateur only ever playing his parents or their acquaintances, and reading books on the subject. Something gave him an inkling that Archie was also a respectable player. Neither was going to admit how good they were in case of defeat. Whoever lost would be able to use the excuse that they weren't very good and pride would be deflected in the fact they neither would be likely to meet again. Chess was George's one strong point and was the only thing that gave him real confidence. He moved along a seat to sit opposite Archie and battle commenced after the ritual of who was to be white.

5

Friday 4th April 1941

That morning at about the same time as George was leaving his parents modest council house for the last time, Kurt was leaving his billet in the northern town of France that he had found himself posted to some months earlier and had come to calling home. It was comfy though, an ancient chateau owned by a noble aristocratic family and occupied by them for six generations. Preceding Kurt's and his colleagues' arrival, and unknown to them, the old lady who had been the sole incumbent for the previous five years had been told to leave as the building was required for the German army. She did not need to be told twice, and left within three hours the same day and moved in with an accommodating friend. Kurt was a pilot in the Luftwaffe and he and his comrades, seven at the end of their last sortie, were the new occupants. All believed in their cause, although not necessarily in the Nazi ideal.

They were in good spirits having had a better breakfast than probably any indigenous Frenchman, and were joking together in the back of the antiquated lorry that had collected them. Fumes from its exhaust, which were probably as lethal as any bombs they dropped, polluted the atmosphere along the regular route. Stuttering and backfiring occasionally the lorry just about managed the one and a half kilometres to the briefing room at the local air field that was now for their sole use. Kurt was a reasonable pilot as were his comrades, but not considered good enough to be fighter pilots though some believed they were. In the briefing room already seated were seven other crew members who were the navigators/bomb aimers. All billeted in a different building as their status was below that of the pilot even though they formed part of a close integral team. Each pilot took a seat next to their navigator.

As they were addressed by their commander, their mood darkened as he appraised them of the day's activity: an attack on an airfield on the South Coast of England. An old Fleet Air Arm Airbase called Ford. They had all been there before and were not too worried about it because the defences were poor. What did worry them was that it was very close to Tangmere, a base for British fighters, and mainly Hurricanes at that. The briefing officer knew it would dishearten his men, but he had one piece of news that he believed would help no end, which he saved for the briefings conclusion. He paused before announcing that a large attack was to be launched by other members of the Luftwaffe from bases close to Calais and inside Germany itself on the port of London. All those in the room realised immediately that the British fighters would be sent from the Southern airfields to protect the capital. Spirits were lifted as the crews were sure they would get a relatively good trip. One thing the briefing officer did not tell them because he didn't know himself, was that the attack on the Port of London was to be a night time take off with the first wave of bombers due to strike at about 7.30am.

At 9.55am, Kurt and his colleagues started to take off and were all in the air and in formation within ten minutes and en route towards England. The cloud base was at about four thousand feet over the coast and quite thick. All the pilots noted this mentally in case they had to make a run for it or try and hide within it. Kurt loved flying, and had learnt when he was in his teens as his Father was quite well off and could afford to have him taught. Now in his early 20s he had lasted longer in the war than most of the other pilots of his generation because he was careful and didn't take chances. He knew that being in a fighter/bomber, he stood very little chance in a dogfight with a proper fighter; something that other pilots did not always grasp and suffered various fates accordingly. Kurt was a survivor, and his navigator was very happy with that. Beneath the clouds, the visibility was good and this helped Jochen get his bearings once the coast was sighted. They tried to keep just below the clouds as it protected them from prying eyes of anyone above.

Kurt stated the obvious to Jochen, "Coast visible ahead."

His navigation, (and leader's plane) had got him to where he wanted to be, and he could see the spire of the cathedral in the centre of Chichester to his Port side and the spire of St John's Church in Bognor to his right. There was a small inlet with little pleasure boats moored at Chichester, but it wasn't attacked as the spire was a perfect landmark for anyone flying in from France. He searched the countryside to the starboard and identified the castle turrets of Arundel way in the distance. From their lofty perch they could see clearly the pockmarked airfield of Tangmere and the relatively unscathed airfield of Ford. Kurt and Jochen had caused some of the devastation at and around the airfield at Tangmere and both looked down on their handiwork with some pride. Not necessarily that they had caused it but had got away unscathed. There was some anti-aircraft fire now exploding below them as the gunners on the ground tried to get the right altitude and gauge the speed of the planes. It was something that did not really worry Kurt as in all his time flying over England he was only aware of a couple of planes brought down by it.

From his leader came the garbled crackled message that the bombs they were carrying should be dropped on the runway itself, and to go straight in to attack in order that they would be as much of a surprise to the defenders as possible under the circumstances of their noisy arrival. Then to turn and strafe the buildings and any grounded aircraft before going home.

'Simple plans are always the best' thought Kurt as he lined up as the third plane to go into the attack. The first plane put a couple of large craters in the middle of the concrete runway and the second left two more craters about a third of the way down. Kurt lined up to drop his two bombs between them.

Jochen called his directions to Kurt and then, "Bombs gone," and Kurt pulled on his joystick lifting the plane back into the sky at an angle to avoid any fire from the ground.

They both strained to see where their bombs had landed, and could only see one crater just on the edge of the runway.

Kurt had known straight away because of the way the controls of the plane reacted, and Jochen checked his instruments and saw that they were still carrying one bomb which had not released. Both knew that they had a serious problem: it was relatively easy to take off with bombs on board, but to land with one that had been armed and ready to drop could be extremely dangerous. Over the radio the leader informed them that they had not dropped both bombs, and Kurt repressed the strong urge to say quite bluntly that they knew. Plane after plane attacked and left the runway unusable to anyone who wanted to land on it, although probably everyone in the attacking planes knew in their hearts that the runway would be patched up and back in use in a few days' time.

Jochen was trying desperately to release the obstinate bomb as the leader turned and started his first strafing run followed by his comrades before starting his dash back to the French airbase they called home. Kurt knew it was no good harassing Jochen who was doing his best to dump the offending bomb and climbed higher to get out of harm's way. Worst was to come for the six planes circling above Ford, who in their attack had failed to notice the returning squadron of Hurricanes making their way back to Tangmere from their early morning scramble to protect the capital. There should have been twelve in the squadron, but they had lost a friend that morning and they were in sombre mood when their attention was directed over Ford. All the Hurricanes were short on fuel, but there was no hesitation by any of them: the six German fighter/bombers had no chance to avoid the onslaught. Only one managed to escape into the clouds and hide from his pursuers before running for home. Kurt saw the Hurricanes diving on his comrades, but his shouted warning was far too late for five of them.

He climbed into the clouds weaving in case someone saw them and then heard Jochen say, "I think it's nearly free."

6
Friday 4th April 1941

Kurt said, "Just get rid of it, and let's go home." He had seen the Hurricanes and did not want to get involved with them.

"Climb and then dive and I'll drop it" to which Kurt pulled hard on the joystick forcing the plane skywards into the clouds. "Now dive," called Jochen and Kurt pushed forward and the plane lurched as it began to plummet towards earth now no longer fighting gravity but embracing its forces.

They burst through the cloud and Kurt saw a slow moving train pulling four carriages.

"Wait" he called and started to line up on the locomotive itself.

Jochen saw what he was doing, and looking through his sights, started to call the course corrections to Kurt. If the bomb released when it now should, it may not be wasted after all.

"Steady" called Jochen and Kurt maintained his dive towards the engine as the driver and the fireman on the footplate looked at the approaching plane with foreboding and a fear of impending doom.

"Now: bomb released" called Jochen, but it wasn't.

Jochen banged the release lever as hard as he could several times with his clenched fist in a fit of frustration. Finally, the bomb left the shelter of the plane as though reluctant to leave a secure home. Kurt was just starting to level out to climb again as the bomb dropped towards the train. The delay caused it to miss its intended target of the locomotive and smash through the wooden roof of the third carriage. It exploded with a deafening noise which turned into a massive fireball sending flames and smoke barrelling through the carriage. The immediate destruction ripped the carriage from the tracks and it seemed to slew slowly away from the rails dragging the fourth carriage with it.

Jean, who like most on the train had no idea of the impending doom about to strike, had been looking out of the window. She was blown right through it as both Archie and George were lifted from their seats and smashed around like peas in a pod before coming to rest in a crumpled heap on the floor. One of the cases that had been pitched about the compartment from the luggage rack was on fire and was close to the two bodies. The other items from the racks were scattered about and were in a volatile condition. Some of the fabric in the seats was smouldering and looking like it would fully ignite at any moment. Wooden slats in the carriage roof and sides were ablaze. A light breeze was fanning the flames, and the danger of the compartment bursting into an outright inferno was great. The majority of the carriage itself had been destroyed by the initial blast and the ensuing fire appeared to be destroying the rest.

Neither Kurt nor Jochen minded where the bomb had landed; they were just relieved that it had gone and they were relatively safe. Kurt swung the plane round and started to climb back towards the sanctity of the clouds not realising they had been spotted by two of the fighters who were now screaming after them. They soon knew when bullets and tracer rounds whistled past them getting closer and closer to the port wing. Kurt dodged and weaved and as he finally made the cloud turned hard to starboard and forced the plane to go as fast as was possible in the hope of escaping his dogged pursuers. Both the pilots of the Hurricanes realised he had an advantage in escaping now he had some of nature's camouflage but they weren't going to give up straight away.

Climbing through the clouds to emerge into clear blue sky and bright sunlight, the Hurricanes' pilots started a fast and frantic search for any tell-tale signs of the lone plane. Each aware they had to land urgently for fuel and to re-arm. Both were aware they had probably missed their one chance of downing the lone German aircraft.

Kurt knew he had to stay in the clouds and believed the Hurricanes would be circling above somewhere like predatory hawks searching for prey. He expected them to be looking in some form of pattern towards the coast which would be the logical route back to France. He had not stayed alive by doing the obvious and headed towards Chichester which would take him close by Tangmere. No one, he concluded would expect a lone German plane to fly past there, and he was right. Within 5 minutes he'd passed Tangmere and believed he could now afford to turn on a heading for France without being seen by the two Hurricanes. Both were actually now on the ground being hastily refuelled and re-armed. Slowly he brought the plane onto the correct course for home still keeping as best he could within the confines of the fluffy white clouds that had been his saviour. Jochen trusted Kurt and had hardly said a word but when they saw the coast of France, he could contain his glee no longer at surviving once more. Navigating straight back to the airfield he jumped down from the plane on landing and insisted on shaking Kurt's hand and promised him the best bottle of Champagne he could find in the local village.

7

Friday 4th April 1941

It didn't take long for help to start arriving at the train as the attack had been seen and reported by the pilots of the Hurricanes and a few witnesses on the ground. Dead passengers were lying where they fell, and some walking wounded were close by the train wandering about in a dazed state before being led to safer terrain by those not affected. Jean was lying on the ground some 15 yards from the train's burning third carriage with her small bag still clutched firmly in her tiny hands. The window she had gone through had been blown out by the blast a millisecond before her, and she had only superficial cuts to show for her unexpected and unorthodox means of departure from the compartment. Her internal organs had taken a shuddering jolt as well, and although shaken about, had not suffered any serious damage: but hitting the tree which she now lay beneath, had knocked her unconscious. She was not going to be seen for some time by the rescuers as the long couch grass that adorned the side of the tracks and around the tree concealed her tiny inert body.

There were small fires still burning in the remnants of the third carriage and the breeze had wafted embers onto the fourth carriage which was beginning to smoulder. Passengers from the last carriage had all escaped with minor bruises and had each thanked God in their various ways. Rescuers and the local fire brigade had arrived and were already attempting to put the pockets of fire out as bodies were pulled unceremoniously from the carriage and laid beside the stricken train. Dignity for the dead had to wait, speed was essential at that time, as some of the embers were starting to spread to the tinder dry grass next to the track. The locomotive had been uncoupled by the relieved driver and fireman from the footplate and moved further up the track out of harm's way in accordance with policy as locomotives were in short supply and had to be saved if at all possible.

Most of the passengers from the first two carriages who were not in shock, went to the aid of their fellow travellers in the third coach. It was a plump woman of about fifty years who looked like nothing would faze her, who went to sit under a tree to recover from her ministrations to the injured. She had been travelling in a first class compartment with her husband in the carriage directly behind the locomotive and was extremely thankful that it was not their carriage that had been hit.

She found Jean. She could not imagine why the little girl was there so far away from the train. Looking down at her, Winifred saw that the small child's eyes were wide open and staring, but they had no life to them. She bent closer. The little girl's hands twitched and tightened around the small bag that she was clutching to her chest.

"Hello. Who are you?" said Winifred in her matronly voice.

Jean just stared back, unblinking, and then began to shake slowly at first and then more violently. Winifred called to her husband who had just administered the last rites to some of the passengers on the ground by the train to bring a blanket quickly. Joseph knew that if his wife needed a blanket quickly there was a good reason. He looked round and saw a dark overcoat lying by the burnt and blackened door to the compartment next to where the mortally injured lay. Snatching it up in his large shovel type hands he rushed to his wife's side and saw Jean lying in the grass shaking violently. Winifred took the coat and started to wrap the small child in it as shock took a tougher grip on Jean. She began to softly wail, and then it turned to a high-pitched scream, and then to dry sobs. Winifred knew that shock could kill; she cuddled Jean and made as many reassuring noises as she could, hoping that the small child in her arms would not become another victim of the reluctant bomb.

8

1986 Angola

"We'll draw straws." Jackson surveyed the twenty-three dirty, grim faces that were all focused on him. "It's the fairest way" he added as if to explain his logic.

They all acquiesced and accepted his decision. He was right not to pick one. There had been twenty-five of them originally, but two had been lost in an ambush. To a man, they trusted him. He was Major Jackson to them, but had never been promoted past Captain. His men were from all parts of the United Kingdom and had all seen some action whilst in the employ of her Majesty's forces. They had been brought together some eighteen months previously by another man they believed they could trust. All assumed that what they had been asked to do had the sanction of her Majesty's Government. It had originally, although only by a handful of senior Government Ministers, and not one had ever committed anything to paper.

Something had now changed. There hadn't been a supply drop for three weeks. The rebels had known precisely where they were going to be. Two of their number were dead and they were lucky it hadn't been more. By sheer good fortune they had fought their way out of the ambush only because the rebels were disorganised and poorly led. Now they knew that they had been abandoned and someone was plotting against them. At least two hundred rebels had come together and were a day behind them, and now they had some good Cuban trained leaders. Even the booby traps that Jackson's men were leaving were being crashed through by the rebel column, killing a few at a time but not depleting their number or slowing them down sufficiently.

Jackson knew it was just a matter of time before the fire fight would ensue. Both he and his men appreciated they were completely outnumbered but were by no means dispirited. They had reached the summit of a hill where they would have a slight advantage. The rebels didn't seem to care if they died as long as they could destroy the British mercenaries and capture the Angolan Prime Minister and it made them all the more dangerous. Major Jackson believed that his men had a good chance due to their weaponry, skill and more to the point, professionalism.

"OK Piper. You've won. Get the man and go."

No one griped. It had been fair. They all returned to their positions and prepared for battle each in their own way. A couple even offered up a small prayer. Most settled down for a rest or had a bite to eat. Their weapons were primed and ready. It was going to be hard but they all believed they would prevail. The rebels knew where Jackson and his men were thanks to information being fed to them from London. They would wait an extra day for further reinforcements before surrounding the hill and mounting their attack. It was a day too late.

"Get him to the safe house and then get back to London. Find out what bastard has betrayed us and if you can, kill him. If you can't, find this copper," and he handed a piece of paper to Piper with a name on it, "and give him my name. We were at school together. He is the only person I trust right now. Be careful Paddy. Don't trust anyone else. Especially those slippery eels in the Foreign Office"

"It will take me sometime to reach Zimbabwe Major. I'll contact you from there."

"I hope so. You've got everyone's ring and coded details just in case."

"It's been a privilege to serve with you."

"Get going Paddy. We should be able to hold them off long enough to give you a couple of days start."

9

Monday 20th December 2010

"Hello Trevor."

"Is that you Graham?"

"Yes. Long time since we spoke."

"Must be getting on for a year now."

"What are you up to lately?"

"Usual. Couple of murders keeping me busy and a nasty little corruption enquiry. You?"

"Still deputy to the Commissioner and pushing paper from one side of my desk to the other."

"How's your handicap coming on?"

"That's what I was phoning about. You still a member at Goodwood?"

"Certainly am. When you thinking of?"

"Tomorrow? The weather's meant to be fine."

"I'm going to be busy in the afternoon. How about an 8.30 tee off?"

"You're on. See you then."

The click of the phone disconnecting seemed to echo round the office like a revolver being cocked. Prodow looked at it as he gently placed it back on its cradle. He scrutinised it as if expecting it to suddenly disclose some useful information.

'I wonder what that was all about?'

10

Monday 10th January 2011

"Yes?"

"We've got a problem."

"What?"

"Our man in the Police is due to retire in a year's time and at present there are two possible candidates."

"Go on. I'm listening."

"The Minister will be endorsing one called Daines: Graham Daines, should he apply. He's honest and would be dangerous to your operations. The other is called Harold Jacobs and would slot easily into the operation for the same fee as present."

"Any others?"

"Not likely."

"Your suggestion is?"

"It would be useful if Daines could be persuaded not to apply or withdraw if he does."

"There's an easier method."

"Problem with that is, they would have to put a serious investigation team onto it and it might come back to haunt you and then we are all in the shit."

"I'll speak to my man and see what we can come up with."

"I'll keep you updated with what's happening this end."

"Leave Daines to me. I'll sort it out."

"Be careful. He's been a problem before and he has some 'iffy' friends."

11

Sunday 1st May 2011

"Hello?"

"It's me."

"Oh."

"I haven't seen you for a while."

"The agency has been sending me all over the place."

"When will you be back?"

"I'm not sure. Probably later this week."

"I want it done then. The sooner the better."

"I'll see what I can do."

"Have you got the pills?"

"Yes."

"The last £1000 is waiting for you to do it."

"Right."

"You're not thinking of backing out? Nothing will be attributed to you."

"There's no problem. I'll do it next time I'm there."

"Good. See you soon. Bye."

"Bye."

The red dot in the phone's display indicating it was busy swiftly faded and died. She snapped the phone shut with a growing anger and stuffed it into her uniform pocket. Upstairs, she examined her made up face and coiffured hair in her medicine cabinet's mirror. Inside, tucked behind taller items was a small bottle marked 'Aspirin'. Its actual contents were a mixture of thirty-seven barbiturate and morphine tablets of varying strengths. She had stolen them from her other clients over the preceding months. Now she knew the time had come and she was frightened.

12

Friday 6th May 2011

Sam looked at the headlines on the front page of the local paper. Some dignitary banging on about a road widening scheme that had been mooted for the route between Bognor and Chichester. Campaigners bleating it would cause an eco-problem if it was approved. A report of a charity bus service being set up and begging for funds and the usual small, totally useless black and white photograph of some prisoner who had walked out of Ford open prison and forgotten to go back. Swimmers whingeing that there were jellyfish off the coast and the council should spend thousands clearing them away.

"This paper gets worse week by week. Why the hell do I buy it?"

"You like the local news" was the response from Chris who was busy in the kitchen, "Or that's what you told me."

Muttering sarcastically under his breath, "Yeah. Right" he picked up his coffee.

Sam hated the new format that the paper had adopted. It was now a small tabloid style; 'easier to hold and read' was how they'd justified changing it from a broadsheet. Opening the paper and trying to drink coffee at the same time still caused problems for Sam. One of the pages dropped a few inches. Putting his coffee on the side table, he shuffled the page back into its precise position and noticed a small paragraph with a heading, 'Local Man found dead'. In no more than six short lines, Sam learnt that George Armstrong had been found on the floor of his home with a piece of paper next to him with the word 'pois' written on it. Police were apparently treating the death as suspicious.

"My God! Of course it's bloody suspicious. This is what should be on the front page!"

Chris came into the room with the morning's mail.

"Any for me?"

"All of it today. Not one catalogue."

Sam dropped the paper onto the floor as he looked at the post before heading off to work.

13
Friday 3rd June 2011

"Course it was her, bloody obvious really, who else could it be?" said Sam audibly to himself.

The story had appeared each week, getting bigger and bigger and creeping interminably towards the front page. Four weeks on, it had arrived. There it was, now taking up the entire front page in stark, bold, black type with a rider at the bottom stating that the full details were contained within its internal pages. Sam wanted every miniscule, morbid fact and was relishing the prospect. The headline screamed out: '*Nurse Charged with Murder*'. Underneath, it stated that George Armstrong, aged 91, ('they always give an age' mused Sam) was found dead at his home in Barnham, West Sussex by his neighbour on the afternoon of Tuesday 3rd May 2011.

Opening the paper, Sam was delighted to see that pages two, three and four appeared to carry the story in all it's full, frank and lurid detail. Sam knew this was the biggest story the paper had ever had and was the talk of everyone within the west of the county. Settling back in his worn, copious leather armchair with a freshly made mug of coffee from a strange looking machine, with an even stranger name, Sam prepared to devour each gory aspect of the story.

'George Armstrong, an outstanding pillar of the community and a retired headmaster, who had only last year won the coveted Southern Counties Chess Championships in a thrilling final, was found dead on the floor of his living room. Mr Chaplin, an elderly neighbour who was going for his weekly game of chess with Mr Armstrong, had found him lying on the floor with a diary and a broken pencil by his hand. Scrawled in practically unintelligible writing on the paper was the single word 'Pois' and nothing else.'

Sam loved the thought of the mystery surrounding that one little word.

'*Mr Armstrong had for many years taught mathematics to the youth of Littlehampton becoming first, deputy headmaster, and finally the headmaster, of the currently named Littlehampton Comprehensive School. Having settled in Littlehampton during the war, he took up his position in 1941 as head of mathematics and remained at the same school until his retirement in 1984. He was a widower of 15 years with no known relatives and lived in the beautifully kept bungalow that he and his wife had bought and cherished when first they married.*'

Examining the two coloured pictures of the large bungalow and the near acre of manicured lawns and flowerbeds, Sam said, 'Got enough money for a gardener' to no one in particular.

'*Unfortunately, in the last couple of years, his health had taken a serious turn for the worst, and he was unable to walk unaided. He had been forced to employ a local nursing agency to supply carers to assist him in the early mornings and late evenings. Within a short time, Miss Olivia Munroe became the regular nurse to attend his needs. Detective Superintendent Trevor Prodow, the Senior Police Officer leading the investigation into the death of Mr Armstrong, told this reporter that the cause of death had in fact been proven to be poison, and that Miss Munroe has this day been charged with murder. Police have so far been reluctant to disclose any further details of the case, but our own enquiries reveal that Miss Munroe has been with the nursing agency for some time and has on at least two occasions been the subject of complaints. We are also informed, by a reliable source, that she has previously made it known that she attended Mr Armstrong whenever possible as, quote: 'They got on well together.'*'

Sam could contain himself no longer. Exclaiming loudly, "I bet she did. He was obviously loaded and she wanted some of it. Probably all of it."

Chris, who had been busy washing the dishes from breakfast in the kitchen, responded to the loud inexplicable statement, "You're probably right dear. Another coffee?"

"Yes please. Use the same mug, saves on washing up."

Chris entered the living room to retrieve the now proffered empty mug, trying to remember the last time Sam had washed up anything in the modern butler's sink. Striding purposefully back to the kitchen, she prepared to engage in combat with the coffee machine's various buttons and idiosyncrasies.

Sam read on: numerous people singing Armstrong's praises and how he would be 'sorely missed'.

'One day' thought Sam, 'someone will tell the truth about a person and say what a horrible shit they had been throughout their life.' It was as though it was prohibited from speaking ill of the dead.

Another picture: this time in black and white of Armstrong himself, sitting in his wheelchair holding the cup he had won the previous year.

"I remember that," murmured Sam, again to no one in particular.

Studying the picture, Sam saw a frail looking old man with drawn features, balding, with tufts of wispy hair mainly falling over his ears. His eyes appeared to be glistening with slight tears of pride even in the black and white photograph and there was a broad smile emblazoned across his face. The caption read, *'George Armstrong wins the Southern Counties Chess Championship.'*

Chris came back into the living room with a freshly made cup of coffee and a small bundle of mail.

"Any for me?" enquired Sam.

"Yeah," said Chris, "all the bills."

Sam dropped the paper on the floor as usual, much to Chris's annoyance and took the mail presented.

"Must you do that?" whinged Chris, "Every morning you read the paper and throw it on the floor when you go to work and I have to pick it up."

"Sorry" said Sam condescendingly, as he looked through the mail which had now become the prime focus of his attention: but made no effort to pick up the paper.

14

Monday 6th June 2011

There was a slight buzz coming from the gathered horde of men and women crammed into the second-floor room that was being utilised as a temporary major incident office at Chichester Police Station. Normally, the majority of them, Detectives, worked from a modern, spacious and newly refurbished but characterless office known as the Major Incident Suite at Sussex House on the outskirts of Brighton, which they were missing and desperate to return to. They had been spoilt over time with plenty of room to move about and contemporary phones and computers on state of the art desks with comfy chairs and other luxuries. Chichester, on the other hand, was a long way for most of them to travel to work in what they regarded as a dilapidated building with antique fixtures and fittings in a refined backwater of Sussex.

There were several civilian specialists huddled together chatting in a corner as if involved in some dialogue of a conspiratorial nature. Occasionally they had been required to leave the confines of their warm laboratories or snug comfy offices based around Brighton and travel to Chichester and its environs. None of them had appreciated leaving the cosy atmosphere inside their buildings for the vagaries of the English summer climate. Each of them quietly believed that it was their specific expertise that was likely to be the defining 'nail in the coffin' which would prove the perpetrator's guilt.

A few of the Detectives present had been seconded from local stations and were enjoying the change from investigating mundane burglaries and drunken assaults. There were two uniform officers who, with their local knowledge of the people and of the area, had facilitated a lot of the Detectives' work. As the incident they were all currently tasked with investigating had occurred in Barnham, it would normally have befallen officers working from the MIT (Major Incident Team) in Littlehampton to have taken on the investigation. The senior officer there, DCS (Detective Chief Superintendent) Trevor Prodow, had deemed that his officers were much too busy to deal with yet another murder as they already had several on the go. His decision had been heavily influenced by the fact that he was fully au fait with the work load of the MIT at Brighton who currently only had one outstanding investigation in progress. Put under pressure from his superiors, who knew he was approaching retirement, he had reluctantly agreed to take on the role as the SIO. (Senior Investigating Officer) To assist him, he had taken a typist and a DS (Detective Sergeant) from his contingent at Littlehampton, who he knew and trusted, to be the backbone of the Chichester office.

Barnham was a lot closer to Chichester than Brighton. Even the hierarchy of the force who were not always renowned for their logic realised a base at Chichester would be more cost efficient. The room was on the top floor in the rear part of the Police Station, tucked away from inquisitive eyes and casual passers-by. An Inspector from Brighton had appeared at the Chichester office on the first day of the enquiry and arranged for the office to be furnished with what he considered to be essential equipment and then had not been seen again. In its time, the room had been used as senior officers' accommodation, Forensic officers' work stations, Traffic wardens' parade room, and other civilian unit's accommodation. It was obviously an office that people did not like as they moved out as soon as they possibly could.

15

Monday 6th June 2011

The office manager who had been seconded by the DCS from the MIT at Littlehampton lived to the west of Chichester and enjoyed the shorter journey to work and easier parking. On the initial day of the enquiry, he requisitioned the first desk by the door as people entered from the corridor in order that he could challenge any unwanted guest, or grant unfettered access to others. He was a man of some twenty-five years' service who had the ability to understand what senior officers wanted, or should have wanted before they said anything. Some had referred to him as 'Radar' in the past which was a name stolen from the film 'Mash' and one which he abhorred.

Ensconced behind his ancient desk, which had seen much better days and, over its lifespan, had lost all its drawers, he surveyed the room. A grey rickety two tier in-tray was sitting on the left side of the desk and was full to the brim with correspondence which all required some form of action. A box file containing indexes and notebooks was standing upright next to the trays. On the other end of the desk stood a black computer monitor with a grubby white keyboard in front of it. In the middle as if warranting pride of place, were a couple of telephones. Their wires draped over the back towards the interior of the office, before snaking their way loosely around the desk towards the sockets set half way up the wall behind him. The unwary passer-by could be guaranteed to catch their foot in one or both of the wires so yanking the phones from the desk.

Paul, the office manager, sat passively observing the gathered officers from his vantage point at the head of the office and cogitated as to what enquiries were still unresolved.

At the opposite end of the room, sitting behind an equally dilapidated desk, was the exhibits officer, Jimmy Green. He was in his late 20's with trendy cut and gelled blonde hair and designer stubble. Jimmy worked hard on his appearance, visiting a salon weekly where he saw a stylist for his hair and a manicurist to maintain his neat nails. At least twice a week he would visit a health club and be coached by his personal trainer for which he paid a King's ransom. His face was free of any blemishes and the nearest he had probably come to breaking his nose was not through sport or any assault, but falling over as a toddler. Several times a year, he would visit Spain in order to keep his tan topped up. In his mind, he knew he was handsome and utilised his unbridled confidence to present himself as an accomplished lothario. Others knew: looks could be deceptive.

Jimmy's real problem was that he didn't know what he was doing as an exhibits officer, having spent his three years assigned to the CID (Criminal Investigation Department) at Bognor Police Station investigating the more menial enquiries his supervisors could find him and trust him to complete. He was a sociable and likeable person who had the 'gift of the gab' and was always ready with an answer. Having been made exhibits officer in preference to one of the officers from the MIT, he had decided on a policy of 'take the lot' so he couldn't go wrong. His desk top barricade, which was concealing the laptop and one telephone on his desk, comprised of stacks of sealed brown paper bags containing various unsavoury items and a few plastic bags with items clearly visible of a less gory nature.

Perched serenely on a corner of his desk swinging her shapely crossed legs nonchalantly, was an exceptionally well-dressed young WPC. (Woman Police Constable) She had on what looked to the other women in the room like a grey designer suit, which had actually been bought off the peg in Chichester's biggest store, 'House of Fraser'. Her court shoes were polished and un-scuffed, and other than petite pearl earrings and an elegant gold coloured watch, she wore no other jewellery. Life's ambition for her was to become a talented CID officer, get promoted to a high rank, preferably CC, (Chief Constable) get married and have children and live happily in a big house in the country.

This was the first murder enquiry that Alison Daines had been seconded to, and she had done well. Having worked with an experienced member of the MIT from Brighton since the inception of the enquiry nearly five weeks earlier, she knew she needed to work with someone else to garner more experience. Still technically a uniform officer, this was she hoped, her passport into the CID.

She was a very well educated and clever woman, and for a twenty-five year-old, did not miss much. Her vibrant bright green eyes had casually surveyed those present and she decided she would now learn more if she could latch onto the office manager. In the meantime, a bit of flirting with the exhibits officer seemed harmless enough.

Overall, the office would probably only just be considered a passable facility by a zealous Health and Safety officer. The furnishings which adorned the room were so old an antiques dealer from 'The Lanes' in Brighton would likely have taken the lot. The room itself was painted in the obligatory dull government beige so popular in official buildings thirty years previously and the floor covering was in a musty flecked grey that was sticky underfoot. The officers who had come from Sussex House could understand everyone's desire to get out of the room as soon as possible.

16

Monday 6th June 2011

Sitting behind a smaller desk which had one leg supported by pieces of cardboard for stability was a man in his late-forties with finger combed, suspiciously black hair. A high forehead with more lines on it than Southern Railways didn't enhance his appearance. Some heartless people would consider it was the sign of impending baldness, but would not have the nerve to tell him. His recovering bloodshot eyes were closed as he recalled his previous evening's excesses in one of the local hostelries with the licensee. He had managed a few hours' sleep, a shower and change of clothes, although due to his ample size they always looked slightly scruffy. No one seemed to bother him and he didn't want to protest.

He'd been a detective for over twenty years and had moved the year previously on a secondment to Sussex Police from the Met. (Metropolitan Police) His task had been to assist in an exceedingly confidential corruption investigation which he had recently accomplished successfully. Whilst he had been completing his paperwork for Sussex, in readiness to return to duties at Scotland Yard, a high ranking senior officer in the Met had called him. John was rather surprised to be told he was being assigned to the murder enquiry to offer any 'useful assistance'. It was highly unusual for an officer on secondment from the Yard to be attached to a provincial murder team, but on arrival at Chichester he had worked out quite quickly why he was there.

The enquiry was already well into its fourth week when John walked into the temporary office. He was welcomed by Paul who had been his original Sussex liaison officer when he had first been assigned. Each trusted the other up to a point, and discussed the original investigation in hushed tones when the office was practically empty and particularly quiet. Paul queried his attachment to the murder as the culprit was known and charged. John batted off the question with a non-committal answer which partly satisfied Paul. Reading reports, watching videos and a brief trip to the scene of the crime soon brought John's knowledge of the murder up to speed.

The original attachment to Sussex had suited John down to the ground. He had been born, and grew up, in Bognor leaving aged 16 for the bright lights of London. His knowledge of West Sussex was incomparable, especially the locations of public houses. Appearing to be older than he was when in his teens, he could easily fool licensees as to his age and he soon acquired the taste for real ale. Most of the time his only problem was how far away to leave his push bike so the publicans wouldn't see it.

In 2009 he'd purchased a luxury flat in Westgate in Chichester in preparation for his retirement, and was gradually furnishing it, when finances permitted, in an opulent manor. He had maintained a small one bedroom flat in Fulham which was known as his 'registered' address while he was employed by the Met, but hardly ever used it. If anyone wanted to trace him, they invariably ended up in Fulham. His Chichester flat was to all intents and purposes to remain unrecorded and unknown. On his retirement, he intended that no one other than those he implicitly trusted would be made aware of it. Various theories had been mooted as to why he had been seconded, but only a few senior officers in different forces knew the real reason, and again, he was happy with that.

17

Monday 6th June 2011

DCS Trevor Prodow strode into the room at exactly quarter past four in the afternoon followed by DI (Detective Inspector) Bryan Groves. Those seated, except John Whiles who remained rooted to the spot eyes firmly closed, jumped up virtually to attention.

Prodow, with a dismissive wave of his hand said, "As you were, now let's crack on and get this job sorted out."

Groves had noticed the complete contempt that Whiles had shown to the Chief Superintendent's arrival and was going to mention it to him later. This was Sussex Police where rank was earned and treated with respect, not the Met where anything goes. Whiles expected Prodow was going to be a quarter of an hour late: whenever he had met him before he had always been a quarter of an hour late, and never once had he bothered to apologise for his tardy time keeping.

Every member of the team was aware that Prodow was the figurehead for the enquiry. Customarily he would not have been so 'hands on' as to the day to day running of the investigation but more concerned with its oversight and with the direction it was to pursue. He was currently the senior investigating officer to six other major enquires, five of which were murders, and three of those appeared unsolvable. Whenever he had a success, he invariably found a congratulatory note in his post from his immediate superior the ACC (Assistant Chief Constable) or more likely a succinct e-mail. If it was deemed that he had committed a misdemeanour or made some perceived error of judgement, it was a personally delivered summons by a staff officer to attend either the ACC's office, or if serious, the Deputy Chief Constable's office. Prodow was, however, the person who decided who was to be charged and when in consultation with the CPS (Crown Prosecution Service) as well as giving all the press briefings. Because of this, he was routinely awarded all the plaudits for his junior officers' work, especially when an offender was convicted.

Paul Brokes, the office manager, moved away from his seat as Prodow walked round the desk towards it. One of the telephones shot off, crashing onto the floor as Prodow's foot caught the wire.

"That bloody thing gets me every time," he growled as he plonked himself down into the vacated chair.

Paul picked up the two main pieces, and replaced the phone on his desk. Everyone watched him in silence as he went to the seat next to John which had been left empty for him. Groves was left standing by the door as all the others who had been milling about in the middle of the room seemed to melt to the sides and lean or perch against the walls or desks.

Prodow was nearing retirement, and knew that this was likely to be his last major enquiry. Since joining the Police straight after his national service, he had an industrious career climbing the promotions ladder slowly on merit, which endeared him to junior officers and not as some of his counterparts, because of those they knew. That's not to say he didn't know the right people: he had mixed with some of the best in the country and had done jobs for them, which had resulted in quiet recognition. Now that this was likely to be his last major enquiry before retirement, he was extremely cheerful that it was an open and shut case. He was going to go out on a high note and he was going to use the press to get his name some prominence so if he did decide to get another job, people would remember him.

The prospect of work did not currently appeal to him as his kids had flown the nest: literally one to America to work and the other to Australia to get married and live in the sun. Joan, his long-suffering wife of the past thirty odd years was the only likely reason for him to seek further employment. He needed to get away from her for a few peaceful days each week. This had already been at the back of his mind, but he could play golf twice a week which would achieve the same result with the benefit of a lower handicap.

Prodow noticed Whiles apparently comatose and smiled to himself at what the others may have thought about him. Opening his murder book at a new page, he wrote the date and time of the office meeting and said in his characteristic booming voice, "Right Mr Groves fill me in."

18
Monday 6th June 2011

Vilf was one of life's losers. His Mother's accent had caused the harried registrar who recorded his birth to write down Vilf instead of Wilf. He'd grown up in Chelsea. Not living in one of the thousands of nice houses that made the place famous, but in a small housing association flat on the Peabody estate occupied by his emigre Mother and a succession of boyfriends. His Father wasn't known by either of them and neither much cared. The Council seemed to like his Mother and showered her with as much money as she appeared to want, which she quite happily accepted. Most of it went to fuel her Heroin addiction and the rest was mainly spent on drink and cigarettes. Very little was left for food and Vilf suffered in his younger life with rickets, but as he grew older he became a proficient shoplifter. Slowly, he built his strength up until he was fifteen when his Mother overdosed on Heroin and left Vilf with nothing, except a strange name.

The Council didn't like Vilf as much as his Mother and basically told him not to sponge off the taxpayer and get a job. For some reason the housing association didn't like him either and kicked him out. Vilf drifted for two years living on the streets by begging and stealing whatever he needed. He met like-minded people who took him under their wing and taught him how to steal cars and sell them to bent dealers for cash in hand. The more money he made from it, the more he wanted. It didn't take long until he acquired a shotgun.

He was not a competent armed robber. Over the years, he occupied cells in prisons up and down the country. Nearly everyone he trusted shat on him if they could benefit from doing so. On his last excursion as a free man, he was renting, with stolen money, a luxury top floor flat overlooking Tower Bridge when he met a woman who thought he was rich and promptly married him. As soon as she realised her mistake, she started to look for a truly rich man and slept with every potential candidate. When she found the 'man of her dreams' it didn't take her long to get Vilf to rob a small Post Office and let the Police know which one and when. The Police paid her what she considered a derisory sum of £2000 for the information that sent Vilf to Maidstone Prison.

She visited just the once to tell him she was getting a divorce. Vilf told her where he had stashed some £12000 that he'd stolen and said she could take it. Sometimes Vilf could be a real gentleman. Women were his weak spot, and he always tried to do right by them however badly they treated him. When 'banged up' he was always a model prisoner showing the officers respect and never getting into any trouble. Then within three years he had been moved to Ford open prison ready for his release two years hence. But since the day the Police put the handcuffs on Vilf, the one thing that had been gnawing at the back of his mind was, who had grassed him up: although in his heart he knew.

Seven weeks at Ford was enough for Vilf. His cell mate was some obnoxious foreigner who had a smuggled phone hidden in his cell and charged fortunes to anyone who wanted to use it. Sometimes when he wanted a secretive conversation he spoke in Russian believing what he said was secure. Vilf saw no reason to dissuade him. He would often find the foreigner's conversations enthralling, and could occasionally hear parts of the other person's utterances. Somehow the man had an endless supply of booze for which he charged way over the odds. Vilf soon established from the phone exchanges that it was left by an insecure part of the perimeter security fence. It didn't seem to matter in an open prison whether the fence was secure or not as lots of the prisoners went outside the main prison during daylight hours.

Vilf believed there were more foreign languages being spoken there than all the other prisons he had been in put together. It was purgatory. All the home grown criminals seemed to be in 'proper' prisons and all the foreigners and 'nonces' were in the open ones. He walked out of the front gate of the prison in the morning at 9 as though to go to a gardening session across the road. Stealing a car within the hour, he was in Central London by midday. Dumping the car, he walked the half mile to a house where he had previously laid low. There he put the final touches of his plan in place.

As the day's de-briefing was in progress, Vilf had a stolen car parked for a quick getaway and was burgling the first of three houses in Petworth. It was in the third house that he found what he wanted – a double barrelled shotgun.

The unlocked garden shed provided the hacksaw that took the barrel down to the length of the fore stock and removed nearly the whole of the stock. If he had realised that the weapon was an antique Purdy worth a couple of thousand pounds, he didn't care as he had a plan and wasn't going to deviate from it. Just because there were no cartridges to go with the gun did not matter because when he had pointed sawn off shotguns at people before, they tended to do what they were told whether it was loaded or not.

19

Monday 6th June 2011

Groves expected the question, but to have been put in such a terse and abrupt way shook him slightly. He stuttered as he tried to gather his thoughts and looked anxiously around the room as if seeking succour from one of the sets of eyes that were boring into him.

"Start at the beginning" boomed the gruff voice of Prodow, "it will be easier for all of us."

Prodow had only met Groves at the start of the enquiry some five weeks earlier, and had come to the quick conclusion that he was only just up to the job and had probably been over promoted.

"Well as we all know on the 3rd May, George Armstrong was found dead at his home as a result of poisoning by one of his neighbours."

The interruption by Whiles came as yet another blow to Groves, mainly because he thought him to have been asleep,

"I think you mean that a male known as Mr George Armstrong was found dead at his home address in Barnham on 3rd May 2011. Death was caused by poisoning, and Mr Chaplin, who was a neighbour, found the deceased."

He was livid that a scruffy, unkempt excuse for a detective had the gall to interrupt and correct him while apparently asleep and still making no effort to open his eyes. Groves had been an efficient DC (Detective Constable) and very capable DS. On promotion to DI, his career seemed to have come to an abrupt halt. He had landed in an office behind a desk which was alien to him, and his main priority seemed to have shifted from solving crime to rebuking junior officers, and enforcing discipline. All his credibility was slowly evaporating.

Years of meritorious service were slowly going down the tubes, and he could do apparently nothing to stop it.

Prodow let Groves off the hook. Smiling again to himself he said, "OK we know the basics" and then addressing Jimmy Green, "How are you doing with the exhibits?"

Jimmy knew the question would be posed at some time and was ready. "We completed the full search of the bungalow on 4th May and among the exhibits I have are the broken pencil and diary, a crumpled tissue, some plaster casts of footprints and tyre marks, some cups and saucers, samples of carpet, tapings, all his clothing and other bits and bobs from around the bungalow."

Prodow winced visibly at the 'bits and bobs' reference but said nothing as he tried to understand the point of all the seized exhibits.

Jimmy was now getting into his stride. "With Mr Groves and DC Tindle, I attended the Post Mortem which was carried out by the Home Office pathologist," and Jimmy paused checking his note book before continuing, "Mr Stubbins. I took possession of samples and fluids of Mr Armstrong's internal organs which I submitted for toxicology to the Laboratory at Huntingdon. They have confirmed poison, but they seem reluctant to identify which one and say they want to consult an outside specialist. We still await their written report. I've got the pictures of the scene from the photographic department, if you would like to see them?"

Jimmy, without waiting for a reply, gave a thick album of photographs enclosed in a blue bound cover emblazoned with the logo of Sussex Police to Alison who duly passed them forward to the next person in order that they reached Prodow who like everyone else in the room had seen them already.

"I've got the finalised video as well if you would like to see it later?"

Prodow nodded his acquiescence, beaten into submission by Jimmy who had hardly paused to draw breath.

"Have you got the bottle of poison?"

Jimmy said, "Oh yes sir, one of the first items, found on the floor in the shed. It's still at the lab. Fingerprints on it have been identified without doubt as those of Olivia Munroe and I'm expecting full reports and statements within the next couple of days."

Prodow said, "Good work. As soon as you get the confirmation from the lab, let Mr Groves know and he will tell me."

Groves was still seething as he realised his name had been used and he hadn't followed the reason why.

Prodow scowling at him said, "When Munroe was interviewed, did she admit anything at all?"

"Nothing. Carly and Zabroski conducted all three interviews and Munroe had the duty solicitor for all of them who had told her to say nothing."

Again, the interruption came but not from Whiles, from Paul. "Governor, you're forgetting the verbal statement she made to the arresting officers in the custody centre when she said she'd put the bottle in the shed."

Groves could have kicked himself; he'd never have forgotten that when he had been an active detective. The only thing she'd said of note and he had overlooked it because he was flustered.

Prodow looked at him in utter disbelief and then totally ignored him as he asked Paul, "Can you arrange transcripts of all the taped interviews with Munroe?"

"Already in hand sir and they are due back tomorrow with covering statements."

"Good. I want you to listen to them for anything else that may have been missed."

"Consider it done sir."

"Thank you Paul. Anybody else got anything they want to add?"

Someone discussed the statement from Mr Chaplin saying his age and shock had made it difficult and perhaps an additional clarifying statement should be obtained, and then other witness statements were mentioned and run through without incident. Paul was jotting occasional notes on his pad as actions required were identified or sprang to mind. There were still a couple of minor outstanding statements to be obtained, but the majority of the investigation had been completed. Statements from some specialists were still awaited, but required no further work from the MIT officers.

Prodow closed his murder book having written various notes within it. He brought the proceedings to an end by telling everyone that because nearly everything had been done, he was just keeping Paul and Doreen the typist to run the office with Jimmy as the exhibits officer and John and Alison as the enquiry team. He confirmed he still wanted the HOLMES (Home Office Large Major Enquiry System) operator at Brighton to continue to liaise daily with Paul and visit the Chichester office once a week. The civilian operator was not best pleased but held her counsel. Thanking everyone profusely for their professionalism and efficiency, he told them once all their paperwork was completed they could all return to their respective duties in three days' time.

Although he had no authority to do so, in effect, he was giving them all a day off without actually saying so.

Groves could not understand why John and Alison were being kept on the enquiry when there were so many better detectives there in his opinion. He didn't know that Alison's father was a personal friend of Prodow and some months prior to the outset of the enquiry had contacted him with a problem. Because of this, Prodow arranged for his daughter to be assigned to what would be her first major enquiry, and John to be attached to it instead of returning to his duties with the Met.

As the officers again began to chat amongst themselves, Prodow called above the rising din to Jimmy, "Can you set the video up?"

But the answer came straight away from Paul that it was all ready to go in the conference suite and briefing room on the first floor directly below the office they were in. Prodow was always impressed with Paul, and had often seen him as the office manager on various major enquiries in Sussex. Paul had been appointed to the Armstrong murder enquiry as soon as Prodow knew he was to lead the investigation and he knew that the temporary office would be set up and running in no time.

"Good man. Let's go and look at it. Anyone else who wants to see it: downstairs conference room in 5 minutes."

20

Monday 6th June 2011

The sunken, recovering eyes of Whiles snapped open, looked around and latched onto Alison. She had her auburn hair neatly cut and short enough not to get in her way. Her eyes were clear and vibrant green whereas his were bloodshot and dull brown. Her lips were thin and had a hint of lipstick and looked as though they were about to burst into a smile, and her eyebrows were enhanced with fine 'pencil' strokes. His eyebrows were bushy and needed thinning and his tight chapped thicker lips had a slight gloss applied via a stick when he remembered. Her cheeks were prominent with a very slight blush as opposed to his puffy ones. Her nose was small and slightly upturned and his was roman, broken and reddish. Alison had clear and smooth skin with a perfect tan obtained from the sun and John just had weather-beaten features from time spent outdoors. His face was host to a couple of scars which when he exerted himself, showed up redder than the rest of his face. John could see she was very pretty, about five feet six inches and of an athletic stature with honed features from regular visits to a gym but not what women's magazines would refer to as beautiful. On the other hand: John was just over six feet tall and had gone slightly to seed and if commented on, claimed he had 'passed a gym in the car but was too busy to stop'. Her clothes were neat and stylish and suited her. John knew he was no style setter as when shopping for clothes he always bought the first item that fitted. He knew that Prodow would have had a reason to keep them both on the enquiry and he guessed that Alison's Father, who he also knew, had a hand in it.

In the late sixties, both Whiles and Graham Daines had been Police cadets together at Ashford Cadet School prior to joining the Metropolitan Police.

They had become firm friends and joined the Police proper on the same day, but after initial training at Hendon, went to different inner London Police Stations. During their service, they had met on various occasions, and at one time worked together on the RCS (Regional Crime Squad) for seven years in a team of ten travelling all over the country doing jobs relating to enquiries emanating in the Met. Due to their successes, they were called upon quite regularly to conduct covert enquiries for the Home Office. The team had all kept in touch and they often met up somewhere for a reminisce with a pint or two.

Both had attended each other's wedding, although due to his work, Whiles soon parted from his wife, while Daines went up the promotions ladder with his wife by his side who gave birth early in the marriage to their daughter. Whiles was aware that Graham was a deputy to the City of London Police Commissioner, and having spoken quite recently to him, knew that he had an application in, and was likely to be promoted to Chief Constable of a Midlands Police Force.

Alison also wondered why she had been retained on the enquiry, as she was not yet a confirmed detective, but then she didn't know Prodow and her Father knew each other, and she was definitely not privy to their original discussion. Her sharp eyes latched onto John's sunken bloodshot ones and she thought to herself, 'Why on earth am I going to have to work with him.'

As if in response, John said to her, "That's us; we need to see this video."

Paul, John, Alison and Jimmy ambled down to the conference room on the first floor, where on arrival, Paul went to the VCR player, picked up the remote control and then joined the others seated a few feet from the drop down large white screen. Some of the officers from the MIT sat about at the back more out of curiosity than to learn anything new. Everyone had already watched the video at least once before. Prodow and Groves came in together and sat directly in front of the screen as the others shuffled their seats so they could see it unhindered.

"OK Paul, start it when you're ready."

Paul, as a precursor said, "This was taken by the photographer approximately one hour after the body had been discovered. The Doctor had already attended and pronounced life extinct, and he may have moved the corpse when he examined it, but he is adamant he hardly touched it and returned it to how he first found it. Both statements from the Doctor and Photographer are already on the file." The image burst into life as Paul set the video in motion.

21

Monday 6th June 2011

Displayed on the screen in pin sharp colour and perfect focus, was the picture of a road with a few entrances on either side but mainly greenery in the form of trees, bushes and hedges. A small square semi-transparent panel in the top right hand corner superimposed onto the film showed the operation name; 'Heartstring' the date, 3rd May 2011 and rolling time including seconds and a compass point which was indicating east. The picture panned slowly round 180 degrees to view the road to the west, which was similar to the first view. Noticeable by their absence was the lack of visible buildings. Zooming in and turning to the north, the picture was directed at one specific entrance that had a long and large laurel hedge to the right side of it running parallel to the footpath and a large privet type bush to the other. All those watching had visited the scene of the murder at least once and knew roughly the layout of the premises and the surrounding area. Whichever photographer had taken the film kept it running at all times as he moved about zooming in at some things and out at others.

The opening grew larger on the screen until it could be clearly visible as a reasonably maintained tarmacadam driveway that ran northward at a right angle from the road for over a hundred yards to a bungalow situated on the right hand side of it. To the left of the driveway, as the pictures showed, was an overgrown beck with a continual trickle of running water in the bottom which seemed to disappear under the privet bush and the roadway beyond. Large bushes, some bearing flowers and fruits were next to the stream providing a border between the bungalow of George and Chaplin's house and grounds. This formed one boundary of the property. On the right of the drive was a large garden with various bushes and trees scattered about in the extensive and orderly well-kept lawn, which was in its turn bounded on the east side by a large conifer hedge reaching in places to at least twenty feet high. Two-thirds of the way towards the rear of the plot sat the large and beautifully maintained three bedroomed bungalow with a substantial sized conservatory overlooking the front garden. A garage was attached to the rear of the premises which then led into more manicured lawns unfolding northwards. An ornamental pond stretched from the end of the driveway on the west side boundary to the large conifers on the other, and behind it at the northern most curtilage of the property was another large hedge comprising of closely planted evergreen flowering trees interspersed with colourfully leaved trees and climbing plants which assured that the property was not overlooked at all.

The bungalow may only just have been visible to a pedestrian on the pavement (had there ever been any) if they had stopped at the driveway entrance, and walked in a few yards.

Prodow said to no one in particular, "That is one bloody big pond."

John retorted, "And not a fish to be seen in it."

Slowly the picture moved on showing the complete perimeter of the house, its outside lighting, and burglar alarm box and a well concealed wooden shed at the rear of the garage to the east of the bungalow with the door propped open. Clearly displayed within were various garden implements arranged on racks, some resting against the walls, a couple of white plastic folding garden chairs and table and an old wooden chest of drawers at the opposite end to the door. Standing on the floor just inside the shed nearly out of sight to the casual observer was a small jam-jar about a quarter full of a clear liquid.

The image lingered on the jar a while and then moved back to the closed door of the garage which as if by magic swung up and into the roof space to reveal no vehicle but about ten racks around the walls filled with full bottles of wine. Both Prodow and Whiles had spent a little time in the garage when they were there, not because it afforded any clue about the murder, but because they both loved good wines and there were plenty in the racks to look at. In front of the garage was a smoothly compacted gravel compound surface leading to the driveway and the camera moved down to show a tyre mark a few inches onto the grass next to the gravel.

Moving on to the closed front door, the camera disclosed that at some time it been painted over and as a result had become stuck and no longer used. A hand had appeared in the picture trying to open it as if to prove the point to any viewers before moving around to the kitchen door which had been left open for the cameraman to enter.

Inside the kitchen was a table with a ring binder on it open at the first page showing a headed nursing agency form displaying George Armstrong's details and medical condition.

Jimmy happily said, "That's an exhibit now governor" and then realised that everyone knew that anyway.

Everything seemed to look alright in the kitchen, utensils were where one would expect them to be, a neat pile of papers were on a work surface with a paper pad and pen next to them and a couple of cups and saucers in the washing up bowl in the sink. Jimmy was happy; he had seized and exhibited all the items filmed. Prodow was starting to believe he had seized everything in the house.

The cameraman left the kitchen via a glazed door, and started down the hallway entering the first room on the right which was a bathroom that had been converted into a large shower room in order that it could be entered by someone in a wheelchair going straight into a specially adapted shower cubicle. Nothing out of place, towels on their rails, and even the flannels in the washbasin were folded.

Further along the corridor and next was the wheelchair adapted toilet and then the corridor doglegged to the right into a bedroom, which was simply decorated and contained a single made up bed, a dressing table and a built in wardrobe. A simple neat and tidy room. Alison noted the curtains were from Laura Ashley, exactly the same as were in the bedroom she used when she visited her parents.

Back into the corridor and into the next bedroom, which was the furthest from the kitchen, and the biggest bedroom in the bungalow and the one that George Armstrong utilised. There was a double bed which seemed higher than most beds, a freestanding wardrobe and a built in wardrobe which contained expensive looking clothes all tidily arranged on hangers. Two chests of drawers containing more clothing all perfectly folded and arranged and a dressing table with relevant grooming accessories all aligned on the top. Next to the head of the bed attached to the wall was a panic button for the alarm.

Alison saw again curtains similar to the ones in her parents' house and said, "He bought his curtains at Laura Ashley."

No one else seemed to care about where the curtains came from.

Moving into the third bedroom, the image showed another single made up bed and built in wardrobe and dressing table. Then it was back into the hall and towards the kitchen.

Prodow said, "Stop a second" and the video image froze immediately. "Where is his dirty washing?"

Jimmy said, "In the bathroom was a laundry basket behind the door that the camera has missed. He did have some in it, all folded."

Prodow said, "It would have been" to the slight amusement of Jimmy. "Keep going" and the film re-started promptly, passing the front door and the cupboard housing the alarm control box and digital keypad and back into the kitchen through the glazed door.

It turned immediately right into the dining room as all those present drew unintentionally closer towards the screen. Alongside the wall on the right as the camera entered was a beautiful French oak wall unit with glazed displays showing crystal glasses in all their glory and against the opposite wall a matching oak sideboard at least seven feet long with crystal ornaments and an antique clock on a Swiss lace runner on the top of it. In the middle of the room was an English oak table covered in a matching lace tablecloth supporting crystal candelabra and surrounded by six carved English oak chairs. Alison was enchanted with the room and mesmerised by its style. It was closest to her dream idea of what a dining room should be. Then the picture moved towards the door next to the sideboard leading to the lounge and conservatory from the dining room.

22

Monday 6th June 2011

Vilf had hidden the gun in the engine compartment of his stolen car. From previous experience, he had noted that when the Police stopped cars they tended to search the inside and the boot. He had never seen them look under the bonnet. They probably did infrequently, but he'd never seen them do so. If they stopped him, he knew the car had been expertly cloned and would pass a basic PNC (Police National Computer) check, even without a displayed tax disc. His new clothes, courtesy of Harrods, although not paid for, portrayed him as reasonably prosperous and consequently in his mind, affluent and respectably middle class.

From his extensive knowledge of the Police, he believed they would have completely forgotten about him within a fortnight of his illegal departure from Ford. He knew that they would have checked his old haunts and acquaintances within a few days, and having drawn a blank would have given up as other matters became imperative and needed prosecuting. The stolen identification was not so good, and would be a last resort as a diligent check would reveal its probity. Vilf could talk for England, and was of the opinion that he could talk his way around any Policeman asking for ID. Hence, he was confident it was highly unlikely he would be identified having being 'on the run' for the best part of five weeks.

Parking in the Earl of March car park in Lavant, Vilf strode into the restaurant section of the pub as though he were a regular. Waiting at the sign, 'Please wait here to be seated' he picked through the few old papers that were still in the rack selecting the Chichester Post. A tall thin lady with a strong foreign accent wearing a tight black trouser suit and an excessively large dark blue apron which went around her twice rushed to meet him.

"For how many?"

Vilf replied, "Just one at the moment. I might be joined by my friend John Whiles if he can get here. Do you know him?"

The woman was still learning her English and Vilf had confused her by not saying a set number. She had been told by the landlady if she had any problems, to call her.

"Wait here" and she practically ran off to fetch the landlady who was serving behind the bar.

After what seemed like an eternity to Vilf but was only five minutes, the woman and the landlady approached him.

"I'm so sorry for the delay. Can I help you?"

"I was just saying I might be joined by a friend, John Whiles, and asked if she knew him."

"It's not a name I am familiar with. Do you want a table for two?"

"Yes. Just in case he can make it."

Vilf was escorted by the landlady with the foreigner in tow clutching a tri folding menu to a table, and after ordering a drink and a main course by pointing at the relevant items from the list of options, he settled down to read the paper.

He believed he had plenty of time. A contact in London had told him that Whiles had left the Met and was working somewhere in West Sussex. There were a large number of pubs in the county and he knew Whiles liked real ale and deemed their paths would cross eventually. Vilf had planned to eat all his main meals in them during the evenings and visit others during the day. Most served coffee and tea as well as alcohol, so he didn't worry about drinking and driving. He couldn't afford to be involved in an accident. His Mother's reliance on alcohol had never rubbed off on him, nor had her other vices for that matter. Someone would know John Whiles and when they did, he would wait for him. For some illogical and unspecified reason, he automatically assumed that he would be told the truth immediately when somebody knew him. His plan had already fallen at the first fence!

The landlady watched Vilf from time to time via a mirror that allowed her to see part of the restaurant while she was serving behind the bar. She had deliberately placed him at a table that she could monitor. Whenever she checked, Vilf was either eating or reading the paper as though without a care in the world. Something was worrying her and she couldn't immediately put her finger on it. He looked presentable, and he was polite and other than confusing her new Polish 'greeter' had not caused any problem.

Vilf was so engrossed in reading the paper, he didn't see the landlady hand the bar duties temporarily to her deputy and go to the phone. She was no longer than two minutes, punching a number into the keypad from memory and leaving a voicemail message. The paper was carrying the details of George Armstrong's murder which Vilf found fascinating. Who would want to kill a ninety-one year old guy who apparently was about to 'pop his clogs' anyway? In his life, Vilf had met some very weird and dangerous people with some exceptionally bizarre ideas, but he couldn't think of one who would consciously set out to kill a defenceless cripple who would probably be dead within the year. Even the thought of a mentally deranged nurse seemed unlikely to him.

It was practically the same thought that John had had from his first day on the enquiry and it was in his mind now as he was watching the video.

23

Monday 6th June 2011

It was a large well-decorated room. The far end of which was opened up as a conservatory overlooking the front garden. Two large picture windows faced the drive, and a large decorative Portland stone fireplace was inset into the opposite wall. Each side of which had three flat polished stone surfaces: lowest of which was largest, decreasing in size with height like a set of steps. A couple of matching book cases were against the wall separating the lounge from the dining room and were mainly filled with books in height determined order. Two neat piles of postcards from people around the world rested on the same shelf as various assorted unopened bottles of spirits.

There was a large three-piece suite in the room which really looked quite lost in the endless space available, and within the conservatory, practically in the centre next to the wall of glass were two cane chairs either side of a matching table accommodating a carved wooden chess set resting upon it. George's electric wheelchair was parked in a corner well out of the way.

Next to the fireplace towards the conservatory end was a small table, which housed a telephone sitting on top of a 'Lifeline' box and an angle poise table lamp that was arranged to illuminate a 'riser/recliner' chair that was currently raised to its highest point. At the other side of the fireplace was a large old fashioned Sony cathode ray television on a moveable handmade wooden stand. On most of the flat stones of the fireplace were several ornaments and the small 'lifeline' button on its cord which should have been around George's neck. Nearest the phone table, a paper pad was on top of a neat pile of four paperback books alongside a wallet.

"All that expensive gear and not a penny in the wallet" said Jimmy.

The film having panned around the room, slowly sank lower. Lying face down on the floor in front of the fireplace as though having been thrown out of the raised chair was a body dressed in an immaculate suit. The body's right arm was raised above its head and the hand appeared to be reaching for a small diary about two inches from its grasp. Nearer the chair and furthest from the grasping hand was a pencil that was broken and splintered. The camera hovered above the diary which had one word written on an otherwise blank, dated page, 'Pois' and a squiggle which tailed off to nothing.

The picture faded sluggishly to black and Paul turned the video off. "That's the end."

Prodow said, "The photographer did a good job with that. Would you send him a note thanking him from me?"

"Be done first thing in the morning."

"Before you all disappear, has anyone got anything they want to say or ask?"

John, after about 5 seconds realising no one was going to speak said, "I have been right through the exhibit books and checked the charge sheet of Munroe and briefly checked the bungalow and there are some items missing."

Everyone was focused on John as Prodow quizzically said, "Go on?"

"He was really neat and tidy, he had two piles of postcards from people on holiday all over the world, and he was a very popular person. Postcards do not usually have the sender's address on but letters normally do. Why are there no letters anywhere: if he keeps postcards why not letters? And why is there no address book?"

Silence.

After what seemed like an age to Alison who was amazed that John could come up with this when everyone else had missed it, Prodow said, "What do you understand by their absence?"

"Easy really: whoever poisoned him probably thought that their name might be in his address book or on a letter, and we may have come across their identity as we trawled through them. So, to prevent that occurring, they stole them."

Prodow spoke quietly, slowly and softly and chose his words carefully, "What you are saying then, if I understand you correctly, is that you do not believe Munroe did it?"

"That sir is correct."

Groves could contain himself no longer, speaking without thinking, "Jesus, are you stupid or what, it is irrelevant about letters and address books, Munroe must have taken them trying to cover her tracks."

Prodow did not want Groves in this conversation, "Mr Groves, I think you are not understanding the relevance of these facts. Munroe is probably the one person who would have no reason to steal these items. She is recorded at the Nursing Agency every time she attends Armstrong, and her details are in the binder that were in the kitchen and her time sheets were also in the binder which are signed by Armstrong in order that she be paid. If someone other than Munroe did it, by removing these items, they may believe we would not trace them. As I think about it, I don't know anyone over about the age of 12, except the proverbial hermit, who does not keep some kind of address book. I think we need a further search of the bungalow, and a further search of Munroe's home address. John, what else should we be looking for?"

Prodow was correct in assuming there was more to come.

"Having seen the way that this man lived and how organised he was,"

Alison interrupted and said with a startled cry, "Of course, a will."

John continued, "he would have made a will, which we haven't found yet."

Jimmy, who felt aggrieved and slighted by the comment, interrupted saying he had made enquiries to try and trace one without success.

Prodow ignoring Jimmy's indignant hurt said, "Well you both seem to be on the same wavelength, get yourselves there first thing in the morning and see what you can find. Mr Groves I would appreciate it if you and Paul check out Munroe's house. This could be a catalyst in our case against her."

24

Tuesday 7th June 2011

The following morning at 7.30, John sauntered into the canteen on the ground floor directly below the conference room to see Alison already there and at the servery buying her second cup of tea.

"I need a pint of this to get me set up for the day."

She looked as though she had been up just long enough to get smartly dressed, as was her wont, and her makeup immaculate but not overdone. A dark trouser suit was her preferred apparel for the day as she deemed it more suitable if searching premises than a skirt. John on the other hand had been up some time, and looked, although showered and wearing clean clothes, as though he had been dragged through a hedge backwards. His hair needed further additional hand combing and his tie needed straightening, but then it always did. His eyes looked like someone had recently stuck a finger in each causing them to be slightly bloodshot.

He had however the ability to rise quickly and move without liquid or food and keep going for several hours before needing a drink. This ability had served him well over the years, as had the fact that he needed very little sleep, to dodge unpleasant surprises and decamp prior to discovery.

At the servery, Alison asked what he wanted.

"Coffee please" and got a cup of tea for herself.

John went to a table and sat with his back to a wall waiting for Alison to deliver his drink.

She took it to the table and said, "I was at that one, (pointing to a table in the middle of the room with a dirty mug on), shame to make two tables dirty."

He chose to ignore the remark, saying "If we go straight to the bungalow we will probably be finished there by midday. I doubt that we will find anything of note, so this afternoon we can try and find which solicitor has his will. Have you got a car?"

Alison who was now finishing her second cup of tea said, "Yes, but we need the keys for the bungalow first."

"I got them from Jimmy last night to save time so we can go straight there."

She realised that she would not be getting her breakfast today.

In the yard, Alison led the way to a nearly new Ford Fiesta that 'blinked' at them as they approached.

"Mine opens with the key in the lock if it's in a good mood."

"Which one is yours?"

John pointed to what Alison had thought to be a suspect vehicle of some kind that had been brought into the yard and left in a corner for a year or two where it had likely rusted and collected debris under the wheels.

"What is it?"

"A Vauxhall."

Alison could not see herself getting into that car under any circumstances: what would she be sitting on, but more importantly, it would destroy her image completely if anyone saw her getting in or out of it.

They both got into the Fiesta and Alison drove them safely and quite swiftly to the bungalow swinging into the driveway as though it were her own and stopped a few yards short of the garage level with the side picture windows in the lounge. The PCSO (Police Community Support Officer) who had been guarding the property overnight and was waiting for his morning relief, acknowledged their arrival. He was sitting in a large marked Police land rover which was backed up against the garage. Being half asleep, he couldn't be bothered to get out of the vehicle and let the night's accumulated warmth escape.

As he unlocked the kitchen door John said, "I'll start in here if you want to do the bedrooms or the dining room and we can both do the lounge."

"A couple of the trained PoLSA (Police Search Advisor) team and Jimmy have already searched this place. Any clue as to what we are actually looking for?"

"Papers. Anything out of the ordinary or in the wrong place."

Alison went into one of the bedrooms as John started in the kitchen. He soon arrived at the pile of papers that were no longer in such a neat order as they had been when the photographer had filmed them originally. Going through them thoroughly checking each piece of paper, John soon realised that none were what they were looking for. Most were instruction leaflets or circulars from local establishments, menus from local take away restaurants, information about taxis and trains from the local station, social services information, and some old utility bills. Folding one of the gas bills, he slipped it into his inside jacket pocket.

He opened every drawer and cupboard, taking stock of the contents and moving everything as he checked carefully. Pausing at one of the double wall units, he examined the contained dinner service before removing each item of crockery to examine it. According to the writing on the base of each item, it had come from, or been acquired from Marks and Spencer's. John jotted a note in his pocket book.

Within 45 minutes, he had finished searching the kitchen and went into the main bedroom where Alison was completing her search of the room.

"Anything?"

"Nothing at all. I've checked everything. Done both the other bedrooms. All the pockets in the clothes are empty, not even a coin. I just need to lift the bed if you are feeling strong enough."

"I think I could manage providing you go under to have a good look."

"Drop it and I'll never talk to you again."

"If I drop it, you'll never talk again to anyone."

They checked the underside of the bed without incident.

Then they moved through to the dining room and Alison said, "This room is what a dining room should be, simply laid out with expensive classical furniture making it so formal that to eat in here you feel you would have to dress for the occasion."

John could not agree with her but decided against saying so.

"If you start one side I'll start the other: choose your side."

Alison went to the large dresser and John went to the sideboard and the pair of them looked in every nook and cranny.

John inquired, "Found any crockery?"

"Yeah. There is a beautiful six-piece dinner service with an inlaid pattern of red roses."

They completed the rest of the search in silence until they finally met at the far wall.

"Why?"

"What do you mean, why?"

"Why the interest in crockery?"

"I'm impressed you realised it was a relevant question."

"So, answer it."

"When I searched the kitchen, I found a basic six-piece dinner service which I believe was his day to day one. How many cups and saucers were in the sink when the photographer went round?"

"Two cups and two saucers."

"Correct. Therefore there should have been four cups and saucers amongst the crockery in the cupboard. There were four saucers but only three cups."

"So? One may have got broken at some time. Means nothing."

"Not necessarily. Maybe it was taken. We need to check with other carers to see if they know how many cups there were."

"You have something on your mind about the cup. Are you going to fill me in?"

"Not just yet. If you want to be a Detective, I've given you something to think about. Consider ABC (Assume nothing, Believe no one, Check everything). It's quite logical. See what you can come up with."

25

Tuesday 7th June 2011

"Right, let's do the lounge" said John and they went into the room now void of George's body.

At the wall units, Alison took one look at all the books and thought she may as well start with them and said so. John went into the conservatory and lifted the cushions from the cane chairs and in doing so knocked the table holding the chess set. He felt under the chairs and under the table as he himself at times had kept items taped to the bottom of tables and drawers. Picking up every chess piece and checking them, he lifted the board to find an old piece of newspaper stuck underneath it, which had been there for some time to prevent the board slipping. Deftly, he peeled it from the base of the board. Examining it carefully for a few moments, he noted the date in 1980 and the story about a school trip to a varsity match at Twickenham. Judiciously he folded the paper and put it into a small clear plastic exhibits bag taken from his right jacket hip pocket before placing it back into his inside jacket pocket.

Alison meanwhile had been removing every book, flicking all the pages and checking each cover and flyleaf and finally shaking them before putting them back from where she had taken them. As she shook a copy of an old Oxford English dictionary, several £50 notes fluttered to the floor. She flicked the pages slowly in order that she could see clearly between them and found twenty £50 notes in total.

"John, what do you make of this?"

He looked up to see her holding the money in her hand, "I don't know; have you considered fingerprints?"

"Oh, sod it" came the reply as Alison's hand slightly uncurled from the notes as she went out of the room to find an exhibits bag from the kitchen table where she had inadvertently left them on arrival at the bungalow.

John moved to the raised chair that was by the fireplace and thoroughly checked it before lowering it to its proper seating position before slumping down into it. As he sat there, Alison came back into the room with the money now in a sealed exhibit bag.

"Tired all ready, you should get more sleep."

John said, "I have often found that if you put yourself in another person's normal place and just look at the world from that person's perspective you may learn more."

Alison said, "It reminds me of an old poem, 'what is this life if, full of care, we have no time to stand and stare.'"

"By W. H. Davies I believe" said John as his eyes slowly scanned the part of the room that he could see from the chair without moving.

Alison thought, 'Knows a bit of poetry. Maybe not such a philistine as he seems.'

He noticed that the side table with the telephone and lamp were higher than could be reached easily by him and Armstrong was several inches smaller which would have made it even harder for him. The lowest shelf of the fireplace nearest the riser recliner would have been a perfect height to place the telephone and lifeline on. John saw that the slab had no ornaments on it like the other flat surfaces. Leaning forward, he examined that side of the fireplace as Alison watched him intently wondering what on earth he was up to now.

On top of the slab next to the chair, he noticed a black pencil mark and said to Alison, "What do you make of this?"

She leant forward, checked it and said," Looks like that's where the pencil was broken by Munroe or whoever murdered him to stop him writing anymore."

"What if he only intended to write 'Poisoned' and he broke the pencil himself?"

"Why would he do that?"

"As a guide perhaps, he couldn't walk, or reach the phone because he was lying on the floor, the only thing he could reach were the slabs at either end of the fireplace."

"Well," said Alison "if that's the case, I am totally confused. How can it be a guide?"

"Because of where he was lying, he would have had to twist his body to reach this slab; there are a couple nearer to his hand. Have another look, you may notice something else."

Alison leant forward again and stared at the slab. Then she looked at the other slabs near it.

John sunk back in the chair closed his eyes and said, "Look what's not there."

Alison was starting to get annoyed when she suddenly realised what he meant. Around all the slabs except the relevant one, was a neat seal of cement holding them firmly in place. Although the cement was there, a well-nigh invisible hairline crack ran down the middle of it. She grasped the edge of the slab putting both her hands on one side, and pulled on it. It slid with inordinate ease from its position leaving a thin wedge of cement on the fireplace and one on the slab itself. It moved from along the whole length of the crack without disturbing any of the cement. Alison was amazed at how easily she was able to move it from its proper position.

Before it had moved more than six inches she could see a cavity opening up underneath. Lying in the cavity was a long brown envelope.

Without opening his eyes John said, "What have we got?"

"There is a brown envelope, but tell me how did you spot that slab?"

John explained that the logical place to keep really private papers was not on the table where the phone was but on the slab next to the legs of the person who sat in the riser chair. They could then be reached easily if needed and it would explain the absence of an ornament on that slab.

"Simple really," said John.

"Elementary" said Alison thinking of Holmes to Watson.

She put on a tight pair of white latex gloves which seemed to be filled with talcum powder and picked up the envelope which was quite old and not sealed. Reading the address out as John wrote it in his notebook, 'Peckham Hill Street, South London'. Nothing else was written on the envelope nor had it ever borne a stamp. Alison shook the envelope and two folded pieces of paper fell to the floor which when gently unfolded transpired to be two war time identity cards: one in the name of Jeffery A. Anderson and the other Jean Anderson. Alison looked into the envelope and saw a third piece of paper which she teased out between her gloved thumb and index finger of her right hand. She carefully unfolded it to reveal a birth certificate in the name of Jeffery Archibald Anderson. The Mother was shown as Molly, the Father as

Edward and the registration area was Cambridge with the date of 11th April 1918.

John said, in essence to himself, "Now what are we to make of this?"

Alison sat on the settee leaving the envelope, I.D. cards and birth certificate on the floor between them.

After a couple of minutes, Alison said, "Could George Armstrong really be Jeffery Anderson?"

John said, "I don't know, but the question that would then have to be addressed is if so, why has he been using the name George Armstrong?"

26
Tuesday 7th June 2011

"It's me. He applied a month ago. It's been kept quiet. They may suspect something. He's got to be persuaded to withdraw."

"There's plans in motion. Don't worry."

"Keep me informed and I may be able to help when I know how you're doing."

"I've got people in the South preparing for this. I don't envisage a problem."

"The Minister wants him. Interviews will not be for a few months so there's a bit of time."

"I'll be ready to go in a week or so."

"I'll speak to you soon."

"Hello Grigoriev. I've sent the Lithuanian brothers to help you and Petrovski. Dimitri will be with you when he's released in a fortnight. Are you ready yet?"

"Another day or two should do it."

"Any problems?"

"Will need some technical help"

"OK. I'll send it as soon as I can. Watch Dimitri. He likes the ladies. That's why he's locked up."

"Will do."

"Call me as soon as you're ready."

"OK."

27

Tuesday 7th June 2011

They arrived back in the office about 2.30pm to find Jimmy, Paul and Doreen all busy with various bits of paper. Doreen's fingers were whipping across her keyboard which was emitting a gentle repetitive clacking sound as she touched the keys. If she could complete all the day's typing by 3.30pm she would have half an hour to read her latest library book which was sitting in the top drawer of the two still residing in her desk. Most days, she managed it. At 4, she would be off home taking the bus to her Mother's, where she still lived, to be in time for her evening meal which was always taken at 5pm on the dot. Doreen, like Lavinia, her Mother, was a person of routine. Men had flitted in and out of her life but her only interest was her passion for books.

Alison showed them the items they had found through the clear plastic bags that she had placed them in. She explained where they had been hidden before giving them to Jimmy who wrote down their details in his exhibit book. Paul asked him to take photocopies of the documents before submitting them for forensic examination, in order that he could inform both Groves and Prodow when they attended the office next. Paul stated he would have a word with the PoLSA officers on their search. He was not happy.

John, who had left unnoticed during Alison's quick briefing, was now being missed by Paul who wanted to discuss some further enquires that could be made about the documents.

He said in exasperation to Alison, "Where's 'Black John' gone off to now?"

Alison hadn't noticed John slip out of the office, but in addition, she had never before heard him referred to as 'Black John'. Being a white Englishman, the only explanation was his seriously black hair, some saying suspiciously black, implying the use of a dye which she assumed probably explained it. But the name rankled.

Before she could answer, John walked in carrying his nigh on thirty-year-old battered brown leather briefcase that had been repaired on at least four separate occasions and bore new metal brackets on the corners holding it together.

Paul said, "Why don't you buy yourself a decent new briefcase and chuck that crappy old thing away, it looks worse than you do."

"This case means a lot to me; a friend gave it to me and I shall have it till the day I die."

Paul knew that anyway, he had heard the story months before from John about how a colleague had been run over when they were together, and before he died he had given him the case. What he hadn't been told was that they were working undercover in the Midlands and had been deliberately targeted, and that John had managed to jump out of the way of the murderer in the stolen car. The locked briefcase had contained some very important evidence required by the Home Office, and John was implored to take the case and run which he did leaving his friend to die alone under the car in a dirty, wet, Midlands street.

Paul addressed John and Alison, "I'll do the enquiries with Cambridge about the Birth Certificate and anything pertaining to it if you two can have a go at the I.D. cards. Keep me informed and I'll let you know what I turn up, and keep your phone on."

The last was directed to Alison as John hardly ever bothered to use a mobile nor had any inkling to own one.

"Jimmy can try and sort out the newspaper and what he wanted £1000 in cash for."

Alison was still thinking of the name 'Black John' and the numerous times she had heard it as a child from her Father and the exploits that seemed to always accompany it. This must be a totally different 'Black John' to the one of her youth. They both went to the canteen where Alison, who had started to take a closer interest in John, noticed that he took a table in the corner furthest from the servery and sat with his back to the wall. As they ate a late lunch, she found herself watching John more closely and noticed his eyes constantly monitoring the room over her shoulders, but she still could not imagine this was the 'Black John' her Father spoke so fondly of. He was just an old detective constable coming up to retirement with the same nickname: but then he had quite impressed her with some of the things he had done and said so far. She could not get it out of her head when John interrupted her thoughts.

"What are you thinking about? You're miles away. You still studying me?"

Before she could stop herself, she blurted out, louder than she needed causing the occupants of the closest table to take stock of her, "Do you know my Father?"

"Ah so that's it. I do, who told you?"

Alison could not believe it. All the things she had heard as a child related to the man seated in front of her. She explained how she had heard about a man called 'Black John' from her Father and just previously from Paul, and put two and two together but couldn't believe it quite made four.

She asked some probing questions really just to confirm to herself that it was the same 'Black John'.

He answered nearly all quite truthfully until he said, "I would be obliged now you have discovered my little secret that you do not divulge it willy-nilly to anyone else."

Strangely, Alison, who didn't know why, agreed readily to the request and then said, "You're a bit like Armstrong. Not what you appear to be."

John moved the conversation away from himself and said, "If we could solve the conundrum of the cup and the I.D. cards, that may open the case sufficiently and take us to the murderer."

Alison was now back on track and said, "I think I could probably find something about the ID cards on the Internet, I'll have a go when I get home."

This was a technology that John had yet to embrace fully. Having heard how useful it could be, he just didn't trust it.

"If you go straight home after lunch it will give you more time."

Alison's stomach was rumbling loudly as the first food she had eaten today seemed to fill the empty chamber and echoed around it. John was too much the gentleman to comment.

To cover her obvious embarrassment, "How do you go so long without eating? Were you a camel in your previous life?"

"I think camels have to eat, it's water they don't need so much of."

"You can be an exasperating sod at times."

"Thanks."

"What are you going to be doing this afternoon?"

"I'll check out the mug and I want to try and find a will." He thought for a second or two. "Here's another quandary though for you to ponder. Jimmy has the last year's bank statements of Armstrong, and they have been checked thoroughly. All his bills have been paid using direct debits. The cheque book has not been used for anything except to draw cash. The largest amount having been £500 and the average £200. First: being a housebound invalid, did he go to the Bank to cash his cheques? And, how did he get there? Or did someone do it for him? Second: and in my opinion more significantly is what did he spend the cash on, and how?"

28
Tuesday 7th June 2011

Vilf was a townie. He loved the buzz of London. The countryside was all right, but not much seemed to happen in it: other than the occasional murder. Villages were too quiet for him but the smaller towns were chiefly passable. Bognor Regis was big enough to have a buzz and it was by the sea. He had reached the age of twenty-three before he'd seen the sea for the first time and that had been at Clacton in company with some woman he had been trying to impress. A few days later, he had helped himself to a swimming costume and towel from Marks and Spencer with the ultimate goal of going into the sea. Unfortunately, his efforts went unrewarded as being arrested and locked up for an old burglary thwarted them.

Now he was in Bognor. He'd been in a café for a sandwich at midday and was sitting on a bench on the prom watching the few 'white horses' that were atop some waves while licking an ice cream. There were a couple of pubs he'd noted doing food and he planned on eating later at one and having a drink in the other before heading back to his lodgings in Midhurst. As he sat staring at the dark grey green sea of the English Channel and pondered the logic of the local authority not repairing the pier, he overheard part of the conversation of the two men seated on the next bench. Cars passing along the seafront road drowned out the majority of it, but he heard enough.

He couldn't bring himself to look because he knew that they would see him, and anything could happen then which frightened him. His car with his gun, which he considered an equaliser was some way off. What he had heard, he believed, confirmed that he was in the right place. Straining hard, he tried to hear more above the sound of the passing traffic on the road behind the prom and rumbustious screaming children desperate to be on the beach and their bawling overprotective parents. Yes: it was Russian, he was sure of it. He'd heard them mention Dimitri. That bloody obnoxious foreigner he had been forced to share a cell with for seven weeks. Had he heard them say he was due out? If true, he would have to speed up his plan!

Casually getting up, he walked the couple of yards forward across the prom and stood for a few seconds looking at the sandy beach and sea beyond while wolfing down the remnants of his ice cream cornet. Then he turned, and saw a single man sitting in the middle of the bench with his arms out resting on the back of it, glegging. Glancing up and down the prom he couldn't see two men together. In the corner of his eye he caught them, just reaching the far side of the road having dodged between the traffic. One much larger than the other. All he could see were their backs!

They were soon out of sight walking rapidly off down a side street. Vilf was not as nimble on his feet and could not get across the road fast enough. He really wanted a good look at them.

Accepting defeat, he made his way back to his car resolving to move his lodgings to Bognor.

29
Tuesday 7th June 2011

Alison left for home as John went back to the office to pick up a full list of local Solicitors in West Sussex that Paul kept in one of his own indexes.

Paul gave him a photocopied list and said, "What do you want it for?"

"I hope one of these will have a copy of the will and we might get to see it."

Paul said, "Don't tell me you're going to get a solicitor to show you any will they have before an inquest."

John replied, "Why is it that no one seems to trust lawyers? They are reasonable people if you speak to them nicely. I'll be in the conference room. The 'phone in there is a direct line and doesn't show up on 1471."

With that he left and made his way down to the empty conference room where he placed his briefcase on a large table, pulled the telephone from the window sill that was it's normal home, and then sat down facing the only door in and out. He was still a very nervous person, and knew that people from his past would love to see the back of him even now. During his service, he had been shot at, caught in bomb blasts and physically attacked and only a few years earlier, a man who John had given primary evidence against, had broken out of gaol swearing vengeance against him. One thing he'd learnt in his career was not to be predictable, and this trait held true in most things that he did. Scanning the three pages of Solicitors and their telephone numbers, he picked one from about half way down the second page at random, and dialled the number.

"Good afternoon. Peters and Morris Solicitors. My name is Maureen. How can I help you?"

"Hello Maureen. This is John Whiles from the Police. We need a copy of George Armstrong's will for the murder enquiry in case there is anything of evidential value recorded on it. Do you think I could collect an endorsed copy and a producing statement tomorrow?"

"Just one moment please" and John heard a click as the call was put on hold.

Mundane music of no recognisable composer commenced its weary dirge. Maureen was soon back on the line.

"Hello Mr Whiles. I can't find any record of us holding a will in the name of George Armstrong at all."

"Maureen, I am so sorry, I have rung the wrong firm." John glanced at the list and said, "I meant to call Petra's."

"No problem Mr Whiles. It was nice talking to you. Have a pleasant day. Goodbye."

"Goodbye Maureen. Thanks anyway."

Both hung up. John didn't really trust lawyers that much either and thought if a firm believed he had knowledge of something in their possession, they would probably be more forthcoming in imparting information.

John continued to dart up and down the list at random calling the firms shown and crossing each one off as he called them. Some were immediately helpful, others were after some cajoling and then a few with blatantly contrary, or plain sheer lazy secretaries told him he should know better than to ask them such things. There were two that told him that he should address his request in writing to one of the partners in the firm. Making a note against these as 'possible' for further attention should the need arise, he continued. Just short of three hours and just prior to 6 o'clock when most solicitors' secretaries were getting ready to go home, John struck lucky.

He'd rung the third solicitors shown on the first page of the list. Aldwright, Sedgwick and Partners of Bognor and spoken to the receptionist who sounded like a teenage girl. In fact she was in her mid-twenties and had only been at the firm for about six months. Today she was by herself as the senior receptionist had stepped out for some cakes for the partners. When John called, her first thought was she had neglected to prepare a copy of the will and was as helpful as she could be. It had been drummed into her, like all other solicitors' receptionists, that she should not divulge anything to anyone over the telephone, but here she was giving John the information. Mr Sedgwick had removed the file only last week and then as a throwaway remark stated that he was probably dealing with the duplication himself. Thanking her for her candid assistance, he said he would call tomorrow to talk to Mr Sedgwick and they both hung up. With rueful resignation, John realised if he had started at the top of the first page of the list, he would have discovered the whereabouts of the will within about fifteen minutes. 'Sometimes,' he thought to himself, 'life's a pain.'

Looking at the assembled pile of jumble inside his briefcase, John found and took out the gas bill, unfolding and smoothing it before laying it flat on the table. Turning to the 'G' page of his address book which he always kept secured in a pocket of the briefcase, John found 'Gas' and the name next to it: Gordon Weeks, with a Croydon telephone number. It rang for so long that John was just thinking of hanging up when he was jolted into action by the voice that answered.

"Weeks."

"Hi there Daily, Oscar here. How's retirement?"

"Bloody hell, I thought you must have been dead by now. Where are you, or shouldn't I ask?"

"Sussex. I've got a little problem though and I thought of you."

"You only ever call me if you've got a problem or you want someone to buy you a pint, what is it this time?"

"I have a gas bill from a guy who was murdered, and I want to know all his banking details. Can you help?"

"Yeah. Shouldn't be a problem. Give us the reference number and I'll have the details tomorrow about 12ish. That do you?"

"Be great." John read out the reference number and Gordon read it back to him for confirmation. John continued and said, *"I'll come up and see you and bring someone you might know."*

"I was right then; you want me to buy you a pint. Mind, it'll still be good to see you. Make it the office then in Crawley. I could do with a day in the sticks."

Both said their goodbyes till tomorrow and hung up.

Gathering all his papers up, he threw them back haphazardly into his briefcase and returned the phone to its exact position on the window sill which was identifiable by the absence of dust. The Police employed a professional team of cleaners who were obviously neglecting their duties in some of the lesser used rooms around the station. Checking that as far as possible he had left no discernible trace of the fact he had been there, he went upstairs to find Paul.

Doreen had gone home a bit before 4 o'clock to Mum and her tea ready to go out early to her book club meeting. Jimmy had 'legged' it even earlier so he could get himself ready for a great night out with his new sexy girlfriend at one of Chichester's noisy and busy night clubs. Paul was looking through the papers scattered about on one of the spare desks, and throwing some away and putting others into his own 'in' tray for further thought in the morning when John walked in.

"Cuppa?"

"Why not."

Paul opened Doreen's large bottom drawer and took out an electric kettle and the accoutrements and set about making a coffee. Sussex Police frowned on kettles in offices if they weren't PAT (Portable Appliance Tested) tested and there was a perfectly good canteen two floors below, hence the feeble concealment. Pauls argument, should anyone have found it and questioned it, would be that the office would remain unmanned while he queued two floors below. Other than Groves, the whole team, including Prodow knew of its existence and location.

John updated Paul with the details of the Solicitor holding the will in order that he could arrange for Prodow to sort out a copy to be obtained for information. He already knew that the lawyers were to act as sole executors thanks to the accommodating secretary.

Both men sat with their feet resting on the edge of Paul's desk as they drank the hot coffee. Paul had searched at the back of the drawer that held the kettle until he found the biscuits that he loved to dunk. They chatted amicably about the case and Groves and how he hadn't a clue considering his reputation as a DS.

Paul said, "Do you think she did it?"

"It's possible but I think unlikely. What do you reckon?"

"I don't know. Everything points to her, but I'm not sure."

John said, "The thing that worries me is the missing letters and other items. For a man who keeps pamphlets and postcards in neat piles, he should have some letters and definitely an address book of some kind. By the way, we are off to Crawley tomorrow where I think we may get some leads on his financial affairs."

"Try to get back sober, Prodow is due in at 4.30."

"You mean quarter to 5."

They continued 'chewing the fat' for a further twenty minutes before they closed the office and made their way into the yard and towards their respective cars. Paul looked disdainfully at John's Vauxhall.

"I don't know which is oldest, the briefcase or the car."

"Nor do I." retorted John laughing at his lie.

30

Wednesday 8th June 2011

Alison had got in early, she wanted breakfast today. She wasn't on a diet and didn't need to be on one, and after yesterday not eating before nearly 3pm she thought she might have wasted away. 'Everyone knows breakfast is the most important meal of the day' she thought to herself, 'so how is he so damn large if he hardly eats anything?' John ambled into the canteen and saw Alison sitting at the same table that they had occupied for lunch the previous day, but this time she had her back to the wall. He went to the servery without speaking to her, and bought a coffee for himself and a tea for her remembering to put in two heaped teaspoons of sugar. Walking back to the table, he placed the tea in front of her.

"Some years ago, I was on a boat going down the Thames when we went past a sugar factory. I could see all these little black things on the sugar cane where it had been offloaded before being refined. When I asked the skipper what they were, he said 'Rats'. I've never taken sugar since in tea or coffee."

Alison looked at him for a few seconds and said, "Good morning to you too."

John sat at an angle in his chair and said, "How did you do yesterday?"

"Not too bad, I've got to make some phone calls between 9 and 5. There are some people connected to the DWP (Department for Work and Pensions) in Newcastle that may be able to help and the MOD (Ministry of Defence) as well as the National Archives. What did you do?"

John filled her in with his afternoon activities of the preceding day, and then said to her, "Do you think she did it?"

Alison, who had just taken a sip of tea, nearly choked on it at the question which she had definitely not expected. She had assumed like nearly all the

78

murder team from the start that Munroe was responsible for Armstrong's murder because she had been arrested within two days of the crime, and had since been charged with the offence of murder.

"You alright?"

"Yeah. I didn't expect to be asked that question."

"Well? What do you think?"

"Yes. I mean no. I don't know."

"Why not?"

"I just assumed that because she was arrested originally and has been charged, she did it."

"Come on. Think. Remember ABC. Where's your proof that will convince a jury?"

She sat silently in meditative thought evaluating the facts that she was aware of, as John sat looking straight at her waiting for her to make some valid comment in reply. Alison wasn't to be rushed. Seconds passed, then a couple of minutes of silence before she replied.

"Right." She took a mouthful of now tepid sweet tea and started. "We know that Armstrong was alive between 7.30 and 8.30am because the morning carer attended to him and filled in the relevant entry in the binder in the kitchen. Then he endorsed her signature with his own. Also, the postie who delivered the mail at about 9ish saw him in the chair by the fireplace and waved to him and got a waved response. At about 2pm, when the postie was going home along the road and approaching the driveway, he saw a small green car turn, in his words 'quickly', out of the drive and across the road in front of oncoming traffic and away towards Barnham. He thought it was a woman driving. Munroe has a small green Micra. When her car was impounded and searched, a really old and out of date pension book of Armstrong's was found under the passenger seat. Could it have been in the stolen bundle of papers and dropped by her accidentally?"

Pausing to think for a few seconds, and take a final mouthful of tea, she continued.

"Munroe said to the arresting officer before the 'brief' told her to say nothing that she went to the bungalow about 2ish to see George to let him know she was doing the evening carers' session, but would be late. When she was walking towards the kitchen door, she said she saw the jam jar with liquid on the floor outside the shed and put it inside for safety. Obviously, she knew her fingerprints would be found so she had this as an excuse. She claimed she didn't go inside the bungalow because the door was locked and there was no response to her knocking. She didn't look through any windows because she maintained she was in too much of a rush to get to another client. Other carers said that Munroe was always asking to be allocated to Armstrong and often tried to change clients with them to do so."

Looking straight at John as though for encouragement and reading nothing in his expression, she persevered.

"There had been two complaints lodged about her in relation to inappropriate comments about client's financial affairs. Other carers were often told by clients that Munroe was more interested in their finances than their well-being. The Post Master in Barnham has stated that just recently, a female had tried to acquire money, unsuccessfully, using Armstrong's pension card in a card reader machine. That person had the wrong pin number and couldn't get anything from his pension account. Mr Chaplin, his chess playing friend, says that Armstrong had told him of a carer who was getting in his words, 'very pushy' and argumentative. There were two cups and saucers in the sink which had both been wiped with a dish cloth and rinsed in water, indicating he knew and trusted the person who put them there."

Considering what she had already said, she knew she was struggling. John stared impassively back at her. Alison was not quite willing to give up.

"Armstrong appeared to have been held on the floor for some time because the pathologist found a large bruise on his back. Maybe until the poison took over when Munroe left him for dead. Chaplin saw him on the floor straight away when he looked through the side window after he found the door locked. Worst of all, she said nothing really during the interviews which gives the impression of guilt, and during the first, only confirmed the handling of the poison jar and a few facts about her training and work as a carer. That's about it."

"So according to your account," said John, "we only have circumstantial evidence, and not much of that either."

She knew before the end of her summary that everything she said was circumstantial and when they took it to court as it was, they would be lucky to get it past the committal stage of the proceedings let alone to the Crown Court for trial.

Reluctantly, she sullenly agreed, "Yeah."

"Never mind, I have arranged to see someone in the office at Crawley who may be able to shed a little more light on George."

31

Wednesday 8th June 2011

Paul was about to make his second cup of tea, and getting another cup ready for Doreen when John and Alison walked into the office.

They greeted one another and John said, "Forgot to ask, get anywhere with the Birth Certificate?"

"No, not yet. I spoke to a very nice lady in the registry office who said she would dig out any other related information she could find today. She's got to find the really old records from the archives and then get an endorsed copy made for us and with a bit of luck she may find out more about the parents. Doubt that it will be any more than what we have but it may make the force go bankrupt; it's going to cost us £7 a certificate!"

John retorted, "Prodow won't like signing your expenses claim for that."

"The address on the envelope means nothing to anyone."

Doreen walked in carrying her library book which she put straight into her top drawer as she sat at her desk and said, "What sort of office manager doesn't look after his staff? They could die of thirst here."

"Yes alright. These two have delayed me, I was just getting it."

After some general office banter where the two older members of the team seemed to quite happily insult each other but take no offence, John asked, "Can you set the tape up tonight so we can have a quick look at it again?"

"Yes. What are you looking for?"

"Where the emergency button for the lifeline was. Can you get Jimmy to find out when the burglar alarm was last serviced?"

"Yes. Will do."

The two left the office, and descending the stairs, went into the yard.

John said, "Let's use mine today" and walked straight to his car with Alison unable to stop him or complain as she was struggling to match his pace.

He slid straight into the driver's seat: the car wasn't even locked Alison noticed, but she wasn't able to open the passenger door. There was a click from within, and the door became free for her to open, and she slid into the passenger seat after first brushing the detritus from it. Now attired in a smart two-piece suit, she did not want it ruined. As she expected, the top of the dash board was covered in a fine layer of dust and there were bits of paper and other assorted rubbish in the foot well, but not enough to be a problem. The seat was remarkably clean once she'd brushed it with her hand. She had noticed what appeared to be a waxed jacket of some kind strewn across the back seat with an old fashioned wooden umbrella lying on top of it. From the rear-view mirror hung and swung what she really hated in any vehicle: a 'smelly' and this was the worst type, in the shape of a Christmas tree.

"It's June for God's sake, how long has that been there?"

"Not too long. I had a couple of them."

'What a fun trip this was going to be' she thought.

With the horror of the vehicle still in her head, John turned the key in the ignition and the engine immediately burst into life and began to purr softly. Quieter than her little Ford. She noticed all the antiquated rocker buttons set into the mock wooden dashboard in a neat orderly line, and what looked to Alison like a steam driven radio set right in the centre of the dash. The car was manoeuvred out of the yard and into the gentle flow of what was locally described as the rush hour by those who had never experienced the cut and thrust of a true one such as the capital's.

She scooped the papers from the floor and before he could say anything, Alison tried to open the glove box by pushing the release button with the intention of depositing them therein. It didn't open.

"It's jammed, that's why they are on the floor."

She pushed them all into the passenger door's pocket that already contained a full unopened can of beer which gave the impression that it was trying to keep everything else out, but she persevered and put the papers to the side of the can. The car sped out of town and into the country and neither spoke.

After a few miles, the silence was broken, "Does the radio work?" and she reached for the nearest dial which she assumed to be the on/off knob. Nothing happened.

"Let me," and as his hand moved to the radio, she saw him gently touch a rocker switch in passing. When he turned the knob, the radio burst into life on radio 2.

'He would listen to that', she thought. "Anything decent on it?" and she pushed the middle of the five pre-set buttons that she assumed to be set on some obscure stations. The glove box dropped open hitting her knees and caused her to jump in shock, not pain.

Inside was a screen about six inches square glowing gently with a slowly scrolling coloured map with a pulsating green dot in the centre which Alison took no time at all in realising was their position.

"What the hell is this?"

John said, "That's my Sat Nav. I very rarely use it, that's why it's in the glove box."

"That's the strangest and biggest looking Sat Nav I've ever seen. I saw you push that switch," and she pointed at a rocker "before you turned the radio on. Is it some kind of control?"

"You don't miss much. Yes, you're right."

"Now I come to think of it, my little Fiesta has two switches, how come yours has," and she quickly counted, "ten. What do they all do?"

"Different things. It's an old car and each switch does one thing; your switches do several things each. Now can you just push the glove box closed?"

It gently clicked into place, and in a sudden rash moment, she tried to open it again by pushing the release button, but it stayed firmly in situ.

The radio played soporific music that was what she thought would be suitable for people in mental institutions to keep them calm and was from some radio station she had never heard of. She let the music drift over her as the car swept along country roads towards Crawley. Alison was thinking quiet thoughts about the car she was in, and how her seat was so clean, how the car started a lot quicker than hers which was years younger, and how sprightly it traversed the roads and just seemed to purr effortlessly along.

"I've never been to Crawley Police Station before. Who are we seeing?"

"Who said we were going to the station?"

"You did."

"No I didn't. I said we were going to the Crawley office."

"Where the hell is it then?"

"It's nearer Three Bridges really, but it's been called the Crawley office for as long as I can remember."

Alison was exasperated and thought, 'what's the point, I suppose I'll see when we get there', and she settled back with her own thoughts, as John smiled contentedly knowing he still hadn't told her much. Surprises are so much more fun: sometimes!

32

Wednesday 8th June 2011

The car slowed and came to a halt against a pavement in a quiet suburban street with enough room for vehicles to park without manoeuvring back and forth. John left the Vauxhall a few feet from a dropped kerb in front of a drive to a private house in order that no one could park in front of him or block him in without it being obvious. They both left the car and Alison noted John locked it on the driver's side with a key, not a fob: 'how antiquated.' Although to any casual observer, they were walking together, John was leading as they crossed the road towards a junction to what appeared to be a very small private road. With a casual glance behind, John turned into the road, and within a few yards ducked into an open gated entrance with some kind of evergreen plant virtually concealing it.

Alison was taken completely by surprise as she was about to walk past. She ducked through it now a yard or two behind John and found they were walking down a crazy paved path which was enclosed on both sides by flint stone walls and a canopy of vines which were clinging to some kind of roof covering. After a dozen yards or so, John reached the end of the passage, and ducking his head; he opened a thick oak door and walked through into a dimly lit room with two tables surrounded by an assortment of odd chairs. He held the door for Alison and shut it behind her.

They entered a windowless room lit by a single light that was trying valiantly and failing miserably. From the bright sunshine outside to the dim light inside took Alison's eyes several minutes to adapt. She didn't know it, but there was a logical reason for the room to be kept in a subtle glow. There was a small bar area with room for one person to stand behind it in one corner with an unobtrusive closed door to the rear of it. The door flew open and a man of at least sixty years burst through it. He was only about 5 feet 8 inches in height but had the bearing of a taller man; upright and alert, fit for his age and modestly attired. His face was slightly rounded and his bulbous nose disclosed the fact that he liked a drink, and as Alison tried to see him more clearly in the dim light, she started to think how much he looked like a picture she had once seen of Captain Pugwash.

"Hi John. Long time no see, you can stay here in the green room for as long you like today."

"We will if that's ok with you? How are you Ginger?"

The two men chatted amicably for a few minutes as Alison tried to make out the colour of the room, and then to discreetly see what colour the man's hair was. It definitely was not ginger, more she thought brown with grey flecks and patches: befitting for a person of his apparent age.

"Ginger, allow me to present Alison Daines to you. Last time you saw her, she was about four months old."

Alison sat heavily down onto the nearest chair flabbergasted. She had no idea who the person was, and for some reason she felt embarrassed that he had seen her when she was so young.

"Alison, this is Jeff Taylor."

"Hi Alison. Really nice to meet you again. How's your dad?"

She was thrown. Totally confused. Who was this man? How did he know her Father?

"Em. He's ok thanks" came her hesitant reply as she tried to recover her composure. "I seem to be at a loss here, who are you?"

"You're a sod Oscar. You haven't told her, have you?"

"No I thought you could tell her. I'll go and see your missus and get the drinks." And with that, he lifted the flap at the side of the bar for Ginger to step into the room and subsequently allowing him to step behind the bar and out of sight through the door.

"Have a cosier seat Alison and I'll fill you in so to speak."

They sat at the table nearest the bar and Ginger began to regale her with an abridged story.

"Long time ago, me and a few mates who were all ex-military were recruited by a private company to become 'official mercenaries' and go and help the Angolan Government who were fighting a long and protracted civil war against what they then called rebels. It was actually on behalf of HM's

(Her Majesty's) Government who supported the elected regime at the time. We knew if we were caught that our Government would disown us and deny all knowledge of us. As it so often happens, our Government changed as did its Foreign Policy, and then things went a bit pear shaped causing us some problems and we had to get out of Angola pretty fast. We found out that the person who had recruited us on behalf of HM Government sold us out for a large amount of money to the rebels so if we were killed or caught he didn't have to pay us. It also seemed to suit some people in our Government if we were killed. So we made a pact that whoever survived would deal with them.

All my mates were killed and I got out by the skin of my teeth and made my way back to England. I knew some older ex-military people who had worked for the same firm and was able to find out that not one of them knew what the person who had recruited us was up to. Rumour had it that he was possibly acting as an agent for contract killers. Soon found that was right when a Russian tried to kill me after I had attempted to make contact with some Foreign Office mandarin. I'd been given your Dad's name as a person I could trust so I found out where he was and went to see him: that was the day of your christening."

"Brilliant!"

"Well things soon got under way with the team and they went after the recruiter and the hit men he employed. The Home Office muscled in and got involved and John's mate ended up dead because they blabbed about it to all and sundry and didn't take the security seriously. Anyway, the shit who sold us out got done for plotting a kidnapping of someone in Guatemala that saw him pull twenty years and you don't want to be in a Guatemalan gaol for a week let alone twenty years. Your old man's team went after the hit men and some got caught and banged up but a lot got away and that's why we still take precautions."

Alison, now composed, said with slight sarcasm, "Surprised you trust telling me then." "Not really. If Oscar trusts you to bring you here, I trust you. Simple."

John burst back into the bar and over to the table with two pints of some dark brew which he put down without spillage.

"Forgot to ask what you want to drink. You definitely would not like this; all the shorts are on the optics and the mixers are under the counter. Help yourself."

"Is that ok with you Jeff?"

"Sure, call me Ginger. Your Dad owns a tenth of this pub, so I'm sure he wouldn't object."

It had dawned originally on Alison that she was either in a private club or in a small back bar of a pub. The fact that her Dad owned a tenth of a public house was suddenly starting to weigh heavily on her mind, and she wondered if her Mum knew of the arrangement.

She walked over to the bar and behind it through the raised flap. Thoughts swam in her head as she squatted down on her haunches to see if there was any orange juice on the chiller shelf. There were two bottles of it amongst a few other flavours, and as she removed one of them a dark object to the very right of the shelf caught her eye. Sitting there, handle backwards towards her ready to be picked up was an automatic handgun.

As if in passing, John broke from his conversation with Ginger and called to her, "By the way, be careful with the gun, it's loaded and the safety is normally off," and then continued his conversation.

33

Wednesday 8th June 2011

Alison was starting to get extremely worried by things she had heard and seen when a small light in the middle of the room flickered and a bleeper that Ginger had in his top jacket pocket went off twice.

"You expecting anyone?"

"Yes. Sorry Ginger, forgot to mention it. Gordon."

"I'll be out the front for a couple of minutes then," and Ginger seemed to evaporate as he left the table and disappeared through the door having lowered the flap on the bar as he left.

"Am I going to get some more surprises?"

"Very probably."

The door from the alley burst open and a man strode into the room that did not look that dissimilar to John in both features and clothing. He looked straight at John and said, "Hi John, see you've got a drink already. We staying here in the green room today?"

Alison believed she had established in her own mind that the room was more a bluish colour. His voice was rasping and he sounded slightly out of breath.

"Yeah. We're happy here. Gordon, I'd like you to meet Alison, Alison this is Gordon."

Alison looked sideways at John and with no irony said, "How old was I when Gordon last saw me?"

Gordon laughed freely and without inhibition before saying, "You're just like your old man, stroppy and sarcastic. I think you were about a year old."

"Brilliant!"

Ginger, who had released the secure catch on the door from the alley by pressing a button next to the small CCTV (Close Circuit Television) screen that he had checked first to make sure he was permitting entry to a welcome visitor, came back into the room. He greeted Gordon and put a pint down on the table for him.

Gordon said, "Your old man told me you'd joined up. How did you get teamed up with 'Black John'?"

Alison said, "I really am starting to wonder now. I honestly don't know. I've never actually believed in fate."

Gordon had swallowed nearly half his pint and had somehow managed to get a whitish froth on his top lip which his tongue cleared in one sluggish sweep. "At least you'll learn a lot. Might not be stuff you want to know, but you'll definitely learn a lot."

All three men were lolling in their seats chatting and drinking and Alison, who was sitting as befitted a respectable young lady wearing a two-piece suit and court shoes, listened in intently but did not join in the conversation.

Ginger was soon onto his feet and said, "I've got to go into the bar to help the missus, it's a busy time. Help yourselves to drinks when you want them. I'll see you later," and with that he glided out of the room.

Gordon said, "Right, down to business, you could have got this information without my input, I presume there is an ulterior motive?" He slid a sealed envelope that suddenly materialised in one of his hands across the table to John who put it into an inside pocket.

"Yes. Someone has been making not very discreet enquiries about me, mainly my habits."

Gordon guffawed, "You don't have habits, any ideas who?"

"No, but I thought I would give you a heads up so you could let the others know. Soon as I find out anything, you'll be the first to know. I'll fill Alison in, because she is with me and because of her old man."

"I presumed that's why she was here."

Alison could hold off no longer, "What the hell are you two talking about? What are you going to tell me?"

John replied, "I promise I will tell you before we get back today. Have a little more patience."

Gordon said, "You still take all the precautions?"

"Yeah: and a couple of my own. I feel confident, but better safe than sorry."

Alison was angry and seething inside but wasn't sure whether she should say something else to let the two of them know how she felt. So instead, she got up and went round to the little bar and from under the counter took a bottle of vodka. Putting at least a double into a tumbler, she added what remained of her original orange juice. Then she slouched back to her seat like a stroppy teenager having decided to say nothing. The two men appeared to Alison to be talking in riddles, but she still listened to what they were saying and took in most of what was said.

At 1.30pm, Ginger came back into the bar carrying a tray with three simple curries on, and two more pints. Placing the pints in front of the men and the plates onto the table in front of the little group told them, "Help yourselves to the eating irons on the bar, I can't stop, it's still heaving out there and Sylvia is struggling." With that, he turned and was gone again.

As if in passing, John said to Alison, "It's his wife, the only person he's frightened of."

Alison had calmed down, and got the knives and forks for all three who were soon making short shrift of the food.

Whilst they ate, Gordon grilled Alison about why she had joined the Police, what she had done so far and what her ambitions were. John quietly listened to her answers without passing comment or asking any additional questions. She began to mellow with the help of the Vodka and talked quite freely to Gordon whom she was really starting to like, and he began to gently tease her comparing her traits with her Father's. When she managed to actually put a question to him though, he seemed to simply dodge the answer with some flippant remark that led to another question for her. Alison would later realise that he had found out a lot about her and her personal life and that she had learnt practically nothing about him.

Ginger came back into the bar and joined them for enough time to say their farewells and Gordon left via the rear door once Ginger had released the lock. A few minutes later, John and Alison vacated the premises going down the alley leaving by the postern gate and straight across the small road before moving towards the junction and the Vauxhall.

34

Wednesday 8th June 2011

The car snuck away from the kerb and off down the road and Alison got a fleeting glimpse of the front of a public house decked out with hanging baskets over hung with a low thatched roof. Tables and chairs were dotted about randomly in the front garden surrounded by people eating and drinking and enjoying convivial company. 'Nice', she thought, 'no wonder he was busy.'

"When are you going to 'fill me in'?"

"We'll get well South of Crawley, and then we can stop in Storrington."

John took a different route back, but soon arrived in Storrington and parked in a car park behind some shops. Walking together, they went into a small tea room where they were lucky to find one small empty table by a window. John sat where he could see the front door and have a view out of the large picture window. Then both had proper tea out of a tea pot, and through a strainer. The only way John could drink it and enjoy it.

"I don't believe your Dad has ever told you what he did for a short time when he was in the Met, but he thinks the time is right for you to know."

"Are you saying you're in touch with him?"

"Of course." Before Alison could say anything more, John continued, "Some time ago, there was a war going on in Angola and a man in the UK saw a way of making some money by recruiting ex-military personnel to go out and fight."

"Yeah. Ginger told me."

"They believed it was sanctioned by the Government and they were promised good money but the guy had no intention whatsoever of paying any of them. It transpired he was in collusion with a couple of junior politicians and civil servants who were all out to make as much money as they could by fair means or foul. Ginger was one of the men who went out to Angola.

The guy took a lot of money from the Angolan Government and then when it looked like the rebels were getting the upper hand, he shopped all the mercenaries' positions and objectives, so they were caught and killed. What he didn't know was that during the fighting, the Angolan Government were so grateful that they had given the fighters each a gold ring inset with nine diamonds which was worth a lot of money. The official Prime Minister at the time controlled the diamond mines and gave Ginger a large bag of uncut diamonds for getting him to safety. After they were all killed, Ginger managed to get the rings to a contact in Zimbabwe and then back to the UK. Ginger has probably told you what happened next."

Alison nodded, "Some."

"Well, your old man was working at the Yard and there were a few of us at your christening,"

Alison interrupted saying, "Either I'm younger than I thought or you're older than you look."

John continued without affront or comment. "After Ginger arrived, we made some enquiries and soon found out that the guy was probably controlling some foreign hit men. Your old man put a team together who he could trust in order that we could do something about them. Then a ranking officer at the Yard with little intelligence who had never done a proper day's Police work in his life without making sure his back was fully covered, decided that the Home Office should be informed, and naturally, it all went pear shaped.

Someone found where we had secured Ginger, and tried to kill him. He was quite sprightly in those days and managed to jump out of a window with his Police minder and get away. We worked hard and found out that a lot of the people we were after lived in the Midlands. While we were there, one of the team got run down after the Chief Constable who had been informed of us working in his area, failed to arrange a backup team although agreeing with the Met Commissioner to provide one."

John paused in quiet contemplation for a few seconds before continuing, "We soon discovered the guy had some powerful friends that he had 'bought' and they were happy to see us fail." Sipping his tea, he scanned the small room, and stared out of the window with glistening eyes still remembering his friend.

"Perseverance put a lot of major people out of jobs and some in prison, and they weren't happy. There are still some that would like to see the hit men who got away earn their keep by eliminating a few of the team and that's why we have to be careful."

Alison said, "So is my Dad a target then?"

"It's possible, and because you are starting to become a little well known, you may become one too because you are his daughter. The reason I'm telling you is because somebody has been making some obvious and blatant enquiries about me in places I frequent in and around Chichester. They do not seem to be trying to hide the fact which is strange in itself. That's why I've told Gordon and Ginger, in order that they can take extra precautions and let the others know. You should just be aware about what's happening around you, and not let too many people know your movements. Gordon found out an awful lot about you in the pub considering what you discovered about him."

Alison said, "The gun under the bar is a bit over the top. What if the locals do a licensing visit and find it? I kind of feel I should do something about it."

"Ginger is probably the main target and needs an equaliser, and the local law probably don't even know that room exists as you can only get in from the rear if the door is released. The door behind the bar has to be released as well. Both doors have steel inserts so would be hard to break down. There's also a record at NSY (New Scotland Yard) of a licence for the gun so it is legal."

John saw no reason to tell her that a condition of its possession was that it should be kept unloaded in a locked and secured cabinet.

Alison was quiet as she thought for a few minutes before asking, "Is all this the reason I was put on the Armstrong enquiry and teamed up with you?"

"Your old man still has clout."

"Another thing Ginger told me is that my Dad owns a tenth of the pub, what's that all about?"

John slurped the remnants of his cup of tea avoiding the few tea leaves that had somehow defied the strainer, and then tried to force another cup from the dregs in the tea pot without success.

"When we wound the job up, we found the nearest and dearest of all Ginger's dead mercenary mates and unobtrusively gave each of them a ring as supplied by the Angolans. One of them, a lovely girl, wouldn't take it, and told Ginger to do something with it that would benefit him and the team. Your old man set him up with his current identity and we found the pub which was for sale, and he bought it on the proceeds of selling her ring and his own ring. Ginger had always had an inkling ostensibly to run a pub. He was a couple of grand short and didn't want to use the bag of diamonds at that time for various reasons. So, the whole team put in just two hundred quid each which was a lot of money in those days to an impoverished copper. Ginger set up an account and puts some of his hard-earned cash into it, and when we retire, we can take a tenth of it."

"That's a bit iffy for Police to be involved with?"

"Why? It's an investment. Lots of Police have investments that they can cash in when they want. Ours is slightly different, it can only be cashed in when we retire."

"So because my Dad is still in the job, he will get a tenth when he retires, and so will you."

"Yes, sort of, there are only four of us still serving, and the others have taken theirs."

"What's happened to the bag of diamonds?"

"That's a long story. I'll keep it brief. Ginger had to be careful with how he dealt with them so as not to attract attention. Someone knew a dodgy diamond dealer and with some inducement, he had them cut in Holland. Then they were sold and investment bonds were bought. The values rocketed. Ginger, using his second alias, and via different countries, bought a large plot of land in Kent which has over the years been developed to accommodate injured and retired military personnel. Some are trained in different disciplines and then subsidised when they set up their own businesses. There are specialists in numerous fields who can experiment there, and develop new products. Many make money and when they can afford it, put money back into the unit. Self-perpetuating."

"I think I understand."

"Sometimes we take large amounts out for bits of kit like the Sat Nav gizmo in the car. At any one time, we can see where other people's cars are by looking on it. We have radios in the cars linked to each other through Ian our technical wizard who owns and works in his own specialist company, and our cars are looked after by Bill, our mechanic. All paid for out of the fund."

"That can't be cheap?"

"Think what a bag of about 100 large uncut diamonds would be worth."

Alison was perplexed, so much information, she'd never had any clue as to what her Dad had done during his service. It was something she hadn't bothered to enquire of him. She had always thought he had been in offices doing boring paper work as he made his way up the promotions ladder, and now she knew so much more, she wondered what else he had been involved in.

"More tea?" said the plump owner come waitress, pulling Alison back from her thoughts.

"Not for me thanks."

John said, "No thanks, just the bill," and paid straight away.

Alison seemed preoccupied with her thoughts as they walked back towards his car.

"Something troubling you?"

"Yes. Stupid really. He's had…er.., no, he's got all that money. Runs an apparently successful pub but can't put decent lighting in a room."

John burst out laughing. "I thought you had worked that out. Try and think about it logically. How we got there. Weather conditions. Security. That sort of thing."

Back at the car, they got in in silence. It was soon tearing back through leafy country roads to Chichester.

"Well. Have you worked it out?"

"I think I actually might have done."

As they strolled towards the office, John said, "Go on then, enlighten me."

"Ginger, or whatever his real name is, is worried someone might try to do him harm by entering down that small passage. He'll see them coming on the CCTV and would have the gun ready. If it's sunny outside, anyone coming in would be at a disadvantage because their eyes would need to adjust to the gloom. How's that?"

"Pretty good. See. You can think things out if you try. Piper."

"Piper?"

"Ginger."

35

Wednesday 8th June 2011

They ambled into the office a few minutes prior to the meeting's alleged start time knowing they would still have plenty of time before the two senior officers arrived to have a chat to Paul. Opening the envelope from Gordon, John found a copy of a Gas bill in the name of Armstrong that was dated three days before his lifeless body had been found. There was a separate piece of paper showing a completed direct debit mandate in a neat, slightly forward slanting style of writing by Armstrong which showed his banking details. On a small collection of other papers was a request from Armstrong to the Gas board in his practiced hand that his bungalow be connected to the main gas supply and their reply. It was stated that he would have to make a financial commitment and he acknowledged by disclosing a debit card's details.

John gave the items to Alison who perused them quickly, and then passed them to Paul. He glanced casually at them not breaking conversation with John on the merits of his day out in Crawley and whether or not he had been drinking a decent real ale. In passing, he threw the fact into the conversation that all Armstrong's financial details had been requested from a Credit Reference firm and were already on file. The producing statement would be available to the office in the next couple of days. John did not seem to be that interested, nor in fact did Paul. At the front of his mind was that John had some ulterior motive in going to Crawley, and that he would only be privy to it if John fancied telling him.

Jimmy came rushing in ten minutes late for the meeting's start time, and was happy to see he had beaten both Prodow and Groves. He had been at the Lab with the toxicologist for most of the afternoon, and had learnt more about poisons than he thought was probably good for him. Now he knew how to administer and use certain ubiquitous poisons to kill people and leave very little trace. His mind had wandered on his journey back to the station to a short list of possible candidates to practice on, of which Groves was premier. Paul gave him the papers that the two investigators had collected, and he sat down and entered them into an exhibit book with gusto which he completed as Prodow and Groves strode into the room exactly 15 minutes late.

Prodow sat in Pauls vacated chair, and Groves saw the seat opposite empty and made for it. The phone flew off the desk and caught Groves at thigh height in the groin before dropping to the floor. All present except Groves suppressed laughter, but Prodow surrendered any pretence, and finally burst out with a loud roar.

"At least when I collect it, it falls straight to the floor. You shouldn't be in such a rush."

Groves was in temporary pain, and furious with himself for catching the blessed wire which he had avoided like the plague every time he had entered the office. To be criticised by Prodow though compounded the pain as he was the only one who on a regular basis had the phone off the desk.

"Right, sorry I'm late," John could not believe his ears, "I've been at the lawyers picking up a copy of the will," and with a flourish he removed a long thin brown envelope from his inside jacket pocket and gave it to Paul.

Doreen, who had been reading her book when both John and Alison had arrived, was studying Prodow now with intense interest as she had never heard him apologise to anyone for anything let alone unpunctuality. Prodow had thoroughly enjoyed the meeting with the lawyer which had adjourned at its conclusion to lunch and drinks in a local club.

Mr Aldwright, the lawyer, had suggested the possibility of him working for the group of seven practices as a legal representative between them and Police when certain of their higher profile clients were arrested. Because of this, he was in an exceptionally good mood and nothing was going to upset him. Paul gave him the briefest of updates which he joyfully praised, and he turned to John in anticipation of an update from him.

"We have been to Crawley and perhaps Alison would be the better to update you." Alison was not expecting a speaking part during this meeting, and seemed to splutter into life like a motor boat starting up on a pond. She was careful what she said, and like Paul extremely brief, and to her shock was also praised by Prodow.

"That's the problem working with an awkward bastard like John, you never know when he's going to drop you in it, but you recovered well." Alison turned a pleasant shade of red. Groves was also showing more interest in Prodow's remarks and couldn't make out what was wrong with him.

"Right Jimmy, your turn, let me have it."

Jimmy was ready and prepared, and set off in a chronological order of the events at the lab with an over enthusiastic detail of results of every day poisons.

Prodow showed great interest in his narrative, and at its conclusion quite openly said, "If any of your relatives drop dead, we'll know what to look for," and sniggered at his slight joke. "Doreen, is there anything you want to add?"

That nearly made her fall off her chair as in all the enquiries she had been on, no one had ever deemed to ask for her opinion, "Err, no."

"What are you reading now?"

"A book on Troy." She'd known for years that he had probably been aware she read in the late afternoons, but he had never once previously alluded to it.

"Mr Groves, anything you need to let us know?"

"No."

"Well that's it, thank you all for your hard work and keep it up," and with that, Prodow was out of his chair and towards the door like a man half his age followed by Groves who reminded Doreen of an obedient poodle.

Paul said, "What the hell is up with him?" but didn't get any response from the remaining little group who had all witnessed the departure with differing degrees of incredulity.

36

Wednesday 8th June 2011

Paul opened the envelope, and removed a vertically folded, certified copy of George Armstrong's last will and testament. He read this a lot more sedulously than the papers John had given him. Apparently, when the will had been made, his wife had still been alive and they had a clause that allowed the first person's monies to go to the survivor. As George had survived his wife, he was her beneficiary. There were no known relatives shown, but the final bequest was that all his monies go to similar charities, which he had listed. Paul gave the will to John who opened it and placed it flat on a desk so that both he and Alison could read it.

"What do you make of that?"

John said, "Very philanthropic."

Alison was studying the list of charities, and said, "Why so many different charities when they are all supporting basically the same thing, why not just one?"

Paul said, "Don't know, and at the moment, don't really care although duly noted," and then to John, "Nearly forgot, the video is ready to go."

Alison handed the will to Jimmy who laid it flat on Paul's desk before pouring over it trying to find something the others had missed that was relevant to the enquiry written thereon. His patience expired rapidly. He soon gave up, and was astonished when Doreen asked to see it. Handing the open will to her, he returned to his fortified desk to get his exhibit book, and a clear bag to place the will in. Doreen had enjoyed the fact that she had been included by Prodow in the meeting although she had no contribution to make, so now she wanted to get more involved.

She studied the will intently as Alison, Paul and John were making for the door and said, "I didn't know he was a smoker."

Paul stopped dead, and said, "He wasn't, why did you say that?"

"These charities are all for chest and breathing complaints."

Paul knew that little things mattered in major enquiries, and that information could be gleaned from the most insignificant of sources, not that he considered Doreen insignificant. He made a mental note to discuss this with her the following day, and then trailed after the others down the stairs to the conference come briefing room to check out the video. John had the remote in his hand and was speeding the video forward saying that all he wanted to check was where the panic alarm and the lifeline button were. Soon the recording slowed to normal speed and the lifeline button was clearly visible because of its bright red coloured button, on the top of the mantelpiece.

"That was out of his reach then, now where is the living room's panic alarm?" The picture moved slowly round and picked up the panic alarm on a trailing lead nestling on the floor under the table with the telephone. They all looked at one another.

Alison said, "He could probably have pressed it."

John said, "Two questions then, why didn't he have the lifeline round his neck and why didn't he press the panic alarm?"

Paul said, "We can't find any records of the alarm company as they went bust years ago, so I don't know if it's been serviced lately. Frankly, I doubt it. I've spoken to the technical branch, but they say it would have to be a qualified alarm engineer to check it. Prodow has authorised it so it's in hand. I will write a note to Chaplin because he will not speak to anyone on the phone because of the press intrusions. The local uniform officer can deliver it later tonight. I'll ask if it was Armstrong's habit of not wearing the lifeline, and if he often left it on the mantel piece."

John didn't bother rewinding the video, he just took it out of the machine and gave it to Paul saying it would be much simpler if it was copied onto several DVDs. They parted company from Paul without returning to the office.

In the car park, Alison started towards her car but was brought to an abrupt halt by John who said, "Remember, be careful."

"All very well for you, I don't know what, or who I'm looking for."

"You're a Police Officer, be suspicious. If something is unusual or someone asks too many questions, take care."

"Great!" and with that she got into her car and drove out of the station into the early evening traffic. Within 15 minutes she arrived home at her nice, quiet, small two bedroomed first floor flat in an up-market part of the Northern most area of Chichester. She left her car on the hard standing in front of her allotted garage, making sure it was locked and alarmed, before climbing the external stairs to her front door. Before putting the key in the lock, she hesitated and looked about from her first-floor vantage point but saw nothing that was unusual. Why on earth, she thought, did she need to worry as she was a baby when the Angolans were fighting each other?

Then she opened the door. There was a swift sudden movement from inside the hall, and an old crystal vase containing roses that was on the hall table hit the wooden floor and shattered sending small shards of glass and water about the floor as a black and white furry cat accelerated towards and past her.

"You stupid bloody idiot! You nearly gave me a heart attack."

37

Thursday 9th June 2011

She was awoken by the phone's incessant shrill at exactly five o'clock, which was an unearthly time in Alison's book as she hated to be disturbed before six. Preferably seven. Checking the luminous dial of her bedside alarm clock, she picked up the phone.

"*Hi Dad. What do you want?*"

The soft voice of her Father came to her ear, "*How did you know it was me?*"

"*No normal human being would ring at this God forsaken hour.*"

"*Early bird etc.*"

"*What do you want?*"

"*See if you want anything and have a chat.*"

"*Dad, it's five in the morning.*"

"*I thought you would be up getting ready for work: you won't get far if you lay in bed all day.*"

"*Who have you spoken to? John or Gordon?*"

There was an imperceptible short pause while he considered his options and decided to be as truthful as possible, "*Both.*"

"*I'm ok Dad.*"

"*Listen to what they say, you will learn more from them than most other Detectives.*"

"*More than from you?*"

"*Unlikely, anyway, now you're up, you can go to work, John's waiting for you,*" and he hung up. She lay in bed looking at the phone still in her hand.

At 7.15am when she walked into the canteen, it had only been open fifteen minutes, but John was in his chair, back to the wall eating what was probably all the unhealthiest choices the canteen was offering for breakfast. The lady at the servery was definitely a morning person, happy to be up early and too chatty by half for Alison's liking. With two cups of tea for herself, and a cup of coffee, she joined John at what was becoming their regular table. He acknowledged with a nod her arrival, but continued eating as she downed her first cup of tea.

Now she was starting to feel human, "When did you speak to my Dad?"

"This morning."

"Don't you people ever sleep?"

"Why waste your life lying in bed all day, anyway, Paul's in the office and he'll brief us."

"What about?"

"The gardener."

"Of course. I should have known!"

With his last fork full of food about to leave his plate, he said, "Sarcasm I presume."

Both finished their drinks and Alison managed two poached eggs on toast before making their way up to the office where Paul was brewing his own tea.

They all greeted one another and as was normal, engaged in general conversation. Paul brought the subject round to the murder and the fact that Armstrong employed an elderly man as his gardener. This had only come to light when a man had walked into the station just as Paul had been leaving the previous evening, and asked to speak to someone about all the Police tape that he had found when he had gone to mow the lawn at the Barnham bungalow. Paul had made a quick appointment for the two to visit the bungalow early to meet the man who had given his name only as Dan Smith.

"Sod's law really. Prodow withdrew the PCSO guarding the place yesterday morning, and this gardener chappie went there in the afternoon."

Alison said, "Interesting coincidence, don't you think?" No one bothered to answer.

In the yard, John's car was in its normal place, but he headed straight past it towards Alison's and got in when she unlocked it. They were soon travelling towards Barnham using the exact same route that she had driven previously. For some reason, she felt quite perky now, even having got up earlier than she normally did and not even having a proper full breakfast.

John hardly said a word as she babbled on about very little including the near heart attack her cat had given her the previous evening. He liked cats and only commented about the cruelty of leaving one locked in a house all day.

She was going to answer but swung into the drive of Armstrong's bungalow, and pulled up behind an open back pickup truck with three different size lawn mowers on the back. The PCSO and his land rover had already gone which afforded more parking spaces and turning capabilities, although the pickup seemed to have been abandoned in the driveway.

Both got out of the Ford as a man well into his sixties walked into view from the side of the garage. He was dressed in a pair of old brown cord trousers with a couple of holes in both legs, 'not designer holes' thought Alison, and an old green fleece over an un-ironed checked shirt which was all topped off with a French beret.

Alison said, "Good morning, we are from the Police, I presume you must be Dan?"

"That's right luv," and Alison visibly winced at being called luv.

"What happened here then?"

Before she could respond, John said, "Dan Smith. You sure? What's your real name?"

"Dan Jones."

"Is that who your wagon is registered to?"

"Yeah."

"You know I'll check?"

"Yeah."

"And you'll be easy to find in that," and indicated the truck, "if you are telling us a porkie?"

"Yeah. I don't like Police Stations at the best of times, so I use Smith."

"Jones doesn't seem much better."

Indignantly Dan said, "What's wrong with it? It's my real name."

John said, "OK Dan, I believe you" and left a pause which Alison took as her signal to outline some brief details which had already been emblazoned across the front pages of the papers and headlined on the television news channels.

When she finished, Dan looked at both of them in astonishment, and started to shake his head.

Alison asked him, "Don't you believe me?"

Dan kept shaking his head. "He told me his pain was getting worse. I suppose it could have been a blessing in disguise. I still wouldn't wish it on anyone."

Pausing in what Alison thought was a respectful silence, Dan suddenly took of his beret and stuffed it into his pocket.

"Come on. Follow me. The time is right."

"Sorry. I don't follow?"

"You'll see luv."

He set off towards the road but walking down the middle of the front garden passing all the unusual and ornamental trees still shaking his head. About two thirds of the way to the road, he stopped, and pointed to a large overgrown mahonia.

"There."

Both John and Alison said in unison, "What?"

It had to have been the only un pruned bush in the entire garden. Dan walked towards it, pulling at the marginally prickling branches and moving them aside as he forced his way forward towards the centre of the shrub. A circular piece of concrete which was concealed from the casual onlooker by the density of the bush became visible on the ground. John, who was accustomed to hiding places, was impressed at how well hidden the piece of concrete was, and it was obvious to him that it was also the cover of a hole in the ground.

"Dan, I'll give you a tenner if you can cut a path into this bush so we don't have to fight our way in."

"You're on" and Dan headed off back towards his truck, and delved into the back seat area for his petrol driven Black and Decker chain saw.

It was clear to both Alison and John that Dan did not proscribe to Health and Safety standards as there was no sign of goggles, ear defenders, protective clothing or anything else.

Alison said, "Shouldn't we get this filmed before he cuts himself or this bush to ribbons?"

"It was on the original video, so no problem there, and I'm fascinated with what's in the hole, aren't you?"

She was, and said so, and watched in anticipation when Dan scythed through the foliage clearing a path to the concrete circle.

With the path cut, John handed over a crumpled £10 note to a grateful Dan who added it to his bulging wallet. Moving to the concrete lid, John tried to prise it open by getting his fingers under it. It was too tight a fit and obviously heavy. John examined the circle of concrete but could see no way of getting any purchase on it. The concrete was surrounded by a thin lip of weathered wood which was obviously what it was seated upon, and was the circumference of the actual hole.

John looked at Dan and said, "How do you open it?"

"You give me another tenner."

"You must be a very rich gardener."

"I do all right."

"OK. A tenner."

Dan was off back down the garden towards the house, but not towards his truck, he went to the shed and both Alison and John watched in disbelief as he opened it with a key. In less than 30 seconds, he was out carrying two jemmies and on his way back down the garden.

Alison queried, "You've got a key to the shed?"

"Cause I have, I'm the bleeding gardener, where do you think all the stuff is kept that I need," and he cast his eyes upwards for a second and tutted.

John looked at Alison, "He's got a point," then to Dan and said, "Have you ever seen a jar of poison in the shed?"

"Yeah, my rat poison, but it was in a packet, not a jar."

"Look Dan, we are going to have to take a statement from you which covers how you came to be the gardener here and a few other details, including why you have only just contacted us."

"Yeah, no problem, I liked George and played chess with him once or twice when we got the board out in the garden sunshine, I owe him. I don't read so never saw anything in the papers and I don't watch much telly. Because I haven't been well lately I missed the last couple of times I should have been here to cut the grass."

"Have you ever opened this before?"

"No, but it's obvious to me that no one would have two identical jemmies that have never had much use other than to prise something open. Let's have a go."

He handed one of the jemmies to John, and they both bent to look for the slightest part that they could get the jemmy into between the wood and concrete. With an exclamation, Dan slid the end of his jemmy into a minute indentation and pointed to another about a quarter of the way round from his. John put the straight end of his jemmy into it, and they both pushed and the jemmies slid down and under the concrete so they could lever it upwards at an angle out of the hole.

The problem was that they needed both hands on the jemmies to keep the concrete out of the hole, and Alison made it quite plain she was not putting her hands under the concrete in case they dropped it. Dan let his side down and was off back towards the shed: he was in and out again in seconds, and heading back with two six foot iron spikes.

"I always wondered why he had these, they must go under it."

They both lent on their jemmies, and Alison slid the spikes under the concrete holding it perfectly just above the hole. Now they could get their hands under the raised side, the two men realised that the concrete would roll over the spikes, and sit on the grass alongside the hole. Not half as hard as it originally appeared, and all three reached the same conclusion that one person could have done it by himself if he knew what he was doing to start with.

John proffered the £10 note, but Dan said, "Keep it, I want to see what's down there."

As the concrete lid was pushed onto the grass, all three peered into the disclosed hole. The wooden lip which the concrete lid sat on was only an inch or two deep with the diameter of the hole about four feet across. At the base of the hole, which was about ten feet deep, was a solid concrete floor, and the circular side of the hole appeared completely bricked around. Dan, who had done some bricklaying in his long career as an odd jobber, could appreciate the skill of laying bricks in what looked like a perfect circle. The remainder of the bush above prevented light permeating right to the floor, but they could all just make out the shape of a box at the edge by the wall.

John said to Dan, "You seem to have all the ideas, have you got a ladder?"

"Dan was on his belly hanging over the side looking into the hole, "No, but I don't think we'll need one. There are some bricks set out from the wall that look like they are steps."

Neither John or Alison had seen them until Dan pointed them out, and Alison immediately jumped at the chance of going into the hole claiming to be the lightest and fittest.

John had to remind her about preserving the item for forensic examination, so it was her turn to run back up the garden to her car to collect what she thought was a big enough exhibit bag and some latex gloves. In the time she was gone, John and Dan chatted amicably and John found out a little bit more about Dan and his work at the bungalow. Alison, in her haste on returning, nearly fell into the hole in her desire to get to the box, but after steadying herself, she found the first brick with her searching foot, and began the short decent. At the bottom of the hole, she could see a lot easier than at the top, and soon had the box in the clear plastic bag. It was a reasonably modern type metal box with a key lock that looked to her like a petty cash box. Frustratingly though, it was locked. Nevertheless, it wasn't rusty.

Climbing out of the hole was a lot harder than going down when her hands were held by John until her feet were half way down, and she jumped the remainder. Coming up, she had to hold on to individual bricks which only protruded a couple of inches from the wall, and it took her nearly five minutes to find both foot and hand holds to get high enough for John to grab her outstretched clasping hand. It was as though she were in a lift, her feet left the bricks and she was pulled clear of the hole and deposited unceremoniously on the grass by the one hand of John. Her skirt had grass stains that she couldn't see, but she knew they would be there. This box had to be worth it.

She took the bag out from inside her jacket where she'd placed it for the ascent, and gave it to John.

Dan said, "The jemmy will open that," but was informed quickly about the need to preserve it for fingerprints and other forensics.

He was disheartened by this as he had known the concrete circle had been there for years and now he had actually seen into the hole and what was there, he felt cheated that he couldn't see the contents of the box. John passed the bag back to Alison and putting an arm round Dan's shoulder gently steered him back towards the house chatting about the garden as they went as though they were the best of friends. Dan was happy to make a statement, and agreed a time to be at the station, and then realised he was late for his next client's lawn. Alison moved her car, and Dan disappeared towards the road, emitting noxious diesel fumes from the truck as he went.

38

Thursday 9th June 2011

They both walked round to the kitchen door and let themselves in and went to the places that they had seen some unaccountable keys during their previous searches. Alison found them in a small saucer which also contained a miniature compass and a material tape measure. It was tucked away in the top corner of a cupboard in the kitchen, and had somehow avoided becoming one of Jimmy's many exhibits.

Carefully taking the box, which showed no sign of corrosion, out of the bag, she inserted the smallest key easily into the lock without resistance and turned it with little effort. It unlocked with a soft click, and Alison opened the lid. Filling the inside was some foam and cut into it was a shape which housed an old Webley .38 revolver, and a box of fifty rounds of ammunition. Both of them stared at it, each with their own thoughts as to why it was there. After what seemed a millennium of silence, they discussed their course of action.

John went into the lounge and sat in the same chair that he had occupied previously. He picked up the phone, and called Paul. The pair chatted about the hole and the find, and agreed on what they should do. Jimmy would be sent to the bungalow with the reprimanded PoLSA team of two specialists to go over the area around the hole and in it, and take possession of the box and firearm and arrange ballistic tests.

As he relayed the decisions to Alison, she realised that there would be a delay of an hour or two while arrangements were made for the search team, and hunger suddenly struck her. Two poached eggs wouldn't keep a mouse going. She made it quite clear that she was not going to wait, and asked if John wanted a sandwich before she headed for her car and to a local shop in Barnham.

John sat in George Armstrong's chair in meditational silence. He looked about. He'd missed something, but he couldn't see what. Pressing the button on the side of the chair, it slowly rose with a whirr to its limit forcing him to stand up. Moving into the conservatory end of the room, he stood stock still looking out of the windows, and down the garden towards the hole. The hackles on his neck rose and made him shiver. He normally felt this when he was being watched. There was no one there. Perhaps it was because a person had been murdered in the room.

Dan had told him he'd been the gardener for the last eight or nine years, and John could see he had done an exceptional job. The only thing he had left was the mahonia which George had forbidden him to touch and told him to allow to spread. John sat in one of the cane chairs by the window, and watched the birds that were enjoying the lawn. It was pleasant just sitting and watching as they went about their business of searching for food. John could imagine George spent a lot of time here with a glass of wine, just watching the birds foraging. He had catered for their needs with several bird boxes in the trees, a small water holder and various feeders scattered about. Dan had told him there were rabbits and that George had forbidden him to kill them or fill their holes in. John couldn't see any rabbits or holes, but didn't doubt Dan at all. The only thing George hated according to Dan were rats. He had several packets of different poisons on the go at any one time, but never in a jar.

Alison drove slowly into view up the drive towards the garage at the rear of the bungalow. John could understand George's hatred for rats, and thought that the small ditch would probably be where they were. When she walked into the lounge, John was still in pensive mood, and she told him she had seen him seated in the window like an OAP as she had driven along the drive. John wasn't offended, but confided in Alison that he was sure that he had missed something.

Before she could stop herself, she said, "What?"

"If I knew, I wouldn't have missed it, would I?"

"See your point, sorry." She stood by the chair looking out of the window towards the hole, and gave an involuntary shiver, "Someone's just walked over my grave," and then, "What now?" as John swung to look at her.

John was brusque to the point of rudeness when he asked her why she had said it. Alison was taken aback by the sudden inquisition and responded with a quip that she didn't know: she just shivered. He explained to her his feelings when he looked down the garden, and she shivered again. Both scoured the garden but saw nothing.

"We've missed something, and it's bloody obvious, and that's why we can't see it."

They discussed Dan and the hole and that he had a key to the shed, but nothing about him worried either of them, including the use of a false last name.

Both went out to the still open shed, just as Dan had left it, and looked about inside. Although Dan had mentioned packets of poison, there were none visible, just a wooden wheel barrow with some grass care rakes, and some garden tools neatly in clips along the side. The jemmies had been in a drawer which had been left open by Dan in his haste, and the spikes had been leaning against the old wooden chest of drawers. The team of two specialist PoLSA searchers had already gone through the shed, and found nothing in addition to the jar of poison. Neither could see anything out of the ordinary. John left the shed and walked very slowly towards the front garden and the hole. There was something else, but he was damned if he could see it, but he was sure it was in the garden.

Alison joined him, and he asked her to tell him exactly what she saw. She listed everything she could, and even surprised John with her knowledge of the names of flowers, shrubs and trees. They walked up and down the garden several times, and found a couple of rabbit holes, but still nothing, and then John with a flourish decided on another course, and headed back to the house and the lounge. He went straight to the fire place and took the lifeline off the mantel piece and pressed it.

39

Thursday 9th June 2011

"Hello Mr Armstrong, this is Wendy at the lifeline control, are you alright?"
The voice, although soft seemed to echo around the bungalow but was coming from the control box at the phone.

John responded by identifying himself and informing Wendy that George was dead. After a pause, Wendy stated that the coroner normally informed them of a death, and arranged for the collection of all the lifeline accessories, but she had never heard of one of their clients being murdered, so she didn't know the correct procedure. John asked her where the microphone was that he was using to talk to her, and she told him briefly how the system worked, and that the control box opened up a telephone connection without the phone being lifted from the cradle. She explained that if there was no reply to her response to the pushed button, she called a nominated person to go to the house, or the emergency services. When John asked who the nominated person was, neither he, nor Alison were surprised that she said, *"Mr Chaplin."* He thanked her for her help, and heard a click which he assumed was the phone being disconnected.

John asked Alison, "Do you play chess?"

"Yes. I think I could beat you."

John sat down in one of the cane chairs which was by the white side of the board and began.

He didn't give her the option of who was to be white.

She was not even surprised by John's laid back attitude, and took the position by black.

Both however, felt uneasy sitting by the window in the conservatory and after a few minutes she passed comment that she believed it would kill enough time until Jimmy could get there, but was surprised when John said that wasn't the purpose.

Alison put the obvious question, "What is the purpose?"

She was rewarded with the ambiguous answer, "I don't know."

They both saw the movement in the hedge on the other side of the ditch towards the furthest part of the drive at the same time, and were already on their feet when Mr Chaplin came into view. With apparent ease, he seemed to clear the ditch and step onto the drive, looking in the direction of the road, and then walked towards the bungalow. John resumed his seat, and started to talk to himself in a hushed whisper.

"No, he's not been watching. Can get here without going on the road though so wouldn't be seen. No motive."

Then to Alison, "What do you think?"

She had anticipated the question, "He found the body, so he had time to do whatever he wanted."

Both watched him approach along the drive and noticed he didn't walk in a straight line because he was looking into the garden. The concrete lid and the newly cut mahonia were not visible from the drive, so he wasn't distracted by that, he was just enjoying Dan's efforts in George's garden.

He got to the back door and walked into the bungalow and then the lounge, but kept as far from the fireplace and where he had found George as possible. They greeted one another, and Chaplin told them he knew they were there because he had been contacted by Wendy at the lifeline control. Then looking at the chess board, he quickly assessed the pieces position and proffered the opinion that Black should resign. Alison looked hurt, but John knew from the opening moves that she wasn't very good and that he could win quite easily. John asked question after question and Chaplin answered without hesitation: he knew that Dan had a key to the shed, he knew he had missed his last appointment because he was ill, that he attended twice a month, once to mow the lawn and once to tend the garden. He said that George was a person of routine and did not like it to be broken. If someone had an appointment with George, they had to be on time, and the nurses knew this.

"Do you know if Mr Armstrong wore his lifeline button?"

Chaplin thought for a couple of seconds before responding, "He often wore it if he was outside the bungalow, or doing something unusual in the house when the nurses were not here."

"Like what?"

"Well. Washing up dirty crockery. Really anything which could cause him to overbalance in his wheelchair."

"Where did he leave the button when he wasn't wearing it?"

"On top of the mantelpiece usually. When I came to play chess, he often asked me to find it because it could often be somewhere ridiculous like in the bedroom or bathroom."

Chaplin who was sitting in a chair that Alison had pulled up for him, sat bolt upright and stared out of the window and down the garden. She saw shock on his face and was immediately worried, she couldn't see what he was looking at. John saw it as well and scoured the furthest point of the garden.

"What is it?" she demanded with a quavering voice displaying a slight hint of fear.

Chaplin turned to look at her, paused and said, "The mahonia, what have you done to it?"

Alison practically shouted at him, "Shit. You frightened the life out of me," and sat down heavily into the chair which she didn't realise she had risen from.

John soon established that Chaplin did not know what was beneath it, and suggested they go and look. On the walk down the garden, Chaplin and Alison chatted about the various shrubs and trees, and Chaplin explained that the bungalow had been built by a nursery owner. Some of the trees were rare to the UK and Chaplin pointed out the differing canopies that each formed. One, a Canadian spruce, attracted squirrels and on cue, two were visible in its higher branches. John stopped and watched them for a few seconds, and Chaplin told him that George tolerated them like rabbits, but he called them 'tree rats'.

Chaplin looked into the hole, and was wondering how in all the time he had been visiting George, he had not seen it before. He knelt down and rubbed his hand round the side and found one of the protruding bricks. John watched, surprised that Chaplin knew what to feel for, but then by way of explanation, he said that it was one of the finest examples of a Second World War Home Guard storage hole he had ever seen. Continuing, Chaplin explained that when it was thought that England would be invaded by the Germans, the Home Guard needed somewhere to keep their weapons safe, and constructed some pits dotted along the South Coast. They were well made so that weapons would not get damp, and the pits would be large enough for a person to hide in if need be. Furthermore, the pits were usually well hidden, as was shown by the fact that Chaplin knew George's garden well, yet didn't know about the pit he was now staring into.

After he had seen enough, Chaplin stood up, and they all ambled back towards the bungalow and into the lounge just as Jimmy drove up the drive. Alison watched him from the conservatory as he went past and towards the garage. Soon the back door opened, and Jimmy and two young PCs, about Alison's age, and dressed in overalls, joined them in the lounge. John explained to them what had happened at the Mahonia bush, and went into the kitchen with Jimmy, and showed him the box.

Jimmy, one of the PCs and Alison went off back down the garden leaving Chaplin and John alone in the conservatory. The other PC had moved to the shed. They spoke for a short while before Chaplin left to go home via the hedge and ditch from where he had originally appeared. John sat by the chess board watching the three moving around by the Mahonia bush, and thought, 'Why not.'

Rising from the cane chair, he walked over to George's chair, stood by it, and pressing a button sat in it as it descended. He found the trailing lead with the panic alarm button by the telephone where someone had moved it to: and tried to push it. Nothing happened, so he tried to push it again but the button was already pushed inside its plastic housing. Somebody had already pushed the button in and it could only be released with the correct small plastic key.

John had already seen the key in the same saucer as the key to the box from the hole. He went straight to it, picked it up and then back to the panic alarm. It slotted home, and the button was released and returned to its armed position. John pushed it again, and felt it slide into its protective plastic sleeve. The alarm should have activated, but there was silence. Turning the plastic key again, the panic button released and resumed the armed position, and John removed the key and put it into his shirt pocket. Sitting back by the chess board, he felt happier about the enquiry now than he did when he first visited the bungalow.

40

Thursday 9th June 2011

It couldn't have been much after 2pm when Alison drove into the empty car park of the Murrell pub towards the end of the road just before the bridge at Barnham. When she followed him into the lounge bar, she was not in the least fazed by the land lady welcoming John like a long lost brother and pouring a pint without asking what he wanted. John introduced Alison to Merle who pulled a large wine glass out and filled it with white wine from a barrel and passed it to Alison. She didn't normally drink at lunch time but thought it would be ungrateful to refuse. For about ten minutes, John and Merle discussed how to put the world to rights before John told her he needed a quiet place to chat to Alison about George's murder. It had the desired effect of him asking her without her realising, what she knew and had heard about it. Merle knew very little, and it was obvious that she had heard nothing from her regular clientele. So John and Alison went out into the pub's small beer garden for a chat.

They sat either side of a rickety wooden table on benches that were fixed to it, and John told Alison of the alarm. She considered it for a few seconds and came to the same wrong conclusion as John; that George probably pushed it and it didn't work. John looked hard at Alison and asked her what else she considered. Alison racked her brains, but could think of nothing else. He reminded her of the fact that he thought they were being watched, and asked her for her views, but she couldn't come to any conclusion. Even when he reminded her that she had involuntarily shivered several times, she said she'd been doing it a lot lately and it was nothing of note. They discussed Dan and Chaplin at length, and decided that they were not involved in any way, but neither understood why there was a jar of poison but none of Dan's packets of it in the shed. Neither could come to any conclusion about the gun.

After leaving the pub, they made their way back to the Police Station and to the office. Paul and Doreen were engrossed with a standalone computer that had been linked to the internet at Paul's insistence. Prodow was agreeing to every request presently and now Doreen was manipulating the internet with speed. They had found the web sites of the charities and the sort of work they did, and both had decided, although they mainly related to respiratory problems, smoking was not a major factor. Doreen was getting so interested in what was happening, that she had still got a few odd bits of typing to do, and hadn't even considered getting her book out. Jimmy was only thirty minutes behind John and Alison, and all of them sat around Paul's desk.

Paul divulged that in the post that morning had been an envelope from the Cambridge Registry Office which contained two birth certificates, two death certificates and a marriage certificate. They all related to Molly and Edward Anderson, Jeffery Anderson's parents. The accompanying letter explained that there was nothing really that could be established from the two witness's names shown on the marriage certificate. A full search had been made by the Cambridge archivist to trace any record of Jeffery Archibald Anderson having been born, married or died without success. The letter went on to explain quite candidly that during the war years numerous offices housing relevant details were destroyed and the birth certificate in the hands of the Police was now a lone original. After due consideration and a confirmation phone call to Prodow, it appeared pointless to pursue their family lineage further.

Jimmy confirmed that he had got 'absolutely zip' relating to the Newspaper and £1000. He really had no idea where to start. With Doreen, he had researched the rugby game and found nothing of note. They could only assume that the paper was available at the time when George needed it to prevent his chess board slipping. If it had any evidential value they were unable to establish it. Having checked back through some old bank statements of Armstrong, they could see that over a year he had withdrawn sufficient funds to live on and stash at least a grand away if he wanted. As to its purpose, they were at a loss and welcomed any suggestions. No one had any.

Alison apologised profusely that she hadn't followed up her phone contacts with the DWP and MOD as to the ID cards, and swore it would be the first thing on her agenda in the morning. Claiming she and John had been so busy during the day, it had completely slipped her mind.

Feigning serious hurt, John begged her not to attempt to blame him for her complete and utter incompetence.

Doreen and Paul took up the offensive by tutting as Jimmy sucked his teeth.

John compounded the matter further by shaking his head and saying, "Dear oh dear" several times.

She was annoyed and told them so which just made it worse.

Eventually, Paul got the kettle out and started to make everyone tea and coffee, Alison taking coffee which she wanted black. Lunch time drinking was something she abhorred. It made one neglectful. Working with John seemed to make it obligatory. They discussed what they had learnt amongst themselves, each putting any ideas that came to mind before the others so it could be fully explored. Some were easily discounted, but other ideas were noted by Paul for further enquiries. Doreen was no longer backward in putting her ideas forward, and some were noted, and the others spotted that she was also very good at playing devil's advocate. At about five, instead of making her normal swift get away, Doreen was still there arguing points, and Jimmy chided her that she would be late for her bus and her Mother's set tea time.

Paul apprised John and Alison that an alarm company was going to be at the bungalow the following day in the afternoon with Jimmy and if they wanted, they could pop along as well. He told them that he was also expecting some documents from Peckham library which may probably help them. He didn't hold out much hope though. John suddenly got up and made his departure bounding down the stairs calling back to Alison that he would phone her in the morning, but didn't say when. Alison watched him to his car and wondered what he was up to as it left the yard at speed. They all drifted away from the station going their separate ways.

41

Thursday 9th June 2011

John's old Vauxhall slid swiftly out of the yard and into the Chichester traffic and round into Avenue de Chartres. No hold up for the railway crossing which was a blessing as he wanted to get to Barnham well before dusk but was taking a longer different route to normal as a matter of precaution. He hadn't seen the newish bronze coloured BMW join the traffic from the parking area by Chichester Basin just down from the Police Station entrance, but he soon noticed it holding station about a hundred yards behind him as he approached the roundabout at the top of West Street. John considered his options quite quickly and decided to keep going as planned and lose the BMW as soon as he could have a good look at the driver. He continued in the traffic round Chichester past the Fire Station and then past the entrances to St Richard's Hospital. Traffic seemed to be getting heavy and the BMW made a bit of ground to close up on him. The driver of the BMW appeared to be lying back from the steering wheel giving very little away as John tried to see any features of him in his rear view mirrors.

At the Westhampnett roundabout, John drove into the entrance to Sainsbury's and then into the garage. Making for the middle petrol pump he watched as the BMW also pulled into the garage and went to a pump at the edge of the forecourt. The BMW could not get any further away if it tried as John had got the middle of the garage covered. Stepping out of his car, John slowly walked to the garage shop and watched the driver of the BMW alight and pick up a pump.

It didn't take John more than a second or two to commit the vehicle and then the driver's foreign swarthy appearance to memory. His small frame and oval head with shaved hair and gratuitously black sunglasses presented the appearance of a thug which was probably what he wanted. After collecting some sandwiches and chocolate from the shop, John ambled back to his car, slid into the seat and without fixing his belt, drove rapidly out of the garage. The BMW did not follow as John accelerated quickly away and along the A27.

It was still clear daylight when John parked amongst the other cars in the Murrell car park. Moving to the boot which was against the wall away from prying eyes, he opened it and foraged in a small bag taking a monocular and torch out. Shutting the boot gently, he took his old wax coat out of the back of his car, put it on and then slipped the two items into the pockets. Locking the car with the key in the driver's door, he walked away briskly towards the bungalow of the person known to Police as George Armstrong.

42

Thursday 9th June 2011

"Everything is ready as soon as you say the word. You were right: that oaf was a crap bouncer but a good builder. Your new man has given us ears, and he has eyes."

"Good. Hold off a little longer."

"We have set the room up. It's comfy enough, but I wouldn't want to stay there!"

"Should hope not. Any other problems?"

"The guy she works with is all over the place. I had a look at him."

"Did he see you?"

"Not a chance. He's an old, out of condition drunken copper. He can hardly walk."

"Can you get him out of the equation without upsetting anyone?"

"Yeah. Couple of smacks should do it."

"Be careful."

"Always."

43

Thursday 9th June 2011

The footpath soon stopped on his side and he had to cross the road to follow his course. He didn't like walking with his back to the traffic because anyone wanting to do him harm would not be seen coming. John had learnt this in his first year as a Policeman and hadn't forgotten his tutor having to jump for cover as a car had tried to run him down. Every time he heard a vehicle approaching from behind, he made a swift backward glance checking for a BMW. In his right hand, he held a small pen like object which was a powerful red laser. Something he had learnt a lot later in his life was that if a sudden very thin bright red light was aimed at a person in a car, it had the effect of making them take immediate evasive action. Not that he had ever used the technique, but he had witnessed it work.

He arrived at the drive entrance to the bungalow and stopped on the pavement. From his pocket, he retrieved the monocular, and placing it to his eye, scanned the higher branches of the visible trees in the garden. After four to five minutes he was happy to move a few yards into the drive. Looking carefully at every bush and piece of hedging before passing it or drawing level with it, and scanning with the monocular the trees as they became visible, he made very slow progress along the drive. Eventually, after what was close to three quarters of an hour, he was still only level with the mahonia and in clear sight of the actual bungalow. Again he scanned the trees, and checked the bushes and then stopped. Something wasn't right. He knew he had seen something, and the hairs on the back of his neck were confirming it. His whole body seemed to be tingling.

Practically jamming the monocular into his still slightly bloodshot eye, he searched the trees, then lowering the monocular, checked the bushes, and then it came to him. The monocular was lifted slowly back to his eye, and he looked up and across into a tall spruce which was practically in the centre of the garden. There was a bird box about fifteen feet up that faced the bungalow and was fixed onto the tree with cable ties. At the back of the tree was a very thin wire hanging down. He'd nearly missed it. An aerial. All the other bird boxes in the garden were at the most six feet off the ground. Whoever had put the one up in the spruce had needed a ladder and that meant it was out of normal reach of anyone, especially a disabled person.

John knew he had found what he was looking for. Without passing the spruce, he went to the back of the tree and looked up. With the naked eye, the wire was hardly visible and just looked part of the fixing of the bird box itself. He knew then that the bird box probably housed a camera in it that would clearly see the drive by the left of the bungalow, the bungalow itself, and the approach to both the front and back doors. On the ground were two small indentations where the ladder had probably sunk slightly when the weight of a person had been on it. Returning to the pavement without having passed the spruce, John looked at the occasional drive entrances on the opposite side of the road as he walked, facing the oncoming traffic, back to the pub and then inside for a 'livener'.

By nine o'clock, John had imbibed more than a 'livener' and returned to his car. Even with a few drinks inside him, he was cautious and checked around for any signs of the BMW, or anything else suspicious for that matter. He was happy and got in and drove slowly in the fading light to an entrance he had seen about 200 yards before that of the bungalow on the opposite side of the road. The road was empty of traffic as John reversed into the drive and into a small open barn where he killed the engine and pushed a couple of rocker switches on the dashboard.

Getting out he went to the boot, and from his bag, took out a six inch long spike with a small round top which resembled a big nail, and after securing the car, went back to the spruce without passing it. Moving to the side furthest from the drive, and about a yard from the base of the tree, he drove the spike into the ground. It stuck up out of the ground three inches. Standing over the spike he put the heel of one hand flat on the head, and his other hand linked on top of it. Then like a polar bear trying to break through ice, he slightly lifted his body and then driving all his weight through his joined hands, forced the spike right into the ground. The circular head was practically concealed by the grass and John moved and coaxed the grass around it until it was completely hidden. Satisfied, he returned to his car.

44

Thursday 9th June 2011
to
Friday 10th June 2011

John got into the front passenger side by opening the door with his key. No internal lights came on because he had disabled them earlier. Opening the glove box by using the radio button, he turned the Sat Nav screen to a very low light resolution, and manipulated a side control. The map showed the area that he was in with a gently pulsating green dot in the middle and a pulsating red dot appeared in the position of the spike. Turning another dial made the map a lot smaller covering a large area of southern England and John saw another green dot in the middle of Kent. There were some black dots also appearing which he ignored. He tapped his finger on the green dot in Kent, and the map switched to the local area just to the south of the village of Meopham with a green dot slowly pulsating in the middle of the screen with a small black number five in the middle of the dot.

His index finger again touched the green dot and this time he held it there for a couple of seconds. A voice that appeared to be coming from somewhere below the dashboard said, "Hello Oscar. You're showing green with a red overtone."

"Hello Ian. I've just laid a 'trembler' and am waiting for a visitor. You're out late."

"Yeah, I'm checking some new kit to put into Alison's car. Trouble with new cars like hers is they have computers in them which can bugger up our old stuff. Soon as it's ready and tested, I'll let you know so you can make arrangements with her."

John knew he would have to broach this with her quite soon but for the time being believed there was no immediate urgency. He didn't know how wrong he was. Even as he was talking to Ian, there were eyes watching the front door of Alison's flat.

After a little further chit chat, John pulled his wax coat with its woollen fleece lining tightly around him as he snuggled down for the night. He could see the lights of passing traffic on the road, but could not make out the vehicles because he was too far away. The glove box had been pushed shut, but not closed, after the Sat Nav had been reset. There was a practically inaudible blip every minute which indicated that the 'trembler' was active but in sleep mode. If anyone walked within ten yards of it, they would wake it from resting and the blip would sound every five seconds. John had a couple of options if that happened. He could try to detain the person there and then, or follow them to an address. The latter was always his preferred method as normally more evidence could be obtained. John considered that as whoever had put the bird box up was obviously technically savvy, there was a lot more to this case than was previously believed.

As the night wore on, John started to get tired as he watched the head lights of fewer and fewer vehicles travelling back and forth along the road. He slipped out of the passenger seat and away from his car to relieve himself of the previously consumed alcohol, and then regained his position in the passenger seat. A single set of headlights was approaching from Yapton, but very slowly. They slowed even more as they passed what John knew was about the front hedge of the bungalow. 'Someone just being nosey' thought John as the vehicle built up speed as it headed out of sight towards Barnham. Twelve minutes later, another set of headlights coming slowly along the road from Yapton again. John was starting to wake up a little and pay more attention as the vehicle practically stopped at the entrance to where the drive of the bungalow was and then accelerated off.

John knew the area well. If the vehicle had driven originally along the road and into Barnham and then travelled around the block via Lake Lane, that would have taken about seven minutes. Then again, it could have taken maybe twelve minutes thought John, especially if the level crossing at the junction with Yapton Road was shut. It was something he thought of. He watched some time and assumed it was nothing. Just a different vehicle. As the clock slid past one in the morning, John drifted into a very light sleep.

---
*

Vilf was still awake, now ensconced in his new lodgings; a pleasant little bed and breakfast hotel close to the sea front. What he had heard on the prom had made him reconsider his options. One thing disturbing his sleep was how he would proceed from now on.

45
Friday 10th June 2011

There was very little noise during the night other than a few nocturnal birds moving about and calling to each other, but as the dawn was shortly due, even that stopped. John knew that there was usually about an hour between the birds of the night settling down and the dawn chorus starting up. Someone once called it 'the blue period', but he couldn't for the life of him remember who. He woke up just prior to his little alarm's activation which was about to buzz at 5.30am and turned it off. It was a habit that he always set an alarm for whatever time, day or night he wanted to wake, and then awoke just prior to its commencement, and in time to stop any excessive noise assailing his ears. For some unknown reason, if he didn't set an alarm, he could not wake at a set time no matter how urgent it was that he did so. Dropping the glove box lid, he checked the screen of the Sat Nav which showed absolutely no activity at the 'trembler'.

Again, he left the car to relieve himself of the last vestiges of his 'livener', before entering via the driver's door. He assumed that no one would be so stupid or blatant enough to remove, or go near the camera with a ladder in daylight, so he took his coat off and threw it onto the backseat. The car purred quietly as it glided off to join the occasional early morning commuter traffic all totally oblivious to any speed restrictions. It wasn't long before he drove into Chichester Police Station and abandoned his car in it's usual position among the rubbish.

In the changing rooms, which were in the bowels of the station, he showered and completed his ablutions before taking a fresh set of clean clothes from a locker. He tried to keep at least a few pairs of socks and underpants in the locker with one emergency shirt and a pair of trousers and shoes: and an old jacket which had hung in there since the day he'd arrived at Sussex Police. Checking the jacket, he noticed a slight musty niff. It had been there too long without having been moved. Time to have it cleaned and aired. Placing his wash bag on the shelf, and his dirty clothes in a linen laundry bag, he dressed putting his blue tie and dark blue suit back on before going up to the ground floor canteen.

He was earlier than he expected. There was fifteen minutes still to wait before it was officially opened at seven by the lady who was already there fussing about with pots and pans and the milk and bread delivery of 6.45. John found a newspaper dated the previous day on a table amongst the dirty plates and cups which had yet to be collected to be washed up and recycled. Picking the paper up, he resumed his normal seat, rocking it back on two legs and started to read. A lot of the contents he considered irrelevant filler and glossed over them. Crime interested him and he soon found some stories to occupy his attention.

The canteen lady erupted from behind the servery with a trolley, and started noisily clearing away the dirty crockery and then squirting a spray of some unknown detergent on each table before giving them a cursory wipe with an old dish cloth before moving on. She called cheerily to John addressing him by name and said she would bring him a coffee as soon as she could. John always meant to find out what her name was, but never seemed to get round to it or remember it if he heard it. The Polish man who was the pot washer, had got the water machine turned on and ready as he awaited his first trolley full of crockery. It was going to be him taking the trolley round for the rest of the day and enjoying the banter with some of the customers who tried to teach him better English, and him trying to teach them just a couple of words of Polish.

*

Alison had not slept at all well that night having been woken by her cat running into her room and jumping onto her bed at about the same time as John was drifting off to sleep in his car. Hannibal, her cat, slept at night in a basket lined with an old blanket in the kitchen. Normally from the time he was summoned indoors at night until just before Alison rose and fed him in the morning. An occasional patrol of the flat was his only night time excursion. Then, before going out for the day to work, Hannibal was required to leave the flat at the same time as Alison either by his own free will or by Alison's hand. The cat knew the score.

She had not been happy when she threw him off her bed onto the floor. As she had woken with such a start, she spent the rest of the night tossing and turning and drifting in and out of sleep. Hannibal on the other hand had very quickly fallen asleep on the floor by her bed where he stayed for the rest of the night. The morning saw her grudgingly feed the cat and then expel him as soon as he had finished.

As Alison entered the canteen at about 7.30, John looked up to see her approaching and noticed she did not look her usual immaculate self although her clothes were right as was her appearance and makeup. She plonked herself down on a chair facing him.

"My bloody cat was lucky to live last night. I am knackered!"

John went and got her two cups of tea and said, "Go on then. What happened?"

Before she replied, she had sunk the first cup and was sipping the second. It was all divulged with passion and some strong expletives about Hannibal thrown in for good measure, but Alison could see John was just humouring her although she felt all the better for baring her soul. When she had completed her story, John truthfully revealed how he liked cats and would have to pop round and see Hannibal sometime. Dismissively she flung in an aggressive aside he would be lucky to get anywhere near her demented pet as he hated strangers. Alison sensed John was starting to take a more attentive interest.

She grew more bellicose as she got into her stride. In order to reinforce her current displeasure about her erstwhile pet now she appeared to have his apparent full attention, Alison related her grandmother's old vase being smashed by Hannibal in his speedy exit from the flat. Swearing blue blind at the fact that her cat had managed to find a way into her flat yet couldn't find his way out wound her up even more. As if to finalise the point she concluded her narrative with one last full blown diatribe directed at the defenceless animal. That made her feel so much better. Slowly she calmed herself down and paused to draw breath before slurping the cold dregs of her tea.

Alison thought she perceived John's demeanour change just slightly, but she could not be sure. Perhaps she had gone a bit over the top in slagging off her pet which she still loved if the truth be known. Maybe she had actually upset him if he was a true cat lover. She may have threatened to have killed her pet in horrendous ways, but they were just words. She didn't actually mean them.

He unexpectedly pronounced, "Do you want breakfast? I think I am going to have some. I'll just pop up stairs and let Paul know where we are" and he was out of his seat and towards the exit.

She could not fathom out what he was up to as Paul knew that they always started in the canteen before going up to the office. Within three minutes, John came back into the canteen with a piece of A4 paper that he had grabbed from the first office along the corridor and scribbled a note on. As he approached her, he held a finger to his lips to silence her and handed her the paper.

46
Friday 10th June 2011

She took it and read:

> Under no circumstance say a word until you have read this.
>
> Do not mention your cat again until we can speak confidentially. I will let you know when within the next hour.
>
> Do not mention anything contentious about the enquiry. Again within the hour.
>
> Possible that we are being monitored.
>
> Categorically, nothing to be said until I check it's safe.
>
> Just general chit chat for time being.

Alison read it twice and then looked up quizzically at John who again put his finger to his lips. She turned the paper over, and with a parker pen, not a basic charity biro like John's, wrote:

> What the fuck has my cat to do with anything?
> What are you on about?

John read as she wrote, and immediately responded with his cheap biro:

I promise to fill you in within the next hour. Please say nothing as overleaf.

We must use my vehicle today so please do not object.

John said, "Right Paul knows where we are. Let's see what's for breakfast".

He ambled across to the servery and ordered exactly the same as he always had if he ate in the canteen. Alison also went to the servery, and ordered as healthy a breakfast as possible, casting the occasional puzzled glance at John. They sat at the table eating and talking about inconsequential items that John had read about in the paper and things that Alison had watched on Television. She bought a second coffee for him and a third tea for herself and when they had finished, John put the now screwed up piece of A4 into his pocket and they both went upstairs to the office.

They found Paul and Doreen were chatting amicably between themselves with a mug each of their favourite brew and on her desk, were a selection of 'dunking biscuits' lying on a tissue awaiting their fate. Both quickly declined the offer of a drink as Paul broke off and reminded both about the alarm engineer being at the bungalow in the afternoon and said Jimmy would be there at 2ish. To her surprise, John stated that they had a couple of brief enquiries to complete but would definitely be there. Paul knew better than to ask what they were. Alison could not have told him even if he had asked. Unfolding the screwed-up paper, John fed it into the industrial sized shredder that ate the A4 sheet in a second as if an appetiser.

They headed for the yard and his car. He went straight to the boot and opened it first with the key and then ran his hand under part of the offside bumper seeking a small push button which he found and pressed. The boot lazily rose displaying the yawning compartment. Refraining from comment, Alison watched him take out a basic square brown wooden box with each side about a foot long with an eye and hook clasp securing the lid. John had to give it a tug because it was wedged snugly between bags filling the whole space. Unlocking the passenger door of the car once he was inside, she got in and immediately started to say something but was loudly over talked by John.

"Right let's go and see this person who says he knows who did this murder."

He started the car and let it idle for thirty seconds, and then pressed one of the rocker switches and held it as a white light above the switch turned red. Holding his finger to his mouth for her to be silent, he opened the box.

Inside, the wooden box was filled with a mushroom coloured foam which had some shapes cut out, and in one was a small silver box about twice the size of a matchbox with three lights and a small switch on the top with an aerial that John extended fully just four inches. He pressed the switch and all three lights came on for a few seconds, one red, one yellow and one green. The green went out leaving the red and yellow still glowing. Alison had watched the light on the dashboard illuminate, and now watched the illuminated red light on the box.

John said, "Where's my pad with the address?" She could see, and assumed that red was obviously not good. He took a small beige covered note book out of his pocket and wrote:

> Red means there is a radio transmitting from within the car.
> Yellow is likely a tracker.
> I know it is not me, and it is not in the car as I have all the electrics isolated.
> It is somewhere on you.
> Do not be offended but I am going to scan you.
> Please say nothing.

Alison was slowly starting to become irritated and annoyed, but did not know what to say or do. John took out a layer of foam from the box which revealed a small paddle like table tennis bat from another lower cut out section and touched a button on the handle as he held it over her bag. A small green light came on and remained illuminated. He held it about six inches above her head and then ran it down her left side and the light stayed green, then ran it up her right side and still the light stayed green. John did not understand, he was sure there was a 'bug' on her somewhere, and was certain the equipment provided by Ian would work properly. She was fuming as she picked up his note book and wrote:

> Happy?

John thought for a moment as to what to write in reply, and then took the note book back intending to write his thoughts. As he put the paddle on the dash board with the intention of picking up his pen, the light turned red and there was a short sounding bleep. They both heard it and saw it: and they both saw it was an inch from where Alison had placed her mobile phone.

John wrote:

Logical. Should have checked it first.
  Now we know where it is, leave it in the car.

Then he said, "I think I must have left the details upstairs. You coming back up?"

As if on cue, but still sullen and openly annoyed, she replied. "Yeah, why not" and they both got out of the car leaving the phone on the dash board.

47

Friday 10th June 2011

They both walked away from the car towards the old Police football pitch which now resembled an uncut meadow and away from the main building.

"We need a long talk but not here. Whoever put that bug in your phone will expect us within a few minutes to get back in the car and go and see this witness who does not exist. Last night I was followed by a foreign, swarthy looking man in a bronze BMW. I would expect to be followed again now, so we are going to go for a roundabout ride towards Singleton. When we go along the valley from Charlton, I will jam any signals being emitted, but to be sure can you take the battery and sim card out of your phone when I signal to you."

Alison said, "What the hell is this all about?"

"I promise I will tell you as soon as we get past Singleton. In the meantime, follow my lead and still general chit chat."

They both strolled back to the car and got in, John now completely satisfied with how things were, and Alison totally confused and slowly losing her temper but hanging onto it well.

"Right" said John, "We're going to be a bit early so we can take our time."

He returned the two items to the wooden box and placed it on the back seat because he was going to need it to check again later. Driving slowly through the yard to the exit leading out onto Basin Road, he stopped to let a woman with a push chair cross in front of him. A small puff of black smoke shot from the rear of a dark Audi parked down by Chichester Basin as it was started up. John thought the problem with nicer hire cars is that they get 'hammered' and the engines suffered as a result and often kicked out smoke when the accelerator was pressed at ignition. It would have been easier if the guy had stuck with the bronze BMW, but it really didn't matter at the moment.

They chatted about nothing in particular as John took a different route out of Chichester to get to the A27, and then he stuck at fifty as he headed towards Fontwell. He smiled contentedly to himself as the Audi tried to drop a long way back as no one else on the road was doing less than seventy. He knew from training and experience that it is very difficult going so slow and not showing out to the 'rabbit'. At the approach to the junction of Britten's Lane, John gave a nice long clear left-hand indicator signal in case his pursuer did not have full tracking capabilities and turned up towards Eartham. Going even slower than the forty mile an hour speed limit, the Audi struggled to go slower still and dropped nearly half a mile back just clipping vision on the bends occasionally. John followed the road to the junction with the A285 and signalled right. There was no sign of the Audi in his rear view mirror which meant the driver did not know the area or have a map immediately to hand otherwise he would have closed up on the approach to the junction.

He waited, and as the Audi came into view made the turn slowly going up the hill and indicated left straight away for the junction about half a mile ahead into Selhurstpark Road. The driver of the Audi accelerated hard to the junction and saw the Vauxhall crawling slowly going up the hill with the left indicator signalling. As soon as John made the turn the Audi followed up the hill to the junction and saw the Vauxhall dawdling along the top road towards Goodwood race course. Another car came up the hill and the Audi was forced to complete the left turn and pulled straight into an open area car park so as not to get too close.

John saw all this in his mirror and said, "There's a really nice pub down in the valley on the right at Charlton, shall we stop?"

Alison said, "If you want. I'm easy."

John hoped this would slow the Audi more and he started to signal right nearly a mile before the turning into East Dean Hill. The driver of the Audi was still in the car park and was looking at a paper ordinance survey map and he saw a PH sign in Charlton. He had been led to believe the radio transmissions from Alison's phone in built up areas were good for about half a mile and 2 miles in open country. Now he believed he could hang even further back and take his time. Confidence was high.

Then the dampener came. John said, "Trouble is in the valley you get a very poor signal on phones and Paul said he would ring you. Never mind. Let's have a 'livener' we're thirty minutes early."

"OK" was the resigned reply.

Confidence was wavering.

John turned right at the signpost to Charlton and could see no sign of the Audi as he started to accelerate dangerously down the hill and swung a violent left at the bottom into Charlton Road. In the opposite direction to the pub. He accelerated hard along the valley towards Singleton as he pointed to her mobile.

She knew what he meant, and turning it off she prised the back open and hesitated when she saw a strange wire. He saw her falter before taking the battery and the sim card out of the phone. Sending up a small shower of debris, he drew into the side of the road braking fiercely. John snatched the phone from her grasp and pulled the wire off it and threw it out of his open window. The battery and Sim card looked ok but there was a very small flat silver square sitting below where the battery had been accommodated. Within about ten seconds, he had prised it out with one of his full remaining undamaged fingernails. Taking a toffee hammer that he kept in the door pocket, he hit it hard enough to destroy it. That followed the wire into the Sussex countryside. She didn't know anyone who would carry a toffee hammer in a car but John having one came as no surprise.

"You can put it back together again but don't turn it on just yet."

The car took off from the side of the road so fast it nearly pushed her out of the side of her seat. Wedged between the seat and the door would have been the final insult.

Elsewhere: Confidence was zero.

48

Friday 10th June 2011

The car was no slouch along the narrow country road, nor through the constricting back streets of Singleton lined with jagged unforgiving flint walls. Then up the steep hill past the Weald and Downland museum towards the crown of Goodwood. As the road turned ninety degrees to the left in order to reach its summit where the race course crossed the road and caused chaos on race days, John carried straight on into a shoddily maintained private road. The potholes were horrendous with some several inches deep. John weaved violently from side to side as Alison hung on grimly with both hands to the grab handle as the car bounced about. Trees and bushes crowded in from both sides forming an unruly canopy destroying efforts at penetration by the sun's rays.

He knew they were no longer being followed as he drove on for half a mile. Then they burst out through the trees into bright daylight. Directly to their nearside was a small chalk car park with a few wooden benches affixed to tables scattered about on the grass adjacent to it. John swung the car into it and parked, then killed the engine. Alison heaved a sigh of relief and thought the car was probably doing the same.

The Trundle was higher up still but only on foot and via a chalk path which led off from the furthest point of the car park. There was a clear unobstructed view stretching from Portsmouth and the Isle of Wight in the west to Littlehampton and the outskirts of Worthing in the East. Another chalk path flattened over time by farm vehicles led down towards Lavant.

Alison had never been there before and was amazed by the astonishing view. It was, she realised, less than four miles from her flat as the crow flies. She could see clearly the outline of the 'Sail' at Portsmouth and a hazy view of the Isle of Wight. The spire of the cathedral in Chichester stood out like a beacon from the surrounding area and the old motor racing circuit of Goodwood laid out below them was busy now as a small airport with little planes buzzing about like bees. The white roof of Butlin's 'tents' at Bognor shone brighter as the summer sun struck them, and the dull grey green gasometer at Littlehampton was still an eyesore. On the horizon, the sea shimmered and danced blue as it reflected the sky.

John pressed the rocker switch and held it, but the light stayed clear. He opened the wooden box on the back seat and took out the smaller silver one and turning it on, extended the aerial. The lights all came on, and this time the red and yellow ones went out leaving the green one glinting in the sunlight. Putting the paddle by the mobile phone, the light shone green.

"Can you turn it on now please?"

Alison pressed the button, and the phone burst into life playing a few innocuous notes of music and asking for a password which she duly entered. Within a minute or so, the phone indicated it was operational and in standby mode. John now, more as a matter of caution, held the paddle next to it and watched as it still glowed green. He was happy but didn't bother showing it.

Alison said, "Time for you to fill me in I think."

"Let's go to the bench because it is going to take a little while."

There were a few other cars already in the car park when they had arrived with people sitting in some of them admiring the view or eating their packed lunches early. Others were empty as their occupants had decided to climb even higher up to the trig point on the very top of Goodwood or just walk their dogs in the adjacent fields. John kept the small silver box with him as they both made their way to one of the furthest wooden tables and then extending the aerial, placed it in the middle of the table as the light stayed green. They sat opposite each other and John produced a bar of chocolate from the day before and proffered half to Alison who took it. He still watched the entrance to the car park: just in case.

"Let's talk about your cat last night, and the time it broke your vase and nearly gave you a heart attack."

Alison said, "The day it broke my vase was when it got back into the flat without me knowing because it is a clever little tinker. Last night was as I told you this morning, although I didn't think you were that interested."

"To be honest, I wasn't, but politeness deemed that I should ask. What made me listen most was when you said I would not get near it because he didn't like strangers."

"So?"

"Come on Alison, think. You are more intelligent than most, it's a logical assumption."

She sat there, and stared at him hoping for inspiration from his rugged face which stared back impassively. Silence for nearly five minutes was nothing for John but was excruciatingly embarrassing for Alison, and caused her to concentrate more than ever. Slowly she started to consider the outlandish which began to make sense.

"Are you thinking my cat ran from a stranger last night, and if so, that means someone was in my flat when I was asleep."

"Yep, that's what happened. Someone entered your flat at about 1am, which is when most people are at their deepest point of sleep, with the intention of bugging your phone. Your cat, who does not like strangers, took flight from the kitchen to where he thought he would be safe, your bedroom. Bet your phone was in the kitchen."

"Shit, that's really frightening. I put my phone on charge every night in the kitchen."

John continued, "The day your cat was in the house breaking your ornaments was probably the first day that someone had broken in, and the cat also got back in probably if the front door had been left slightly ajar for the burglars' fast exit. Your cat then having been locked in when the burglars went was likely to be desperate for the loo and that's what he was waiting for, someone to open the door and let him out."

Alison stared at John for a good minute now not at all embarrassed by the silence. Her brain was whizzing through lots of 'what if's' and she was imagining the worst of all which in her view would not have been her murder. John still stared back at her with his totally impassive look. Then he broke off a piece of chocolate and put it in his mouth as he watched a beautifully kept old Morris Minor with two elderly people in it drive slowly into the car park and park so they could admire the vista without alighting.

"Say something. I'm going mad! Someone has been in my flat when I have been in bed, anything could have happened! You just sit there with that blank expression on your face as though it's a common occurrence. What the hell is happening?"

John said, "I was hoping you had read some of Sherlock Holmes."

Alison interrupted him by shouted at him, "What the hell are you on about?"

"Try to think rationally because when you get angry you don't think straight. Remember, eliminate the obvious and what remains, however implausible, must be the truth."

She just looked straight at him with incredulity forgetting for a second her night visitor and said, "That's not how Holmes puts it."

"I know, but it's my take on it."

She leant back on the bench to try to relax and unclenched her hands that she hadn't realised were now in fists.

"Try some chocolate, it's not bad. Might help you think clearer because you haven't finished. You know there is more."

She did, but was trying not to think about it.

"Come on. What else have you thought?"

She glared straight at him, and said, "My flat's bugged too, and probably my car because I always park outside my garage when I get home at night. Never put it inside. But why? This has nothing to do with the enquiry, has it?"

"Now you are starting to think logically. First though, we are going to have to sort out your safety. Can I use your phone?"

49

Friday 10th June 2011

John tapped out the number from memory, pressed the main button and waited for the connection to be made. Ian answered within three rings as he always did because that was how long it took him to remove his mobile from his shirt pocket or pick it up from next to his bed, check the caller ID and then acknowledge it.

"*Hello*" was all that he said now because he didn't know, and his phone didn't recognise, the caller's number.

"*Hi Ian. Oscar here. I'm using Alison's mobile. We've had a little problem.*"

"*You ok?*"

"*I am now. We lost a tail and now we are recuperating at the top of Goodwood sitting on the green grass of the Sussex Downs enjoying the view.*"

"*Not in a public house? Times they are a changing.*"

"*Cheek.*" He explained the phone having been bugged.

Alison was not concentrating at the moment about what was being said because she was lost in her own thoughts which again were turning towards dire consequences for her well-being.

She heard John say it was "*professionally done*" and then mention "*amateurish surveillance techniques*" but they were just odd words that penetrated her thoughts. What brought her back to immediacy was when she caught the phrase "*three at the most, possibly four.*" Something in that phrase really started to worry her because she believed she knew what it meant and then she shivered as her thoughts ran amok. Alison fought to think straight and concentrate on why it was happening to her and formulate some questions where the answers would make sense of it all.

John disconnected the call after the words, *"I'll sort it out with her after I have spoken to Simon"*.

"Who's Simon?" was all she could say although she had her questions stacked up and all ready for when he hung up.

"Ginger's boy."

"Why do you want to talk to a boy? Can't you ever speak without talking in riddles? You are so infuriating that at times I could quite happily hit you over the head with a truncheon."

With a sly smile, John said, "You need to purge yourself of all these violent thoughts, it's not good for you" and totally failed to answer her question as he started to dial again.

"Hello Ginger. Oscar here" and he went through the rigmarole of where he was and that he was using her phone before asking if Simon was available. Ginger was really happy that John had obviously got some work for Simon, as he'd been living at the pub since he left the army and was frankly getting under his parents feet. Simon had done a few jobs for others on the 'old team' and his own contacts, but nothing in the last two months other than helping out in the pub in the evenings.

Alison got up, and stretching, said she was going to have a walk around and wandered over to a ridge that had probably been part of the old fortifications when the ancient Britons were running about in the area. She was settling down now and starting to regain her composure. When she was young, her Father had often referred to her as 'plucky' because he saw her stand up for herself on many occasions, but now she was older and times had changed she was referred to as 'feisty'. Her forthright attitude and quick temper had often been the reason she hadn't kept boyfriends for too long as it frightened them off.

John went through all the facts of the 'burglary cum bugging' giving Alison's full address and vehicle details and then looking straight at her, described her in a genuinely fair but flattering way. He told Simon briefly about the enquiry they were on mentioning the bird box and that they had absolutely no idea who had committed the murder or why.

Simon said, *"Firstly then you have a murder with someone somehow involved who has technical knowledge. You can keep tabs on that one as that's what you're paid to do."*

John appreciated the droll humour as Simon continued.

"I'll liaise with Ian when we hang up and sort a few things out that I will need and I won't be in your area for about six to eight hours because I may have to go to Kent for them. Are you going to update her old man?"

John replied in the affirmative saying he was not going to enjoy the conversation and then they agreed contact details with Simon ending the call by saying confidently, *"Once I'm there, she'll be safe."*

A statement that John thought maybe over confident.

John dialled the number as he watched Alison standing on the ridge, staring into the middle distance lost in her own thoughts.

The conversation was going well he thought, especially after Graham had calmed down and listened to what had been planned. Maybe shouting and losing one's temper ran in the family although in John's long association with Graham, today was the first time he had heard him raise his voice. Alison walked back and sat down on the bench and knew intuitively straight away who was on the phone.

She signalled to John as best she could that she did not want to talk to him and as if on cue John said, *"Do you want a word with her, she's right next to me."* and handed the phone to her.

Mouthing the words, 'You bastard' at John she engaged in conversation with her Father as John walked away.

50
Friday 10th June 2011

John had assumed her position on the ridge to give her the privacy that Father and daughter conversations deserved. It was as if the ridge promoted deep and meaningful thought because he seemed to be looking straight at the Cathedral spire without seeing it as he considered the options to be taken. Alison finished the call by throwing the phone onto the table hitting the little silver box of tricks that still showed the unwavering green light. Her Father had imparted a lot of information in such a short time that she was still having trouble disseminating it. He'd concluded with strong words impressing upon her not to lose her temper as was her wont as it could have disastrous consequences for her and those around her. She knew what he meant but didn't like to be told so, and did not like him telling her to do as John told her.

The noise of the phone hitting the box on the table told John the call had been concluded and he walked back and resumed his seat. They sat opposite each other in silence for a minute or two.

"Calmed down now?"

"Yes" was the curt reply.

"The questions that you had for me earlier, I'll answer now."

Alison had already formulated new more pertinent questions and said, "My dad said they could be after either one of us, so why haven't they gone after you?"

"About a week back, I heard from some people I know that a man who had a weather-beaten appearance was asking after me and my whereabouts. Since then, I have only been to my house once and I knew I was secure. I don't know if someone is looking for me or deliberately looking for you. Remember, it was me that was followed."

Alison thought for a few seconds and said, "My flat has been broken into at least once while I was at home and probably been bugged. We know my phone was bugged. If anyone wanted to do me harm they could have already done it, so I can only assume it's you they are targeting."

"That could be a logically acceptable conclusion, but better safe than sorry, Ginger's boy can keep an eye on you."

Alison was starting to get a little riled again.

"If it's you they are after, I don't have a problem and don't need a 'babysitter' because I can look after myself. I have done some taekwondo and judo."

John smiled, which infuriated her even more. He explained to her that if the people were as serious as he and her Father believed, she would not stop them. Although she now assumed they were after him, erring on the side of caution because they had been inside her house was the logical thing to do. John did not for one minute consider that he was the target even though he did not understand someone bandying his name about so evidently.

Then he told her that one of the places where a person was most vulnerable was when they were in bed, normally in their own home where they felt safe. She did not like his matter of fact, impassionate attitude when discussing her personal safety but saw his rationale.

"Why do you think there are three or four of them, and how will Simon by himself be able to protect me if you say they are so dangerous?"

John was still smiling and said, "You have to think cogently Alison and consider everything. You know the first time I was followed was by a BMW, and today was an Audi. That implies two. There are two exits from the Police Station yard onto two different roads. Are you forming an opinion?"

"You can be the most irritating, sarcastic and sanctimonious sod at times."

"So I have been told. There may be a third tucked away somewhere by your flat and the person running the show. Simon has also done some martial arts so between the pair of you, it's possible you'll survive."

"What are we going to do about my flat and car?"

John lent forward putting his arms on the table and told her exactly what was to happen that evening. She could not think of anything more ridiculous under the circumstances, but was coming to the conclusion that he knew what he was doing plus her Father trusted him so, 'hey ho'. He asked to use the phone just one more time and she just waved her hand in surrender as if to say, 'Yeah, whatever' and went for another short walk to the ridge to admire the view again.

This time her thoughts turned to Tennyson and she remembered his words: '*You came and looked and loved the view, long known and loved by me, Green Sussex fading into blue with one grey glimpse of sea*' and she could see exactly what he meant.

When he had finished the call, she walked back and he gave her the phone saying, "Don't let it out of your sight for the time being, we don't want it tampered with again. The charge should last a few days and can be boosted from the car power socket if need be. Now to Barnham."

51

Friday 10th June 2011

They went back to the car and John put the little silver box back in its protective foam and then put the wooden box back in the boot wedging it between the other bags holding it securely in place. Alison pulled her seat belt tight, pushed herself as far back into the seat as possible and had hold of the grab handle with her left hand and the edge of her seat with her right ready to be slung about as they retraced their tracks down the pot holed road. John drove so slowly along drifting nonchalantly from side to side missing the majority of the holes that it hardly caused the cars suspension to consider operating. When they reached the main tarmacadam road, she relaxed and let go of the handle and the seat knowing full well that her caution had been superfluous and seen by John. Both were inwardly laughing.

On the way, they spoke about the murder and Alison was of the opinion they were struggling until John just happened to mention the bird box. She looked hard at him as he drove and confirmed her assessment that he was the most infuriating person other than her Father that she had ever had the misfortune to come across. He didn't appear to ever take an insult to heart which often had the effect of annoying a protagonist even more. Like her Father, she hadn't seen him lose his temper or even hear him swear other than a few mealy-mouthed expletives that wouldn't bother a nun. She would have loved to have emulated their traits but thought it may be an attribute that came with age. John told her of the night he spent in the barn and mentioned the headlights of the two vehicles slowing to practically a halt by the bungalow.

She scowled at him. "Are you really such a dinosaur? Have you ever heard of the internet? Don't you know what a flash download is?"

"I'm proud to be regarded as a dinosaur. Did you know they were on the Earth for millions of years longer than we humans have been its occupants? Yes, I do know what a computer is and I have a rough idea of how it is connected with a modem to communicate with the internet. Not a clue what a flash download is though. Pray, enlighten me."

Her eyes bore into the side of his head as he stared forward ostensibly concentrating on his driving. Then Alison explained in words not quite of single syllables how it worked.

To push her explanation home, "Just imagine. A camera could be placed, for example, in a bird box, and it could record a timed video file. Normally a day or two would be recorded at a time. A person with a laptop would approach, for instance in a vehicle. Then as long as the right electronics were paired and when the receiving equipment calls for it, it would send it wirelessly as a 'flash' download to the receiver's computer. To be sure of receiving the full video, a vehicle carrying the receiving equipment would have to stop or pass by very slowly. Say for illustration, at the end of a drive."

Her voice had risen towards a slight crescendo as she spoke. "Do I detect some sarcasm there?"

"Oh yes, you unquestionably do!"

Still looking at him as he drove, she said, "You probably wasted your whole night in that barn."

He glanced at her and said, "Has that made you happier?"

"Bloody ecstatic!"

"It'll make you even happier then knowing I'll be in the barn tonight."

"I'll be dancing for joy!"

She was smiling so much that when they arrived at the bungalow Jimmy could not help but notice and comment. They all went inside to wait for the engineer and Alison stole a long glance down the garden from the conservatory. She saw the bird box but the hole just looked black with no camera visible.

No shivers from her now.

52

Friday 10th June 2011

The engineer arrived and asked, as instructed, explicitly for Jimmy who identified himself with a flourish of his warrant card and with an air of superiority, implied he was the person 'running the show'. They all crowded around the alarm control box and input key pad with trepidation.

As he was the expert he was afforded more room and looking at the key pad, he said, "Does anyone know the code?"

None knew the actual code and Jimmy again exerted his authority by declaring that he had been assured that as an expert it was something he could establish. Unfastening a small metal case full of tools, Joe, the engineer, removed the front panel of the alarm control box using a key from a bunch of about thirty that were rattling about in the bottom of it. Dropping the panel on the floor, several irate but frightened spiders made a dash for cover. Now playing slightly for those present, he looked at the electronics and hummed and ha'd to himself and rubbed his chin as if calculating a major mathematical conundrum.

Then as if it had come to him in a vision from above, he said, "Yes," and started tapping the keys on the key pad. Within a minute he rattled off four numbers which Jimmy recorded as the code.

Had the truth be known, Joe knew the 'back door' code of the alarm the minute he saw the box affixed to the outside of the bungalow as he drove up the drive. With that knowledge, he knew before he even walked into the kitchen that he could find the code that was programmed. Joe was an expert with alarms and often got called by the Police for help and was aware that he was the first choice for any callout and was determined to maintain his premier status. Still milking what he considered his silently appreciated applause he stared at the electronics inside the box.

"Yes. Dear me!" Taking a small insulated screwdriver from his case and placing the point into the innards of the control box, he said, "Look."

Jimmy, John and Alison all strained to see what he was pointing at. Before they spotted anything, Joe appeared to be speaking rhetorically.

"Well. What do you make of that?"

He didn't have to wait long. Jimmy jumped straight into his trap.

"What?"

"That wire is disconnected. Plain as day. It has been deliberately disconnected. Can't come undone by itself."

They all kept scrutinising the inner workings of the box. The harder they looked, the less they saw.

"No moving parts, no strain on the wire. Fancy that!"

All three kept studying the wiring indicated and could just make out a small wire that looked exactly as they believed it should have looked.

"Strange." More chin rubbing. "Been disconnected and then the wire cut back to the sleeve."

John was now sure it had something to do with the panic alarm in the lounge and said so. Joe had now seized command.

"Come on," and set off with John in his wake and led the way into the lounge. He picked up and armed the panic button with a key from his pocket and told John to press it only when he called and not before.

Joe had hijacked absolute management now from Jimmy who just stood gawking at the innards of the control box. He was none the wiser as to what he was seeing and the longer he stared, the more confused he became. It could have been the workings from a doorbell or the latest space craft for all he could decipher. Joe was a portly man having lived a sedentary lifestyle but his fingers were long and thin and were extremely dextrous. They were in the box swiftly working now on the practically invisible wire and connecting it to its appropriate station. John stood in front of the fire where George had gasped his last breath holding the panic alarm as Alison walked in.

"God knows what he's doing with that alarm. By the way, you look a right lemon standing there holding that."

"Thanks."

"Anytime" and she sat down on the sofa. Two minutes later, John heard the engineers yell: and pressed the button.

A piecing oscillating siren erupted from the alarm control box temporarily deafening Jimmy who was still standing right next to it. Joe had expected and anticipated the racket it would make and hurriedly punched the code into the key pad to silence it. He joined John and Alison in the lounge and re-armed the panic button and again reiterated his instruction to John to press it only when he called. The yell came and John pressed the button: nothing, not a whimper.

"Yes is the answer to your question. It is the panic button wire" shouted the engineer who knew he would be making a statement and knew the Police were prompt payers who never quibbled at his allegedly exorbitant bills. So, Joe was happy to help as best he could and remain the engineer of choice for Sussex Police.

Jimmy had regained a bit of his hearing having been momentarily deafened due to his proximity to the internal bell and asked Joe if the external alarm bell had activated as it should have.

Joe with some disdain said, "Didn't you hear it? It was loud enough."

John and Alison walked back into the hallway as Joe was crouched down tidying up his tools in his case. Thanking him for his help John asked him when he thought the alarm was last serviced.

Still with his attention directed at his case, Joe said, "I can only say that it was in 2011 by someone called 'Gary'."

All three stared at the back of Joe's head and Alison said, "How on earth do you know that?"

Joe stood up and pointed to the front panel of the control box which was still lying on the floor and said, "When an alarm is serviced, the engineer should put their contact number, date and sign and print their name on a pad. There's a piece of paper stuck on the inside of that panel with all the service dates and engineers details. The last one is incorrectly completed by 'Gary' who serviced it this year. No proper contact details, name or date. Simple."

Alison picked up the panel using gloves and handling it only on the very edge turned it over to find the paper stuck firm. A list of sixteen previous engineers were recoded correctly and the last was 'Gary'. Joe expressed sadness that a member of his profession was unable to follow basic procedures by filling out four easy boxes. There were sixteen people that had managed it and even the most illiterate engineer could surely have looked at how they had achieved it and used their efforts as a guide.

Then, "Mind you, he couldn't be very competent if he'd left that wire like that." Both John and Alison were not at all surprised at 'Gary's' competency as both were now forming an opinion.

Jimmy and the engineer sat at the dining table and at his dictation, Jimmy wrote the statement which was a detailed account from the arrival to the present time and the incidents between as recalled by Joe.

John and Alison went into the lounge and down to the conservatory where Alison said in hushed tones, "I can't see it."

"It would be a useless bit of kit if you could. You don't need to whisper by the way, I have checked and there's nothing in the house."

Alison asked him how they were going to be able to trace 'Gary' if indeed it was his true name. John was not too sure, and told her he knew there was no paperwork relating to the burglar alarm inside the house.

He mused aloud, "Has it been deliberately removed? Possibly. Is Gary the person who put the bird box up? Possible. Did he undo the wire? Likely. Why? Did he kill George? No idea."

She looked at him and said, "For once, we're both on the same wavelength. There is just one other question I'd like to add: are the murder and my burglary related in any way?"

"No. I can categorically say no."

John was still discussing the case with himself but loud enough for Alison to hear, "Did he pay for the service by cheque? Look at bank account. Did he use a credit card? Check what we know or credit agency. Go through all burglar alarm engineers listed with yellow pages or Thompson's for a 'Gary'. Jobs for Paul. Check internet. Job for Alison. Sit in cold barn all night to see who drives slowly by. See if someone sets off 'trembler'. Job for an idiot."

"I completely concur with all that. Now is it too soon to go and get some decent food."

53

Friday 10th June 2011

They sat in the car on the drive once he had pulled past the spruce with the 'eye' in the bird box, and both looked at the Sat Nav as Alison was given a lesson on how it worked. John told her that Ian was working on some new equipment for her car which would be a lot more modern and sophisticated than the stuff in his. Claiming her little Fiesta only had a small glove box, she couldn't work out how Ian could conceal the Sat Nav.

John's simple answer was, "Just because something is in plain sight does not mean it's visible."

Alison was bemused. 'Another stupid statement' she thought. 'Pointless pursuing it' but she just couldn't help herself.

"Whose quote is that then? Holmes, Maigret, Poirot, or some other fictional character?"

"No. It's mine. Feel free to use it if you want."

"You're so bloody insufferable. I think you're as bad as my Dad."

She learnt quickly, manipulating the Sat Nav with ease. Throughout the country, the younger generation seemed to be so much savvier with modern technology. They picked it up like they were born to it whereas the older generation had had their moments many years earlier and were now quietly proud it was their children's turn. John not being actually old, just a dinosaur and proud of it.

Both saw that Simon was approaching Arundel on the A27 and appeared to be moving quickly towards Chichester. He was going to be in position a lot earlier than expected. She expanded the view and saw Ian's car was moving about near the M20 and John searched for and found her Dad's car travelling along the A3 towards the M25.

"You can speak to him if you want."

"No thanks. I don't need a lecture now."

She asked about the box with the aerial and how it worked to which he said he had "No idea. I turn it on, green is safe, amber is a tracker and red a listening device. It only works accurately up to five yards. The paddle up to about two feet. It's all getting old. There's a couple of small magnetic tracking devices called either a 'sticky' or a 'lump' in the box which you slap on a car, then it shows up on the Sat Nav as red just like the 'trembler'. Trouble is the magnet's not that powerful, and a knock like a pot hole could dislodge it. Ian can fix a proper tracker which can't be seen and won't come off. I really need a new car and the updated gear that you will have but I'm happy at the moment with what I've got. Mind you, that's where the best bit of kit comes in."

She couldn't stop herself from asking although she knew it was a set up question.

"What's that then?"

He took the toffee hammer out of the door pocket offered it to her and said, "This of course."

"Modern technology it isn't. So what do you do with that? Break up frozen chocolate?"

"If you get close enough to put the 'sticky' on, you give the rear nearside light cluster a gentle tap with the pointed end and then you can see a bright white light at night, and when the vehicle brakes: anytime. Makes it easier to follow."

Alison looked as stern as she could and explained to him he was suggesting various illegal actions including criminal damage and use of unauthorised equipment and reminded him of the gun in the pub. Looking as shocked as he could, he claimed ignorance of all and stated he would amend his ways: next month. Tucked tightly under his seat and out of view to inquisitive eyes or groping hands of any searcher was an identical gun to the one in the 'green room'. John decided the time was not yet right for Alison to know that fact.

Joe the engineer had completed his statement with Jimmy and was now in his van behind the Vauxhall in the drive. The van was an old diesel like Dan's was that rattled constantly especially when it was idling. The row it made precluded the use of a horn. He was hoping to get home to Brighton as soon as he could for an evening out 'on the town' with his wife on his future revenue from Sussex Police. No need to harass with a superfluous horn as the Vauxhall pulled off up to the road and swung right and towards Barnham and he went left towards Littlehampton and eventually, Brighton.

John pointed out the entrance to his night time habitat in the barn as they discussed where a person would leave a vehicle if they were going to remove the bird box, bearing in mind they would need a ladder. Both had differing positions and both would be wrong.

54

Friday 10th June 2011

They drove back at a leisurely pace to the yard at Chichester where John parked in his usual place which always seemed to be vacant for no evident reason. Walking up to the office, Alison pestered him for the use of the anti-bugging box which he steadfastly refused citing, 'it may be an unauthorised device' which riled her beyond belief. As they entered the incident room, she was stridently threatening John with a range of hideous assaults after preferably days of indescribable torture. Prodow was sitting at Paul's desk waiting for the kettle to boil and burst into a booming laugh at the threats he'd heard issued.

"He's finally got to you: not bad holding off for a couple of days. You have promise. Most just want to kill him in about twelve hours."

She went redder than she had ever been and didn't know what to say spluttering something about not meaning the menaces. Prodow was still chuckling and told her not to apologise as it was just water off a duck's back to John: and then offered to make them both tea.

Doreen was swiftly, in her estimation, growing old. Her birthday was in another month and she would hit thirty-five. Although she looked her age thanks to premature lines around her eyes and bags beneath them, she rarely bothered with makeup. She liked to keep her long fair hair pinned back in a sort of loose bun which was in vogue prior to the war. The great war! It made her look appallingly frumpish to any potential suitors. To endorse the fact, she was always dressed in a knee length skirt and white blouse and black shoes. She tended to buy items from catalogues in multiples so there was always something to wear that was identical to the day previously.

One thing she had in spades was a great personality with compassion for those in need, but her Mother was her problem. Being an only child, she felt it was her duty to care for her in her old age, and Lavinia took full advantage of it, dictating terms as though Doreen was still a child. Any man who had the temerity to appear on the scene was soon put off by the authoritarian matriarch. Books had become Doreen's life and deliverance.

Now, Doreen was busy typing and stole a peek at John and raised her eyebrows and pulled an expression as if to say, 'I don't know what he's up to.' Paul was close on their heels entering the office with three cardboard cartons of cakes and a couple of spare packets of 'dunking' biscuits all in a Waitrose bag. Prodow seemed very happy and greeted Paul's return.

"Got the cakes, good. I'll let you finish making the tea as you know where everything is. Unfortunately Mr Groves can't make it today which I know will upset you all," and he guffawed before continuing, "We'll wait for Jimmy and then get started."

Paul got all the cups out and a couple of 'borrowed' plates from the canteen on which he placed the cakes. A new carton of milk was removed from the small exhibits fridge which thankfully rarely contained anything else. Maybe a blood or DNA (DeoxyriboNucleic Acid) sample inhabited it for a couple of days prior to delivery to the laboratory for analysis, but nothing else. Most importantly, the milk was not likely to be contaminated. Alison had nearly resumed her natural colour and was examining a computer screen in an effort to look busy, and John just sat at a desk doing nothing. Prodow happily engaged Doreen in conversation about her latest books and said he had read a few of them and went on to discuss their merits.

Paul was engaged handing out the teas and coffees when Jimmy entered the office. Once Jimmy had submitted the statement to Paul and been served a tea by Doreen, Prodow told everyone to have a cake. Then they all settled down to see what he had to say. He started off by saying that Olivia Munroe was going at the end of the following week to the crown court at Lewes for pleas and directions by the Judge as to the conduct and progress of the impending trial. All the relevant disclosure papers had already been prepared by a retired Met Detective who was employed as a PCW (Prosecution Case Worker) in the major incident room at Brighton and the CPS had been briefed by DI Groves.

Sipping his tea, he paused, then bit into an individual fruit tart savouring the fruit.

"From what you have all achieved and found out up to now leads me to believe she is probably innocent. In addition, we are still no nearer to confirming the victim's true identity. The problem is, unless you have ascertained new evidence today: we don't know who did it. I feel that I am going to have to tell the prosecutor and then the Judge. Comments?"

Jimmy was up for the challenge, and discussed in detail the engineers visit and 'Gary'. As he spoke, Alison caught John's eye and noticed him shake his head from side to side very slightly. They all discussed methods of tracing 'Gary', and Paul took on the onerous tasks that were mooted and agreed. From what Prodow was saying, they appeared to have a week at the most left in which to sort the matter out before Munroe was released and the whole squad would be re-formed to start the enquiry up again. Paul suggested asking the Judge to remand the matter for a fortnight to give them more time to truly identify the victim and prove either way Munroe's involvement if any. Prodow accepted that it was the immediate course of action he had considered and would pursue it.

Alison apprised the group that she had eventually been able to speak to the records clerk at the MOD who was surprised to hear that the ID card marked Jeffery A Anderson was still in existence. They had been informed during the war by the local Police that Mr Anderson, who had been a procurement official, had been killed during an attack on a train by German aircraft near Drayton Railway station in West Sussex. Cause of death had been recorded 'as a result of enemy action'.

There were, according to the person at the MOD several riders to the report which informed the clerk at the time that Anderson's wife had been killed when his home address had been destroyed by a bomb on the very same day. A search of the house found no trace of Jean his young child, so she had been listed as 'Missing. Presumed dead'. No other enquiries were made to trace relatives.

The last report was according to Alison the most interesting.

"The lady said that Jeffery Anderson had at the outbreak of war been issued with a .38 Webley revolver and fifty rounds of ammunition. Neither of which had been recovered. I told her we had recovered a Webley and ammunition and she has given me a serial number of the missing gun."

She handed the paper with the number on to Jimmy who went to his Exhibit Book. They all sat quietly and waited.

Jimmy said, "It's identical."

John said, "Why did Armstrong have it hidden in his garden?" No one answered because they were all thinking the same.

Paul broke the silence.

"I think Alison needs a congratulatory round of applause after our unwarranted criticism yesterday, she has redeemed herself."

They all started to clap and Alison grew redder. The pucer she went the louder and faster they clapped.

"Sod you all!"

Everyone burst into laughter including Alison. Gradually, they all calmed down.

Then as if imparting a confidence, Prodow went on to say that he had decided to retire as soon as was practicable, and between them all, he had been offered a job for two days a week working for the solicitor's where he had obtained the will. He had the small gathered host to thank for that as it was they who had sent him to the firm in the first place, hence his 'lavish' outlay on the cakes. There was then various chit chat between them all with John as the only person present proffering the opinion that the case would be solved before he retired. Doreen excused herself and left to go home for tea and onto her second book club meeting of the week.

Prodow left the office and as he was approaching the head of the stairs, called to John from the corridor. It was obvious to all that he wanted a private word, and John followed him out to see what was on his mind.

As soon as he could speak quietly enough, he asked, "Are you going to be able to work this other matter out in time?"

"Yes."

"How's Alison getting along?"

"She's good."

"Before I retire, I'll arrange for her to be transferred permanently to the CID if that's what she wants" and with that, he bounded off down the stairs calling his farewells as he went. John went back into the office and after a short time both he and Alison left Paul and Jimmy in the office and headed for Alison's sporty little Fiesta.

55
Friday 10th June 2011

They drove less than half a mile to the huge car park at Chichester Gate keeping their own counsel en route. She parked as close to Frankie & Benny's restaurant as she could and they went in for a meal. The two cakes she'd consumed had only served to prevent her stomach letting everyone know she hadn't eaten properly for some time. It didn't matter now, anywhere would have been sufficient for her because she was so hungry she felt she could have 'eaten half a cow.' Then the concept instantly repulsed her, but didn't do anything to put her off. She knew there was going to be no holding back or eating healthily. It was going to be the full monty! Thoughts were swirling around in her head, drifting in and out. 'How the hell does he go so long without food or drink?' Then she came to the illogical conclusion he must have been a camel in a previous life. 'Is this what lack of food does?'

Both were acknowledged with enthusiasm by the young 'meeter and greeter' called Davide, who Alison thought wore a pleasantly perfumed cologne. Asking them to follow him to their table, he spun round and took off like a greyhound with Alison dogging his heels. The two cakes she'd eaten earlier had failed to alleviate her hunger and so weren't worthy of recognition.

Within five paces John slipped and clattered to the floor. Neither Davide nor Alison, who had both heard the commotion, bothered to turn round or break step in their reckless pursuit to reach the allotted table. Gathering himself up, and apologising freely to the person who aided him from the floor, he followed them to the designated table. The menu was thrust into her clutching hands as the 'meeter and greeter' sped off to find his next customers.

Within seconds a waiter was next to the table asking for their drinks order. It was bordering on harassment.

Alison could not have cared less.

As soon as they were alone, John took a mobile phone out of his pocket and turning it on found the saved numbers and dialled Alison's mobile from the list. She looked astonished as her phone rang from within her handbag.

"Now you have my number on your phone."

"Where did you get that from?"

"When we came in, Simon gave it to me when he helped me get up off the floor."

Alison raised her gaze to the door and the route they had taken to the table but saw no single diner.

"Sometimes you really worry me."

They ate a full nourishing meal and both checked the clock on the wall at regular intervals until 6.15pm when they walked to the till and paid Davide. Both noticed his French accent had slipped slightly towards 'Estuary English'.

Whispering to her, "Shows you can't believe everything that people want you to believe. That's a good lesson for you!"

Alison chose not to reply.

Leaving by the main door, they sauntered from the gloom within the restaurant into the bright low light of the evening sun. Both paused and took a few seconds to readjust to the daylight. Then strolling a further fifty yards along the pedestrian precinct, they stepped into 'Lloyds' an upmarket, busy and bustling wine bar. Buying a good, slightly overpriced chardonnay, they took their bottle and glasses to a couple of comfy looking seats under the stairs. There were a few other people from the Police Station in the wine bar having an early drink after work before heading off home, who acknowledged them in passing. They chatted about their histories with Alison revealing a lot more about her past as she drank more wine than did John. Very heavy set men in black suits started to appear and take up strategic locations around the wine bar and at the front door. All the bouncers, or 'door personnel' as they preferred to be called, liked to be in place well before 7.30pm.

Just prior to 7.30pm, John reminded Alison to keep her phone where she could see it. As if an act of precocious defiance, she took it from her bag and plonked it on the low table in front of them next to her glass.

"There. Happy?"

"I am."

John said goodbye and made his way to the exit where he engaged a bouncer in some friendly banter for a few minutes before walking off back towards the Police Station.

He followed the footpath as it meandered through the precinct and round past the fitness centre which was deserted. Then he intentionally staggered a little as he walked at a ponderously sluggish pace. Within seconds he heard footfall quickly gaining on him from behind. Suppressing the urge to turn, he continued along the footpath. A soft voice seemed to echo in his head from his right ear.

"*They are five yards off. Turn around… Now.*"

As he pivoted about, something hit him on the right shoulder which knocked him to the floor. A sharp pain to his rib cage caused him involuntarily to curl into the foetal position. The shoe he saw was a dirty brown brogue as it passed his eye and glanced off his nose and onto his cheek. That really hurt more than his ribs. Then he heard the call from a distance that he had been waiting for.

"Police. Stop where you are" which caused his attackers to immediately run in the opposite direction.

"Are you ok John?"

"I ache like hell. Did you get it on film?"

Ian said, "Yeah. Two of them. Definitely foreign. Your cheek is bleeding quite badly. I think you need a couple of stitches. I'll call an ambulance."

"Cheers."

*

It only took four minutes from the anonymous call being received for an ambulance to arrive. The paramedics also thought he needed a couple of stitches and a once over from the A and E staff at St Richard's Hospital. Being relatively early in the evening, the casualty unit was practically empty and the staff were snatching hot drinks and taking a quick breather ready for the drunks and assaults that would fill it later. The ambulance crew deposited him on a trolley in the casualty unit and left after handing him into the care of an officious nurse.

Clipboard in hand, she took down his answers recording his personal details in the boxes provided.

When she had what she wanted she said, "The doctor will be with you shortly. These notes will be entered onto a computer and you can have a printout should you wish."

Before he could consider a reply, she had left the curtained cubical. John lay on the trolley and reflected on the assault. They had a blunt weapon which had struck him on the shoulder. His head had not been the main target although by turning it may have put them off, but he thought not. If they wanted to cause serious harm, they would have probably used a knife. By turning, he hoped to have protected his head and body from any knife attack. Only one kick had been made to his ribs and one to his face. All in all, he had not been seriously assaulted and he knew the object was to temporarily incapacitate him which would mean him having time off work. Now he knew for sure, they had confirmed the target was Alison.

The doctor pulled the curtain aside and strode into the cubicle leaving it open for all to see in.

"What the hell have you been up to now?"

"Hello Carol."

A nurse stepped into the cubicle with a small silver tray containing odd looking instruments and pulled the curtain closed behind her.

"Don't bother Zara. I'll sort this idiot out."

Looking slightly bemused, the nurse deposited the tray and left the cubical to find the staff nurse in charge to press her concern at the doctor's behaviour towards the patient. She would not have worried had she known the casualty doctor was a very close personal friend and their beds had been shared more times than either could remember.

Carol examined him and offered 'blanket stitch' if he wasn't going to see her within a week, or 'ace needlework' that would not leave a scar if he promised a visit. A visit was promised and the stitches were inserted neatly and uniformly small. Once they were completed, she insisted on checking his rib cage as she stated she wanted him in full working order for his visit. Assessing his ribs to be bruised but not broken, she arranged for an x ray the following day just to make sure. He tried to get up off the trolley and she tapped him on the forehead gently with some tweezers to knock him back down so she could check his shoulder. It also seemed to be ok but requiring a confirmation x ray. Massaging it with both hands, she leant forward and whispered in his ear letting him know exactly what was being lined up for his visit. He swore to himself he would be there within the week.

56
Friday 10th June 2011

"The cop is out of the way. Probably a broken rib or two. Should put him off sick for a while."

"Any problems with him?"

"No. Not really. They had to run before they made sure. Some other Police were in the area."

"That could be a problem. Could they be recognised?"

"No. Too far for them to have been seen. They weren't even chased. No problem."

"I hope not."

"She'll be alone now."

"Be careful."

"She's easy."

"Keep a grip of it. No more problems."

"OK."

57
Friday 10th June 2011

At 8.pm, Alison was unintentionally sinking gradually deeper into the soft leather of the armchair that she had made her own since arriving. It was due to the amount of wine she had already consumed and now the remnants that she was trying to wring from the bottle and the dregs in her glass. Her mobile, now sitting next to the bottle on the low table where she could keep it in constant view started to flash a bright white light. It began to vibrate and started to dance across the table and then played a cardinal version of Bizet's Carmen which attracted a few turned heads due to its excessive volume. She hadn't sorted it out after she and John had dismantled it.

She examined the screen which appeared blurred. A displayed number was pulsing with a blue light which meant nothing to her but that was no bar. Clamping it to her ear she answered in a slurred voice.

"Hallo."

Ian introduced himself to her and she blurted out that she thought he was somewhere in Kent because she'd seen it on the Sat Nav. He mildly rebuked her for mentioning it over an unsecured phone line in a wine bar and then gave her a sanitised version of what had happened to John. Brushing off her questions about his injuries, he told her that John was just getting checked over at St Richard's and would be out within a couple of hours at the most. Continuing without giving her any chance to interrupt, he revealed he had filmed John's assailants and the assault. He said that he had already e-mailed a copy to both Ginger and her Dad in an effort to try to identify, via their respective sources, the attackers.

Her head seemed to rapidly sort itself out and she started to think rationally. Now she could think clearly and speak cohesively she managed to interrupt.

She assumed that the hospital receptionist would inform the Police about the assault.

"I'll go back to the Station and start an investigation. It will be a lot simpler if I took a role in it as I have more idea of what is happening."

"I cannot emphasise enough that you take no part in this matter. Your father is adamant. John will be devastated if he knows you are getting involved. He told you something may happen. It has. Should any Police investigator speak to you about it: you know nothing. You have been having an after work drink. Am I making myself clear?"

"But why?"

"Matters are being dealt with that you are not yet aware of. Allow the normal Police procedure to be instigated. Take it from me, you will not be asked to take part in any investigation."

A pause before a sullen reply, *"OK."*

Changing tack, she whispered loudly down the phone with her spare hand cupped over the mouth piece.

"Well, it now looks definite that John is the target. So, tell me, why was my phone bugged? Probably my car and flat as well!"

"I cannot tell you."

Now confident enough to butt in, *"Or you won't tell me?"*

"Your father will keep you informed as needs be."

"I'll be waiting till kingdom come in that case."

"Don't get upset. Things seem to be speeding up. You will probably be the first to know as it is," and then the phone went dead.

She took it from her ear and slowly placed it back on the table watching it all the time.

'What did he mean by that?'

The man standing by her seat said, "Can I join you?"

Caustically, without looking at him, she replied. "No."

"You should look after your phone, anyone could pick it up. How's John?"

Her head whipped up to stare at him as her left hand grabbed for her phone knocking the empty chardonnay bottle off the table. It bounced on its base and rolled back under the table without breaking.

"You were lucky. If it had been full, you could guarantee it would break. Sod's law."

He slid a small sports bag under the seat as he sat down assuming John's vacated chair with its commanding view of the entrance and front of the wine bar. Placing the half full glass of Spitfire beer that he was nursing onto the table he looked at her.

"Well. How is he?"

She couldn't stop herself from answering grumpily, "Apparently, all right." Alison hated the fact that often in her life when people asked her questions, she answered instinctively without thinking: invariably truthfully. Over the years, it had cost her some friends. It was a trait she was desperately trying to stop, and failing each time especially with well over two thirds of a bottle of wine on board.

"I'm Simon."

"I'm Alison."

"I know."

"Smart arse."

She liked him. He had a permanent smile etched across his face as he spoke. Laughter lines suited him. Even the small lines engraved across his forehead enhanced his looks, although she wasn't sure about the designer stubble. His features were soft under his short, neatly groomed fair hair which she thought had slight copper tints giving it a little gingerish hue in places. The miniscule indentation of a dimple on his chin just had to be there in the same way that any ear lobes on such small ears would have been wrong. It was a face that exuded strength and confidence and even the very gentle lump half way down his nose where it had been broken while he was in Sierra Leone looked as though it was a feature from birth. Alison saw the warm brown eyes, bright and clear which complemented his face. She reckoned about thirty years old and was only one year out. No taller than five feet ten inches wearing what could only have been a designer suit made by hand to fit over a body that was honed to practical perfection. No tie and suede shoes were the only things that upset the whole appearance in her eyes.

"What do you think?"

"Pardon?"

"You have checked me over, what do you think?"

For the second time in one day, Alison went a bright red with embarrassment but this time had no computer to hide behind. He laughed freely without malice and then apologised for being so insensitive and rude. She liked him even more but was not going to show it. His cologne wafted towards her and she remembered precisely where she had first caught its fragrance.

Leaning towards her, he lowered his voice, "There is only the one person watching your flat."

Alison was taken aback by this, and regained her natural colour a lot faster than previously.

"I went straight there when I arrived and could just make out the person who is watching wrapped up in a very large parka practically asleep in the back of a van and not paying much attention. The van has 'BT Telecoms' written on the side. It looks natural enough and doesn't stand out much. It's parked in a bay directly opposite your road at the junction and has a clear line of sight on the front door of your flat. Have you noticed it at all?"

Shocked by this new revelation, and again slurring her words slightly, "I can't remember seeing it today but I think I saw it there yesterday. I thought they were working on something."

"That's the reason it has BT on the side. To put you off remembering it. You're going to have to start noticing this sort of thing."

Alison was creeping sluggishly towards a sulk. She was fighting it and still winning. Within the hour, she'd been rebuked and chastised by Ian and now criticised by Simon. She was just able to hold it together because in her heart she knew they were both right. The alcohol was stifling her combative streak. As she listened, her thoughts wandered as he seemed to prattle on how it was so easy for the 'watcher' sitting in the back of the van to monitor any listening or video devices within her flat. It was something at the moment that she did not want, or care to know. Simon concluded by telling her how simple it was for the 'watcher' to see any movement towards her flat as it was the last in a block and the only one with outside stairs in the small cul-de-sac.

"Thanks for the information."

He did not hesitate in his narrative, and informed her that when they were inside her flat, she was to give him a guided tour, so he could check where any bugs or cameras were and decide how they were going to continue. Reminding her to be judicious in what she said once inside her flat, he told her if she had anything contentious to say she was to write it down.

As if by way of a culmination, he picked up his beer glass, downed it in one, and said, "This is a good brew. I'll have another before we go. I'll get you a J20. You need to sober up a little" and got up and went to the bar.

Alison watched his back as he navigated through the crowd and only then realised she still had her mobile phone clenched in her left hand. She stuffed the phone into her bag and thought, 'Why do they all tell me what's happening and what I've got to do and I don't get a damn word in edgeways.'

He returned with his beer and her apple and raspberry J20 still in its bottle with an empty tall glass upended on it which he set down before her. She poured the juice from the bottle into the glass and took a sip. Wincing from its sweet taste she forced a full mouthful. Not that bad really.

Resuming his seat and swallowing a third of the dark liquid from his pint in one movement he queried, "You didn't answer the question."

"Truthfully?"

"Of course."

"Smart arse. Wants a shave. Needs proper shoes. Wear a tie with a suit. A really aggravating sod."

Simon burst out laughing not offended in any way and said the only one he didn't agree with was proper shoes. He liked his suede shoes because they made no noise.

They chatted amicably for a while as they finished their drinks and he finally said, "Let's go and play!"

58
Friday 10th June 2011

Graham had been busy. He had spent a great deal of time on the phone to Ian who was on his way back to Kent.

"I want to be ready."

"I'll bring as much as I can with me. The rest will have to come in during the night. You are certain no one has ears or eyes on you?"

"The technical boys from the City do occasional sweeps so I have had them do them every three days. Nothing. The surveillance team are running practice sessions by following me. They would spot anyone else watching the house. Nothing."

"I presume GCHQ (Government Communications Headquarters) are monitoring your phone."

"Yes. That's why I am using a 'burner' now."

"When do you think it will happen?"

"I don't know, but I want to be ready."

"I'll have to be there all the time."

"You can use the spare room."

"Where's your wife?"

"Having a holiday."

"Who does your cooking?"

"Me."

"I'll bring someone with me. I don't want to be poisoned."

59

Friday 10th June 2011

Doreen strolled into the church hall at 7.15pm and straight up to the little canteen counter where they only sold tea and coffee with a biscuit on the side, and asked for a tea. It took the two ladies, who were volunteers, five minutes to make it and present it with a custard cream. They lived for rumours about people they knew or had heard of. It didn't matter who told them or what it was, providing it was salacious. So, gossiping was the main motivation for them to be there and the sale of tea and coffee was secondary but a good means of introduction to lots of people who could impart tittle-tattle.

There were always small groups using the facilities of the church hall which were second to none in the surrounding area. With her tea slopped into the saucer, Doreen went to the small side room that was the setting for her book club meetings and sat on one of the eight chairs that another volunteer had previously placed in a circle. Being the first in, she had her pick. As usual, she lowered her bag onto the floor next to her chair and teased a book from it whilst balancing her tea in her other hand. There had never been more than a dozen people and normally only seven or eight which the caretaker knew. His attitude was why leave more seating out than was likely to be required. It would only mean he had to spend more time putting it away later. Therefore, he only ever left eight chairs out.

Elderly women shuffled into the room in dribs and drabs carrying cups full to the brim trying valiantly not to spill any as they took their seats. Each carried a handbag that was so large the book to be disseminated and discussed that evening could be borne quite safely in them with all their other treasures. Placing their bags on the floor whilst balancing their cups however was beyond each of them. To a fault, they all managed to slop their cups' contents to some degree into their saucers. Tissues were extracted from some of the bags and placed under cups to mop up the worst spillages. Ten people had entered the room, and the last two leaving their bags and drinks on the floor, scuttled out in search of additional chairs. The meeting was scheduled to start at 7.30pm but didn't get under way until ten minutes later. Drips from the cups and saucers that had landed on clothing had to be mopped up immediately with generous 'tutting' from the victims.

All those present had known each other for several years of attending the book club meetings and roughly knew what each did and where they lived from long forgotten conversations. The majority were retired, and just a few were still young enough to need to work. Paid members ran to only thirty-four souls, but most only ever appeared on special occasions. Doreen, who was the youngest was the most regular attendee and was often asked to take the meeting when the organiser was unavailable. Gladys kept everybody on her database informed of what books were being read and reviewed and when. She tried to run the meetings in a chronological way, but was often unable to control the direction of them due to the forceful personalities of some of the members; one of whom was present tonight.

Sally hadn't been to a meeting for some months, and was not really there to discuss some book she hadn't heard of until Gladys e-mailed her with the title. She'd got her husband to buy it for her in order to appear knowledgeable although she hadn't bothered to read anything other than the fly leaf. Then as the meeting was half way through, she declared to no one in particular how she had been following the local mystery regarding George Armstrong's death and wouldn't it make a spectacular novel?

"I've followed this since it was first reported in the papers. How do they get their information? They seem to be leading people to believe that Olivia Munroe is a really devious murderer. One thing that I do not understand is why would she want to murder an old man of ninety-one years who was a cripple and nearly at the point of natural death? I reckon she had to be after his money."

Gladys knew straightaway that Sally's intervention was not going to be helpful. It was clear that a different discussion was now to be had. Everyone present had followed the papers as the story of the murder had unfolded and all had an opinion which they wanted to share. It was obvious that the meeting was now lost and hurtling off at a tangent. She knew she could not bring it back on track and decided to let it run its course.

Sally had sown the seed. All those present seemed to agree that it did not seem a logical murder in accordance with any of the murder mysteries that they had read or discussed. The papers had implied that there were financial implications and possible irregularities without actually saying so. Doreen may have been the youngest but was by far the shrewdest person present. She attended the meetings every week and was mindful that Sally, who was only five years her senior rarely appeared unless she had an ulterior motive. As soon as she had mentioned George, Doreen could see she was going to be asked if she knew anything because they were all aware she worked for the Police as a typist on major enquiries. Sure enough, someone asked her and she was ready and fielded the question by 'confidentially' letting them know that the case was going to Lewes crown court within the week where Munroe was to be asked how she would plead. Then if she denied it, the case would be set for trial and all the evidence, of which she was not party to, would be heard.

They still engaged each other with possible scenarios as to why Munroe would have done the deed. Sally had gone remarkably quiet after her initial remarks and was listening intently to all the banter and submissions. No matter how they tried, they could come up with no other possible suspects, and all enjoyed, bar Doreen, the conversation and hypothesising regarding Armstrong's death. She had noted how Sally had 'stoked the fire' as it were, and then sat back and revelled in the others' deliberations.

On her way home, she cogitated as to what had been said. It was, she concluded, a reasonable question to put to Paul the following day. She was aware there were no real financial implications as yet disclosed so why kill someone who is nearly dead anyway?

Sally was also thinking of the murder as she made her way to meet her husband for a drink and to discuss why on earth anyone would want the old man dead. 'It's got to be for money. It just has to be. He had a few bob. How was Munroe going to get it? Why kill him before you've got it? Stupid bitch.'

Normally the meeting concluded at 9pm in order that the caretaker could check that everything was back in its rightful place, lock up and go home for 9.30pm. The women from the book club were the last group out of the church hall and when he checked their room, he found a pristine copy of a novel about the fall of Troy. He took it, and gave it to his wife who said it was the author's last book before she died: then opened it, and started reading her first book in years.

60
Friday 10th June 2011

John left the hospital in company with a young uniform officer who offered to drive him back to the station to collect his car. It was only about a mile, and when they arrived without having been involved in an accident, John was extremely thankful. He was sure that the only reason they hadn't crashed was because they were in a marked Police car and everyone around them became very cautious and got out of their way.

Now he walked slowly, because it was too painful to walk quickly, to his car. Getting in caused a sharp pain to his ribs on his left side, but sitting in the Vauxhall's worn seat was so relaxing and pain free it was a joy. Manoeuvring through the Police car parking area to the exit at the back of the station he turned right into Kingsham Road. Accelerating rapidly to the end of the road he looked for signs of anyone following. Then driving through back streets and into Oving Road he was held momentarily at the red traffic lights at the junction with the A27 before following the road towards Tangmere.

No one pursued him and he didn't understand why. His only conclusion was that his assailants were confident they had put him out of action and away from Alison. Most people would have checked just to make sure and the simplest way would have been to follow him. He checked the rocker switch on his dash. It showed clear. Pulling up sharply into a side road, he forced himself out of the car and to the boot. He removed the small silver scanner from its wooden holder, turned it on and watched the red and amber lights go off leaving the green one glowing. Moving it about the car and checking his wax coat on the back seat it still shone green. Putting it back into its foam resting place, he eased himself back into the driving seat and checked his dashboard light once again as an additional precaution. Still clear.

He was satisfied. No tail. No bugs. He made his way leisurely but directly to his temporary bedroom in the barn. On passing the Murrell, he looked longingly towards it but could not bring himself to stop. As soon as he was in position, he pulled his fleece on and his big wax coat over it: turned the Sat Nav on, checked there was no movement shown at the 'trembler' and fell quickly into a light sleep having first set his little alarm.

*

Gary was in the Oyster Catcher pub at Clymping where he had gone after work and met a couple of friends for a drink. They were sagacious people who after a couple of pints knew any more could be a driving problem, so had gone home leaving Gary to sup alone. He did not want any trouble with the law either so had gone onto diet coke while he read one of the pubs free daily papers to kill time.

Simon and Alison made their way from the wine bar towards her car and both got in. Simon's hand removed a little silver box from his pocket similar to John's but smaller, and turned it on. Only the amber light came on.

"That's good, it's only a tracker."

"I hope your right."

"This is the top of the range latest unit, never been wrong."

She had given him the keys because she was still slurring her speech and she knew she would make a breathalyser cough. He drove towards the North of Chichester and was given unnecessary directions by her before she closed her eyes and dozed. As they approached the turn into her road, Simon gently nudged her to open her eyes and she saw the van in the bay with a bronze BMW parked behind it. Pointing it out to Alison he told her they should proceed as planned. He drove face in to the front of her garage and parked.

While still sitting in the car, Simon said, "Remember. Whatever happens, I'm your cousin Simon, my dad's Graham, same name as yours and I'm here for a week's holiday. OK?"

"You really know how to inspire confidence." and they both got out of the car laughing.

Alison led the way up the stairs to her front door, and they both entered the hall. As soon as the front door was shut, Simon took his small silver scanner out of his pocket and turned it on: the light went straight to red. He moved it about the hall but found nothing as he spoke about how nice it was for her to invite him for a holiday and her uncle sent his regards. She in turn responded and led him into the spare bedroom where he dropped his bag as they engaged in general chat. Again, he found nothing but was not surprised as it was a room she obviously didn't use much. When he indicated to her to move on, she led him to the kitchen. The lights on the little box all flickered on as he held it close by one of the wall cupboards which held tins of food. Then it settled to a solid red. Bending slightly to look under the pelmet of the unit and gently running his fingers along the inside of it where he could not quite see, he pointed and held up his index finger to imply one.

They went from the kitchen into the lounge as Simon moved the scanner in his hand over the sideboard and other odd bits of furniture including the TV and hi-fi units around the walls. The lights all flickered on as he held it over the landline telephone unit before settling to solid red, and he held up two fingers. He was moving about the lounge checking low and high, and all the furniture but found nothing else. Normally he would have expected to find another in the lounge, but concluding that it was not a very big room, he accepted that one would probably be sufficient and they moved back into the hall and to the bathroom. That was all clear, and Alison showed him into her bedroom glad she had tidied up in the morning and made the bed on rising. He moved about with his little scanner, and all the lights flickered as it hovered over the landline phone extension next to her bed. As the lights settled again for a solid red she felt goose bumps rise on her arms and legs and then she shivered involuntarily. He held three fingers up, although that was totally unnecessary as far as Alison was concerned.

Eventually, he turned the scanner off contented with the fact that there were only three listening devices. He took it into the spare bedroom where he placed it into what looked like a phone charger and plugged the lead into a wall socket. All the lights came on and started to blink at fifteen second intervals. Still chatting about inconsequential things, they made a cup of tea and both went into the lounge and settled down to watch the TV for the rest of the evening.

Although Alison was fighting to keep her eyes open, she had noticed as he was moving about the flat earlier, that Simon wore no jewellery, watch or wedding ring. Something she had never looked for, or noticed, on a man before. She felt obliged to tell him about her cat living in the kitchen at night and that she left for work at about 6.45am. He in turn told her he liked to go jogging every morning and would she like to come with him. The thought of even being awake before she needed to get up and get ready for work filled her with dread, but she cheerfully agreed. When he said 5am, the shock of the hour was evident on her face, and he laughed freely and gave her the option of declining.

61

Friday 10th June 2011

John awoke at 11.15pm when his alarm clock sounded. The assault had taken more out of him than he thought because it was the first time he had actually heard the alarm go off. His face was starting to ache, and he was desperate to itch where the stitches were, but knew it would not be wise. Rubbing his sore ribs, he tried twisting his body slowly from one side to the other while sitting in the seat to see just how they were holding up. Both his ribs and shoulder were sore in the fact they throbbed constantly, but he could manage them. Swallowing a couple of tablets courtesy of the NHS via Carol, he gulped a mouthful of water from a bottle. The pills were washed down as he grimaced at the tastelessness of the water. Taking a clean, still folded handkerchief from his trouser pocket, he pushed it onto his face where the stitches were but didn't move it. The relief that a small piece of cotton gave him was amazing: the itch was eradicated within seconds. A bit of blood shone on the cotton when he removed it, so folding the handkerchief carefully with the blood contained in the middle, he returned it to his pocket.

The very soft bleep from the 'trembler' pulsing at regular intervals from the Sat Nav remained constant as John fixed his gaze towards the road and the front of the bungalow. Not many vehicles were moving along the road, but still too many for anyone to engage in clandestine activities. John eased himself from the passenger's seat and had a mooch about the barn in an effort to stretch and force his body to work normally before going to his wooden box in the boot and taking nearly all the foam out to reach the bottom. A battery was connected to a plate on which sat four magnetic discs about an inch in diameter and a quarter of an inch deep. As he pulled one of the discs from the plate, another bleep emitted from the Sat Nav proving to him it had activated. Slipping it into an empty pocket of his waxed jacket, he returned all the foam and equipment into the box before flopping back down into the driver's seat. Putting the toffee hammer into his other pocket, he settled back down again to just watch.

*

Gary was sitting in his van at the furthest point of the car park of the Oyster Catcher under a tree out of range of the car park lights and CCTV security cameras, with his wife. Her car was in the middle of the car park with other patrons' vehicles who were still to leave. They were engaged in a heated discussion.

"We have got to get that bird box back. If anyone finds it, we could be right in the shit."

"It's me who's got to get it. I'm the one who's taking the risk."

"It's been nearly two months, give or take a week. The Police are well finished at the bungalow by now. It should be easy."

"If it's that easy, you do it."

"Don't be silly. You know it won't take you more than five minutes."

"I don't like it. We can leave it longer."

"Why? What's the point? You know the 'old bill' have only been there during the day lately. If you're that worried, do the van."

"It's still a risk."

"I've told you. They are convinced it was the nurse. They aren't looking for anyone else."

"Who the fuck was it then?"

"I don't know. Just get that box back."

Gary had recovered the images for the day of the murder without originally first realising it. He had whizzed through the tape at four times speed just like he usually did. He'd seen the green car, the Micra, which he thought he recognised as the nurse's car. A person all in dark clothing with a hood up arrived in it and entered the bungalow via the back door. Just like the nurse normally did. He didn't bother to slow the images to normal speed, just kept on. Within thirty minutes the person left and went to the vehicle and drove off. Just like the nurse normally did. What confused Gary then was some ten minutes later, the green Micra was back up the drive. The nurse got out and went to the back door. She was clearly identifiable this time and he recognised her as the usual nurse and noticed she was now wearing her uniform. She didn't go into the bungalow, just to the back door and then left. Strange thought Gary, must have forgotten something, but he noted the time.

It was four days later that Gary downloaded the next 'flash' film onto his laptop. The box recorded a maximum five days before it recorded over itself. He saved the film to a DVD from his laptop three days later but still did not view it until nine days had elapsed. Gary had not seen or heard any report of George Armstrong's death because he did not read the local papers and could not be bothered to watch the news. As soon as he viewed it however, all he saw were uniform Police Officers, Police vehicles and CID officers swarming all over the place. He was on the phone straightaway, panicking. Once he had calmed down, his wife told him to check the internet and buy a local paper. There was a piece about the murder on an inside page giving the date it had occurred. Again, he was back on the phone.

Gary prided himself on being a strong local body builder although compared to his diminutive wife, he was a comparative weakling.

62

Friday 10th June 2011

Gary and his wife had sat in their study with his laptop open on the desk. She'd shut the door and turned the key in the lock. No one else lived with them and there was no one else in the house. The paperboy, postman and milkman had made their deliveries so they had been and gone. They had secured the house but Sally knew that there was always the unexpected. No one was going to be allowed to interrupt them. Gary put the DVD in and then opened the folder revealed on the laptop as 'G.A. Barnham' and then the film covering the date 3rd May 2011. He started to play it from 7am in double time. This was going to be the longest either of them had watched any film together. It was one neither wanted to see and would not have paid to see. It was a film though that was imperative that they watched.

A nurse in uniform cycled into view at 7.30am and leant her bike against the side of the lounge. Then she walked past the conservatory to the back door and after several seconds went inside.

"That's her normal time. Same woman nearly every morning. Only inside for thirty minutes maximum. I think she unlocks the backdoor and shed with keys. Before she leaves, I often see her shape pushing him into the lounge and putting him onto his chair."

Leaving after thirty minutes the nurse walked back the same way to her bike and cycled off down the drive. Next to travel up the drive at 8.11am was a red post van. The postman left his van level with the front of the conservatory with the van's door wide open as he walked towards the back door holding a few items. They watched him go to the back door and enter the bungalow. He was back out in twenty-five seconds on a reciprocal route to his van. There was visible movement from inside the lounge.

"The old guy waves every morning as the postie walks back to his van."

Once inside the van, the postman turned around in the entrance to the garage and drove away from the bungalow back towards the road.

"Run it on to the next person."

Gary lent towards the keyboard and sped the film up but only to treble speed. Neither took their eyes from the screen and he tried hard not to blink in case he missed something. Then the green Micra came into view and he stopped the film. Both examined the vehicle's image. It was the back of the car as it had driven up the drive towards the bungalow. The car's rear number plate was covered in mud and not readable on the video.

"Can you be sure that's the nurse's car?"

"It looks like it, but I can't be sure."

"Can you zoom in?"

"Yes. But watch. As it moves in the image seems to blur."

They watched as Gary started to enlarge the image of the vehicle. It blurred and was useless. Returning it to normal size, he clicked the image and ran it on one frame at a time. Eventually the car pulled onto the drive to the garage and was side on to the camera. The driver got out but was close to the limit of the view from the camera. They wore a large wax jacket that was a common unisex brand, similar to one that Gary wore when he was working outside in the cold, wet weather of the winter months. The hood was being worn up and drawn right down over the head so the person was nearly invisible beneath it.

"It's summer for God's sake. Who wears one of those coats in the summer?"

His wife replied, "Someone who does not want to be recognised."

The person walked out of sight round the back of the garage and the bungalow and then reappeared approaching the back door and straight towards the camera. The coat was large and low-slung and the hood was pulled way down hiding the facial features entirely. Once at the door they watched as the person hesitated a few seconds, looked about and then walked straight into the kitchen and again out of sight.

"It must be the nurse; she knew the door was unlocked and went straight in. He knows them so they were expected. Look at the sun on the lawn and the flowers. Why have they got such a heavy coat on?"

"Shut up! Just watch."

The camera showed movement in the lounge on and off for some time but not clear enough to see who, or what was happening. Then the wheelchair appeared at one side of the conservatory.

After thirty minutes, the person exited the kitchen door still wearing the coat with the hood up.

Gary said, "It's the nurse. She's done her thirty minutes That coat though is weird."

"Stop going on about the bloody coat."

"They have been in there thirty minutes. That's how long the nurse is in there every day. Just earlier than usual. It's probably a new nurse trying to make a good impression."

Both watched as the person stooped and placed an object on the floor as they walked away from the camera back towards the rear of the bungalow and out of sight.

Gary paused the video. "What's that on the floor?"

"Can you zoom in?"

"No, it just blurs."

"Why put something there? Surely they could have left it inside the house if they didn't want it."

Sally thought for a few seconds.

"Perhaps they wanted someone to pick it up or move it."

"Why would they want to do that?"

"Jesus Gary. Think. If someone picks it up they would likely as not leave fingerprints on it."

"I still don't get it?"

"It's as though it was left there to be picked up by a certain person. It could be a set up to frame someone."

"What. The nurse?"

"It's feasible."

Both considered the possibility.

"Let's see what else happens."

Gary set the video running. The person reappeared from behind the garage and went to the Micra and got in. It completed a turn and started back down the drive towards the road. Gary froze the image but it was impossible for either to see the driver as the sun was reflecting off the windscreen. Both could clearly see that the front number plate was also covered in mud and reflected nothing.

Gary looked at his wife.

"What do you think?"

She still stared at the frozen image on the screen.

"I don't know. Could be the nurse, but why the coat? Fluke that both number plates are caked in mud."

"What if they knew about the camera?"

"How could they? You put it there. I haven't told anyone. Have you?"

"No. Of course not."

"In that case, no one else knows about it. If that person killed him, maybe they were just taking precautions. I would."

"Yeah. I suppose that's logical."

"Let's see the next bit."

Gary set the film running again at normal speed. They did not, nor could they afford to miss anything. It was ten minutes later when the green Micra drove up the drive and the film froze. Both examined the image of the car but the sun was reflecting off the glass of the rear windscreen causing a 'flaring' of the image. Even playing it one frame at a time made no difference. It was impossible to make out the number plate at all. The vehicle stopped practically in the same place as previously, and the driver got out with their back to the camera and walked round the back of the bungalow and out of sight. As the driver came into view walking towards the kitchen both could see it was a female wearing a blue nurses uniform.

"That looks like his usual afternoon nurse."

She stepped past the item on the floor before reaching the back door but didn't go in. Standing outside for only thirty seconds or so before turning around to retrace her steps. She bent and picked the object off the floor and went to the shed. Opening the door, she deposited it just inside without actually entering herself. Gary froze the image.

"I see what you mean. She's picked it up and that means her fingerprints are on it. The person who left it there knew she would see it and move it. Framed!"

Sally sarcastically said, "Well worked out Gary. Just one small point you may have overlooked. What if she was the person who put it there?"

"Do you think she was?"

Exasperatingly she said, "I don't fucking know. Just play the video."

They watched the nurse close the door of the shed and walk off round the rear of the bungalow and back to the car. It began to move. It turned around and started back down the drive towards the road. Again, the flaring, this time from the front windscreen which distorted the entire image of the front of the vehicle and the driver.

Gary was worried and wanted confirmation.

"What do you reckon?"

"I think the nurse could have killed him. She came back because of that thing that was on the floor. It had to be moved out of sight. She realised she'd left it, so came back to hide it."

"You could be right."

"Course I am. The Police have got the right person. Makes a change."

Both weren't sure though: but for their own reasons could not and would not tell the Police. They watched the tape until Chaplin arrived and then the Police and ambulance.

"Well, it looks like she did it. Don't know why and frankly I don't care."

"Would you have done him?"

"Likely."

63

Friday 10th June 2011
to
Saturday 11th June 2011

Reluctantly, after some gentle bullying he agreed to do it that night. He kissed his wife goodnight before she slid out of the van and keeping close to the edge of the car park and the overhanging foliage made her way back to her vehicle. She sat in it waiting for another car to manoeuvre and then left to make her way home to Birdham. Gary knew it was pointless trying to get it before 1.00am as there was too much movement about the area and he would be spotted by some 'busy body' who would be bound to call the Police. Just then, some boisterous late departing patrons returned to their vehicles and left the car park in a queue. It suited Gary as he drove out behind them. He travelled via the backstreets to a small industrial estate off Ford Lane where he knew there was no CCTV, and parked behind one of the units. All of them had their own alarms, some of which Gary had installed, and he knew there was no night working or security.

He was cautious. Getting out of the van he walked slowly about the units making absolutely sure no one was still about or working late. Once he was satisfied, he went to the near side of the van and opened the sliding door. Taking out a small telescopic light aluminium ladder which he could easily manoeuvre with one hand, he put it in the vacant passenger seat.

Climbing into the back of his van, he opened one of the storage boxes that he had built and fitted himself and propped up the metal lid. Then with a small posidrive screwdriver from his toolbox, he removed the backing to it. Two magnetic number plates were revealed and displayed and were stuck firmly to the underside of the metal. Gary had to pull quite hard to prise them from their hiding place before jumping out and affixing them over the van's original ones. At night, no one was likely to spot the false plates which he had no intention of keeping on for very long.

Pulling his dark blue overalls out of another of his boxes, he put them on over his clothes and checked he had wire cutters in the pocket. On both side panels of the van were magnetic 'boards' showing his firms details and company logo which he peeled off and threw onto the floor in the back of the van. Sliding the door shut he got back into the driver's seat. To all intents and purposes, it was now a simple, inconspicuous, plain white van.

Remaining where he was, he turned the radio on softly, and sang along to the songs he knew, and listened to those he didn't. Gary was more nervous now at the thought of removing the bird box than when he had removed others previously. In the past, he was always able to collect them without problems as and when he wished because he and Sally were always in control. They had known when the person they were watching via the camera footage was going to have serious medical problems because Sally arranged it. It was so simple then when no one was at the premises for him to take his bird box down. He was even brazen enough sometimes to do it within daylight hours. It beat skulking around at night! This time, someone killed George before they could cause him harm, and they were no longer in control. Sally had not even managed to obtain any monies from him before he was murdered. Whoever had done it had no finesse.

*

By 11.30pm, Alison had gone to bed after watching Simon standing on the toilet seat to get a clear view from the high dormer window in the bathroom to the junction where the van was now alone. He'd mouthed the letters, 'B M W' and made a movement with his hand to let her know it had gone. She said 'goodnight' and was asleep in five minutes from her head hitting her pillow knowing she had made a rash commitment to get up early to go jogging. Simon had gone to the spare bedroom and taken a butterfly knife from his bag, and put it between the headboard supports and the bed. He wasn't anticipating anything untoward occurring, but like John, he tended to err on the side of caution. When he was content, he got into bed and drifted into a very light sleep waking only once during the night when Hannibal did his patrol of the flat at 2ish, and on realising there was an unknown person in the room, fled.

*

John remained vigilant and wide awake ready to take off after whoever drove too slowly past the bungalow. He reckoned that if it was to happen again, it would not be before midnight when there were still a few cars moving about. The later the better for him because it would make it slightly easier for him to follow any culprit without 'showing out'. Midnight came and midnight went without anyone slowing, or showing any interest, at the bungalow. By half past twelve, John was coming to the conclusion that it wasn't going to happen, and his thoughts started to turn to Carol, the casualty doctor.

*

Gary was getting restless, and the music after midnight was so soporific, he could take no more and turned it off. Then time seemed to slow down for him and practically stand still. He kept checking his watch, ten past, then quarter past, then not quite twenty past. He thought 'Sod it. I'll do it now' and set off for the bungalow. As he was getting nearer, fear started to play on his mind and he decided to drive round the block just to make sure.

64

Saturday 11th June 2011

John saw his headlights approaching from Yapton, and could see he was not travelling at the speed of previous vehicles. Nothing else appeared to be moving along the road. He started the Vauxhall as the headlights slowed to practically walking pace, and then began to accelerate towards Barnham and past the entrance to the barn. Without turning any lights on, and disabling his brake lights, John moved to the junction with the road and could see the tail lights of the van nearing the Murrell Pub in Barnham. Pulling speedily onto the unlit road he accelerated, still lightless, after it. Gary was nervous and thought he saw some movement behind in his rear view mirror as he passed the Murrell. He swung under the railway bridge and turned right towards Lake Lane. No one was following him, and he decided it was just a trick of the light and he was being hypersensitive. Nothing followed him because John had turned his lights on as he passed the Murrell and kept on the road round towards the railway station having seen the tail lights of the van turning into Lake Lane.

John knew straight away the vehicle was going round the block and would again approach the bungalow from Yapton. As soon as he reached the railway station, he swung a complete 'U' turn and drove as fast as possible back to the entrance to the barn and reversed into it and as far back inside the barn as possible. He killed the engine and disabled all the lights and got out as fast as he could disregarding all the additional incurred pain to his ribs and shoulder. Running the fifteen or so yards in a lop-sided manner to the junction with the road he squatted down and hid behind a large thorn bush. Now he was close enough to see the index number of any passing vehicle. He was ready.

Gary was in no hurry going around the block, checking his mirrors all the way, making completely sure he was not being followed. He stopped at one point in a small pull-in for nearly two minutes to see if anything drove past him. Nothing. Sally and he had not survived for so long by being careless. Looking at his watch for the umpteenth time, he saw twenty to one. He moved off and completed the block as he drove back into Yapton and turned towards the bungalow. No lights anywhere, from houses or cars, he was safe: or so he thought.

He drove at a snail's pace along the road towards John, who saw his headlights approaching. Then they were turned off as the vehicle swerved across the road to the entrance of the drive to the bungalow and stopped. It was way too far off for John to see any index number. Scrabbling in an inside pocket, John found his small monocular. It didn't have night vision capabilities. It was adequate. The driver's door opened and the interior light came on for a couple of seconds, as John saw the ladder being dropped just inside the drive.

Having twisted to manipulate the ladder over his body, Gary slammed the driver's door making more noise than he wanted in the stillness of the night. The interior light dimmed to extinction. Properly seated in the driver's seat, he turned the headlights back on and continued towards John's concealing bush. Putting his monocular back into a pocket John waited. Three quarters of the way between the bungalow and his hiding place was a small parking area for a nursery, and Gary pulled into it and extinguished the lights and turned the engine off. Sitting motionless in the driver's seat, he surveyed the road scanning for any movement. Not even a fox moving. He was soon satisfied and he got out of the van leaving it unlocked and ran as fast as he could the hundred and twenty yards or so towards the drive to the bungalow.

John fathomed that this was going to be more than a 'flash download' and assumed he was going to be taking the bird box down. His Sat Nav would confirm movement via the 'trembler' but he was too far from his vehicle to see. He had time to run in his Quasimodo type way, which seemed to help stop the pain in his ribs, to the van. Making a mental note of the vehicle and index number, he stuck the magnetic tracker from his pocket under the rear offside wheel arch and gave the nearside light cluster a gentle tap with the toffee hammer. The noise it made was similar to a breaking stick, and the hole it made was no more than the size of an old one penny piece. Now his ribs had started to rebel and were hurting more than ever, but he forced himself to run back to the entrance of the drive for the barn and the sanctity of his car.

Gary had already been up his ladder and cut the bird box free and was moving back along the drive to the road carrying both. Waiting a couple of seconds, he checked the road again for movement and saw nothing. John was already back in his car popping a couple more pills and swigging water. It was an easy jog back to his van, and Gary believed it would be just as easy to do it with the ladder and bird box together which he would hide in the hedgerow if he saw vehicle lights. He would be safe when he was back in his van. As he set off jogging, John was confirming by his Sat Nav that the 'trembler' had been activated and the tracker was operational and functioning. John judged the surveillance was going to be easier than he thought. One of them was wrong.

Gary made it to the van without incident, and put the ladder and bird box on the front passenger seat before jumping in and driving briskly away heading back to the industrial estate at Ford Lane. His adrenaline was overflowing. John watched exactly where he was on the Sat Nav without even moving. Casually he drove out of the barn and followed at a respectable distance as he monitored the vans position without fear of notice. The nearer the industrial estate Gary got, the faster he drove, and as he pulled harshly into it, he bounced over a rubber speed hump dislodging the tracker. It rolled on its edge towards the first unit where it came to rest after it bounced off the side. John saw the vehicle stop according to the Sat Nav.

Gary jumped out of the van as it came to a halt and yanked the side door open. He grabbed the two magnetic boards from the floor and stuck them back into position on the side panels of the van. Ensuring that they were straight and in exactly the same position as previously, he ran to the front of the van and recovered the false number plate and then the one from the rear. Inside the van, he stuck them back inside the lid of the storage box and then screwed the lining back onto it.

He was so full of adrenalin his heart was beating so vigorously he could feel his chest moving. But now he felt safe. The ladder was slotted back in its rightful position and the overalls were hung behind the driver's seat and looked perfectly natural. His laptop was now sitting on the passenger seat in what was its typical locus. The only item out of place in the vehicle was the bird box lying on the floor in the back of the van. He could get around that if any nosey copper asked too many questions.

Firing up his laptop, he opened a programme and typed '*HA*' (*Home Address*). Within milliseconds there was an electronic voice saying, "*Map prepared and downloaded.*" A map flashed up on the screen which was comparable to a Sat

Nav, but Gary very rarely needed to look at the map because he just used the electronic voice to guide him. '*Continue when ready.*' Fully relieved and slowly coming down from his adrenalin induced high, he pulled smoothly out of the unit and started on a circuitous journey home.

John had parked parallel to the road by the entrance to Ford railway station keeping an eye on the Sat Nav and occasionally looked across the fields to the darker outline of Arundel Castle against the clear moonlit night sky. As Gary flew past on his way to join the A27 at Arundel, John gave the van a blasé glance as it was level with him and saw a colourful logo and sign writing on the side. He shut his eyes and let the pain in his ribs continue to gently subside after his strenuous activities.

The road was straight with undulations for over a mile and then swung round to the right just before it reached the outskirts of Arundel itself. When John opened his eyes again, Gary was just arriving at the bend and braking to slow down. Immediately, John's gaze was drawn to the white spot surrounded by red at the nearside of the van, even at a mile's distance. Galvanised into action, John took off in pursuit knowing without the tracker he didn't have much hope.

Gary turned left into Maxwell Road, a small side road which led into a maze of other streets. His laptop was 'speaking' to him from the passenger seat and was guiding him to the A27 without passing the ANPR (Automatic Number Plate Reader) camera at the main roundabout at Arundel. John hurtled past the entrance to Maxwell Road and on reaching the roundabout just by the River Arun saw there was no sign of the van in any direction. Picking the road leading up to Whiteways Lodge, he accelerated hard up the hill towards the crest, but long before he got there, he knew he had picked the wrong road.

Gary had joined the A27 and was accelerating up to the speed limit as he headed towards Chichester and onto Birdham keeping within the limit at all times. His laptop was still directing him with its 'electronic voice' to avoid all the ANPR cameras. This night was different. He still had a fair dose of adrenalin pumping round his body and for once chose to ignore all his laptops protestations. Tonight, he wanted to get home as quickly as possible and decided to ignore its constant rerouting until he got to the first roundabout on the Chichester bypass.

65

Saturday 11th June 2011

Alison had an alcohol induced, undisturbed night's sleep, awakening with a jolt as her screeching alarm clock told her it was 5am. She hit the top of it with venom, stopping it abruptly, and fighting the urge to turn over and return to the arms of Morpheus, put her feet on the floor and sat stationary on her bed yawning. Simon called in his cheery voice from the kitchen asking if she wanted a coffee before they set off. Replying as politely as she could muster for the time of day in the negative, she forced herself up and into her jogging gear and shuffled into the kitchen to find him ready and raring to go.

'What,' she thought, 'possesses a normal human being to rise at this unearthly hour to put themselves through hell when they could have another hour in bed!' Furthermore: 'why on earth did I agree to go with him?'

He said, "Couple of miles this morning?"

"Yes, why not." she heard herself saying and hoped he wasn't as fit as he looked.

Simon bent to tie a lace as she locked her front door and he slid a very small sliver of wood between the door and the jam. Her phone stuffed into one small pocket and keys in the other she was set. Then they set off out of the cul-de-sac and left at the junction passing the watcher's van and to the immediate 'T' junction less than fifty yards from it. Turning right, they ran on along small residential side streets towards the fields leading towards Goodwood aerodrome. He knew that no one would follow them and told her that the person in the van looked like he had been there all night. She hadn't run this fast for years, and to her it did not constitute a jog but a full-on sprint. Alison could not understand how he could speak so easily whilst running as she was struggling for breath. Within a mile, they turned onto a signed footpath leading into a field, and within a few yards, he stopped.

"Thank God for that," she gasped, "Why do you run so bloody fast?"

"That's a jog. I normally run about five miles before breakfast."

They walked slowly along the footpath as she regained her composure and discussed her flat and the listening devices. Deciding to lie a little in order to calm her, Simon actively advocated how he could not understand why they would want to bug her flat if they were primarily after causing John some harm, unless it was in the hope of finding out his location. Not one person wanted to tell her she was the target, they wanted her to work it out for herself. They were all surprised she had not come to this logical deduction. Simon had assumed she knew but was refusing to accept it. When he asked her if she knew where John lived, she said she knew his registered address, but did not always know where he spent his nights. There was, thought Simon, a tad of disgust in her voice, or he may have mistaken it for jealousy.

He told her he would recover his car from the car park later in the day and place it nearer her flat and asked where he should meet her when she finished work.

"No more alcohol for a while that's for sure, so no pubs. Lakes Café if you can find it."

Then, "I'm sure I can. Ready?"

She sighed, "What?"

"Race you back" and he turned and started running but not nearly as fast as previously allowing her to keep pace with him.

As they ran up the metal stairs to her front door, he wasn't sweating or even breathing heavily, but Alison was out of breath and 'glistening' as she preferred to say. He saw the small sliver of wood on the floor and taking the keys from Alison's hand, unlocked and pushed open the door. No unexpected surprise: they both went inside with Simon to the fore. Quickly checking the flat for any intruder, he held up his thumb signalling the all clear. In his room, he checked his bag which he instantly knew had been searched. Items of clothing had been lifted on one side and not quite replaced correctly. It was a little thing but unnecessarily careless. The little box with the scanner wasn't there because he had secreted it earlier behind the toilet and he knew no one would have had time to do a thorough search while they were out.

His room had been given a 'once over' by someone who hadn't apparently enough time to put things back exactly as they were. Checking his knife, which on reflection he knew he should have taken with him on his jog intrigued him. It was to all intents and purposes undisturbed and where he had left it. But it was the wrong way round!

'Strange,' he pondered, 'Everything has been neatly done up till now. Interesting.'

Alison got ready for work, and finally after a frantic search found the spare front door keys in a kitchen drawer which she gave to him.

"Why are they always in a different place to where you thought you'd left them?"

"Sod's law."

"Yeah. Right."

She hurriedly tossed Hannibal out knowing already that she was going to be late even having risen before the sparrows. Simon watched her from the front door as she got into her car and sped away passing the watcher's van which did not move. To the station was no more than ten minutes at that time of day and there were early morning and night workers on the move which Simon hoped provided safety for her. It was the start of the Chichester rush hour.

At the front door, he checked both keys in the locks. The one for the five lever deadlock was a little stiff, but the Yale was very slick. Anyone with a small credit card could have slipped the Yale. Shutting the door, he slipped both keys into his pocket and went into the kitchen. Filling the kettle to its maximum, he turned it on and it instantly started to make a low hiss which he knew would increase as the water got hotter. As the crescendo built he quickly started to open the draws in the kitchen and soon found a small collection of keys at the very rear of one. It wasn't the draw Alison had found the door keys in. Turning the kettle off and emptying most of the boiling water, he reset it on its electric base.

Recovering the scanner, he completed a further sweep of the flat finding just one new bug in the base of the light on the locker beside his bed. It was not at all well-hidden compared to the others and would easily have been noticed by an observant person without any technical assistance. Simon smiled although he was worried. It was as though someone wanted him to realise the room had been searched.

His thoughts swung back to Alison who was so obviously the target; he was amazed she hadn't realised.

66
Saturday 11th June 2011

John had found and recovered his bug from the industrial estate and sworn an oath at Ian who had previously drummed into him the bigger bugs with more magnets were the more efficient ones albeit harder to conceal. 'What's he expect me to do? Book it in for a service? Roll under the van and stick it on?' He was aching more now than he had done all night, and decided against a visit to Carol preferring his own bed. Knowing it might be a risk; he approached his flat in Westgate, from West Street and drove past the block. No one was watching from Westgate itself so he returned and drove into the small courtyard where his garage was in a block of six, and opening his door remotely, he reversed inside. There was plenty of room in the garage for him to get out unimpeded and no one seemed to be about.

Ignoring the remote control, he slammed the door to his garage shut, and walked as quickly as he could along the short footpath to the front door of the foyer of the three flats in his block. Unlocking it, he entered leaving it to slowly close by itself, and ignoring the small personal lift, struggled up the one flight of stairs to his front door and inside. His flat was the largest of the three sitting above the two on the ground floor. The block had been well built with exceptionally good sound insulation and John had never once been bothered by noise. Tonight, or now today, was no exception.

No one attacked him or appeared to be watching his flat. He deactivated his burglar alarm and had one minute to check his main security system. In the kitchen was a single dirty plate and mug standing on the draining board waiting to be washed up. John opened the cupboard under the sink not to look for the washing up liquid that was kept there, but ostensibly to look for a small 'dot' light. There was a dull green light displayed as though for a completed cycle of a washing machine or dishwasher, but he knew it meant no unauthorised person had been inside his flat while he was out. He flipped a switch on a panel practically concealed amongst his cleaning utensils to neutralise it. Going straight to his bedroom, he threw his clothes onto a chair and set his little bedside alarm clock. Then he slept the sleep of the dead.

Rising at 5.30 quite normally just prior to his alarm clock going off, and forgoing the en suite shower, he went to the main bathroom, and ran himself a bath. Tipping half a bottle of Radox in, he languished in the soothing properties it offered. Gradually the aches and pains seemed to be washed away and when he got out of the bath, he felt rejuvenated. Searching for clean clothes and a fresh suit, he got dressed with hardly a twinge of pain, and retracing his steps to the garage, freed his car and headed for the Police Station. When he got to the station, his parking space was vacant but still full of the debris that had been blown there over the weeks and months, and could go no further. The maintenance staff seemed to ignore his space when they completed their weekly tasks. It didn't stop him parking.

Holding his newly acquired mobile in one hand, he tapped away with one finger to carefully type out a text message to Simon. '*Can you be available at lunch time for a meeting somewhere in Chichester?*' The reply in less than a few seconds was swift and confirmed his availability and queried where. John hadn't been to the cafe in the cathedral for some time so suggested there at 1pm. It was only a little place in the cloisters with a large garden full of tables, but served a very pleasant lunch. Every day in the summer it was packed mainly with retired locals and the occasional cathedral visitors who stumbled across it by accident. Once agreed, John left the haven of his car, and headed for the canteen walking through the door and to his regular table just after 7.am.

Within a couple of minutes, a harassed Alison joined him. She studied the stitches on his face for a few seconds and then asked him how he was.

"I'm OK, but I have a feeling that my assailants would have preferred me to have had a few days off to recover."

Alison was bemused, "Why?"

"We'll get to that later."

It was not worth her pursuing it any further because past experience had taught her that he would only tell her when he was ready. Instead, she bemoaned the fact that she thought Simon was some kind of sadist, and by way of explanation, described in embellished detail the morning's exercise.

John laughed loudly at the thought and then suggested that she should get the coffee because he was still suffering and to get up would be much too painful.

They both drank more than they really needed and ate what both would consider a cholesterol inducing breakfast. When neither could drink nor eat any more, they went to the office climbing the stairs at a leisurely pace to accommodate John's now exaggerated gait. On entering, Paul asked how John was, as the assault had become common knowledge at the station, and offered them both a drink. He was rather put out by the pair declining so swiftly and abruptly.

John decided the time was now right to inform Paul about the bird box and his two nights' activities in the barn, also to a degree, updating Alison in the process. There were a few 'minor' discrepancies in his telling. Mainly, he had spotted the bird box by chance and having discussed it with Alison agreed he should spend a couple of nights to see if anything happened. He did not mention the deployed bug or 'trembler' to Paul but made a mental note to update Alison as soon as he could.

When it came to the part of the van, he said he couldn't get to it quick enough due to his debilitating injuries. So, he claimed he had no alternative but to try and follow it. Regrettably, he'd lost it as it went towards Arundel but had been fortunate enough to get the index number which he gave to Paul and asked him to do the PNC (Police National Computer) checks. Once they had the driver details, it would be simple work to check and arrange a search warrant. Paul said he would get straight onto it via a secure and dedicated computer terminal downstairs specially used for all forms of official PNC searches.

As soon as he'd left the room, John enlightened Alison as to the whole sorry saga of the bug and it falling off, which she found somewhat amusing. Then he broached the serious subject of the broken rear nearside light and what was really troubling him.

"When the light got broken."

"When you broke it."

"Semantics. Don't interrupt."

"Sorry."

"When the light got broken, the van was a plain white VW. When it passed me in Ford, it had a colourful insignia and some writing on the side. It does not bode well. The driver has taken precautions in order not to be identified. It implies to me that it was not a one-off occurrence."

"It's just magnetic boards that are stuck on the side. Lots of vans have them because they are cheaper than sign writing and can be transferred between vehicles. You're worrying unnecessarily."

It wasn't long before his fears came to fruition as Paul came back into the office and told them the index number belonged to a van with a registered keeper in Manchester. John glanced towards Alison,

"Well that just puts the icing on the cake."

Her reply was more to the point, "Bollocks."

Paul looked from one to the other, "Have I missed something?"

John sighed contritely and said, "No. We were pinning our hopes on that."

"Are you sure you got the right number?"

"I believed so. Registered keeper in Manchester. Something is not right."

Paul said he would check it out with the force area covering the keepers address but John was rueful.

"I'm not holding out much hope."

Doreen strode into the office and sat down at her desk and tucked her book into her top drawer. She caught the last part of the narrative as Paul was telling John about the vehicle in Manchester. So to bring her up to speed Alison filled her in with the rest of the abridged story while the two men discussed various aspects of the case. Paul was of the opinion that the whole case against Munroe was likely to crash as soon as the Judge heard the basis of the evidence. They agreed all should be revealed to Prodow at the late afternoon meeting.

Doreen considered just having a chat to Paul quietly when no one else was in the office, but it seemed right that she should include Alison and John.

"While I was at my meeting last night a woman who hardly ever turns up disrupted it half way through by bringing up the murder. She kind of threw in the question, 'Why would anyone want to kill an old man who was already on death's doorstep'. She implied the main reason would likely be money. Then she sat back and just listened to what everybody else thought. I'm aware that some monies were taken from his account prior to his death, but I don't know if it was relevant. Is this something worth considering?"

Paul said, "It's something we have considered and Jimmy has the last year's copy of his bank statements. They have been looked at by the analyst but please get hold of them and we will go back through them."

John said, "The main reasons people kill are primarily for profit, then come things like jealousy, revenge, being 'dissed,' honour, and for some, enjoyment. Any of these may be the motive for poor old George pushing up the daisies."

Alison added, "Don't forget murder to cover something up. That's my favourite."

Paul said, "You two are real joys." He offered Doreen a cup of tea, and was gratified that someone appreciated him in the morning.

67

Saturday 11th June 2011

"The time is right. Can you do it as soon as possible?"

"Today if it looks good."

"Tremendous."

"What about the 'bugger'?"

"He doesn't need to know any of this. He's done his job."

"Do you want him eliminated?"

"What does he know?"

"Nothing. Everything she said has been rubbish."

"Let him be. We know where we can find him if we have to."

"What about the stuff in her flat?"

"Tell him to clear it out, and the one on her car. Do her phone when you pick her up."

"There was a problem with that. It went wrong the other day. I was behind them listening to their chatter and they went into a dead spot and then nothing. The 'bugger' couldn't get the signal back."

There was silence on the line.

"You there?"

"What did he say about that?"

"Said it's never happened before."

"What do you think happened?"

"It had been working fine up till then. It might be a contact come loose."

"Soon as you get the phone, check it and let me know."

"OK."

"Anything else I should know?"

"There's a guy turned up to stay with her. Some relative."
"Fuck's sake."
"It's not a problem."
"Make fucking sure it isn't."
"Everything's under control."
"We're relying on you. Don't fuck up" and the phone went dead.

68

Saturday 11th June 2011

John wanted to go through what the small team had found out over the last week or so in conjunction with the enquiries and paperwork completed by the original investigating officers. Taking the working copy binder from Paul, both John and Alison left the office and headed for the car park. Before getting into Alison's car, John reminded her of the bug, and was swiftly rebuked rudely as to her possible forgetfulness. As she drove to St Richard's Hospital for John to be X-rayed, he went through salient details of the investigation with her omitting all mention of the bird box and the lost van. Just in case the bug had been changed for a 'listener'.

They parked in the hospital car park after Alison had collected her parking permit and checked on a display board how much two hours was to cost her. Muttering to herself, she considered it to be an extortionate amount for a couple of hours. She was not alone in this as the official patients' group were also bleating in the local press that people had to pay to park at the hospital to visit inpatients. 'Maybe,' thought Alison, 'that's why people call the ambulances more as a phone call is free and it's a lot more convenient than parking.'

Walking through immaculately clean and polished corridors decked with fresh flowers arranged by someone who knew what they were about, both entered the X-ray department. It was hygienic with insipid greenish walls and strange machines in small side rooms barely large enough to swing a cat. Nurses and doctors were rushing about making sure they were outside the rooms and the doors were closed before any machine was activated, then rushing back in when it had been turned off. After furnishing his name at a small reception area, they were shown to a seating bay by a larger lady wearing a blue tabard that was struggling to stay in place. She appeared harassed but in control of who went where and when.

Speaking quietly between themselves, they concluded that Munroe had either been set up as the 'fall guy' for the murder, or was cunning enough to present evidence that would make it seem so. As a result of the matter of the bird box and missing van which had come to light while Munroe was being held in custody, they plumped for the first. Then they considered if she could have an accomplice which in turn would cause them to go for the second option. The third scenario was she had nothing to do with the murder and was in the wrong place at the wrong time and it was committed by someone else at present unknown or unsuspected.

Sitting in silence, they both stared ahead at the green wall lost in their own thoughts considering all the possibilities.

Alison broke the silence first and said as if in a rhetorical manner, "I like the last. She had nothing to do with it. We have no idea who did it. The bird box man is the key."

The large lady came rushing over to where they were sitting causing both to recoil and look at her as she said sarcastically, "Please answer when we call your name as it helps the department to run smoothly. Room 2A if you could manage it. Your daughter will have to wait here" and she turned and rushed off.

John got to his feet and said, "I concur fully. Daughter! God help me," and went into room 2A.

Within the minute, the quiet hustle of the department could hear muted laughter emanating from room 2A. Alison had no idea why, but she started to go a very slight tinge of red.

69
Saturday 11th June 2011

Walking back gingerly to the car having been given a reasonable bill of health by the radiology department who had managed to aggravate the pain in his side, John told Alison that he planned to meet Simon regarding the other matter. Having lost a pound coin in the machine while paying an already exorbitant rate to park, she was primed to ruck about anyone or anything. Hannibal had suffered her wrath someday previously, and John didn't respond to threats or criticism and over the years she had slagged off her Father too many times to mention. Simon was in her sights. Bursting into an outwardly uncontrollable diatribe, she again appraised him of her attitude toward Simon although he noticed that it had mellowed considerably from her first tirade.

At the conclusion, John said, "I ache a bit so can you drop me off by the St Richard's Walk footpath at the end of the grace and favour cottages in Cannon Lane? Then you can nip back and park at the nick and return the working copy binder to Paul. It's only a short stroll for a fit young lady like you to walk back to the café."

She looked quizzically at him. He was up to something but she couldn't suss out what.

"Yes. If I must."

What he didn't mention was that it would give him time to talk to Graham and discuss tactics with Simon.

John alighted from the car with no discernible signs of discomfort in the eyes of Alison. It enforced her belief that he was up to something and it involved Simon. She drove out of the small service road of Cannon Lane back onto South Street and the half mile or so to the Police Station where she parked up at about the same time as John entered the café. Simon was already there sitting at the furthest table from the door with his back resting on the cold stone wall. He was leaning back in the chair with the front two legs well off the floor. John pulled one of the other chairs round to sit not quite level with him but to have a clear view of the entrance and his back also towards the stones of the old cathedral wall. They greeted each other both in the knowledge that they had not been followed into the café.

The stop at the service road just off South Street had been noted. When she drove back out they saw she was alone. They assumed, incorrectly, that John was either in one of the grace and favour properties or had walked through the precincts of the cathedral into West Street and away. Not one of them knew there was a café in the cathedral's cloisters. Now Alison's car was stationary in the car park at the Police Station.

Four men huddled together in the railway station forecourt. A plan was hatched not by committee but by the smallest member of the group who saw a speedily rising opportunity. None of the others would dare to question him such was his status, and each would indubitably do his bidding. His predilection for violence was well known to them all.

He was gambling. It could be a possible fruitful early outcome. If she was going to walk back to the grace and favour cottage they could take her en route. If she was going to drive anywhere, he would revert to his original plan and take her when she got home. He dispatched the largest of the men in the BMW to Chichester Basin to keep an eye out for Alison leaving the station either on foot or in her car. His instruction was only to alert them to her walking but to follow if she left in her car. The little man did not trust him unreservedly and recognised he stood out like a sore thumb on the pavement due to his bulk.

Simon and John were soon deep in a conspiratorial conversation after a three-way discussion with Graham about the threat to Alison and what they were going to do about it. Graham had hesitantly agreed with Simon and asked John to keep him apprised of any developments. All had known from the outset that she had been the subject under scrutiny and the initial rumours that someone was asking about John was possibly a deliberate red herring. Anyone seriously trying to find him could have managed it without having to seek information from other members of the public. To follow him, or break in and bug his flat or car however would have been a totally different kettle of fish. They all concurred that the assaults object was to isolate Alison leaving her alone and vulnerable.

Even so, they believed that she would be safe while at work in the Police Station or moving around the busy streets of Chichester. Whilst in her flat was where they agreed her to be the most susceptible and that was negated now by Simon's presence. Neither thought her to have been in imminent physical danger as whoever had been in her flat during the night could have caused her untold injuries. They had to make it a little easier for her to be taken.

As they were discussing how to proceed, two softly spoken foreign men, one with an adequate command of English had taken station either side of Alison. Each had a vice like grip on an arm at her elbow causing her intense pain as they forced her face first across the back seat of the Audi which had been parked in South Street outside Tesco Express. It had happened so quickly that she had no time to cry out in pain or for help before she was lying across the seat with a strong hand on the back of her neck forcing her face down into its cloth covering. Someone had got into the vehicle directly behind her and she could feel them sitting on the backs of her legs preventing any movement. Her left hand seemed to be bent behind her back at a ridiculous angle in such a way that it was throbbing and giving the impression that if it moved further, the pain would intensify. One person now had perfect control over her.

Her bag that had been slung over her shoulder was now wedged under her chin with the metal clasp digging into her neck. It was causing her a supplementary but unremitting pain. She tried to speak but when she opened her mouth it seemed to fill with the upholstery making her mute. The mobile phone that she had taken to carrying in her hand had fallen from her grasp hitting the kerb and shattering the screen as it bounced into the road and fell under the Audi.

Three pedestrians had noticed Alison being rammed into the back of the vehicle and saw one of the men get straight in after her. They watched as the other man walked casually round to the driver's door and say loudly enough for all to hear in an accent that none could quite place, "Kids huh! They'll be the death of me". With an embellished movement, he cast his eyes upwards and shook his head from side to side as if to signify that they should know exactly what he meant. It was good enough for all three to accept that what they had observed was nothing untoward but a simple family matter. Within minutes, all three pedestrians had practically forgotten the incident as they resumed their relevant pursuits.

The Audi was driven slowly away from the kerb, and the back nearside wheel crushed Alison's mobile phone to destruction as the vehicle completed a 'U' turn in the road and moved off towards the bus station and the level crossing beyond. A softly spoken accented voice told Alison that to struggle was futile and would only cause her infinitely more excruciating pain. As if to enforce the threat, her wrist suddenly felt like it was about to break causing her to whimper into the cloth of the seat and dribble onto the fabric as she cried silently out in pain. Tears welled up in her eyes and rolled onto her cheek destroying some of her makeup. She could see nothing except the stitching on the grey fabric as the car gently rocked and swayed as it followed the road's contours. Alison felt the vehicle manoeuvre round a couple of roundabouts and then accelerate along what she thought was the road towards Selsey.

70

Saturday 11th June 2011

After what seemed like a lifetime to Alison, but was in fact no more than twenty minutes, the car stopped with the engine ticking over. The driver shouted and received a reply from someone, but Alison couldn't hear what was said. A couple of minutes later it moved off again and she felt it bumping along what she thought was an unmade-up road. As the vehicle bounced up and down and snaked from side to side, the pressure on her wrist intensified and decreased as the person holding it was swung about within the vehicle. Eventually the car came to rest and the engine died as the driver got out and returned to the nearside rear door where she had been forced in. A cloth bag was prised over her head and draw strings were pulled and tied but caused no pain. The smell within the bag however, which was totally unrecognisable to her, caused her to retch but not quite vomit. She could still breathe and although her world was now utterly sightless, she was no longer mute and could talk.

"Why have you done this to me? I'm a Police Officer. You're in serious trouble" but before she could say anymore, her wrist was released and the person sitting on her legs got out of the car.

She immediately felt hands on both her ankles and she was pulled unceremoniously half out of the car so she was kneeling on rough ground. Her bag which had been over her head and on her right shoulder swung back down and was grabbed by unwelcome hands which opened it swiftly before dropping it down. Alison felt instant pain to her knees as grit and stones penetrated her black chinos and left very small tears in the material as she held onto the seat to try to preserve some form of balance. The hands had left her ankles and now took hold of her arms again at the elbow and she was forced to her feet.

The driver said, "Keep quiet. Speak only when I say. Do you understand?"

Alison said, "What's this all about?" but suddenly felt a hand slap her face from above the bag.

"Do you understand? Yes, or No?"

"Yes."

They forced her forward, and she heard the driver say there was a step, but she still stumbled when her toe caught it. The surface changed to smooth stone as they entered what she perceived to be a building, and she was piloted to a back room. Once inside, she felt the distinctive cold metal of a handcuff being affixed to her left wrist.

A different voice that exuded sheer menace said in a soft accent she couldn't quite make out, "Listen carefully as should you disobey what I am now going to tell you: pain like you have never experienced will be administered. This room is blacked out but has a light built into the wall. Do not try to disable it. The handcuff is on a chain so you can move to the toilet in the corner. It is a flushable toilet, so do not abuse it. There is a sink and towel next to it, do not abuse it. The bed is wooden but comfortable. Again, do not abuse it. Food will be provided at regular intervals via the hatch at the base of the door. You will not shout or make noise, as we are the only people who will hear and we like silence. The room will be kept at a constant heat. When you hear the door slam, you may remove the hood. Do you understand? Yes, or No?"

Alison thought for only a second before uttering the word "Yes" exceptionally quietly.

The door slammed with a sound that implied solidity. Alison pulled at the hood which had been tied loosely around her neck, and after two tugs, yanked it off over her head. She breathed deeply and looked about her prison. A dim light emanated from behind a metal grill half way up the wall above the bed. It cast eerie shadows around the room but gave enough light to see by. The chain was attached to a bar in the middle of the floor which had been set into the concrete with no visible fixtures. Taking hold of the chain about a foot from the bar, she pulled as hard as she could to no avail: it did not budge or even give the impression that it would. She saw the dark shape of the door located in the wall opposite the bed but could not see any handle or lock. Moving to it, she confirmed no handle or lock on her side of it but saw the hatch which was closed tight at the bottom of it. She kicked out malevolently at it in the vain hope it would fly open, but was not surprised when it didn't. Checking the toilet, she saw even in the poor light that it looked pristine.

Set in the wall at the end of the bed appeared to have been a window which had been bricked up from the inside by someone with limited skills. Mortar was covering most of the brickwork where it had not been scrapped off as it had oozed out as the bricks had been laid on top of one another. Alison examined it closely and saw that it had been built up from the first bricks that had been sited on the wooden window sill. Where the bricks had met the side of the window and the top, they were well set, but the first row on the sill looked to Alison like the weak point. They were deliberately meant to draw the eye and prevent her looking at the ceiling in any detail which was out of reach to her unless she stood on the bed. It was at the extreme limit of her restraining chain and above the remit of the wall light. Had she been so inclined to check, she would have found it to have been a thin plywood covered in very fine plaster.

Sitting on the bed, she removed her bag which had resumed its original position on her body, with the strap over her head and on her right shoulder and the bag resting on her left hip. From within, she removed a small packet of wet wipes and her emergency repair nail file. She took off her ersatz designer chinos and scrutinised them with foreboding. They were way past redemption and although her legs were aching, they now played second fiddle to her favourite chinos. Flattening them out, she laid them on the bed and tried to stroke them back into shape.

Painstakingly she removed the remaining few stubborn bits of grit still stuck in her skin and saw small globules of blood form but none flowed. Lifting each leg in turn she washed her knees at the edge of the sink. The pleasant smell of lemon from the soap caused her to take off her jacket and blouse from her right side and let them slide down the chain to the floor on her left. Unable to free them completely, they were laid as flat as she could manage before she had as close to a strip wash as possible in the smallish sink. It felt to her as if she was washing away the pain and cleansing any thoughts of the men who had abducted her. Using another wet wipe, she finally wiped her knees for the last time with the soft sterile tissue impregnated with anti septic balm which she hoped would prevent any infection. Her nails had suffered badly during the previous hour, and she diligently set about repairing them as best she could. The owner of the eye that observed her through the small spy hole set in the door close to the top hinge could not understand the logic.

Wherever her phone was now, Alison had no idea and did not really care. She knew it was only a matter of time before Simon came to get her. As she dressed, she checked her clothes, cleaning in the sink a couple of marks from her blouse and tried to brush the creases out of her jacket with her hands. Her chinos, she decided, were past salvation because of all the little nicks and small tears, but she struggled back into them without ripping them any further. Looking forlornly at her favourite pair of black shoes that were now scuffed beyond repair, she put them under the bed. Then she sat on the bed, crossed her legs, rested a hand on each knee, holding each thumb to middle finger and shut her eyes and drifted off into deep meditation.

The man who had sat on her legs in the car and struggled to speak any English spoke to his brother in Lithuanian explaining what he had seen through the spy hole. Laughing constantly as the chronicle continued, the driver explained it was just the product of the British elite.

71

Saturday 11th June 2011

"Mr Daines?"

"Yes. Who is this?"

"We have kidnapped your daughter."

"Like hell you have."

"I would suggest you check."

"I don't know how you got this number but do not bother me again."

"You are the deputy to the Commissioner of the City of London Police. You have applied to be considered for the role of Chief Constable for the West Midlands. I am correct?"

"How did you know that?"

"How we know is irrelevant. If you want to see your daughter again you will withdraw your application."

"I will not withdraw."

Then he hung up.

"What do you reckon Ian?"

"That should have wound them up."

"Was it enough to get the mast?"

"Yeah. GCHQ will have it as well in about five minutes."

The phone rang.

"Leave it. That should get them rattled."

"I hope you're right."

"They will do one of two things, either keep trying to get you, or phone the mole to discuss what to do next. That would be what we want."

72
Saturday 11th June 2011

In the cathedral café, John and Simon were wondering where Alison was, and what was delaying her. Simon's phone vibrated on the table top and he saw who was ringing.

He said to John, "It's Graham again. They must have her already" and he answered.

Graham spoke calmly, quietly and quickly.

Simon responded as succinctly as he could and said, *"Now they have told you what they want, it's up to you to flush them out then we can respond accordingly."*

"Can you keep her safe for a few days?"

"Yeah. We'll go and see what the score is tonight, and keep you up to speed. Anything your end, call me straight away please."

"Right. Can I speak to Oscar?"

The phone was passed to John and Graham told him *"Don't take any action to rescue her. It's imperative that I can identify the ringleader. I know you, if you think she's suffering, you'll try and get her out. I'll keep in contact with you and Simon and inform Prodow."*

John asserted that Alison's safety was his prime concern, and was slightly shocked when Graham said, *"She knew the risks when she joined the force."*

Graham rang off and both sat in abject silence for a few minutes as they tried to assess what action he would take to identify the ringleader.

John broke the impasse saying, "I suppose we had better find her so we at least know where she is and how many we are dealing with."

"Yes. It won't be too much trouble. May I suggest we use my car later tonight as it hasn't been seen by anyone?"

"Seems fair."

Simon pronounced his intention that he was going to spend the afternoon checking out Alison's flat firstly to make sure it was not still being watched and secondly that the inside had been cleared of all bugs. They acceded that John was to return to the Police Station and speak to Prodow as to what was going to be said about Alison's disappearance. Then an agreed meeting place at St Richard's Hospital car park was made before both went their separate ways.

Both knew that Alison would be alright for a week or so at the least wherever she was, and that Graham would be making all the right moves as he received the phone calls from the kidnappers. John made his way out of the Cathedral grounds and into South Street checking all the time for anyone following him or just hanging about watching. Reflections in windows displayed sundry people on the opposite side of the road and behind him on the pavement a group of motley school children loudly making their way back to afternoon remedial classes. He walked purposefully through the bus station and then over the level crossing and into the Police Station via the front door and to an office on the ground floor. No hint of injury or impediment was manifest to a casual observer. Knocking once, he barged straight in where he found a uniform Sergeant of some vintage whom he had heard was completely discreet.

After introducing himself to the startled sergeant and explaining that he was actively engaged in a covert operation, he asked if it was possible to view the recent town CCTV from around Chichester. Still recovering from the onslaught of John's entry, the sergeant weakly replied as John knew he would, in the affirmative.

"Can I see the video from the camera in South Street?"

"Yes." His composure now regained and discussing a topic he was fully conversant with, the sergeant pressed on. "You need to fill out one of our forms and we will view it as and when we can."

"Sorry sergeant, but this is incredibly urgent and will be authorised by DCS Prodow, or higher."

The sergeant, who was known only by his last name of Murray looked quizzically at John.

"You do realise that if you view it, and it is later required for court, I am duty bound to disclose you accessed it, and that could be a problem?"

"Let me be frank. The chances of it getting anywhere near a court room is highly remote."

"On your head then so be it" and Murray shifted from his padded desk chair and sat down heavily on a small metal chair that took the strain heroically. His hands darted dextrously across an immaculate keyboard that was sited in front of a large monitor. It looked like a brand new piece of kit but was over a year old and lovingly cleaned every day by Murray when he was in the office. John dragged, rather than lifted another metal chair and sat next to him having first secured the office door. The monitor burst into life with a coloured image from high above the bus station looking towards the Cross along South Street.

"What times are you looking for?"

"Between 1pm and 3pm."

Fingers caressed the keyboard and the monitor flickered and showed 1pm in the top right corner with the current date. Then the video began to play. John asked if it could be sped up but still viewable. Again the fingers hardly seemed to move, but the video was moving at three time's normal speed.

Within seconds, John saw the Audi stop in the disabled parking area outside Tesco Express in South Street facing the Cross in the city centre. He asked for the video to play in normal time, and the Sergeant obliged.

"What are you looking for?"

"I'm not sure yet, but it will become obvious."

Three men, all apparently quite tall as they seemed to unfold themselves from the vehicle, moved to the pavement. Where the vehicle had stopped was nearly half way to the Cross and as such identification of anyone on the video at that distance when the camera was panned out to its maximum was virtually impossible.

After a couple of minutes, one walked towards the camera.

John pointed to the three men and said, "Is it at all possible to get any kind of photo image of them?"

Murray, without a word pointed over his shoulder to a printer on a separate desk as it erupted into life with a loud clonk. Crossing to it, John waited as a coloured A4 size photo slowly spewed out. He picked it up and saw the clear features on an enlarged image from the video which showed the man who had followed him into the garage. The next two images were good enough for identification purposes, but nowhere as decent as the first. They struck a chord with John as he remembered both from his brief sighting of them as they set about assaulting him.

"What have they done?"

"You should see in a couple of minutes." Both sat back in their chairs and watched the screen as the first man walked back towards the camera and to the Crown Court steps where he stopped and lit a cigarette. Witnesses and defendants from the Crown Court who were nicotine addicts were also outside either having a last gasp before sentence or to calm their nerves prior to giving evidence. He blended in immediately. The other two propped up the building level with the Audi by the entrance to Tesco Express as though waiting for partners who were busy shopping inside. They didn't elicit a glance from any passer-by.

Murray said to John but more to himself, "Not a uniform officer in sight. I briefed five of them this morning. Where the hell are they all?"

After seven minutes had elapsed, Alison strolled into view from under the camera at the bus station and into South Street.

"Isn't that PC (Police Constable) Daines? She used to be on my section."

The man on the steps jogged across the road in front of a bus and followed behind Alison at no more than five yards. As she approached the Audi, it was clearly obvious that she had noticed it as her face was turning towards it as she drew closer. When she was a few feet away and level with it, she was looking straight into the car as the two men moved from the entrance of Tesco's coming behind her taking hold of her arms. The following man passed by her and opened the back door of the Audi as he continued towards the Cross. Alison was thrown into the rear of the vehicle.

"Fucking hell." The images stopped. Sergeant Murray turned to John and said again, "Fucking hell. What's this all about?"

John said, "She's been kidnapped, but for the moment, no one must know. Can you play a bit more?"

The video started again and they watched as one man got straight into the back seat after Alison, and the other walked casually to the driver's door and got in. Then the vehicle slowly moved away from the kerb and completed a U turn travelling towards the camera when the video stopped again.

"Do you want an image of the Audi?"

"Yes. It may be useful. I think it's a hire car."

John asked if a full video recording could be put onto a DVD for later use.

Sergeant Murray agreed and said, "What are you going to do about Alison?"

"It may sound strange, but it's all in hand and under control."

John told him that Prodow would need the DVD and would explain more to him later in confidence.

"I'll have it done within a couple of hours and I will bring it up to your office."

"Please only give it to me or Prodow, and make no comment as to what or who it is about."

"One proviso. Alison was one of my star probationers. I want in on any rescue and arrests."

"You've got my word" and John left the office clasping the four coloured photographs.

73

Saturday 11th June 2011

Simon got off the bus and started to walk the last mile towards Alison's flat via the side streets. It didn't feel right as he was walking along one of the tree lined roads. He slowed to a practical crawl and looked constantly at his foot as though it was causing him a problem, or he had trodden in something nasty. Slowly he became sure there was someone following him, but he couldn't see who or where they were and he was the only pedestrian. Using occasional reflections in windows, he scoured the area behind him but saw no one. No one was in front of him nor were there parked vehicles anywhere in the road. All the houses had driveways and some vehicles were parked in these. Simon looked at all the cars he could see, and none looked suspicious in any way. Stopping, he held onto a wooden gatepost and removed his shoe. Hopping about on one foot as he ostensibly tried to sort something out with it: he scrutinised the surrounding area. Whoever was following him had not been on the bus or got out of any vehicle, but seemed to pick him up within a hundred yards of the bus stop.

Simon was well versed in surveillance techniques as having been trained by both military and Police he was good at it himself. His training had also included anti-surveillance methods, and how to spot a 'tail' and lose it if needed. There was no doubt in his mind, there was someone following him, and he knew whoever it was: they were exceptionally good. Putting his shoe back on, he continued, now apparently happy with it, at his original pace towards Alison's flat. It was irrelevant that someone was following him as it was obvious where he was going and he knew he had not been followed from the cathedral. As he turned into the side road just before the entrance to Alison's cul-de-sac, he was astonished to see the van still parked in the lay-by. Walking quickly into the cul-de-sac and then up the stairs to her front door, he realised that they must be waiting for him.

Before he opened the front door, he took his mobile phone out of his pocket as though he had received a text, and pressed a few buttons. Hannibal came up the stairs and showed recognition and no fear as he pressed up against the legs of Simon. Putting the key in the lock he opened the door and Hannibal instantly bolted back down the steps as a large fist travelled towards Simon's face. Simon accepted he was going to have to be subservient for a while, and as the fist hit him, he rode the punch but fell to the floor screaming in deceptive agony. Rough hands hauled him to his feet by his lapels as he snivelled.

"Please don't hit me" as he was dragged into the lounge and deposited onto the settee.

The owner of the fist was a good six feet six tall and built like the proverbial brick outhouse. He was wearing an ill-fitting black suit with a white shirt and poorly knotted blue tie. His face was podgy and reddish and where he had shaved it looked as though the razor had been blunt and just dragged any hairs out. Dark sun glasses covered his eyes, which didn't add to his menace. It was clear to Simon that he was not very fit, but due to his size, would intimidate the majority of people: a heavy in some parlance. Simon had no fear of him and knew he could deal with him when needed, but for now he played the whimpering coward.

With a heavy accent, the gorilla said, "Phone" and held out a frying pan of a hand. The mobile was placed into it.

He heard the front door open and close and a man, entirely opposite to the first, entered the room. This person was only about five feet seven inches tall with no carried fat, and was dressed smartly, but casually, in designer jeans and T shirt with a very light zipped up fitted bomber type jacket. His grooming was stylish, with gelled highlighted fair hair and well clipped eye brows. No glasses were needed by him as his steel blue eyes implied menace. A straight nose and small downturned mouth seemed to augment the threat. Simon could tell immediately that this was someone to be treated with respectful caution.

"Please don't hurt me" whined Simon as he cowered on the settee.

His phone was passed over and the smaller man examined it before pressing some buttons. In a soft accent which was closest to Russian, he asked Simon why he did not have anyone's names or phone numbers stored in the directory.

Still sniffling as best he could, Simon said he didn't have any friends of note, so did not see the point.

The smaller man leant forward so his face was within a foot of Simon's and said, "The girl who lives here, where is her number? Where is your family number?" Simon rattled off the number from memory of Alison's phone and another number which he said was his family number.

Then, "I remember the main numbers so I don't bother with a directory." Pulling back, the man walked slowly round the room looking at the phone and tapping buttons. Simon had totally erased the directory and log prior to opening the front door and knew that without the right equipment, no one would be any the wiser.

The little Russian tossed the phone several feet towards the gorilla who seemed to pluck it from the air with one of his racket like hands. Then as Simon watched, he held it in the palm of his right hand which folded around it and slowly squeezed it crushing it beyond repair. Then with slight irony, he dropped it into the empty waste paper basket. Some people that Simon had worked with in the past could do the same party trick, but today for effect, he feigned fear and anxiety.

Again, the smaller man leant to within a foot of his face and with tacit menace said, "Your girlfriend has gone away for a while. So for now this flat is all yours. Should you make a rash mistake and decide to speak to the Police about what has happened today, my friend here will pay you a surprise visit, and take you on a one-way trip. Do you understand?"

Simon, simulating as much fear as he could muster, shrank lower into the settee and moaned that he did.

Without further comment, the little Russian turned and went towards the hall and front door followed by the gorilla. As the large man was passing Simon he raised the back of his hand quickly as if to strike, but strode on laughing.

Speaking in Russian, the smaller man said, "Leave him Petrovski."

74

Saturday 11th June 2011

Giving their departure a few minutes, Simon went into the bathroom and recovered his scanner. Flushing the toilet just in case he was being listened to, he completed a full scan of the flat, paying particular attention to where he had located the bugs originally. He was gratified to receive a negative result which was what he had expected. Standing on the toilet lid, he stretched to see out of the high dormer window and saw that the van had already gone. Using the house phone, he called his Dad and asked him to let all the others in the team know his phone had been destroyed and his new number would be forwarded within three hours.

The two had left the flat and walked past where the parked van had been, and then into the tree lined road and to an entrance of a detached house about a hundred yards from the gatepost where Simon had removed his shoe. A large silver Saab sat in the drive, and they both got into it with the smaller of the two in the driver's seat. With absolute disdain for his larger accomplice, the little Russian glared hard at him.

"What?"

"Can't you remember simple instructions. I should only have to say it once."

He reluctantly directed his larger acquaintance, a Russian as was he, to replace the 'For Sale' sign that he had previously uprooted and thrown beneath the front hedge. The broken back door was of no consequence to him. Unenthusiastically, and without good grace, the large man clambered out of the vehicle and complied. Once back in the car, they drove off towards the centre of Chichester each wrapped up in their own thoughts. The smaller man was not comfortable because there was something that was troubling him about Simon although he could not put his finger on it.

*

As the little Russian had passed the van on his way to Alison's flat, the man in the back who loved his job of bugging, watching and listening to people, got into the front and drove off. He was a freelance operator who liked the solitude the rear of his van afforded him. On leaving the army he had considered various occupations but did not want to become some sort of desk jockey tied to the same routine day in, day out. The outdoor life was his goal and the added spice of something unusual had appealed to him. A friend of a lawyer had set him off in the right direction with a request to follow a street trader who was engaged in some extracurricular marital activities. He was hooked!

Within a year, he had established himself as a credible investigator with a bona fide licence and bought a new car and his van which he had set up himself. All his equipment had been bought from retailers in Tottenham Court Road or Edgeware Road in London where it was freely available to anyone for a price. If he couldn't buy what he wanted, he had the ability to build it himself. Although in his early thirties, he had acquired a reputation for reliability, confidentiality and accuracy. Mostly, he was self-taught, but had attended evening classes in electronics and computer sciences and kept himself up to date with current trends by reading relevant publications and internet articles, and liaising with fellow experts.

Mainly, lawyers or private detectives kept him reasonably busy with matrimonial matters for which he was handsomely rewarded, but what he liked most was the 'off the book' work which was completely illegal and invariably paid for in large amounts of ready cash. This had been one such job which was paying £1000 a day with an initial retainer of £5000. The whole of the bugging of Alison's flat, car and phones had been done by him, and he had also cut and made keys for her front door.

Included in the price was a daily DVD of all conversation within the flat and video of comings and goings, and recordings from her phones. Equipment was also supplied by him within the price that would enable someone to maintain discreet mobile surveillance on her Fiesta and audio on any of his placed bugs. His 'piece de resistance' was the ability to listen to any conversation within the proximity of her mobile phone be it turned on or off. However, it was a very cheap hand made device because he wasn't going to throw money away!

He had been half asleep reclining in his chair in the back of his van watching his screens the day that Simon had first gone to Alison's flat. That he immediately recognised him was an understatement as they had shared a bivouac on Brecon Beacons when they were being assessed for the SAS (Special Air Service). This had thrown him into a dilemma: he was being paid well, so did he inform his employer, or did he pass a message to Simon. It was a conundrum that he sat and pondered for just a couple of seconds.

75

Saturday 11th June 2011
to
Sunday 12th June 2011

Prodow, who had already been brought up to speed by Graham, had hustled a tardy DC into ferrying him from Littlehampton to Chichester. He slapped his ID onto the reader on the outside of the rear door which was as sluggish as the DC. It eventually clicked its acceptance and was practically smashed from its hinges as he burst through and bounded up the two flights of stairs and exploded into the office. Doreen and Paul were busy arranging papers.

Puffing from his exertion, "Where's Oscar?"

"Here Guv."

"Paul, Doreen. Can you give us ten minutes?"

Both Paul and Doreen looked at one another and Paul shrugged before both left the office. Calling after him, he added, "Paul, can you make sure no one disturbs us?" and he slammed the office door shut.

John relayed the events in Chichester as Prodow regained his relaxed poise. The four copies of the pictures were pulled from his pocket and unfolded for Prodow to examine. There were two sharp knocks on the door which caused the photos to be unceremoniously stuffed back into John's pocket.

"What?"

The door opened and Murray in full uniform and carrying his flat cap under his arm marched in shutting the door behind him. John introduced him and Prodow told him to sit down.

"I've got your tape" and he removed a DVD from within his cap and passed it to John.

Prodow said, "How did you get past Paul? He's like a brick wall normally."

"I told him you had called me to attend in full uniform for an urgent assignment."

"He's getting soft if he bought that Murray. Can I call you that?"

"Sir, you can call me whatever you like."

"OK. Let's reconvene in your office in ten minutes and view this tape."

"Then if you will excuse me, I'll go and set it up" and he opened the door, placed his cap on his head, and marched out shutting the door behind him.

"I like that man."

Paul watched Murray's approach along the corridor towards him.

He stopped briefly by Paul and said, "By God, he can dish it out" and then descended the stairs.

In the office Prodow told John that they were to explain Alison's absence was due to a bout of mild food poisoning and she was to be reported as sick and temporarily unfit for duty.

Prodow opened the door and called Paul back in, "Paul, we're finished now. I have been told Alison is sick and I'm sending Murray to go and see her and check if she wants anything."

Paul knew Prodow well enough to know when he was lying, but he knew better than to challenge him.

"OK Guv'nor." He settled back down with Doreen and his papers.

The three had assembled in Murray's office. Murray was twenty-five years a uniform Policeman, and twenty years of that, a sergeant. Weight had crept on over the years and he was a stone over what he wanted to be although he could still comply with the fitness regime imposed by Sussex Police. His head was the roundest that John had ever seen and his hair had been practically shaved from it. He could have stood in for 'Humpty Dumpty' thought John, and he gave the impression of being a genial mannered officer in the mould of 'Dixon of Dock Green'. His job for the last ten years had been teaching new recruits the way of Policing. Some of them had incurred his wrath, but all had learnt well, and most had benefited from the experience climbing the promotions ladder. Knowledge was his strong point and his aim was to ensure it would be passed on. They viewed the tape in silence.

*

Simon marched back to the bus stop opposite the one he had got off at earlier, and caught the bus into Chichester bus station, bought a pay as you go phone in South Street and then got a taxi from the railway station to the hospital. He knew he was not being followed. Murray had snagged the use of an enquiry car that was so small, two burley coppers filled it. Agreeing to drop John at the hospital, he reiterated on the way that he wanted to be in at the arrest as he had always thought highly of Alison when she was a uniformed officer on his team. John readily consented although he believed the kidnappers would be dealt with by the Home Office.

Because he was so early, John walked the corridors of the hospital to kill a few minutes and then went into the café run by the WRVS (Women's Royal Voluntary Service). Normally he would probably have bought a coffee, taken one mouthful and left the rest because it was practically undrinkable. This time he looked round then made his way to the car park and saw Simon sitting in his Lexus fiddling with his Sat Nav. It was in full view in the middle of the dash board as though a standard fixture. John got into the passenger seat and after exchanging greetings watched as two red dots flashed slightly out of sync in what appeared to be the middle of a field near Lagness.

"Two bugs! Taking no chances then?"

"I dropped one into her bag, and stitched one into her jacket just to be sure."

"You are domesticated. Sewing taught in the army now?"

"Don't take the piss."

They updated each other with the events of the previous couple of hours, and John showed Simon the pictures. The smaller man who had attended Alison's flat was identified by Simon and John stated he was the person who had followed him into Sainsbury's garage. Studying the other two facial pictures took them no further. Simon described the large man who had struck him and christened him the gorilla but explained he had been referred to as Petrovski. That meant with the two kidnappers from the car, there were at least four and the watcher.

"The watcher is no problem because he has gone now." John looked at him curiously. "Take it from me. I just know."

Both agreed a full meal would be beneficial as they were going to be out late, so they went to Frankie and Benny's where they were fawned over by a nauseatingly effeminate waiter. For nearly three hours, they sat and chatted sipping occasionally from glasses that the waiter took pleasure in filling as often as he could from their one bottle of wine. Each ate their fill working their way through the starters, mains and sweets as if they had not a care in the world.

John needed to get his camouflage gear and some additional items from his car at the Police Station and by 11.30pm, both men were in full dark green outfits. John's was from the Met Police and Simon's was courtesy of the military. Each had a pocket containing a small torch and a little electrical device called a 'dog dazer' which had come from a place in Battersea. The idea was that any aggressive dog would be rendered harmless by an ultra-sonic noise. It had worked on various occasions in the past, and the fact it came from Battersea gave it credibility. Simon carried a set of skeleton keys and a butterfly knife in easily accessible pockets and a large soft sports bag full of items in specifically designed pouches.

They sat quietly together digesting their meals in Simon's car and dozing until about midnight. Then having checked the map of the vicinity on his Sat Nav decided that a parking area about a mile and a half away from where the red 'blips' were would be suitable to safely leave the car. A single drive along the nearest road to the 'blips' would, they hoped, give an idea of the sort of place where Alison was being held. Both knew a single pass was leaving themselves open to detection from an observant person, but it was often worth a risk. Simon set off towards Lagness, and the nearer he got, the less traffic there was until practically none at all. The nearest road was not much better than a badly made up single track lane with passing places that looped off Pagham Road and joined Lower Bognor Road which was the road leading to Bognor. No one would naturally use it as it was infested with pot holes and was a longer and slower route than staying on the normal side road.

As they drove slowly along the road by the beams of his headlights dodging the bigger holes, nothing immediately stood out to them except what looked like rubble had been fly tipped into a ditch completely filling it to the top. Behind it, the hedge was very sparse compared with that either side and of the rest of the lane. No buildings had been visible on the Sat Nav nor were any evident along the road except for an old Norman Church that rested solemnly at the junction with Pagham Road. Simon drove two and a half miles round the block to where they were to park, and left his Lexus between other overnight parked vehicles. He took a scanner from the boot and they both set off on foot along the road ready to jump into the ditch if anyone should approach.

76
Sunday 12th June 2011

Alison had given up her meditation after less than four hours which had only enhanced her irritation as to how long she had been incarcerated. During that time, she conceded reluctantly and still with some slight reservation, that she was probably the target all along. As her reflections had swirled about the fog within her head she came to the logical conclusion that she had been put with John deliberately so he could keep an eye on her, and Simon was only there for her protection not John's. Simmering with that thought had led to her vexation with both for permitting it to happen. Where had they been in her hour of need? They were meant to be protecting her. She kept running through how she was going to make them pay and continually rehearsed in her mind caustic words that she would use to cut them down to size. Her kidnappers did not seem to currently inhabit her philosophies.

Slowly, as time marched on, Alison started to calm down and began to think plausibly. Nothing had been said to her as to why she had been kidnapped. Her thoughts unjumbled themselves and started to line up in a cogent way. Then she finally accepted it: she had been the target from day one. Both Simon and John had known and not told her. All the others had known and not one had deemed to tell her.

'Bastards. The canteen staff probably knew' and she began to boil again. Even her Dad knew and hadn't bothered to tell her. A tear began to rise in one eye. She fought it. It gave up and retreated.

Words already spoken started to spin round in her head. It was when she was calm that it all seemed to come together. Forcing herself to think, she looked around her gaol. 'Keep calm and I'll be all right.' The first thing she

231

would do was get out of the handcuff. It didn't take her long with the aid of a fluff stuffed paperclip she found at the bottom of her bag amongst assorted little keys and an old plaster. Straightening the paperclip, she slipped it over the ratchet and using the provided soap rubbed it around her wrist. Slowly pushing the ratchet closed, it stuck on the paper clip and skated open just far enough for her to slip her hand out of the metal bracelet. The ratchet hadn't been locked, so she ran the clasp through leaving it open and loose enough to slip on and off her wrist with ease.

Then it was to the door. Now a proper examination. The lock and hinges were nothing she could beat but she stumbled upon the spy hole. Considering her options, she decided to leave it uncovered. Lying on her stomach, she lined herself up with the hatch and tried to work out whether or not she would fit through the aperture if she could cause it to be left opened. Tight. Very tight. Too tight. Not possible. She checked the walls running her hands all over them looking for a weakness but came away thwarted. Where the window had appeared to have been bricked up revealed no apparent flaw. The floor was solid concrete and the plumbing came up through it. Pipes were so small a rat would have had trouble navigating through them.

She sat on the bed and upended her handbag's contents onto it. The junk she carried and never used astounded her. 'Sods law' she thought as she spotted an old handcuff key from the same style as had been tethering her. She'd moved it when she found the paperclip. 'Look at everything. Ignore nothing. Concentrate.' The new current handcuffs the Police used had a different sort of key. Putting it into the lock of the bracelet she turned it and winced at the pain she'd endured getting her hand out.

Some safety pins all clipped together. An unknown button. Three keys that she would have sworn she'd never seen before. A grubby old nail file covered in fluff. She took it back to the door hinges and tried to use the blunt end as a screwdriver to undo the screws. Not strong enough: it bent. At the window she tried to use the point to scrape out the mortar. It bent.

A note book and an address book. Her new makeup, lipstick, comb, mirror and nail repair kit which she was not going to use for anything other than its true function. Tissues, a purse, seven pens and a pair of trendy sunglasses in a case were the main fillers.

Looking forlornly at the items splayed out across the bed, she could see nothing that would assist her in her quest for freedom. She wanted to become more positive as she scooped them up and tossed them back into her bag.

'There's always a way out, it's just a matter of finding it.' Swinging her legs onto the bed, she sat looking around. The light cast differing shadows. 'Stupid putting a light on a wall. What's wrong with the ceiling?' and she looked up. She jumped up and stood on the bed and could just reach the ceiling. Pushing with her fingertips, she could feel it give a little. Now she knew there was a possible way out if she needed it.

At 9pm on the dot, the hatch had been lowered and a large pizza box folded in half was pushed through into the room followed by a bottle of water. Nothing was said and then the hatch was slammed shut. Alison stayed on the bed because she was sure someone would be watching through the spy hole. She didn't move because the handcuff was not on her wrist but resting on the bed behind her and hidden from the spy hole's view. After twenty minutes she worked on the assumption that anyone watching would be bored and leave, so she picked them up. The pizza was nearly cold and she forced herself to eat a third before giving up. Just past 11, she slipped her hand back into the handcuff, laid on the bed and pulled the blanket over her and fell asleep dreaming of Simon.

77

Sunday 12th June 2011

Simon made allowances for the speed John could manage along the road. He kept himself fit and exercised daily, whereas John was older and hadn't exercised for some years other than walking to out of the way pubs or liaisons. Eventually they arrived at the rubble filling the ditch and the short sharp use of their small pencil type torches revealed tyre imprints across it.

John was slightly out of breath and whispered, "Thank God for that, I thought we'd never get here."

They were just starting to cross when the sound of an approaching engine signalled imminent danger and then headlights became visible approaching. Both ran and dived into the base of the hedgerow that was to the right side of the rubble bridge, and waited for the lights to pass or cross the rubble as well.

John watched with trepidation, but relaxed as the headlights did not slow as they approached and then scooted on by. Both were surprised at the speed of the vehicle which seemed to know the location of the pot holes and missed them all with minimum manoeuvres.

Getting to his feet, and glancing after the vehicle, he whispered under his breath, "Shit, shit, shit."

Simon asked in a quiet but concerned voice if he was alright.

"No. That van that just went past had my mark on the near side light cluster and I still didn't get its number."

"Nothing you can do now: let's crack on" and John knew he was right.

It was an overcast night. The first quarter of the moon provided intermittent light as the feathery clouds parted. Once across the rubble, it became obvious that the hedge had been removed completely and replaced with a large wattle door cloaked with branches and foliage. Close to, even in moonlight it was noticeable but to a passer-by on the road it would have surpassed muster. Examining it, they established that anyone alone would probably be able to open it just wide enough for a car to pass through.

Simon said, "Neat and clever. Someone knows what they're doing. I'll take the lead. Stick in my shadow."

John gratefully replied, "OK."

They opened the gate just enough for each to squeeze round trying not to disturb it too much.

Stretching away from them was a straight dirt track between two fields and through his night vision monocular, Simon could see the clear outline of two buildings. He switched to thermal vision and one of the buildings showed a concentrated heat source, but no human forms. Moving to the side of the now clearly designated, compacted, dirt track, they snuck off it onto the edge of a ploughed field that had deep furrows which could twist an ankle of the careless. Slowly, quietly and cautiously they stole forward with Simon leading and keeping to the periphery of the field. After nearly a quarter of a mile, he stopped, and when John was close to him, whispered.

"There is a small stick" and pointed close to the track, "with a piece of cotton tied to it. I would think there is another on the other side. It looks like a check to see if anyone passes this way. I don't think it is any form of warning, just for information."

They skirted the stick leaving the cotton intact and stretched across the track as they continued warily forward. In the gloom another half a mile ahead, they both saw what looked like a brick built barn. As they approached, the light of the moon showed it to be in a dilapidated state with part of the roof and walls missing, and an outbuilding to one side. No vehicles were visible, and no lights could be seen. Simon checked again with his monocular. Both left the field and moved back onto the track, and as they approached the outbuilding first which had shown the concentrated heat source, they heard the feint unmistakeable hum of a generator originating from within. Simon indicated to John to stay where he was, and then moved swiftly forward taking his scanner from its small box which had been secured in the thigh pocket of his camouflage gear and activated it, checked the outbuilding.

Inside he found the generator, a large water barrel containing in excess of a hundred gallons, a heating system and some form of sanitation unit marked 'macerator'. Wires and tubes left the building and ran towards the barn. He returned to John and in seriously hushed tones, told him what was there. Slowly, manoeuvring past the outhouse towards the barn, the pair surreptitiously approached with Simon leading.

The entrance to the barn had no door on it, but the floor which was compacted rough soil, was tiled in a line two tiles wide, leading to a door in the middle of a wall built inside the barn. The small scanner started to flicker as it detected the bugs planted on Alison. Again, Simon signalled John to stay put, and he set off following the wall within the barn and disappearing from John's view. Less than a minute passed, and Simon came back into view from the other direction. Whispering to John, he told him it was a brick built box within the barn and his scanner indicated that Alison was inside it.

78

Sunday 12th June 2011

"Where are they then?" said John, "They have cleared off leaving her unguarded."

Simon replied, "Strange. The place seems to run itself. The only thing to let them know anyone has been, is that piece of cotton. Not really high tech considering the gate at the rubble bridge and these two buildings."

"Suppose we should tell her we are here."

"You know she won't be happy. Are you going to tell her?"

"You're meant to be her minder, you tell her."

"Coward."

Simon crept to the door and signalled the spy hole to John. They took it in turn to look through it, and in the dim light, saw Alison fast asleep on the bed.

John said, "She doesn't seem to let being kidnapped stop her from sleeping."

"She sleeps like a log. I knocked a glass over the first night. She never twitched."

Simon found the hatch and opened it, and called loudly to Alison, who just turned in her sleep.

Then he shouted, "Alison."

It garnered a sleepy reply, "What?"

"Wake up."

She slowly sat up on the bed. "Who's that?"

"Who the hell do you think it is; Santa Claus?"

"Simon. You rotten bastard. You've left me here to rot. Wait till I get hold of you."

"Alison, I have some bad news" and he told her that she had to stay where she was for the time being, and quickly blamed the fact on her Father.

She was wide awake now and told Simon precisely what she thought of her Father and exactly what she thought of him.

Simon said, "Look, we have to go now."

She butted in, "Who is with you?"

He willingly named John knowing her rancour would be quickly transferred. She then obliged as she let it be known what she thought of him too.

John said, "I did bring a large bar of chocolate, but if that's your attitude, I'll keep it."

Demanding it be passed to her, she said she would reconsider her opinion of him if it tasted alright. He pushed the bar through the open hatch, and they said their farewells, and left.

Retracing their route back to the car in silence without incident, they removed their camouflage clothing, and got into the vehicle. Once inside, they felt confident enough to discuss Alison's predicament. It was obvious to them that the kidnappers had spent a fair amount of time preparing the outhouse and building the room inside the barn. As a result, they believed without a doubt that she was not in any imminent physical danger, but agreed that Simon should keep a close eye on her, and visit her once a night if possible. If a safe place could be established during the day, Simon should try to identify all the kidnappers.

He drove back into Chichester, dropping John off at the Police Station, and then carrying on to the Nuffield hospital on the main road north out of the city. Simon swung into the entrance and went to the car park at the rear which for some reason had no CCTV. There was a dozen or so other cars parked and the Lexus looked as though it belonged there. As he walked out of the grounds, he was caught for a fraction of a second on one of the many CCTV cameras inside the hospital itself. Turning left onto the main road, he jogged the mile and a half round the back streets to Alison's flat noting that there was no surveillance.

As he got to the door, Hannibal joined him, and they went in together.

Simon said, "Now I wonder who fed you tonight?"

A soft voice from within the lounge said, "How did you know?"

"I can smell the recently opened tin. Nice to see you again Barry."

"You've still got it."

*

John was troubled, but not for Alison. The sight of the disappearing van on an isolated pot holed desolate road to nowhere in the middle of the night now commanded his full attention.

'Where had it been? Where was it going? Had it been downloading video from an unsuspecting potential victim? Was someone in grave danger? Worst still: was someone lying on the floor breathing their last?'

Dumping his badly folded camouflage clothing back into the boot of his car and replacing his accessories in their respective receptacles he walked to the back door of the Police Station and tapped his ID on the reader. The gentle click of the door lock releasing allowed him entry to the practically deserted station and he climbed the stairs wearily to the top floor and punched in the numerical code to open the secured office door. Collapsing into the first chair, he fired up Paul's computer. Not being very proficient with some of the systems, he managed quite quickly, amazing himself in the process, to get the Sussex Police mapping system to load.

Searching the locale, John soon found the barn where Alison was resident. The mapping didn't display the compacted earth track leading to it from the side road, but it did reveal it was at a confluence of four fields and was doubtlessly used by a farmer originally to store equipment or fodder. Some half mile distant to the rear were drainage ditches and a small rife which formed boundaries to other fields. John checked the surrounding area and saw no houses within a one and a half-mile radius, but noticed the small church at the junction with Pagham Road.

The pot holed side road was not a short cut, nor did it really help getting to or from any specific places as there was a faster straighter route. It seemed to be ostensibly just a detour into the countryside 'Perhaps the original road prior to the new one being constructed decades ago.' John saw the van must have entered it from Lower Bognor Road and would exit onto Pagham Road in the direction of Chichester and would just cut out the junction of the two at the Royal Oak Pub: one of his favourites. John manoeuvred the mouse panning in and then out and then all around the area to no avail. The van could have come from Bognor and could have been going to Chichester or beyond. It was anyone's guess.

John turned off the Sussex mapping and opened an internet search engine bringing up Google Earth. He opened the street view facility with the resolution as large as possible and slowly surveyed the route that the van had taken along the pot holed road. Then he followed the logical faster route from the junction where the van had turned off. Lingering on the Royal Oak, he admired the simple flower decked frontage and the large car park, where he often left his car, that was always full in the evenings. Following the road to the junction where the van had re-joined it, nothing stood out. 'Why had the van taken the pot holed road?' The answer evaded him. He looked at the time on the bottom of the screen and saw it was the middle of the night and turned the computer off without shutting it down and went home to bed.

He awoke with the answer!

By 7am, he was in the canteen sitting in his usual seat at his normal table. The cook, who liked John because he always referred to her as a chef, called to him. He cheerily acknowledged her question and she set about preparing his usual breakfast. Just a few hours' sleep had done wonders for his thoughts. At eight o'clock, he was going to be seeing the helpful Sergeant Murray.

79

Sunday 12th June 2011

Simon had said goodbye and goodnight to Barry nearly two hours after his arrival at the flat, and a bottle of good chardonnay courtesy, unknowingly, of Alison. Barry needed to leave during the hours of darkness for his own safety as well as Simon's. Revelations by him about what he had been doing and who for was enough to make Simon exceedingly more apprehensive. So when he went to bed with a contented Hannibal curled up asleep next to his feet, the chair wedging the front door was just an additional precaution. He slept fitfully constantly thinking of Alison and how he had grown to like her, and how he would not allow anything untoward to befall her.

Normally he would have gone jogging first thing in the morning, but he needed as much sleep as possible for the upcoming events. Likelihood being that sleep in the next couple of days was not going to be available. Also, should anyone still be about watching, the change in routine would give the impression that he was frightened. Hannibal was the first to rise at about 7.30am, which was considerably later than usual, and Simon was left in no doubt by the animal that he should also be up and providing it with food. An open tin of cat food smelt even worse in the morning than in the middle of the night, although Hannibal did not seem to object.

Simon conducted his ablutions, and was inexplicably drawn to check the parking space at the end of the road. No sign of the van, which he expected, but in its place was a bronze BMW with someone slouched down in the driver's seat. So, he thought, someone, probably the smaller of his tormentors, did not buy his act of cowardice. It was going to pose a problem that would take him well over the best part of a day for him to resolve completely. Then he would have free reign to do what he wanted unhindered.

The taxi arrived in the cul-de-sac at 9.30am, and as is the way of most cabbies, he lent on the horn for about ten seconds without a care for any night workers just meeting Morpheus or late sleepers still in his arms. To get out and go to a door and ring the bell or knock had been foreign to them since the introduction of the hansom cab. Simon opened the door and acknowledged the din: gently used his foot to kick a reluctant Hannibal out: picked up his bag, locked the door and went down the steps and into the back seat of the taxi. In the BMW, Petrovski was in no doubt that Simon was leaving never to return.

He contacted the smaller man by use of one of Barry's provided walkie talkie radios, and told him what he had seen. Then listening intently, he sulkily agreed to follow and report further. Rattling noisily, the taxi turned round and set off for Chichester railway station with the BMW in pursuit and making no attempt at all of remaining incognito. Simon knew he was still being followed and was happy that the cab was so slow that his Mother could have kept up the pace. While he was paying the taxi driver he unconcernedly watched the BMW stop at the rear of the taxi rank. Then with his bag over his shoulder he walked into the ticket office and joined the short queue.

As his turn arrived, he loudly asked for a single one-way ticket to Crawley. To insure he had been overheard, he asked if one had to change at Horsham to get to Crawley. The woman in the ticket office looked at him curiously as she confirmed it was not necessary. Moving towards the platform, he studiously made a determined effort not to look at Petrovski who was still in the same suit and tie, and looking awkward in the ticket office.

Simon stood motionless on the platform staring inexorably across the tracks at the opposite platform's waiting room windows. He could just make out the reflection in them that disclosed Petrovski the gorilla was on a mobile phone and gesticulating wildly with one hand. As the call was terminated Petrovski put the phone into his pocket and looked up at the departure boards. It took him a while to work out when the train was leaving, and Simon watched him speak to the ticket collector at the barrier, before hurriedly leaving the station.

Strolling nonchalantly back to the ticket barrier, Simon said to the same collector, "Did you tell that large man what time the train gets to Crawley?"

The ticket collector glared spitefully at him, "Yes, and if he is a friend of yours, you might like to teach him some manners. Rude was not the word for him."

"No, he isn't a friend" and Simon went back along the platform to wait.

Petrovski was on his way to Crawley twenty-five minutes before Simon's train even entered the station.

By fluke, the train was a fast one to Horsham where it was joined to another couple of carriages before travelling on to Crawley. Simon knew that the car park at the station was on the same side as the arrival platform for his train. He'd lived in the area for nearly all his adult life and knew the layout of the station inside out. When he alighted, he crossed the footbridge to exit the station at the opposite platform and walk down a small passage to a residential road. He walked slowly as he descended the footbridge and soon glimpsed Petrovski who was watching him from the car park. The mobile phone was again clamped to his ear, and he was still gesticulating wildly with his spare hand. There was no chance of Petrovski getting back to his car and finding his way around to the residential road before he had disappeared. Simon smiled as he watched Petrovski start to run towards his car in the vain hope of seeing him again. Not a chance in hell.

80

Sunday 12th June 2011

Sergeant Murray was 'miles away' head down shuffling and scrutinising papers as he made his way towards the briefing room from his office when John collared him and asked to see him as soon as he could in private.

"I've got to brief the local city's officers before I send them out to their respective patrol areas. I'll speed it up if you want to wait in my office?"

"If I could, it would help." John waited patiently for him in one of the flimsy metal chairs with his eyes closed but with his mind working overtime. After twenty minutes, a flustered Murray burst into his own office muttering apologies for the time he had taken, plonked himself in his comfy chair and asked how he could help.

"Something is bothering me about the automatic number plate reader cameras. I'm only thinking specifically of the ones scattered about Sussex. Am I right in thinking that their locations are not disclosed to the general public?"

"That's right. Further to that: they are not disclosed as a matter of course to Police Officers and even if they were, there are too many to remember."

"Can you get their locations from the internet?"

"Not to my knowledge: no. Mind you, it's changing daily."

"If someone knew where all the cameras were: could they travel from one place to another without passing any of them?"

Murray put his hands together as though in prayer but rested his chin on his fingertips. He pondered his answer carefully not to be rushed.

"Mostly, I think the answer would be Yes. There are probably some journeys that a vehicle would take that it just could not avoid passing one of them. To know and remember every location though, even in Sussex, would be impossible. Then of course, you would have to know every back street to avoid them."

The two men sat in an unembarrassed silence. Seconds moved to minutes. Neither moved. John had his eyes closed as he was deep in thought considering several scenarios. Murray just watched him. His eyes flicked open.

"OK. Changing tack slightly. Do the cameras take images of the front or rear of the vehicles?"

"It basically depends on which way the camera is facing. It doesn't matter which side of the road the camera is on."

"My next question then is; do they take a picture of every vehicle as it passes?"

"They certainly do. Every vehicle that passes has its photo taken showing the index plate be it front or back. Some cameras even show who the driver is. With a given index number, it is possible to search not only the Sussex cameras, but everyone in the country showing exactly which camera was passed, where and when. You can practically say where any vehicle was at any given time if it was on the move."

"Right. Here's the scenario. A white van has possibly travelled for a short distance somewhere on the A27 between Arundel and Chichester. The index number is not known, but the back of it may: no, definitely can be identified. So only cameras showing the back view are worth checking. Is that a possibility?"

Murray looked astonished.

"Do you know how many white vans must travel between Arundel and Chichester? Hundreds if not thousands." Turning to his keyboard, he tapped away and said, "It won't take long to identify all the cameras taking images of the rear of vehicles, but to check them all for a white van could take days, if not weeks. How sure are you that it's travelled on the A27?"

"I'm not. I'm guessing it went that way."

"I see. It's a lot of man hours for a guess."

"If I could tell you the date and say a one hour time slot, would that speed it up?"

"Certainly. It still may take a day or two especially if it's in the rush hours."

"No. It's between 1am and 2am."

John wrote the date and time on a memo pad and handed it to Murray.

"That would make it even quicker. I'll crack on with it today and see how far I get and let you know later."

"Thanks Murray. I'll be in the office most of the day."

As John was opening the door to leave, Murray said as if an afterthought, "I suppose if the entire camera locations were loaded onto a computer and superimposed onto a map, the computer could possibly be programmed by a competent operator to give a route that would avoid them."

"Now that would be very interesting."

As he climbed the stairs, John thought that would be a truly useful piece of kit to add to his car's Sat Nav.

He spent the rest of the day reading the file and chatting to Paul and Doreen about the case, even continuing over lunch. Alison was mentioned in passing by Paul, and John told them it was some sort of stomach bug that was keeping her away. Eventually, mid-afternoon, Murray called him and said there were three cameras that showed the rear of vehicles as they passed. The first was just outside Arundel near the White Swan Public House, the next was prior to the roundabout at Fontwell and picked up traffic that joined from the A29, and the last was just past the junction with the A285.

Then Murray said, "I checked the three cameras against the local map and found a simple route around each one of them using side roads. Further to that: there were six side turnings that would also have gotten around them but by a much longer detour."

John was immediately disheartened.

Murray let him stew for a few seconds.

"Do you want to see what I found?"

"I'll be there in a second" and John nearly fell down the stairs in his haste to get to Murray's office.

"I've got three white vans for you, but none of them went past all three cameras" and he handed John the three sheets of top quality photo paper which displayed the coloured image of the rear view of each van with the number plate prominently displayed.

John stared at each in turn but could not make out if there was any hole showing from the rear nearside light cluster of any of them. Murray could see he was looking for something specific and handed him a large magnifying glass. He still couldn't make out any hole.

"Can you do a PNC search on all of them?"

"Already done" and he handed John three small bundles of paper.

Within seconds, John had all the information available about each vehicle, and its registered owner in his hands.

All three were locally registered vehicles, and John saw one was registered to a private address in Birdham, and the other two were registered to companies in Chichester. Things were starting to look up. John was profuse in his thanks to Murray, and promised him a lunch at Frankie and Benny's one day soon. He practically galloped back up the stairs to the office and told Paul what Murray had found and that he would be working late checking the three vans during the evening. Although the sight of it in the Lagness area heading generally in the direction of Chichester the previous night had given him the idea of checking the ANPR's on the A27, he didn't disclose the fact to Paul or Doreen.

Searching the back of a small drawer in a filing cabinet, Paul took out the tiniest magnifying glass that John or Doreen had ever seen.

"Is that the best you've got?"

"It's good enough for what I want" and he hovered it over the image of the van registered in Birdham.

"There is some logo and sign writing on the side, but I can't make out what it is because of the angle of the image."

Doreen, whose eyes were younger and use to small writing, took the magnifying glass, and told them it was the head of an animal, she thought a bird.

Firing up the Sussex mapping system on his computer, Paul printed off three sheets showing the locations of each registered keepers address. Because it was nearer Lagness, John decided that he would check out the address at Birdham first: he knew he was due some luck.

It came startlingly quickly from Doreen who was examining the PNC printout of the details of the registered keepers.

She said, "I know this name: it's the same last name as the woman at the book club who was very interested in the progress of the enquiry. Look at the first name of the keeper."

81

Sunday 12th June 2011

Doreen kept staring at the image of the van as it passed the ANPR camera alternating with the PNC printout. Neither John nor Paul spoke for fear of breaking her train of thought. She used the magnifying glass, and tilted the page with the image as though it would show a different view of the van and the side. Carrying it to the window, she turned it, held it up, lowered it, moved it away at arm's length and then close to her eyes.

"It's a hawk. Hawkeye security systems: Birdham."

Paul snatched the picture from her and put it flat on his desk and with John glowered at the image, which neither could make out.

"Jesus Doreen: how on earth could you see that?"

"Reading practically unintelligible written statements of Police Officers gives you an eye for it."

She studied the PNC and said, "The surname is the same as the lady from my book club and I think I remember someone saying she lived in Birdham. I met her husband once when he picked her up from a meeting. Too much of a coincidence, and I know neither of you believe in them."

John said, "Have you heard of 'Hawkeye' before?"

Doreen, who was firing up various programmes on her computer said, "No. I'll see what I can find" and her fingers danced on the keyboard just like Murray's did, except with a more delicate touch. Soon, a web site belonging to 'Hawkeye Security Systems' filled the screen with the home page displaying an image of a Harrier Hawk with the name of the firm emblazoned below it in red. The contact details were on the bottom of the screen, and married those recorded on the PNC. There were two pages showing images of houses with different sorts of alarm systems prominently displayed, and two pages of industrial premises, again with different alarm systems displayed. All were recorded as being 'professionally and satisfactorily installed and maintained by Hawkeye Systems'.

The last page gave details of servicing conducted on all known alarms by 'Hawkeye Systems' either yearly for a set retaining fee, or on an 'as and when' requirement. In slightly larger and bolder print, a call out service was offered. Paul asked Doreen to print off a complete copy of the web page for the file.

"Just remember Paul, at the present time, I can't say if it is the same van that I saw that night. I need to see the back of it to confirm either way."

At a later date and for lawful disclosure in court, he would confirm any identification made by him was as a result of the small hole in the rear nearside light cluster which showed a spot of white. As to how the hole had got there in the first place would remain a mystery as far as he was concerned. John could not explain the false index plates and hoped that later enquiries would resolve the issue. He would be able to confidently confirm, if asked in court, that he requested Murray to check for the rear view of white vans because that's all he was looking for.

More luck arrived their way very quickly afterwards in the shape of Murray as he burst into the room. John introduced him to Doreen as he knew Paul of old and needed no introduction there. Paul pulled up a spare chair and invited him to sit down as he looked perturbed, and offered him a drink. The Sergeant sat jadedly in the worn but comfy offered chair and eyeing the kettle and accoutrements sitting on a spare desk said he'd love a coffee and didn't realise that drinks were permitted in the offices.

As he was speaking, Prodow, again without Groves in tow, came into the room and seeing Paul preparing the kettle asked, "Got anything stronger? I've had a pig of a day. An old case is in court, and it isn't going as it should."

Paul delved behind two box files on a shelf and produced a bottle of malt whiskey which had never been opened.

"For celebrations, commiserations and when needed."

Doreen emptied the coffee from the cups back into the jar and took the tea bags out of the others. Luckily, she hadn't added milk or sugar. She handed an empty cup to each of those present including Murray who took it rather hesitantly. Murray was not sure what to say with a senior officer in the room.

Prodow just said, "Don't mind me" and Murray no longer prevaricated.

They all sat around Paul's desk reverently holding mugs with at least two fingers worth of malt in each as Prodow was rapidly brought up to date.

Murray said, "After seeing John I tried searching the database with the registration numbers and got no additional responses for the van from Birdham for the whole of that day. The other two hit lots of other cameras around Chichester. I thought I should check the index numbers of all three vans against any ANPR sightings a week either side of the day. The two vans registered to companies in Chichester were in and around West Sussex most week days and into the early mornings. The van from Birdham hit the same ANPR on Chichester bypass at eight odd times during the working days but no other cameras. It just seems to disappear."

He paused, breathed in the vapours emitted by the malt, and let a little of the liquid enter his mouth.

"I decided to check all the enforcement cameras. That took a lot longer than I anticipated, but it reminded me about the video cars."

Prodow said, "What video cars?"

"One of my probationers who I keep in touch with joined the traffic unit and is now a sergeant based here at the Chichester garage. I had a chat with him earlier and asked if any traffic cars were videoing that night. Several were and what they recorded has been downloaded to the independent traffic computer system."

"I have a feeling that you are likely to enforce a top up."

He continued, "I gave him the three vans' index numbers which he has searched for. He had to view all the video they recorded because it is not a searchable database of index numbers, but because it was a van and only an hour period, it didn't take him too long. A traffic car was returning to Chichester after dealing with an accident in Selsey when it recorded a van travelling in the opposite direction at a junction near Birdham."

Prodow said to Paul, "Get that bottle. I've a feeling I might be getting late turn CID to take me home tonight."

"It was the one registered to the Birdham address."

"I still need to check the back of it before we can say for sure."

"I asked my colleague if it was possible to get from the A27 to where the Police car videoed it without passing any ANPRs. He has access to the computer showing all the locations of every ANPR in Sussex at the same time. I hung on for a while as he worked it out and when eventually he came back on the line, he said, 'Yes'."

82

Sunday 12th June 2011

Jimmy strolled back into the office just as Murray was leaving. Doreen, who was not a seasoned drinker, thrust a mug into his hand and poured more than a reasonable amount of malt into it.

"What are we celebrating?" Doreen sat back behind her desk and waved her hand knowing it was pointless for her to try and update him as she was struggling with her diction. The others were all regular drinkers and Paul updated him.

Jimmy said, "Must be good news day. I have been with the toxicologist and the botanist. They have finalised their examinations and completed their statements. To summarise: it appears that what actually killed George was a combination of three different poisons. The main one being a small amount of cyanide which alone would probably have done for him due to his age and infirmity. It appears to have come from the crushed leaves of a passion flower which contain cyanogenic glycoside. They have been allowed to break down to produce cyanide. Then there was a honey type compound made from the nectar of Rhododendrons which produces grayanotoxins. Apparently, it used to be used as a poison but wasn't very strong in this case although yet again, due to his age and infirmity, it may have just about done for him. Lastly, we have cytisine which is derived from Laburnum and induces convulsions, coma and death. However, it was so mild it would unlikely have been sufficient to kill him by itself."

They were all watching and listening to Jimmy in awe that he had it all in his head and didn't need any notes.

He took a gulp of malt and his eyes instantaneously watered, "Blimey. That's strong."

Prodow said, "I'm worried about you. If any of your acquaintances die mysteriously, you're going to be a very strong candidate as the culprit."

"Not me guv'nor, don't like the idea of prison. By the way, the bottle in the shed contained the complete concoction."

"How did Munroe, if it was indeed her, make it and then get him to take a swig of it?"

"The Botanist said all of the plants that have been utilised are common plants in English gardens. She believed the slight aroma emitted, mainly the almond type smell from the cyanide, could be disguised in something with its own strong taste or smell. Scotch for example."

Doreen put her mug down before she dropped it.

Paul said, "So the Botanist was a 'she'. No wonder you've been spending time there."

"I'm taking her to Blanc's to show my appreciation for what she has done. I think it's only right."

"Is she pretty?"

"I don't think that is at all relevant."

Jimmy handed the two statements to Paul and then retired behind his desk with the mug in his hand. He had finalised all the exhibits, and was preparing them for what he, like the others, believed was a pointless court hearing. Statement bundles had already been completed, and the two supplementary ones would have to be served as additional evidence. A complete set of disclosable evidence had already been prepared and had been provided to the defence. Enquiries from counsel had all been answered in the official manner. There was a full list of all the witnesses, and the running order that they were to be called. Everyone had been contacted, and their availability established. All of them hoped that an adjournment was obtained, but they were ready for a trial. If needed, they were in a position to go against a defendant who they had all come to believe was innocent.

Prodow confided to Paul, but loudly enough for all to hear, that he was becoming very impressed with Sergeant Murray, and what was Paul's attitude on him becoming his deputy. Paul quite liked the idea because he hardly ever got any time off when he was office manager on a protracted or confidential enquiry, and with a deputy, he would not be tied to constant working. Prodow said he would speak to Murray, and if he agreed, he would arrange with the station commander for him to be attached to see how he got on. With that, Prodow was gone to find the Sergeant.

Simon spent a long time in a house just a few hundred yards from the end of the passage seeing the wife of an old friend who had been killed during the second gulf war. They had been friends for years, and whenever he could, he would pop round for a chat. When either were attending any official gatherings, they would often ask the other to accompany them as their escort. There was nothing untoward or sexual in their relationship, but both were aware that tongues often wagged. Neither worried or cared as they were at ease in each other's company. He easily explained that although it was nice to see her, he had used a visit to her in order to avoid a person who could cause him problems, and indicated the BMW as it cruised past. She took no snub at the fact, and asked if he wanted lunch.

Eating a simple chicken salad, they chatted of long gone episodes, some happy, others sad. It was good therapy for both of them and Simon stayed a lot longer than he was going to. By late-afternoon, he left his temporary hide out, and walked back to the station and bought a ticket to Barnham. His attitude was simple, if Petrovski was still in Crawley and saw him, then so be it. He had no need to worry though as Petrovski was already back in Chichester being admonished for losing him. The smaller man was not sure if Petrovski was just inept, and there was nothing to fear now Simon had left on a one-way ticket, or he was totally incompetent and had been fed a simple dummy.

Arriving at Barnham railway station, Simon walked out to the busy little taxi office and took a cab to the Nuffield Hospital in Chichester. Watching the taxi leave for its return journey: Simon started to jog towards Alison's flat, taking a longer, completely different route to any he had taken before. His bag was on his back, and his butterfly knife was easily available should it be required. The nearer he got, the more cautious he became. He slowed to a walk and checked all about, but was sure he was alone as he entered the road with the completely empty lay-by. Walking along the cul-de-sac towards the steps he noticed nothing untoward, and he started to climb.

Suddenly he felt something lightly touch his leg. Looking down he saw a black piece of cotton had been tied to the metal stanchions and stretched across the steps: but what he'd actually felt was Hannibal being affectionate. The cotton was practically invisible in the dappled light, and would have broken as he entered the front door. A low tech idea just like on the track to the barn which would let the setter know if anyone had passed by. He stepped over it, as Hannibal ducked under it, and they both entered the flat. By way of a reward, the cat was given two full tins of different cat foods which kept him happy for over an hour as he gorged himself excessively. Simon did not bother using the lights. It appeared that someone was still not sure of him.

83

Sunday 12th June 2011

At 7.30pm after the so-called rush hour, John, who was close to the drink driving limit left the station in his old Vauxhall having first made sure it had not been tampered with, and made his way to Birdham. Reaching the road in question, John noted that all the properties were large detached houses set back on generous plots of land. Slowly driving along the quiet road, he located the one he was interested in. After a short distance, he parked half on and half off the kerb to allow any other vehicles to pass by relatively unimpeded, and got out. Walking back and past the open five bar gate leading to the property, he saw a reasonably new Ford Focus and a new Honda parked on the ornamentally tiled drive, and the white van facing him. He had a dilemma: did he enter the drive and go to the front door on some spurious reason in order to see the back of the van, or did he wait for it to leave, and check it then. In order to remain unobtrusive, he chose the latter option.

It was not easy for him to find a parking place where he could see the drive unimpeded without being seen himself. In the end, he chose a place nearly a quarter of a mile away where he could make out any movement on the drive in the dying embers of the evening sunshine, and then check using his monocular as to which vehicle was manoeuvring. Overall, John was reasonably happy that he would not attract any unwarranted attention, and hunkered down to wait. As the light slowly faded, he started to struggle to keep his eyes open. Having been up half the previous night and with a fair amount of alcohol on board, he was feeling the combined effect. He began to hope nothing would move during the twilight hour because it would be harder to see than if it was completely dark when a vehicle would have to turn its lights on.

As it happened, John had no trouble when the vehicle left the drive. Before it even moved, the drive was illuminated by two powerful flood lights that flashed on making it as bright as day as a figure left the front door. Watching through his monocular, John could see a male get into the van and his heart dropped a beat. He definitely looked similar to the person that had been at Georges bungalow in the middle of the night, but at this distance, John could not swear to it. The headlights came on, and the van turned out of the drive to approach his position. He waited with baited breath as the van drew nearer and then passed him.

"Thank you, God," said John under his breath.

Considering that the van driver used quiet side roads, and appeared to dodge all ANPR's, John was not contemplating trying to follow it. He started his car and set off back towards Chichester Police Station travelling back onto the main road. As he entered Birdham village on the main road with its half a dozen strewn out shops, he saw the van stationary and unattended outside the only Chinese take away restaurant. Skidding the Vauxhall to a halt by the side of the road, John jumped out of the car and opened the boot throwing his camouflage clothing out of the way as he opened his scanner box desperately looking for a bug.

He knew he hadn't more than a minute or two as he scurried forward having left his car with the lights on and unlocked. Inside the take away, John could see the back of the only male customer who was proffering a card in apparent payment and he saw a bag sitting on the counter. Moving into the road away from the side nearest the take away, John slapped the bug under the front wheel arch where it stuck. He kept walking across the road doing a looping turn and returning to his car. Before he had got back to the Vauxhall, the van had gone.

John opened the boot again and tidied up the mess he had made before getting back into the car and turning his Sat Nav on. There were three contacts: two faint ones were from Alison and one strong one from the van. He hadn't realised how close he was to Lagness. Tuning the Sat Nav, he enlarged the map and isolated the bug on the van which he saw was now back on the drive. Happy as he could be, he went back to the Police Station via a Chinese take away in South Street. 'What's good for the goose is good for the gander' ran into his mind.

84
Monday 13th June 2011

Leaving his car in its usual spot in the car park, he climbed the stairs to the office, sat at Doreen's desk, and after a quick search, located a fork and set about his Chinese meal. There was no rush so he turned on the unofficial office radio and listened to Sussex Gold playing the hits from the sixties. 'Proper music that you can hear the words to' he ruminated. The recent burst of activity had cleared his head, and he no longer felt tired or had any urge to rest his eyes. 11.30pm saw him return to his car and set the Sat Nav in motion. No need for him to leave the yard now until he had a reason. That would be at midnight.

The Sat Nav told him the van was on the move and travelling along back streets, sometimes zigging and zagging about, practically doubling back on itself, which indicated to John it was avoiding cameras. Twice he watched as it travelled down tracks which cut through farm buildings. It was mostly heading East, and after thirty minutes, John left the yard and took the main road out of Chichester and along the A27 passing Arundel and parking up at the roundabout by the junction with the A280, just prior to the outskirts of Worthing. When he stopped, he was already three miles further East than the van. John watched the blip on the Sat Nav as the van slowly, and by a ridiculously circuitous route arrived at Angmering.

John kept watching, his eyes now glued to the Sat Nav. Seeing the blip slow right down to a practical halt for nearly a minute as it ventured along a side road off the village spurred him into action. He gunned the engine of the old Vauxhall holding it in as low a gear as possible for maximum acceleration to get to the road. The van, according to the Sat Nav, had resumed speed and continued to the first turning which it took on the right. It was plain as day to John looking at the map that the van was likely going around a large block. The Vauxhall lurched and rocked about as John forced it faster and faster to the road and then stopped with a screech of tyres and a shudder. A gap between a couple of vehicles was just large enough for the Vauxhall to squeeze between and park. John killed all the power leaving just the dull light from the Sat Nav which showed the van over half way round the block. As soon as it was due to enter the road, he killed the Sat Nav and ducked low in his seat.

The van passed him and braked to a crawl, and John saw the nearside light cluster with the small white light circled by red. As it was about to pass the entrance to a large detached house, it again practically came to a standstill and John could see the glow of what looked like a computer screen illuminating the cab area. For virtually forty-five seconds, John watched the van and the glowing light inside the cab: then the light was extinguished, and the van started to accelerate.

Staying where he was, he reactivated his Sat Nav and watched the bug on the van show that it was doing what looked like a reciprocal route. When it was a mile off, John eased away from his parking spot and drove to the entrance where the van had practically stopped. He took note of the house details before driving back by a direct route to the Police Station, and parked in his usual place over all the accumulated debris. Before turning his Sat Nav off, he saw that the van was still on its reciprocal route currently weaving around Oving.

Searching his pockets for his ID to open the back door, John went upstairs to the office and fired up Paul's computer to look at the mapping system of the area round the house in Angmering. Satisfied, he opened the CAD (Computer Aided Dispatch) system of all calls or incidents recorded by Sussex Police, and typed in the full address. Declining to search, the computer returned a help screen asking for additional information, which John read and then completed. Logically, the computer required a date to search by, and he thought that incidents going back six months were ample, and all other parameters requested by the computer would be left as default. Now reasonably satisfied, the computer deemed to complete a search.

It wasn't fast as it was an old system, so John relaxed with his hands linked behind his head. Slowly, it displayed a call to the emergency services four months previously by a neighbour requesting Police but mainly an ambulance as the elderly occupier, Peter Masters had collapsed with stomach pains. Then less than a month previously, again a call for an ambulance, this time by Police themselves who had been stopped by a postman who had discovered Peter

Masters in his garden unconscious. Two calls only, and the computer divulged full details about Masters including his age of eighty-three, no known relatives, telephone numbers, Doctor's details, Hospital details, and social services information. The printer burst into life from its night time slumber, and spewed out sheets of paper, some with useful information on, others with no more than two lines of gobbledegook on. Reading it all, John saw similarities with George Armstrong, and worried for Masters.

85
Monday 13th June 2011

Simon had spent a few hours in the flat mooching about in the dark, and had taken advantage of some food from Alison's kitchen cupboards which he had cooked on the gas hob by the moonlight coming through the window. Dozing on the settee with Hannibal next to him completing his nightly ablutions, he considered when he would leave to go to Lagness. Midnight would be best and he should arrive at the barn about 1.am. A shower appealed to him as he was going to spend at least a whole night and day dug into a field and by the end, he would stink, so starting clean would be a benefit.

Getting to his feet, he made his way into the bathroom, and instinct told him to check the lay by. Stepping onto the toilet he looked out of the window. No van as he knew Barry had finished his contract, but he was astonished to see the bronze BMW shining in the fluorescing glow of a street light. Surely Petrovski hadn't seen him arrive back, and if he had, why would he park so patently obviously in the lay by where he stuck out like a sore thumb. As he watched, Petrovski got out of the vehicle with slight difficulty due to his bulk, and started towards the flat. Simon darted out of the bathroom and to the bedroom grabbing his butterfly knife and then into the hall facing the front door. No lights were on and only his phone was on charge in the kitchen face down and on silent. Nothing disclosed that the flat was occupied.

Simon waited apprehensively in the hall, and soon heard movement on the stairs outside. Then as the sound got louder he heard Petrovski puffing slightly as he reached the front door. Petrovski lent on the door with his left hand as he bent to examine the cotton, and the door moved slightly with the borne weight but held firm. Tension was building in Simon as he braced for him entering the flat. He decided he would have to hit him hard in the throat to keep him silent and disable him, and then if necessary he was going to use Alison's new vase from the hall table to render him unconscious. Hannibal walked into the hall, and sat down next to Simon also watching the front door.

No sound of any key in the lock, but then Simon heard Petrovski talking apparently making a phone call from outside the front door. His gruff voice clearly audible and carrying clearly in the late evening's tranquillity. It was to let his shorter compatriot know that the cotton was still intact. Simon knew a little Russian and realised that he was asking what he should do.

After what felt like hours, Petrovski said "OK" and started clumping noisily back down the stairs.

Moving silently into the bathroom, Simon jumped onto the toilet seat and watched him walk slovenly back to his car, and drive off. Hannibal now bored, ambled into Alison's bedroom, jumped onto her bed, curled up and went to sleep.

Standing under the hot water of the shower, Simon knew that he was still not trusted, and was astonished that Petrovski hadn't entered the flat. He could only assume that the smaller man did not trust Petrovski to enter as he may destroy something or get caught inside. There was always the possibility that he didn't have a key with him, but Simon didn't dwell on that for long.

Just after midnight, he left the flat having first checked the lay by and then making sure he didn't break the cotton. Lifting a riled Hannibal from the bed, he deposited the spitting animal outside and onto the stairs and then with his bag over his back, he jogged to the hospital to collect his car. Putting his camouflage clothes on in the unobserved car park, he set off driving to the parking space used before when he was with John. Taking his bag and additional items from the boot, he jogged to the rubble pile, remembering an old army instructor who used to say, 'repetition leads to complacency which leads to mistakes that lead to disclosure and then you die'.

Once through the camouflaged gate in the hedge, he scanned the barn with the night sights and then switched to the thermal imaging. Still no persons present, or more to the point, no one visible. With slightly more of a cavalier attitude, he made his way to the barn but used the opposite side of the track in a similarly ploughed and recently planted field. The stick with the cotton was roughly where he expected it, and on arriving at the barn there were still no vehicles. Making a cursory check of the outhouse to be sure it was clear of humans, he moved stealthily as he entered the barn.

Something was different: and he saw a video camera balanced on a brick which immediately caught his eye. In fact, he couldn't miss it, it was nearly in his way. The recording device was to the side of it. Noting how he had entered the barn, he knew he hadn't yet crossed its line of vision. Where it had been placed was where it would capture movement and light emitting from the hatch should anyone decide to open it. Even the power lead ran out of the barn and into the outhouse where it was attached to the power supply by the generator. It was not very subtle and not one that Barry or any of his acquaintances would have used. Simon wasn't sure if it was the only one, or if it was a decoy.

The next two hours were spent checking the barn thoroughly by climbing over the broken-down walls in order not to cross the camera lens's view, and then going back through the outhouse checking it a lot more carefully. Then just to be sure, he retraced his steps to the road finding nothing but the stick with the cotton.

'Strange. One camera. Senseless. Why so obvious? Why not leave a guard?' His army instructor's words flitted into his mind. 'What the hell have I done to cause anyone to suspect I was here?' He crossed the track and started back towards the barn on the original side that he and John had used.

Five yards before the cotton he found it.

A very small digital camera concealed in a furrow a yard off the track in the field pointing across the road. The little recorder with its battery pack was encased in polythene and totally covered by a layer of soil. It's what he would have done and he cursed himself for being so predictable. Someone knew any one travelling towards the barn would probably not use the same side each time. Had he or John left a tell-tale footprint to cause suspicion? The camera was going to confirm the wary jailers inkling; someone was going to be aware of his presence.

Simon knew he had to disable it in some way so as not to arouse any further doubt, and uncovering the recorder, he turned it off. It was an older type unit with its own power source and had proven efficient in the past and was still used by many people and some private agencies. There were a lot better systems available, but they were much more expensive. Simon lowered the camera slightly a few degrees and turned it at an angle as though knocked by a passing animal or not properly checked when deployed.

Now it just showed part of the track but not the opposite side of it or the edge of the opposing field. A problem that he knew may occur was if the date and time had been set to show on the video. Most people: and he hoped the person who set this one: never bothered as they only needed to see if anyone passed by. Checking the video picture, he saw it had been set and he swore under his breath as he disabled it. Depending on who originally set it up and whether they were confident that it had been done correctly would determine any further scepticism.

Restoring the recorder to its covered position, he set it to start recording from the beginning of the disk knowing it would record over the time it had caught him as he passed by on the other side of the track.

86
Monday 13th June 2011

Returning to the barn as carefully as he could not to leave any footmarks in the soil, he climbed over the lowest part of the wall to move to the rear of the camera on the bricks. It was aimed across the entrance towards the door to Alison's prison and would only pick up movement in the gloom. Should the hatch in the bottom of the door have been opened, or the door itself, the image would just have shown a slight light emitting from the room. That would have been enough to alert anyone who viewed the video as to his presence. It appeared to Simon that whoever had placed it there expected an intruder to find it and then turn it off again notifying the viewer to his presence. He gently put his camouflage hat over the camera lens so preventing any light reaching it and then went to the door.

Holding his small torch in his mouth, he illuminated the lock on the door which had a simple three lever deadlock that he knew he could pick and had come prepared for. In the boot of his car, he had an electric 'pick gun' but he tended to use that for better quality serious locks or even five lever deadlocks. The 'pick gun' was very quick but made a little noise so he was using the old fashion method of using a lock pick set. Taking what looked like a penknife from his pocket, but was actually marked as a 'jacknife', he opened it up and removed the tension tool. Fanning all six lock picks, he selected the one he needed pushing the other five picks back into the knife handle. The bolts top and bottom of the door were superfluous to a person outside and moved without noise, but to anyone inside, were an additional deterrent to exiting. Within ten minutes he had the door open and went inside to find Alison asleep in bed with a blanket wrapped round her.

Gently he shook her shoulder through the blanket and she woke with a start. Turning to face him, she started to rise before she remembered she was completely naked having washed out her underwear in the sink the night before. He could see that one of her eyes was puffy and was badly bruised and there was a minimal trace of dried blood on her nose. The blanket fell off her shoulders exposing the top half of her body, and she grabbed the fallen blanket pulling it back up over her breasts.

"Why do you do this? Is it to embarrass me?"

"Sorry. I thought I would come and keep you company for a while."

She held the blanket to her as she sat up and told him she was naked so she wouldn't be getting up. Simon sat on the bed having tapped her on the leg to get her to move them to make room for him, passed a non-committal reply and noticed in the dim light her unmade up face was smiling.

They spoke for nearly an hour about what had been happening to each of them and her Father. She became tearful as she told him that she had been given two meals and a two litre bottle of water via the hatch but saw no one. When the food was passed through she had asked for books or something to read but got no response. The only time someone had entered the room, she had been told to put the cloth bag on her head. Whoever had entered took the remnants of the chocolate from her bed and asked her where she had got it from. Although she claimed it had been in her bag, the person had called her a liar and hit her several times round the face. Slowly, tears welled up filling her eyes and she started to cry and grabbed hold of Simon hugging him to her as the blanket fell.

"Get me out of here, please."

Simon knew straightaway what had given her captors the suspicion. The bar of chocolate was so big it would have filled her whole bag and no one had seen it or could remember having seen it. The doubting was not enough for them to leave a night guard. He held her tight for a few minutes.

"You know you have to stay here a day or two longer?" and she cried more than she had done since she was at school.

She hung on to him as though her life depended on it, "Promise you will come and see me every night?"

He swore he would and prised himself away from her. She sat in the bed no longer worried about her modesty, trying to compose herself for his leaving.

Making the comment as he left the room, "If you're going to parade around naked, may I suggest you cover the spy hole" turned her tears to feigned rage.

"Make sure you bring chocolate tonight you bastard."

87
Monday 13th June 2011

Simon had locked the cell door and recovered his hat as Alison buried herself under the blanket and cried herself back to sleep. He believed that the person who had found the chocolate was the one who had set the cameras. Or more likely, ordered one of his minions to do it. The little Russian. If he had been convinced that Alison was lying, Simon was sure he would have had someone there all night.

'That would have been predictable. This guy knows what he is doing.' He wouldn't have settled for a couple of cameras and a piece of cotton. Now he knew he had to be extremely cautious but capricious.

Instead of digging himself a hole to stay in under the hedge near the rubble entrance which would have been the accepted position, he went past the barn and to a dirty drainage ditch in the field beyond and dug into the damp bank with his little fold out spade from his bag. As day was playing host to the dawn chorus, Simon had settled down in his temporary pit on his groundsheet and under his tarpaulin covered with camouflage netting and bits of undergrowth he had added to it for aesthetics. Setting his binoculars in front of him with a small voice activated recorder and mobile phone, he knew he would not move again until midnight.

Shortly after 8.30am, Simon was brought out of the semi-comatose state that he had adopted some hours earlier to conserve energy, when he saw a silver vehicle on the track approaching the barn. Raising the binoculars, and speaking quietly to the recorder, he watched as the Saab stopped and Petrovski got out of the passenger side and removed one of the sticks with the cotton attached and threw it onto the track. The vehicle continued on to the muddy and gritted parking area outside the barn, and the smaller man alighted. Simon watched as he seemed to scour the ground leading to the entrance of the barn. It was clear that he was looking for his footprints which Simon knew were not going to be found as he had previously taken the trouble to erase them. Even in the moonlight, when he had approached the barn earlier, it was clear to him that the ground had been dampened deliberately and all tyre and footmarks were missing. Apparently satisfied, the smaller man pulled a puffa type coat from the car before he strolled into the outbuilding.

Turning the binoculars back to Petrovski, Simon saw him crouched down on his haunches looking at the small screen on the recorder that he had uncovered. Petrovski did not have the stamina to stay crouched too long and soon stood up seemingly bored with his duty. He was less than diligent as he occasionally raised his head and looked about as the recording continued unobserved. There was no sign that he had noticed or seen anything amiss, and before it was possible for the video to have played right through: Petrovski was resetting it, and hiding the monitor. Sullenly, he started the short walk along the track to the barn, hands buried deep in his pockets.

On reaching the car, he got into the passenger seat and started fiddling with the radio before lying back in the seat. It was a full fifteen minutes later that the smaller man left the outbuilding and ignoring the now sleeping 'gorilla' in the passenger seat, took a bottle of water and a paper plate covered with foil from the back seat and walked into the barn. Twenty-five minutes later, he was back out with an empty plate which he tossed from the driver's door into the rear of the vehicle with his coat before settling behind the steering wheel. The 'gorilla' wound the seat up to a normal sitting position and then got out of the car which moved to the track before stopping.

Simon could not understand what had delayed the little man in the outbuilding and was racking his brain as to what he had seen in there. The generator and the other equipment could easily be checked in a couple of minutes. Had he missed a hidden item? Then he thought about twenty-five minutes in the barn. He wouldn't have watched Alison through the spy hole for that long.

'What the hell is he up to? What have I missed?' Now he became anxious. Wide awake and worried, he was starting to imagine he'd missed a camera.

Still keeping the binoculars glued to his eyes, Simon watched as Petrovski dragged his foot over the tyre marks and then went to the outhouse, and walking backwards to the barn, dragged his foot over all the footprints he saw.

On reaching the Saab, he got in, and it started back along the track. When it was level with the camera, it stopped and both men got out. Petrovski walked the few paces and replaced the sticks with the cotton, and the smaller man went to the camera.

Uncovering the monitor, he watched it for a minute before summoning Petrovski to him and pointed across the track and then reset the camera clearly chastising him. As Petrovski set about secreting the monitoring equipment, the smaller man crossed the track and walked a few yards back towards the barn and then turned and walked towards the road. He was still looking for footprints. A man Simon was beginning to develop a begrudging admiration for with regards to his thoroughness.

Simon had been cautious but had not checked for any tell-tale footprints in the mud at the side of the track. The two cameras had drawn his complete attention to the detriment of the basic simple things. Was that the intention the little man had wanted the cameras to have? Chastising himself for his stupid ignorance he vowed to be more thorough. His old instructor would have probably had apoplexy if he knew how laid back he had become. When night fell he would prioritise a full search of the outhouse and the barn before anything else.

He knew he had kept off the ridges and stayed in the furrows as the mud within them was mainly solid because the sun had been prominent for several days baking the soil solid. Where it was in shade nearer the barn, it was still slightly damp and footmarks, if there were any, would be more evident. As the night's activity shot through his thoughts, he became confident that precautions taken by him around the vicinity of the cameras were adequate.

Slowly the smaller man walked back to his car, lent in and pulled out his jacket. Without putting it on, he removed a small pair of binoculars from one of the jacket pockets. The hedgerow by the road was where he focused his attention scanning back and forth. Then he turned, and scanned the fields, several times looking directly towards Simon's position, but never stopping his traverse. Eventually satisfied, he got back into the vehicle joining Petrovski, and left pausing only for Petrovski to hold the hedge open to allow the car to pass through and over the rubble bridge. Simon knew the man was a shrewd adversary, and would have to be treated with the utmost respect.

He felt so much better having seen him take the binoculars from his coat pocket.

88

Monday 13th June 2011

John was in the canteen earlier than usual sitting half dozing in his normal chair trying to work out a scenario as to how he could explain his presence in Angmering and his potential computer enquires with regards to Masters. The best way was to keep it honest: just don't mention the bug. He saw and recognised the rear of the van and was able to follow it which was true in a fashion. Without any input from him, the cook brought him breakfast placing it on the table in front of him.

She stood facing him and said, "You've got to get some sleep. You're looking older by the day."

Thanking her, he pointed out she was invariably in the kitchen earlier than his arrival and if she went to bed late, she also lacked sleep.

"How do you stay looking so young?"

"Pond's face cream. If you used it though, someone would find out in this place and you would attract more men than women." She laughed at the thought as she wiped some of his table with a dirty looking dish cloth before returning to the preserve that was her kitchen.

In the office, he sat drinking coffee and listening as Paul was explaining to Murray systems of paper and computer filing and the vagaries of major incidents that were essential to all investigations. He moved on to explain the role of the office manager, and the fact that he, (or she) was really the backbone of any enquiry, and should be able to recall statements and facts from memory. If unable to recall a fact, the office manager should be in a position to go straight to the item that would divulge the relevant information. This ability was imperative if the manager was to be trusted by the senior officer leading the enquiry. Paul continued on expounding that the main task was of deputing the various officers attached to the major incident team to conduct specific enquiries as they arose during the course of the investigation.

After he'd finished, he looked at John, Jimmy and Doreen and said, "Did I miss anything?"

John said, "I don't know. I do what I'm told and that's the end of it as far as I am concerned."

"Huh. I wish."

Doreen was more forthcoming and suggested that Paul explain the system of HOLMES which all Police forces used. Murray said he was fully aware of its existence, but didn't know precisely how it worked. Still having outstanding commitments at Chichester, Paul and Murray each checked their diaries and agreed a day and time to go to Littlehampton where Paul would show Murray the system in all its glory.

Doreen, having already established Murray's preference, busied herself making drinks for all present. She had also established that the Sergeant liked to be called Murray: not Sergeant: nor whatever his first name happened to be: just Murray.

With refreshed mugs either in their hands or on the desks in front of them, Paul said, "Now when someone has completed an enquiry, they return with the information either on paper which goes in my top tray or they give a verbal account, or both. As you were here at seven this morning, and have noticed that there is no report from anyone in my tray, we must presume we are going to be honoured with a verbal: nay more probably, a verbose account."

Jimmy said, "Not me."

"In that case, I presume you are implying me."

John began his account explaining locating the address in Birdham and describing at first the house and then the two cars on the drive with their index numbers. Continuing, he explained the van's presence and how he only saw the back of it when it drove past him, and it was only then that he was able to confirm without doubt it was the same one that he had seen some nights previously in Barnham. They were all engrossed with the narrative and their now forgotten drinks were starting to cool down. Stating he was returning to Chichester, he spotted the van and decided to try to follow it. More by luck than judgement, and anticipating some of the circuitous routes taken, he claimed to have seen it arrive in Angmering and noticed it linger at Peter Masters' house.

When the van had left, John said he was unable to follow it, so he returned to Chichester and using the computer had searched the CAD for the address. He handed a sheaf of papers to Paul.

"To precis: four months back, Masters, who is in his eighties, was found collapsed with severe stomach pains by a neighbour and went to St Richard's hospital. Three weeks ago, he was found collapsed in his garden and again was taken to hospital. Learned medics appraised him of their opinions as to the reasons for his collapsing which he held to be guesswork at best. When he spoke to his local PC, he couldn't understand why it had occurred as he had always been fit and healthy. It is worrying that the van was in the locale."

As if to reinforce his discourse of earlier, Paul asked how John could have got the registration number of the vehicle so badly wrong when first seen in Barnham. Within seconds, they had all agreed that the vehicle used false plates, but could not understand why it hadn't in Angmering.

To give him a little test, Paul asked Murray "What would you do now?"

Murray was quickly off the mark, "I would bring it immediately to the attention of both Mr Groves and Mr Prodow and seek authority to obtain a search warrant for the house and vehicles. I would arrange a visit to Mr Masters as soon as possible by John and the local uniform officer to confirm his wellbeing and if necessary arrange for his ongoing security. I would ask Mr Prodow for authority to assemble a few of the original officers to conduct the execution of any warrant. I think that's all to start."

"Good enough for me. It's all yours. I'm going to have a big boy's breakfast for the first time in months" and with that, he left the room.

Murray was on the phone for less than five minutes before asking John if he could get to Angmering to meet the local officer outside Masters' house without delay.

"Really Murray you shouldn't ask, you should direct. Other than Doreen; treat us all like your probationers and you'll get on fine."

"Then shift yourself. Now."

"OK" and John downed the dregs of the nearly cold coffee, and left the room. Once inside his car, he turned his Sat Nav on and saw the van was stationary at a small industrial unit between Birdham and Chichester. He knew he had to check it, and accelerated swiftly towards the exit nearly hitting an angry and temporarily bellicose uniform officer in his haste. Hardly slowing at the exit, he swung left and towards the industrial unit in the opposite direction to Angmering. No one followed him.

The unit was surrounded by a sturdy wire fence topped with razor wire, and a substantial metal gate which was wedged open, and by the grass growing around it, had been for some considerable time.

'So much for security' he thought as he cruised by. Turning round, he drove back and stopped in a bus stop pull-in and held a piece of paper high enough for anyone observing him to conclude that he was probably lost. He saw there were four separate large prefabricated workshops in a 'U' shape facing a central parking area big enough for about twenty cars. Each workshop had a large roller shuttered opening door to accommodate a vehicle the size of a small lorry. Next to each of the workshops was an office with a pedestrian's door and a window. John could see that two of the units directly faced the entrance from the road and there was a unit at right angles to them at each end. The unit to the left side had the shuttered door raised no more than four feet which was more than John required to see that the van was parked inside. That was all he needed, and he was rapidly off towards Angmering.

89

Monday 13th June 2011

When he arrived, John parked partially on the verge outside the house behind a small blue Kia that was already parked there. Any decent villain in Sussex could have identified the Kia as being an unmarked Police car as it was practically the only small car on the road painted in a non-metallic blue. The middle aged woman sitting in it was on the phone as John parked, and went to the passenger door. Hanging up as he got in, both introduced themselves and she said she had been the local officer for some time and knew Masters from brief visits in the past. She confirmed he was an elderly gentleman who had been active in the community for many years mainly as a local councillor and also an organiser for a group known as U3A. Recently he had resigned from both organisations sighting ongoing medical conditions as the reason. Claire was aware he had suffered from some form of internal problems that had caused him to collapse on two occasions.

Explaining very briefly about the murder of George Armstrong, John told her that enquires had led to Peter Masters, and he needed to ask a few questions without alarming him in any way. She had read, like most of her colleagues, the newspaper reports and seen television news items about the murder and the subsequent arrest of Munroe.

"I thought you had already charged a woman with the murder. How do you come to be here?"

"It's a bit complicated, but between us it's possible she didn't do it and Mr Masters may have succumbed to a similar poison."

Claire considered the remark and asked that due to his age and frailty, and in order not to worry or distress Mr Masters unduly, that no reference should be made about sudden death. John acceded it was probably wiser not to tell him that he was working on a murder enquiry at all, and he would be vague if questioned as to where he was based.

They both left the vehicle and walked up the gravelled drive towards the front door. On the tile hung frontage of the house towards the apex of the roof, John saw a burglar alarm box. Looking at the one tree in the front garden, he saw about twenty feet up nearly hidden in the lower branches, a bird box. They knocked on the door which was opened within seconds.

A small insignificant man looking older than his eighty-three years dressed in a dark suit which was a bit too big for his frame, stood there. His skin was sallow and loose with no fat to stop it drooping, especially under his chin and his neck. The shirt was clean and although he wore a tie, it was too big around the neck. Grey sunken eyes that had once been clear were now dulled and practically lifeless. White flecks of hair were combed back above his ears as though stuck down with some old fashioned gel. John instantly saw the similarities with George.

Masters smiled engagingly acknowledging Claire as a casual acquaintance, and John introduced himself before both were invited inside. The house was well kept and maintained, and dust was at a minimum. In the hall were small pieces of furniture which had all the hallmarks of being antiques. Entering the lounge, John saw two three-seater settees and five individual upholstered chairs scattered about the room and more furniture of unknown provenance. Peter Masters invited them to sit wherever they felt comfortable which John considered was a little test from a clever and shrewd person. Picking one of the settees, John was glad to see Masters take the other. Claire joined John.

Both engaged with Mr Masters and exchanged pleasantries about the weather and location of nearby shops before he asked how he could help.

Getting quickly around to the fact he was aware that Masters had collapsed a couple of times, John said, "I'd like if I may to ask some questions and record your information. What I ask may seem trivial but it may help others should they find themselves in a similar predicament to yourself."

"I'm happy to help in any way I can. I consider it part of my obligation to my fellow man to assist in any way possible."

"Your answers may assist others who need the help of the emergency services. Can you please tell me if you have any relatives?"

"I am aware of only one living relative, and she is a cousin who lives on the South Island of New Zealand. It is possible that there may be others. I have never actually had time to conduct proper research into my ancestry."

"I have been told by Claire that you were an energetic member of the local council and chairman of the U3A. As a result, you were actively mobile in and around this area of Sussex. Your collapse has apparently forced your resignation from both. Do you consider yourself still as mobile, or are you now housebound?"

Masters paused as he looked at John and his eyes moistened.

"I always considered myself independent and with the ability to get around unassisted. Now, as you succinctly put it, I feel I should remain housebound in order that, should I collapse again, I will be somewhere that will not place too much of a burden on anyone. I'm saying, I will probably die, and I would prefer it to be here."

Now John paused. Claire stepped in, "I'm sure that won't happen."

John continued, "Do you have any form of help: carers for instance?"

"I do. Some obnoxious woman from the Social Services visits once a week. She told me it was a free service that the council provides. I expected to pay towards it, but I have been assured it's free. News to me."

"What does she do for you?"

"She normally cleans the toilets in the house and the bathroom if she feels up to it. More often than not, she just sits and chats or makes one of her bizarre cups of tea."

"I never asked: what's her name?"

"Sally."

"When did she first approach you?"

"Strange really: she was conducting a survey in the area to make sure that the Social had everyone's details on record if they were over eighty. It was the day before I first collapsed. She visited me when I got home from hospital and insisted that the Social Services should monitor me weekly. Unfortunately for me, she was assigned as my carer. Is it apparent I am not enamoured by this woman?"

"Have you thought of acquiring a 'lifeline' system?"

"Claire has recommended that I should get one," and he nodded in Claire's direction, "but Sally told me that they weren't much use as most people didn't like wearing them."

"Moving onto security, I notice you have a burglar alarm. Can you tell me; do you have panic alarms?"

"Yes. A few. One in each of the three bedrooms, one in the hall and one in here by the phone."

"Who services your alarm?"

"To be honest, I can't remember but I could find out from the service paperwork. It's done annually."

Masters was completely at ease answering all and every question that John put, but said his voice was going because he was talking so much, and asked Claire if she would be good enough to make him a coffee. He told her where the kitchen was at the end of the hall and where all the paraphernalia could be found. Both officers also accepted the offer of coffee, and Claire left to complete the task.

As the door shut behind her and before John could ask any more questions, Masters said, "I know you're a Policeman. The questions you are asking are relevant to something you are dealing with and that is obvious to me. They have no bearing on helping others who may be quote, 'in a similar situation as me.' Please answer me this. Am I in danger?"

Without hesitation, "Yes."

"How can I negate it?"

"Do not talk to Sally or anyone at social services or to the alarm engineer without first calling me. If you can afford it, have a few weeks' respite care somewhere away from here."

He thought for a while and decided where he was thinking he may go, and then they exchanged details.

John said, "Would you have any objections if I arranged for an alarm engineer to visit and test your system. Sussex Police would of course pay any charges?"

"If it would assist in any way, I have no objections. I'm here every day."

"You never know. You may be back out and about as a councillor before you know it."

"In that case, what else do you need?" John spoke quickly and Masters continued to be as frank and co-operative as he could be and it soon became clear to John what was happening to Masters, and what had probably been lined up for Armstrong.

90

Monday 13th June 2011
to
Tuesday 14th June 2011

As the day wore on, Simon lay in his pit half dozing, trying not to move as the sun bore down on the tarpaulin warming him to the extent that beads of sweat began gathering on his forehead. Vibration from the phone now in his pocket forced him to move his right hand as he searched for it and then clamped it to his ear. John was talking, asking how things were going, and how Alison was holding up. Simon was concise but thorough as he explained the night's activities and the morning visit from the two Russians. He requested that John update Graham and find out if Alison could be fully included in the loop.

Replacing his phone, he started to settle down when he noticed the sun glint off something by the hedgerow near the rubble bridge. Through the binoculars, he searched the undergrowth and brush and thought he saw movement but couldn't be certain. Suddenly his attention was lured back to the wattle gate as it was pushed briskly aside by the front of the bronze BMW as it cleared the rubble bridge. Was that what had drawn his eye? He wasn't sure. The occupants he thought, were too lazy to even get out and have one of them hold it open for the car that would be terribly scratched by the briars and scrub.

Revving more than necessary, which produced excessive engine and exhaust noise, the BMW continued recklessly towards the barn along the track throwing up a small dust cloud in its wake. Arriving just prior to the twigs with the cotton, it slithered loudly to a halt. Both occupants, the two original Lithuanian kidnappers, who had been inside the car got out and slammed the doors excessively noisily behind them. Chatting amicably, one moved a twig and then they both stood by the car lighting, and then smoking, cigarettes.

Simon knew they were a diversion.

The little man was setting his trap. It had taken him a day to arrange which was a day too long. The cameras had been placed in their respective positions to be found. Once discovered they were easily avoided. The one in the field would have had two main purposes. If found, it would let the little man know by the timing being out. More importantly, it would have conveyed the fact that whoever had found it was no slouch. As a rider, it may also have made the finder more confident and blasé leading to a serious blunder.

Simon knew there had been too many coincidences. The chocolate. A possible footprint somewhere. The camera's timer being wrong. It would have worried him too and he would have taken steps. The puffa jacket had only been used to conceal the little man's binoculars. Taking them out of the jacket in full view had been the little Russian's mistake. The time he had spent in the outhouse and the barn had been used to scan the area without being observed himself. Something Simon would have considered if he had been in the opposing position.

He turned his attention back to the hedgerow and saw movement at its base. Someone was crawling along on their stomach dressed completely in dark clothing but wearing a wristwatch that caught and reflected the sun. Whoever it was did not realise their presence was being announced by the small piece of glass strapped to their wrist. Maybe the little Russian had seen him earlier: but then he would have taken instant action: perhaps he'd spotted a footprint: more likely thought Simon. Watching carefully, he saw the shape move under a large green wayward shrub and disappear. Keeping his binoculars to his eyes, focusing hard on the shrub virtually three quarters of a mile from his pit, he saw a dark shape break off a few lower branches and toss them to one side. A watcher was in place, and from his actions, was going to stay for some time.

Simon glanced towards the two stooges at the cotton trap who were getting back into the BMW. Again, slamming the doors behind them. He was more interested in the quality of the watcher than them, and had not witnessed any bag being carried as he had crawled into his hiding place under the bush. Keeping all his attention on the large innocuous unruly shrub, he could just make out the dark shape of a person's head looking out but without binoculars. This was someone new. An unknown quantity.

The BMW had reached the barn and stopped to allow the passenger to leave the vehicle carrying a polystyrene box from a Chichester cafe company. Simon checked the time: 3.30pm. It was a lot too early for an evening meal. No plate came out with him as he exited the barn, rubbing out a few, but definitely not all footprints and tyre marks before getting back into the BMW which had manoeuvred and was waiting for him by the mouth of the track. It was obvious to Simon that the watcher was to be there for a long time and the apparent removal of the tell-tale marks was therefore only a token gesture.

Once the cotton had been replaced by the passenger who was now doing all the chores, the BMW arrived at the false hedge. This time it had to be held open for the vehicle to pass through and over the rubble bridge. With a blatant glance towards the watcher under the hedge, the false gate was closed, and the BMW joined the side road, now driving normally without any over revving of the engine.

The man under the shrub, although originally in the glare of full afternoon sunshine, soon found as the evening progressed, that the temperature was dropping steadily. His lunchtime meal was acting upon him as were the several expresso coffees he had drunk. Being diuretic, they soon ensured that he had to relieve himself. Simon watched as he crawled out from under the shrub and urinated to the furthest side of the bush from the rubble bridge before crawling back into his hideout. Smiling to himself, Simon knew he carried a special bottle for such occasions so he did not have to break cover. One thing he now knew was that the watcher was not very well equipped, probably not trained and categorically not that dedicated.

As dusk turned to night, the moon casually lit the hedgerow and fields when ephemeral clouds permitted. Simon who was quite comfortable in his pit half dozing saw movement by the shrub and brought his binoculars to bear. He'd changed them to night vision earlier by the flick of a switch, and could see the bush and surrounds clearly, but in a ghostly green hue. The figure of a man had broken the cover of the concealing shrub: not crawling, but nonchalantly walking along the track towards the barn unaware that he was visible to anyone with night vision capabilities. At the cotton trap, he casually stepped over it, then stopped and waved at the camera on the earthen ridge before continuing to the barn. The nearer to the barn he got, the nearer he got to Simon and the clearer he became in the binoculars.

Skirting the parking area, Dimitri moved to the back of the barn and climbed over the lowest part of the broken wall. He passed in and out of Simon's view as he mooched about finally settling for a perceived position of concealment by sitting in a corner on a higher part of the wall facing the entrance. He couldn't resist a short spell at the spy hole before taking up station. The square prison holding Alison was laid out in front of him with the door to it now just out of his eye line. His back was towards Simon who had decided on his course of action. Covering the glow emitted from his mobile, and lowering himself further under his tarpaulin, he rang John.

The conversation was short, and John told him, *"Do as you think fit."*

As the call terminated, Simon saw the time displayed as just past midnight.

Crawling from his pit, he edged slowly and silently towards the barn and the back of the man. Checking through his night monocular every few yards he ensured the man did not move position. Forty minutes to cross the field, another five to establish he was still undetected. The last fifty yards were painfully slow, but Simon knew any noise could be a catalyst for him, and maybe Alison. He had to keep out of the view of the camera on the bricks as well while he dealt with the man on his perch. Ten yards from him, Simon stopped: there was a peculiar noise! Listening intently, he realised the guy was asleep, and snoring! Picking up a chunk of the broken wall that filled his hand, he moved up behind the slumbering man and struck him with it viciously on the side of his head.

Whilst asleep, Dimitri had been wedged in the corner: when struck, he was dislodged and sank to his side lying as though fallen from his roost. Simon climbed over the broken wall and raised the man's head and placed the piece of the wall he had used under it. To all intents and purposes, it may have looked to a blasé observer like the man had fallen and struck his head on the broken piece of wall which now bore a slight smear of blood. Simon doubted it would fool the little Russian, but had no reservation about his cohorts.

Balanced on another piece of the broken wall close to where Dimitri's right hand had been, was a black GSH-18 Russian handgun with the safety catch off.

91
Tuesday 14th June 2011

He'd covered the camera lens again with his hat and was inside the prison in less than five minutes. The lock was getting easier for him to pick the more often he did it. Alison was wide awake and waiting for him. She was in her bed and wearing just her brief underwear.

"You're late. I've been waiting ages."

"I had something to do before I came in here."

She shuffled her feet over to one side. As he sat on her bed, she hugged him.

"How much longer have I got to stay here? I'm going mad."

"There's been a little problem" and he told her how he had been engaged during the day. "The man who was watching came to the barn and was sitting on the wall. I had to wait until he fell asleep and then I knocked him out by tapping him on the head with a bit of a brick. He will be out for some time."

"I'm going to cop it in the morning. I can't take too much more."

"I'll keep an eye on you. You'll be fine. Trust me."

"I actually do" and she held him tighter.

They chatted on and off for over an hour, and occasionally, Alison, who had hung onto his hand since he'd entered, pulled him to hug her which he willingly complied with.

As he was about to leave, she told him, "You smell a bit you know."

"So would you if you lay in a ditch for getting on 24 hours."

"By the way: where's my chocolate?"

"I couldn't find a shop in my ditch: sorry."

"I've got a couple of cold chicken wraps if you want?"

Simon grabbed one and crammed it into his mouth whole.

Then swallowing it said, "I've got this if you're interested?" and took out of a pocket a large flapjack.

"You can be a right bastard at times. Give."

He passed it to her and told her, "No crumbs on the bed and I'll take the wrapper" and held out his hand. Once the wrapper was off and in his pocket, he stood to leave and she practically jumped out of the bed and kissed him.

"Look after me."

He made his way back to his small dug out pit, clearing away footmarks that he had left on his sluggish journey towards the barn. Recovered all his gear and putting it into his bag, he made a final thorough search ensuring nothing of his was left. Then with his spade, he replaced all the moved soil and turves back to their original positions before checking that everything was as it was prior to his arrival. It looked alright in the moonlight, but he knew a person would find it if he looked closely enough and knew what to look for. Now he had to move further away just in case.

Traversing in an arc, he came across an electricity pylon that he'd seen the day before. There was rough ground around the base and a small foot track leading away from it and the barn. He followed the track for about twenty-five yards and then went into the field just prior to one full of yellow topped mustard. Digging into a large ridge, he carefully placed the removed soil further along it. Reversing his tarpaulin, he brushed it as clean as he could with his hands and then covered it in as much mud as he could manage to get to stick before crawling under it. His view through the binoculars was good even at the further distance. Settling down for a few hours' sleep, he knew he was going to have to be alert from early morning.

The starlings woke him as they sat on the power lines at the pylon, seemingly chatting to each other as loudly as possible. There was a soft red glow in the sky and a thin mist sitting a few inches from the ground. He was warm enough and aware the sun's summer rays would soon burn it off with any residual dew. Putting his binoculars to day time viewing, he could see the barn from a different angle: still the back and one side but not so much to the front of it. There was a restricted view of the parking area at the front, which he considered was sufficient.

It was 8.45am when the BMW came bouncing over the rubble bridge and pushed the gate open with the bonnet. The abrasive damage caused, apparently, was of no concern to the occupants who only stopped on arrival at the cotton trap. One of the brothers alighted from the passenger seat and went to the cotton trap first and then back to the camera uncovering the monitor. His brother sat in the driver's seat smoking a Turkish cigarette. Crouching down on his haunches, he had no problem staying in such a position as he watched the night's activities unfold on the monitor. When he reached the part where Dimitri had waved at the camera, he called his brother over to watch it as well.

They both laughed.

Both men continued to watch the remainder of the tape without taking their eyes from the monitor until they completed the night's recordings, and then reset it. Getting back into the car, they resumed their journey towards the barn and then out of Simon's view. He knew it wouldn't be long before they found the body where he'd left it at the back of the barn. One brother had gone to the outhouse to check the generator and other equipment there, and the other had entered the barn.

Even at the distance he was: Simon heard the yell.

"Dimitri."

Alison heard it as well, and it filled her with dread and fear of what was to come. All the starlings heard it, and the chatter stopped for ten seconds before they decided it was not worth taking to the sky for. The brother in the outhouse heard it and knew something was badly amiss. He ran to his sibling's side. Both men stood stock still and gawked at the cold corpse on the ground not wanting to touch it. Thirty seconds later, they were on the phone and it wasn't for an ambulance.

92
Tuesday 14th June 2011

The Saab drove over the rubble bridge and stopped allowing Petrovski out. Simon watched from over a mile away as he started to systematically search the hedgerow to the right of the bridge. He could see a long machete in one hand and a small item in the other which Simon knew must be a gun. Petrovski was being thorough this time, slashing at bushes with the machete when he couldn't see right in to them. Already the Saab had disappeared from view at the front of the barn, and Simon expected a full search was about to take place.

The two Lithuanians walked rapidly into view from the front of the barn and down the track towards the rubble bridge and started to search the hedgerow to the left of it. They were being thorough, but a lot more cautious than Petrovski as they moved along. Through the binoculars, Simon watched the smaller Russian walk casually down the track to the camera and monitor. He watched the complete footage as though not believing what he had obviously been told. His eyes never left the screen. At the conclusion, he lifted the monitoring kit and camera onto the side of the track. Grigoriev knew that if anyone was responsible for the corpse in the barn, they knew how to avoid the cameras and it was now pointless.

Ambling slowly back towards the barn, the little Russian could not help himself from scrutinising the fields either side of the track for any footprints, or tell-tale marks. Thinking it through as he walked, he could not comprehend that if someone could avoid the cotton trap, both cameras, 'neutralise' a guard, then they must have been able to enter the prison. If they could do that, why hadn't they rescued the girl? Why hadn't they picked up the gun which was in an obvious position? Perhaps he was being paranoid and there was no one and that's why the cameras hadn't seen anyone. His placed guard could have dozed off and fallen banging his head. Lots of coincidences and he hated coincidences.

Turning towards the hedgerows, he whistled to attract the attention of the Lithuanians and Petrovski, and waved them back to the barn. Petrovski was reluctant but obedient, and the other two could not have been more grateful. All eventually disappeared from Simon's view as they gathered outside the barn by the cars. The small Russian knew what had to be done, and soon Petrovski walked into view at the back of the barn carrying the corpse over his shoulder, followed by the two Lithuanians. A burial party which was heading for the drainage ditch vacated by Simon. It was the obvious place to put a body.

Alison was waiting for the response to the plaintive cry to Dimitri and it came with the soft words.

"Put the hood on."

"I'm hungry. I need food."

"Put the hood on."

She did, and she heard the door as it was opened. A strong hand grasped her neck, and she instinctively grabbed it with both her hands in an effort to release the pressure. The chain of the handcuff hanging from her wrist.

"Who was here?"

"What do you mean?"

Now no longer a slap. The clenched fist that hit her on the side of the face caused her to cry out in pain.

"No one was here. Don't hit me."

Her fingers on her left hand were enclosed in a palm and slowly squeezed together increasing in pain. Alison screamed in agony as her thumb was slowly and deliberately dislocated.

"Please don't hurt me, no one is here" and she started to cry and collapsed to the floor, her dropping weight freeing her hand and neck.

The stamp of the foot on her knee and the kick to her ribs was an angry gratuitous parting gesture before she heard the door slam shut. She lay still on the floor unable to reach or get onto the bed, or even take off the hood.

Although he couldn't see, Simon knew that Alison was going to be questioned and not politely. He knew that he could not stop it and hoped she could withstand the pain that was being inflicted. In his new pit, he heard the muffled screams and had to listen to them. It was clear that the little Russian was the interrogator and leader of the group and Simon resolved, come the right time, that he would suffer as much.

93

Tuesday 14th June 2011

John had pondered how he could explain his find at the industrial estate as he drove back from his meeting in Angmering. He could not disclose the bug he had been fortunate enough to have planted on the van. Having got around how he had come across Masters, another coincidence would probably raise the eyebrows of the sceptical. It was still the only solution he could come up with. Looked at logically from his point of view, the vans probity had been discovered not originally via the bug or 'trembler', but by observation and the initial manipulation of a toffee hammer and good investigative skills. Some lawyers he thought, may conclude it was an act of criminal damage and question why he did not apprehend the suspect there and then. He could answer them albeit in a roundabout sort of way.

Sitting in his parked car amongst the debris of previous seasons and the prevailing winds, John drew his thoughts together. For just short of ten minutes he sat there seemingly staring into space. An officer that knew him walked past on his way to his own vehicle and waved. Getting no response, he shook his head and walked on. Eventually John stirred and entered the station and climbed the stairs. In the office, he briefed Murray and Paul while Doreen, who was making his coffee, listened in about the interview with Masters. They all agreed, including Doreen who was now becoming more involved, that he had to move out of his house as soon as possible and if necessary at Police expense. All concurred that the alarm engineer should visit in company with Jimmy at his earliest convenience to establish whether the panic alarms had been disabled. Paul had no doubt that should finance be required, Prodow would sanction it.

Sipping his coffee, John said, "Murray, I know you told me to go straight to Angmering. I didn't."

"See Murray. That's what I mean. You tell them to do something and they totally disregard you."

"I went to Birdham to make 100% certain I had got you the right address and details for the warrant."

Murray said, "So your saying you didn't believe the details on the PNC?"

"They have been wrong in the past as we all know."

Paul said, "Can't say that I do. Where's this going?"

"On the way back as I was heading off to Angmering, I was driving past the first industrial unit just North of Birdham on Main Road and got caught behind a bus pulling out of a bus stop. I happened to glance in and saw the van inside one of the units. No 4."

Murray said, "Did you get the name of the unit?"

"I couldn't see one anywhere."

Doreen started to hit the keys on her keyboard and within seconds had Google maps showing Birdham in street view. They crowded round her computer as the map scrolled North along Main Road.

"Stop. That's it." The image showed the entrance to the industrial unit.

Murray said to Paul, "I'm popping down to my computer. I think I can identify it from one of the Sussex mapping systems I have access to."

He rushed out of the room. Within five minutes he was back with the full address. Doreen began typing out the information at Paul's dictation for a warrant. She added the full postal address as Murray told her. Paul already had one typed up warrant and information for the home address, he now added the second. All that was required now was Prodow's authority to seek a magistrate and apply formally for the granting of the two warrants. Never a predetermined postulation.

Paul was getting on well with Murray who was a quick and enthusiastic learner. Between them, they'd demolished half a jar of coffee with Doreen, and agreed a modern coffee machine that made a mug at the touch of a button would be a better option than a kettle. None believed that they would get away with it though. Paul called Prodow and confirmed his afternoon visit to the office and was told Groves would also be there. He informed Prodow that a warrant was already prepared for the house, but they needed to apply for another for a workshop on the industrial unit.

Prodow said, "Get Jimmy up to speed and you can brief me later. I'd like him to make the application. We'll get there earlier. Say 3.30pm and Paul?"

"Yes?"

"I won't be late."

Murray who had skimmed the working copy of the file, and was reasonably au fait with it, had come to the undemanding conclusion that all the evidence pointing to Munroe was circumstantial and insufficient to gain a conviction. Now they all poured over the bank statements that John had obtained from Masters and it was all there, literally in black and white, as to the goings on. Monies had been taken via cash that Masters had not seen or noticed as he had given up checking his statements after his first collapse. For some reason, which the Doctors were unable to diagnose, his vision had been affected, and letters and figures seemed a tad blurred.

Jimmy got back to the office from yet another visit to the laboratory and was quickly told of the Masters interview and the documents to be appended to the exhibits. He'd soon added them to the growing inventory in his book. Then during a brief discussion about Masters inability to read figures clearly Jimmy instantly explained a side effect of one of the poisons was the disruption of the optic nerves. His knowledge of the various poisons was becoming second to none. When Paul informed him that Prodow wanted him to obtain the warrants, he considered it the greatest compliment and endorsement as to his ability. He felt an inch or two taller.

Everyone in the office was starting to feel positive.

Prodow entered the office at exactly 3.30pm followed closely on his heels by Groves. Whiles was at the desk with his back to the wall facing the door and his eyes closed: not due to an evening out, but sheer tiredness. Paul moved for Prodow, and Groves headed for an empty seat catching his foot in the telephone cable yanking one of the phones off Paul's desk.

Prodow in true hypocrite's manner said, "You need to look where you're going" as Paul replaced it.

Coffee was taken by all, including Groves, without protest, and Paul introduced Murray to him.

"Right. Let's crack on. Who's going to brief me today?"

Paul said, "Murray can do it" which confused Groves more than ever. He had learnt his lessons over the previous days that he'd do best by keeping his mouth shut. Looking for, but not seeing Alison in the office, he nearly blurted a question out as to why she wasn't there. Then he stopped himself as no one else seemed to be missing her. Murray was an old hand at it, so his briefing for Prodow was clear, concise and full of detail. Groves had missed a few meetings due to other commitments, so he listened carefully as he would have done when an active DS. He felt as though he was dropping back into the mix when he concentrated on the case and not the officers themselves.

At the end of the briefing, Prodow sat still with his hands together and fingers just touching his lips as if in prayer. Murray was a chin stroker, and sat gently rubbing it with his right hand. John sat with his eyes closed and Jimmy scrutinised the small crack that ran from the top of the door jamb towards the ceiling. Groves was thinking and looking into the middle distance while Doreen looked at each person in turn.

For a full five minutes there was silence, and then Groves said, "For the love of God. If we know of one person, how many more could there be?"

Murray added as if a post script, "It looks like something went wrong with Armstrong though. His bank statements that we have do not show the same as Masters."

Prodow said, "I agree with you Mr Groves. How many more could there be? Now you are up to speed, how do you think we should proceed?" It was more a question of hope that something new could be brought to the table that had not yet been considered. Prodow did not hold out much expectation though.

Everyone was surprised when Groves responded as a good DS should.

"Right then. I'll bring the full team back together for the morning at 5am here. We'll split them into two teams and hit the house and workshop at 6.30am. Paul can lead the team at the house and Murray can lead the team at the workshop. Doreen: If you can get in for 6.30am please and man the office with Jimmy. There will have to be a deputy exhibits officer at each location and they will acquaint Jimmy with what is found. He will co-ordinate all the exhibits. John will attend the location of the van to confirm it's the right vehicle. You Sir, and I will be on hand from 5am and will be at one or other of the locations as and if needed. Interview teams can be decided when we know how many suspects we have."

Prodow looked at Groves in a new light and as if to endorse what he had said, "Any question?"

Paul said, "None. That's what we anticipated and we will be ready."

"Good. Crack on." Prodow scribbled quickly in his murder book. It was filling a lot more rapidly lately.

Paul and Murray had drawn up the two teams and set about phoning everyone and Doreen sent backup e-mails.

"Oscar and I need to speak about other issues, and I may need him elsewhere."

John didn't bother to open his eyes, he just nodded. Groves didn't even give him a second thought.

John and Prodow sat together in Murray's office with the door closed. Prodow questioned him as to how he came to be in Barnham on the evening he first saw the van. John explained how everyone that went in the conservatory end of the front room had a feeling that they were being watched, and he told of spotting the bird box with the wire at the back. Not being sure is why he went there for two nights. They agreed it had to be divulged and that the following of the van was not a problem as they thought the index number was sufficient to identify the vehicle's owners. It justified any loss of the vehicle. How were they to know it was on false plates? John didn't mention his bug.

John went on to explain how he had watched the house in Birdham waiting to check the rear of the van and was able with a lot of luck to follow the vehicle to Angmering and locate Masters. A bird box with identical fittings to Armstrong's was identified in the only garden tree. All the rest fitted together with John telling him that he went to have another look at the house, and saw the van in the workshop by chance.

Prodow looked at him quizzically and said, "You sure you can explain that all in court if you have to?"

"Yes. I was lucky."

"You're telling me!"

94

Wednesday 15th June 2011

5am saw an assortment of twenty-two officers, made up of detectives, uniform PC's, and two SOCO's (Scenes of Crime Officers). They were gathered in the first-floor conference cum briefing room, some still trying to get the sleep from their eyes, others full of beans. All were dressed casually mainly in old jeans and top in anticipation of getting dirty during the searches. The noise they were making as they nattered amongst themselves was amplified due to the time of day and no extraneous noises from outside. They had all worked at some time on the murder enquiry and most were surprised to have been recalled to it, even for one day. Those from Brighton who had probably risen from their beds at 3am in order to be sure of arrival at 5 could tolerate one early start. More local officers had probably not set their alarms much before 4.15.

Prodow and Groves entered the room dead on 5am. Instant silence! They could have heard a pin drop. Not one of the officers had expected them before 5.15am. Some looked around and others casually glanced at the wall clock.

"OK folks, thanks for coming at such short notice. I'll keep this brief. As you know, we charged Munroe and the evidence was a bit weak. There have been some unexpected developments which lead me to believe she may be innocent. Those same enquiries have produced two very strong contenders for the crime. Mr Groves will be handing out a briefing sheet to each of you at the conclusion of my résumé. It gives full names and description of each person, and the addresses."

He paused to clear his throat. Not one eye left him.

"We all know Armstrong was poisoned with a concoction of unusual substances. Details of which are also on the briefing sheet. Therefore, gloves are to be worn and I would recommend you do not lick your fingers or put them near any open wound. Do not drink anything from the premises and that includes water. We have a medic with us who will ensure any wound can be appropriately covered. It has also been arranged for a paramedic to be on standby between the two premises."

Some looked at nicks on their fingers and other little cuts visible on their anatomy. "I want any liquids seized that are out of place. The SOCOs will advise you on this. I want all computer equipment seized and that especially includes any form of media. Are we all clear so far?"

There was no dissent.

"Good."

Prodow resumed, "Each team will go in at 6.30am and the house will be led by Paul and Murray will lead at the workshop. Stand up Murray so everyone can see who you are."

Murray stood for several seconds before regaining his seat.

"Myself and Mr Groves will be floating between both searches, but as I know most of you and I have complete confidence in you all, I will be having breakfast while you are crawling about getting dirty. I know you will appreciate that I have to keep my stamina up."

A titter ran around the room.

"Any questions before you leave?"

One wag said, "Basically anything that looks wrong."

"You got it."

Groves handed a briefing sheet to each person as they joined their prearranged team.

Jimmy, who had made the appointment the previous evening with the Chairman of the Bench (of Magistrates) at his large house in Boxgrove, had enjoyed a convivial sherry as he expounded his reasons that the warrants should be granted. The Magistrate acceded to Jimmy's request and after signing them proposed the toast, "To an efficacious conclusion."

Raising his nearly empty schooner, Jimmy drank to it, although he wasn't quite sure what it meant.

Now he handed the signed relevant warrants to Paul and Murray, as each gave a further group briefing to their teams and then all descended the stairs and to their allotted vehicles.

Came the appointed time, and Murray led a small convoy of vehicles as he entered the industrial unit through the wedged open front gate and up to the workshop entrance. Paul led a similar small cavalcade of assorted vehicles into the drive of the large house in Birdham.

Calling Murray by radio, he let him know that the van was not there and Murray declared there was no sign of it at the workshops. John was sitting in the position he had been in previously when he had watched the house, and hearing the radio, turned on his Sat Nav. The van was on the move and in the backstreets of Chichester in the general direction of the industrial unit.

John took off with spinning tyres to get in a position between the van and the unit. He got to half way and stopped in a pull-in for a bus stop and waited. Murray's team were in the process of forcing an entry into the workshop. As soon as he saw the van, he radioed Murray and told him that the van had just passed him on a direction towards the industrial estate.

Instantly Murray called to his team, "Get the vehicles out of sight, the van is on its way here."

People ran to their cars and drove to the rear of the other units, and there they waited. Within minutes the van drove in unhindered through the open gate and then reversed up to the workshop. Gary jumped out and opened the roller type door. A DC watched from his hiding place and waited patiently until the door was completely open before giving the signal. That's when the officers led by Murray drove round to the front blocking the van in.

Gary Simpson saw them coming and knew exactly who they were without being told, and ran inside the workshop hotly pursued, now on foot, by Murray and a couple of the officers from the first vehicle. He had set the door to close behind him but the failsafe mechanism which touched one of his pursuers stopped it still half open. They were all shouting who they were, which was really quite pointless, and called on him to stop. Inside the workshop it was gloomy with the weak rays of the rising morning sun entering via the half open door. Officers who had chased him in were struggling to see in the murky light towards the rear of the unit.

Slowly as their eyes adjusted they could make out benches along one of the sides and across the back of the workshop which were full of antique and modern tools. Electronic equipment and shelves of VHS tapes, CDs and DVDs lined the other side. He'd disappeared: somewhere near what looked like the main workbench for the computer side. Murray went to one end of the bench and an officer moved towards the other side.

Gary burst out from beneath the bench with an antique half inch wooden handled chisel in his hand which he rammed hard into Murray's stomach and then withdrew it ready for use against others.

Murray went down.

Two officers grabbed for Gary Simpson's arm but couldn't hang on as the chisel was swung about and thrust at them in upward stabbing motions. They dodged and danced and an officer backed off with a gash on his face. Others moved forward and a can of pepper spray was discharged fully into Simpson's eyes and nose with no discernible effect. Some of the officers had extended their batons and advanced cautiously towards him. One officer was already calling for an ambulance as he stood in a protective stance above Murray. Three officers rushed forward striking Simpson as hard as they could on the shoulder and upper body. The chisel slipped slightly from his hand, but was recovered quickly and waved menacingly at any advancing officer.

Prodow ran puffing into the workshop having abandoned his car somewhere in the middle of the units. Groves who had been in the car with him, ran in a few seconds later. Prodow moved to where Murray was on the ground holding his stomach and knew it was serious.

Groves approached the dancing adversaries and told all the officers to move back.

"One chance Gary. Put it down now."

Gary Simpson looked at him in shock that one person might threaten him. Then he saw the four-foot piece of metal rod that was from the front of his garage that Groves now had in his hand. If he was hit with that, he knew it would hurt and he would not be able to use his small chisel against it.

He dropped the chisel.

"Now, get on the floor, on your belly, and with your hands behind your back."

95

Wednesday 15th June 2011

The paramedic who had been sitting in his marked car with the engine running was there within two minutes and did not like what he saw. The larger ambulance arrived quickly due to the hour of the day and the camaraderie emergency service personnel had for one another. Murray was stabilised by them all as they chatted over him. Still conscious, the pain was excruciating and getting worse. Murray was finding it hard to breath. Desperately, he wanted to curl into a ball because his body was telling him it would be best. The medics were insistent he tried to lay flat and he wanted to do what they said.

No jokes: laughter would do him damage. Paramedics from the ambulance conferred with their colleague and called for the helicopter. They wanted Murray taken to Southampton where there was a specialist working. St Richard's, although nearer did not have a surgeon available at that time of day.

Shortly after, a helicopter was hovering over the unit and the cars were speedily moved so it could land. A woman of world weary experience wearing a red coat with the word 'Doctor' emblazoned across the back was first out. An officer led her into the unit where the paramedics were starting to struggle. Murray had passed out. A small pool of dark blood was already seeping from under him as they tried to stem it's tide. She dropped her bag next to Murray as she knelt beside him. All his clothing had been cut open showing a small puncture wound in his abdomen, but where the chisel had been withdrawn, it had pulled bits of intestine out of the small hole. What other internal injuries he had they could only guess at. One of the paramedics was holding a drip which had been inserted as they set about stabilising Murray and giving strong pain relief in preparation for his flight.

Both the Doctor and the paramedics were talking to each other in what most of the listening officers thought was probably a foreign language. Gary Simpson was sitting on a work stool, handcuffed, watching the proceedings and being guarded by three of the biggest officers as they waited for a marked Police van from Chichester. On its arrival, he was escorted to the custody centre by the three officers and two additional uniform officers. When the Doctor and paramedics were satisfied with their temporary handiwork, Murray was lifted onto a stretcher by all the medical personnel and loaded into the helicopter, which was gone as soon as the Doctor was helped back on board by the pilot. Prodow and Groves went back to their car and agreed Groves should go to Murray's side at Southampton Hospital as soon as he could.

They started the search of the unit at 7.25am after the helicopter had left, and kept the temporary exhibits officer busy as they seized and listed all the VHS tapes, CDs and DVDs. Prodow had taken on the mantel of team leader in Murray's absence and watched all the media being 'bagged up' with growing foreboding. Due to the quantity, he could work out it couldn't all relate to Armstrong and Masters.

How many others? This was starting to turn into a nightmare! He knew the CC (Chief Constable) would have to be told and he was going to have to hold some of the officers back to conduct more enquiries. The CC he knew, would probably be more concerned about Murray. He could not retire so soon now. Then it started to drizzle.

'Bollocks'.

A young uniformed officer reluctantly approached him. He'd never engaged in conversation with such a senior officer before, other than his Dad. How to start.

"Excuse me sir." A slight tremble in his voice.

"What?"

Nervously he pressed on.

"Murray deputed me to search the van if it was present here at the briefing this morning."

"Well, get on and do it."

"No sir, I mean I have searched it."

"Then I suggest you go and help the exhibits officer."

"No sir. I do not seem to have made myself clear."

Prodow glared at him. "Spit it out."

"I've found a few items."

"Go on?"

"There's a bird box with a small camera in it hidden under a toolbox, and a set of index plates hidden in a lid of another equipment box."

For a few seconds, Prodow glared at him.

"Show me."

They both walked to the van and the young PC Robertson pointed out the index plates and where he had found them hidden. Then pulling a fixed tool box away from where it had been mounted, he showed Prodow a previously hidden compartment which housed a birdbox.

"I haven't touched either of them sir."

"Why did Murray depute you to search the van?"

"I think he knows I am interested in going on traffic sir."

"When you get back to the office, give Paul your name and contact details."

"Have I done something wrong sir?"

"No. Any other vehicles that ever need searching: you're going to be called first. I don't know how you found these, but Murray had justifiable faith in you. Well done son."

96
Wednesday 15th June 2011

At the house, the search was relatively easy and the single occupier present, Sally Simpson, was being as co-operative as possible. She had permitted entry to Police knocking on her door at 6.30am and took very little interest at the proffered view of the search warrant or her copy. On being asked, she explained to the officers that the study was shared between her and her husband Gary. He had his paperwork for his business on one side and she had hers on the other. Joint paperwork could be anywhere.

The woman detective asked, "What do you both do?"

"He has an alarm company and I am a social worker at Chichester."

The officer and two others sat in the study and systematically started to go through all the paperwork. It was to take them over two hours.

In the filing systems, they found paperwork relating to Sally's previous employment as a chemist at Boots. All Gary's bills and invoices and customer particulars. Details pertaining to people under the supervision of the social services at Chichester. The detectives knew that the information should never have left the security of the local authority and was also subject to Data protection. The list of names continued to grow as more papers were unearthed. Then they came across the personal papers including individual bank statements and joint bank statements going back just over ten years. Each officer was 'bagging' and recording seized items that they considered of note. At the conclusion of the search of the study, there was a two foot high large pile of exhibit bags on the floor.

One of the officers searching the kitchen had come across a large jar in one of the cupboards under the sink that looked like the sort used by brewers. It was over half full with a clear liquid.

He called to one of his female colleagues and asked if she had any idea what it might be. Neither could decide and summoned the SOCO. Paul who was accompanying Sally about the house was called.

The officer who had found it said, "Can you please tell me what this liquid is?"

Sally looked at it and dismissively said, "That's distilled water. I buy it in bulk and use it in my iron. Tap water is really hard in this area and furs it up. Distilled water makes the iron last longer."

Both the SOCO and detective nodded slightly, and Paul moved on to another room with Sally.

Once she'd left the room, the officer said, "That's bollocks. No one would buy distilled water in bulk. Can you take a sample?"

The SOCO who often worked with the officer said, "I knew you were going to ask."

Before he did, he took several photographs of it in situ.

Sally Simpson was taken to Worthing Police Station at the end of the search of the house at 10.35am. At the workshop, the search, which had commenced a lot later than planned due to Murray's injuries being treated, concluded at 11.45am.

All the exhibits were taken to the office by the officers who had found them and handed to Jimmy who piled them high on his and the adjacent desks. Each SOCO gave him blue covered exhibit books they had completed relating to each property and went through them with him. They ensured that everything was correctly recorded and that the relevant seized item was sitting on one of the desks. It was all double checked. There could be no mistakes.

People drifted in and out of the office and visited the canteen to stock up on late breakfasts or early lunches. Prodow, who had been shocked, and pleasantly impressed, by Grove's actions and the manner in which he had resolved the situation, checked with him on Murray's progress. Then at 2pm, they all reassembled in the briefing room.

97

Wednesday 15th June 2011

Prodow started the meeting by giving them the news that Murray would be in hospital for some time as the surgeons had to operate on him to sort out his intestines and some other internal organs. A few of the squeamish squirmed at the thought. Murray's wife, who was a teacher, had been quickly found and taken to the hospital and the situation was being managed to find his two daughters and take them. Paul was setting up accommodation for them all in a top hotel at Police expense, not authorised by Prodow, but the CC himself. Then he moved on to more mundane matters of who was to conduct first basic interviews, and who was to remain on standby for any enquiries.

Jimmy had commandeered three 'hot desks' in the office and he had put all the exhibits from the house on one, the workshop on another and the van on the third. The items from the workshop being the majority, were spilling onto the 'van's' desk. He was sorting through the property seized from the house and located the small sample of liquid. This was his passport to get him back to the lab and his latest muse. John was rifling through the exhibits from the workshop and eventually discovered what he was looking for. Clearing it first with Jimmy, he took the two bags he wanted.

He interrupted Paul who was in a deep discussion with one of the interviewing officers and told him he had found the tapes. The conversation was put on hold as all three flew back down to the conference room where some of the officers on standby were sitting about chatting and nibbling snacks. Paul rudely hustled them away from the viewing equipment and John took five DVDs from the first bag and found the one marked with the relevant date, and tried to insert it into the machine. Only Paul and John were aware of what was likely on it. Paul yanked the screen down as John realised the machine was not switched on.

"Bloody technology."

The machine took a few seconds to warm up before it accepted the DVD and started to play it. An image appeared on the screen with a day and date shown in the top right corner. All those in the room saw the date on the screen and stopped their chatter, and those furthest away lifted, or dragged their chairs to a better viewing point. All saw, and recognised, a picture of Armstrong's property from a height looking down showing the front of the bungalow towards the conservatory. To the left of the screen, part of the drive leading towards, and then past the front door and onto the garage was visible as was a part view of the short path leading towards the front door. On the right of the screen and of the bungalow could be seen the paved area from the rear of the garage to the back door and the wooden shed. Everyone in the room had instantly realised the value of the tape.

John sped the playing speed up and slowed it when he saw the morning nurse and the postman. Nothing attracted their attention and it sped up again. Then he saw the green Micra approaching the bungalow along the drive and stopped the images. Everyone drew slightly closer, but no one present could make out the number plate. Paul spun round and asked one of the officers to go and get Doreen who seemed to have a way of reading the undecipherable.

She was soon at the controls of the machine going slowly backwards and forwards.

"The only letter I can make out is an 'E' which is second from the end. They all stared at the index plate and not one could get close to seeing it. Doreen played the tape at half speed at John's request.

The car stopped just at the limit of the cameras view, and a person got out wearing indistinguishable clothing and a hood pulled down over their face.

Doreen said, "That's a woman."

John said, "How on earth do you know that?"

"Look at the shoes. The way the walk is trying to be disguised. There's hair pushed up under the hood and it's sitting slightly too high at the back. The hand holding the front of the hood is using two fingers daintily where most men would probably grasp it."

The female officer in the room said, "Yeah. I see that."

All the men present accepted without question Doreen's assumption.

Slowly the tape continued as the person moved out of view and then reappeared on the right of the screen walking past the shed and to the back door and then inside without knocking or hesitating more than a couple of seconds. It seemed obvious to everyone that the person was aware of the camera and the number plate had been deliberately obscured. As the tape continued at normal speed, there were moments when a human form could be glimpsed as if a shadow in the lounge, but was unidentifiable. Then, as the person left the back door, they appeared to hesitate as though locking the door. Doreen slowed the tape again, and stopped it immediately as the person began to walk away from the camera.

"See the shoes? Look at the way that coat hangs. It looks like a man's."

A voice at the back of the assembled group shouted, "Wait" and they turned as one to look who had spoken.

The young officer, PC Robertson who had searched the van was lifting himself out of his chair, and walked to the front of the room within a few feet of the screen. He examined the image held still on the monitor

"When I was going through the van, I saw a jacket identical to that in one of the lockers."

Paul said, "I presume you brought the van in?"

He confirmed he had and said he'd go and get the coat. Doreen, who had only been distracted by the shout for the time it took her to turn to see who had uttered it was again examining the image.

"It looks like there is a little tear at the edge of the right pocket."

John and the others returned to view the screen searching for the tear on the pocket.

Paul said, "How do you see things like that?"

"Elementary. The day you lot can learn to write will stop me seeing things. So I think I'm safe."

She let the recording continue, and the person walked back past the shed bending down once. Doreen stopped the tape.

John said, "Yeah. We can all make that out. Doreen, what's written on the side?"

"Now you're just taking the micky."

Paul said, "I think it says poison."

A couple of others in the room added their jibes.

"Not to be taken orally."

"Wash hands after use."

"Keep away from children."

Doreen said, "Anymore and I'm leaving" which provoked raucous laughter.

The tape continued and the person seemed to rush back and into the car, turn it round and start back down the drive still holding a hand over their face. The glare of the sun did not seem so pronounced on a large screen.

Doreen stopped the tape: then let it play at normal speed, then rewound it and played it exceptionally slowly, rewound it again and played it one frame at a time, and then stopped it.

"The first letter I think is a G and the numbers at positions 3 and 4 are definitely 06."

Again, the gathered officers stared at the number plate. Some moved to the side, some stood up to look down and others sank in their chairs as if to look up. The image was the same however they looked at it. Not one other person could confirm or disprove Doreen's identification.

Paul said to John, "Problem. Munroe's number plate starts with an H and it is 08."

"Can I watch the rest?"

John told Doreen he had no objection, and she played the tape quickly and soon saw the arrival of Munroe in her green Micra with the number plate fully readable and Munroe easily identifiable. They all saw her leave her vehicle, put the poison inside the shed, knock on the back door and then leave after looking at her watch. Then the arrival of the neighbour and the emergency vehicles. The tape ran till 1.16am and finished.

Paul said, "Anyone got any comments about what we've all just seen?" All was quiet in the room.

Then Doreen pronounced, "Well. It's blatantly obvious to me that the two vehicles are different, and the person who killed him was not Munroe."

98
Wednesday 15th June 2011

John placed the tape back into its holder and into the correct exhibit bag with the four others. Then taking the fifteen DVDs out of the other bag, he searched for and found the one he was looking for using the date conveniently written on the holder by Gary Simpson. The room had been slowly filling as news of the played DVD and its content was becoming common knowledge among the officers. Putting it into the machine and pressing play brought up the image, again from a height looking down. It was, as John told the gathered audience, a view of Peter Masters' house showing part of the driveway to the left and all the parking area at the front and side. The front door was the main focus and there was colourful foliage to the right of the house which appeared quite dense. Again, visible in the top right corner of the screen ran the date and time the recording occurred.

Addressing those present, he told them that this was another premises that Gary Simpson had visited. Doreen, who was now in complete charge of the remote control, was whizzing the images through at four time's normal speed. She was quick, and stopped it to see a mid-morning delivery from the postman, and was into the afternoon before she stopped it again. Sally Simpson had driven her Ford Focus onto the drive and parked at an angle to the camera. Several in the briefing room confirmed it was her as she went to the front door.

Doreen said as if a stage whisper to Paul, "She was definitely not the person in or out of either of the Micras at Armstrong's place."

No longer than thirty minutes had elapsed before Sally left the front door, put a thumb up to the direction of the camera, got into her car and drove off.

John said, "That proves she knows about the camera."

The images started to speed up again as Doreen's gaze never left the screen, and her fingers automatically seemed to know where each button was on the remote and what they did. At 6.15pm the front door opened and Masters was frozen on the screen as the images stopped dead. Doreen manipulated the controls and enlarged the picture until the front door was filling the screen and then started again frame by frame. Masters was shown on a cordless telephone in the doorway holding on to the door jamb with his spare hand.

In the slow motion of the images, his legs seemed to slowly buckle at the knees, and he lowered himself to the floor. His hand holding the phone gently unfurled letting it fall from his grasp, and it beat him to hit the floor. He lay in a crumpled heap on the tiles of his own porch step.

Doreen held the frame frozen as they took in what they had all just seen. Then it was running again but only at double speed. Eight minutes later, a Police Officer in uniform reached Masters and an ambulance was six minutes behind. He was tenderly lifted onto a trolley, still apparently unconscious, and placed into the back of the ambulance which left the cameras view.

John said, "That's all that's relevant on this tape."

And Doreen ejected the DVD.

A general hub bub ensued in the briefing room as it started to become apparent that there was a lot more about to be uncovered in the ensuing investigations. Paul approached two of the officers and arranged that all the VHS tapes, CDs and DVDs were copied as soon as Jimmy had confirmed their provenance. Another was tasked to list every different address shown on the covers and holders of the recorded material and compile a list with Doreen. Mapping was asked for with every address where recordings had been made.

Paul looked at John and said, "There must be well over a hundred different addresses going back quite a few years. We need an urgent chat with the boss."

Everyone with a task appointed, set off with a purpose, and John, Paul and Doreen climbed the stairs back to the office. Prodow was sitting behind Paul's desk with a telephone wedged between his chin and neck like a fiddler holds his fiddle without using hands. He was scribbling on a piece of paper and talking rapidly and kept using the word 'Sir'. The three waited for him to finish. Before he put the phone down he told them the Chief Constable would be visiting at 11am the following day.

"That's a whole morning buggered up. Can't he get up earlier and be here for 8. He's got a driver for God's sake. He could sleep in the car if he's that bloody tired."

They briefed him on what they'd seen.

"I thought as much. How many do you think there may be?"

Paul said, "When Jimmy was given all the tapes, he reckoned there may be well over a hundred different addresses shown going back up to ten years."

"Fuck's sake."

John said, "The bad news is, I don't think either of them did for our George."

"Jesus Christ Oscar. Have we got any good news?"

Doreen said, "Yes. I've got a new type of coffee."

After a brief second or two of laughter, Prodow apologised to her for his bad language.

"OK. Let's try it. I've sent Bob out to Tesco's to pick up four bottles for later. It's going to be a very long night."

The young officer knocked on the door of the office.

"Don't stand on ceremony son, just walk in."

"Thank you sir. I've got the jacket you want from the van."

Prodow had not been told about the jacket and looked perplexed.

Paul said, "Let's have a look."

Doreen said as if to clarify, "I think this officer believes the jacket the murderer was wearing was identical to this one."

Paul said, "It looks the same. Shit. Look at the pocket."

He held the jacket so they could all see the pocket with the slight tear.

"How the hell did you see that Doreen?"

Prodow said, "Fill me in for Christ's sake."

Paul updated him. Within a couple of minutes Prodow was congratulating both Doreen and the young PC Robertson.

"Paul, get this guy's details. Any enquiry with a vehicle, he's your man."

John added, "Problem is, we don't think either of them did it, but that's Gary's coat. How do we explain that?"

99

Wednesday 15th June 2011

It was a very long day for Alison. She had no food and was given no water. She was on the floor for over an hour drifting in and out of consciousness. Her thumb was throbbing and hurting her badly, her side ached and she felt two teeth were loose and her cheek hurt. Although she hadn't stood up, she could feel her knee was sore and knew it would not bear any weight being put on it. With an enormous effort, she wrenched the hood off tossing it to one side and then forced herself to crawl to the toilet where she threw up. Kneeling before it, she realised she had to get up and get to the sink. Her knee had been forgotten as she was being sick but soon took over as the predominant pain.

Forcing her legs to straighten, she gingerly stood and gripped the sides of the sink for support. Sliding her hand out of the handcuff and dropping it to the floor, she no longer cared about any pretence of it still being correctly in place. Filling the sink, she let her head drop as far into the water as possible sending some splashing over the edge. It felt invigorating, and she only took her head out when she needed to take a breath. The cold water lingering on her lips tasted disgusting, but she knew she had to drink something. Two mouthfuls were all she could manage before returning to grasp the toilet.

For a person who hadn't eaten much she was shocked at the amount she expelled.

Pushing herself away from the sink she aimed at the bed and fell onto it. Sleep enveloped her within minutes and when she awoke there was a two-litre bottle of water lying by the hatch with a small bag of sweets. Still no proper food. 'Who put fucking sweets through? I need substance!'

Resolving not to cry again, she felt her two wobbly teeth and concluded they were likely to fall out. She wasn't going to hasten them. Her side ached and the only way to stop the pain was to lie on her back and remain still. From her limited knowledge of first aid, she knew she had at least one broken rib. The thumb of her left hand was at a strange angle and swollen at the base which was gradually turning a weird colour of black. Getting to a sitting position with her feet on the floor, she rose as gently as possible and picked up the water and tottered back to the bed.

Simon had watched the search and then the burial, which was not the best he'd seen, but adequate under the circumstances. The two Lithuanians had conducted a supplementary search in the drainage ditch and the area around it, and Petrovski had searched towards the pylon and the mustard field. He walked along the footpath looking into the fields but didn't leave the firm soil for the ridges and troughs in them. The mustard field attracted him like it would a bee, and he did conduct a detailed search of the first two planted rows.

They were all recalled to the barn by midday via a loud piercing whistle from Grigoriev, and Simon watched the Saab drive towards the rubble bridge with the small Russian driving and Petrovski in the passenger seat. It only stopped for Petrovski to put the camera and monitoring unit into the boot before leaving. The BMW, which didn't seem to be handling the track as well as the Saab, followed with the two Lithuanians inside. No one bothered with the twigs and cotton.

Staying put under his tarpaulin, Simon was running out of water and was out of food as well, but didn't have the additional problems that Alison was facing. He was also able to last a lot longer without either thanks to his training with the Army. Because of the way the little Russian had organised the searching of the area, Simon appreciated he was no amateur. The search may have appeared random to an untrained observer, but Simon could see he was conducting it methodically. Had the actual searchers known what they were doing, they would have soon located and identified his original 'pit' and eventually have found him. Simon knew what his own next move would be if he was in the little Russian's position, and he was worried.

He hated big savage dogs.

There was nothing for it. He gathered all his kit and packed it away. It was easier for him to disguise his present position by digging it over and dragging additional earth over it, but he knew a trained dog would identify the spot.

If the little man was worth his salt, that was what he would arrange next. His hope was that the handler would assume the dog had found a trace of some animal and move on. Forlorn hope really. Making sure he left no marks, he got on the path, and ran to the barn. Praying he had time, he saw the camera had gone from the bricks and he opened the small hatch.

"Alison."

No reply.

Louder, "Alison."

A faint reply, "Yes."

"Are you OK?"

"No."

"I'm going to call your Dad and get you some food tonight. Can you hang on?"

"If I have to. Did you leave the water and those stupid sweets?"

"No. I think it must have been the gorilla, he was the only one who I saw come anywhere near you."

"Get me something nice, I'm desperate. I'm so hungry."

"Where does it hurt?"

"Everywhere."

"I'll be with you tonight."

She couldn't be asked to reply; it was hurting to just talk. Slamming the hatch shut made her jump slightly, and Simon was gone.

There were tyre marks and footprints all over the parking area which sped up his departure. No need to cover his imprints now. Running flat out in the middle of the track with his bag on his back, he passed the broken cotton and reached the wattle covered gate. Expecting a trap, he opened the gate slightly so he could squeeze through with his butterfly knife open and in his good hand. The road was empty! Fear for Alison spurred him on as he ran as fast as he could back to his car. Tossing his bag into the boot of the Lexus, he found a 'trembler', jumped into the driver's seat and took off.

Throwing caution to the wind, he drove to the rubble bridge and stopped, blocking the road. Jumping out he scrambled into the ditch by the side of the rubble and found a small fissure and drove the 'trembler' into it. Still no one attacked him. Getting back into his car he drove away. He decided to wait till a little later in the night before visiting Alison just in case the cautious little Russian should make a surprise visit. No dog handler would still be about after midnight, so he hoped he'd be safe.

Evening meal time did not happen for Alison which was a problem. She'd thrown up several times, and the lack of quality food had only made it bile. The little Russian may have missed it deliberately to see if anyone else took her food or water.

Simon drove on to the Nuffield hospital car park where he got out of his camouflage kit. Tidying the boot of his car, he reorganised his bag. His camouflage gear stank. The clothes he wore stank. He stank. He decided to take all his gear to Alison's flat to wash. It was only the ground sheet and tarpaulin that he left in the car. Her washing machine would have given up the ghost if he tried to put them in it. The smell from them he knew would soon permeate to every corner of his car. Couldn't be helped. Locking it, he slowly jogged back cautious in case there were different eyes watching. Carefully stepping over the cotton, he went into Alison's flat. Still no attack.

Wedging a chair under the front door handle, he stripped and threw his clothes into her washing machine before heading for the shower. Longing to linger awhile under the steaming water, he was soon out and wearing a clean set of clothes. A swift check with his scanner confirmed the absence of any bugs. Barry had cleared his but Simon knew other people could have left some. Sitting on the settee with his mobile in hand he started to dial Graham's number.

Then he froze for a second before picking up his knife. A faint noise at the front door had put him on edge. It sounded like scratching. Slowly, he went to the door and quietly moved the chair out of the way and gently took hold of the handle. Not knowing what to expect, he rapidly opened it.

Hannibal walked nonchalantly into the flat.

100

Wednesday 15th June 2011
to
Thursday 16th June 2011

Simon hung up. Graham had utilised aspects of the City of London Police Force, and the unit run by an acquaintance from within GCHQ at Cheltenham. They had heard 'chatter' but it was so fast that they couldn't locate the source, other than the general areas. Birmingham and London. Both were obvious considering the threats and his information, so it was no surprise. They could only narrow the radio masts down to one of three in Birmingham. The Metropolitan Police who ran a large unit specialising in tracking and locating mobile phones via the masts were unable to assist. Ian had spent a few days living in Graham's house and exploited every bit of equipment he had or could think of. As he often sold his inventions to the Government, Graham held out more expectation that he would solve the puzzle. They were all getting nowhere fast.

He called John. They discussed options. Graham had told him he wanted to leave Alison where she was. John wasn't happy and said he would speak to Graham himself. It did not get him anywhere. Graham was adamant, she had to be left where she was for a little longer. Simon knew she was hurt but not how much. John was in his car and turned on his Sat Nav when Simon told him he had set the 'trembler'.

"It's sleeping."

"That's what I am going to do. I'll be back there tonight and I'll let Alison know what's happening."

"I'll phone you if I see any movement."

"Cheers. They are monitoring it from Kent as well."

Hannibal was not hungry when Simon put down some food.

"You little tinker, where have you been?"

The cat looked at him with unadulterated contempt. Then walked off towards Alison's bedroom. He was soon back, and appeared to glare at Simon as he walked into the spare bedroom and jumped onto the bed. Both slept soundly for six hours. On waking, he phoned Kent just to confirm there had been no movement at the 'trembler'.

"Well Hannibal. Your mistress is going to be peckish. What do you reckon she would like?"

The cat looked at him and then with an aloofness that most cats possessed, went to the food and ate it.

On leaving the flat, Simon was going to put Hannibal out, but the cat knew and looked disdainfully at him, then with a superior air, walked out unassisted. Leaving the cotton in place, Simon soon reached his Lexus, and was nearly overcome by the stink from his dirty tarpaulin. Driving with all the windows open into Chichester, he parked and walked the short distance into North and then East Street and stocked up with various items of confectionary. He would buy some hamburgers later. Sitting in his car with the windows still wide open, he watched the world go by. The bugs on Alison had long since died, but his 'trembler' was giving off a small bleep every minute. Still in sleep mode. He saw John's signal pulsing. Opening his map wider, he saw Ian and Graham were also in their vehicles. It had been a busy day for all of them.

Midnight came and went with no one crossing the rubble bridge. Wondering what the little Russian was up to was starting to drive his thoughts all over the place. The two brothers, Petrovski and the little Russian had left roughly at midday. No one had visited or checked on Alison since. He started to think the worst may have happened, but realised that he had spoken to her after they had last been there. 'What the hell is he up to?' He called John and asked him.

"God knows. It's strange. Could it be some kind of trap?"

"I'm going to see her at two whatever. I think she may be hurt badly."

"I'll go to the Royal Oak. They never get to bed much before one. It will give me time to have a wander round."

"Be careful John."

John who had imbibed a few large scotches earlier in the office drove towards Lagness. His aim now was to drive round to the rear car park, have a 'swift half' with the licensee and then mosey about as though drunk. Simple he thought until he arrived. At the front of the pub was the bronze BMW and the dark blue Audi.

Both were parked directly under the wall mounted CCTV camera which faced towards the road and probably caught some passing traffic. The conclusion that John had come to for Gary in his van to have used the ridiculously potholed, excessively long, short cut.

He kept on past. As soon as he reached a safe spot a mile further on, he called Simon.

"Their two cars are at the pub. No sign of them though. I don't believe they would have been invited for afters, but you never know."

"Can you put in a surreptitious call to your friends there?"

"I'll give it a go and call you back."

Seven minutes later, John called Simon who had moved to the car park of McDonalds in Portfield Way.

"The pub's empty and they haven't seen anyone by the cars. I don't like it. Where the hell are they?"

"John, I've got to get to her. I've looked at the map, and I think I can get in from the back."

John scrolled his Sat Nav map about and said, *"It looks like you can but it's a good two miles across fields."*

"I'm going for it."

Driving through McDonalds, he bought three burgers and a milk shake and then set off.

101
Thursday 16th June 2011

The Lexus sped to a small side road that turned into a dead end. At the end, Simon pulled onto the verge and got out. Picking out of his bag the items he needed, he reluctantly put his camouflage gear back on. He wedged the burgers and milkshake inside his coat, and set off. His monocular which he set to night mode, spent an inordinate amount of time glued to his eye.

Without it he would have twisted an ankle and never have made it. What he really needed was a full fixed head kit of night vision gear, but in its absence, the monocular had to suffice.

Simon scanned constantly watching the ground and suspecting a trap. He saw nothing untoward, and knew that the only one of the four who could probably evade him would be the little Russian. As he neared the barn, he turned the monocular to thermal imaging. Still nothing of note. The closer he got, the more cautious he became. His watch showed ten past two. He'd made fair time.

Realising if someone was concealed and had night vision capabilities, he would be seen whatever he did, he pressed on.

No one was waiting for him at the barn. With his thermal imaging, he scanned the fields around. He checked the hedgerow either side of the wattle gate. Something at the very edge of the monocular moved way over by the church. Turning to focus his attention towards the church, he thought for a second he saw the image of a human and then it disappeared. Straight away he knew that there would be someone else hidden at the other end of the road.

Now he was happy.

"John. I know where they are."

"Where?"

"One's in the church and another must be at the other end of the road. I just caught sight of the one by the church as he shifted position."

"That's two, be careful, there are four remember."

"Perhaps they are relieving each other."

"Call me with an update on Alison."

"OK."

"Stupid place to leave the cars in full view."

"Yeah. Very slapdash."

He went into the prison to find Alison awake and lying on her back in the bed. She smelt of puke, and her hair was straggly and plastered to her head in places. Her skin looked sallow and her eyes were puffy and one was colouring and would soon turn black. She didn't sit up and he could see she was in pain. Her hands clasped the water bottle.

"What did they do?"

She lisped as she whispered in reply, "I have two teeth about to fall out, and a mouthful of blood."

"Open your mouth."

"Can't."

"What else?"

"The bastard just broke my thumb. With one hand, slowly."

"Let's see."

She just held up her hand and Simon knew what the trap was. It was a clever ploy. Simon realised the thumb had been dislocated deliberately by the little Russian who knew if there was a night visitor, they would probably be able to reset it.

"Can't feel it."

"You're not going to like what I am going to tell you."

It was a horrible colour already.

"It's only dislocated. I think it was done to find out if you were being visited. If I reset it, they will know."

She looked pleadingly into his eyes.

"I can't Alison."

He knew that the longer it was left, the worse it would get and harder to fix.

"My side. I think I have broken ribs."

"May I?" and he pulled the blanket back exposing her body. She couldn't have objected even if she had wanted. Putting his hand on the bruise that had

315

already started to form, he felt gently about. His hand was warm and had a soothing effect. He could feel ribs that moved which should not have done.

"I think you have at least two broken ribs, try not to move too much."

"Really? Will I have to stop my exercises?" Looking at him, "Food?"

"I've got you a choice of hamburgers."

"Christ."

"This time of day, that's all I could get."

"I can't chew."

"I could knock you up a stew."

"Chocolate?"

He produced a couple of small bars of different flavours and the milk shake. The drink was like a nectar to her, and she held individual pieces of chocolate in her mouth and let them melt at their own pace.

"You smell."

"So do you."

She thanked him for the water, and when he looked bemused, she said, "The water bottle you put through the hatch for me, with those stupid sweets."

"I didn't put it there."

"Who did?"

Simon said, "I think I told you earlier that I thought it was Petrovski."

"I can't remember seeing you earlier."

"I was outside calling through the hatch."

She started to cry, "Why didn't you come in to see how I was?"

"I'm sorry, there were things I had to do."

"I was hurting and you had 'things to do'?"

"I should have come in. I'm sorry."

She sobbed in silence. Eventually she regained her composure and grasped his hand.

"I forgive you."

"Thanks. Where's your bag?"

"What?"

"Where's your bag?"

"Under the bed. Why?"

Simon found and opened her bag and took out what she had thought was a small button.

"This has gone flat" and he dropped a new bug into her bag.

Alison started to cry again.

"Now what have I done?"

They chatted about very little, and there were lengthy periods of silence. He held her good hand and broke off the odd bit of chocolate and put it in her mouth.

"I can't take this much longer."

"I'll call your Dad."

"Get me out Simon."

102
Thursday 16th June 2011

For most of Wednesday evening, and into the night, Jimmy, John and Paul were in the office talking tactics and Paul was jotting notes in a new pad he'd acquired specifically for the oncoming investigations. Prodow had already started a new murder book in anticipation of potential revelations. Doreen spent several hours going through the Exhibit books and looking at all the media as she completed a typed list of 212 addresses. When she'd finished, and gone through it with Paul, he put various officers' names against each address. Then she set about printing off a map displaying the area around each one. Due to the lateness of the hour and the length of time she had been working, a detective was deputed to take her home.

On walking through her front door, there was no hint of a welcome. Her Mother berated her firstly for leaving so early in the morning and disturbing her sleep in the process and then arriving home at a ridiculously late hour. With no thought or concern for her daughter's wellbeing, she informed her that her ruined hot evening meal was still in the oven, and then muttering to herself, climbed the stairs to bed four hours later than her regular time. Doreen who had hardly uttered a word, just watched her struggling up the stairs.

Prodow had returned to the office at 9ish and had agreed that the interviewing officers, six in total, should remain the same. Neither of the Simpsons had yet answered any questions put to them, which had probably been their lawyer's advice. Paul had stipulated forcefully the following morning's briefing for everyone (except the Chief Constable) was due for 8am. There would be no excuses tolerated for absence, other than Murray's. Then as everything was being finalised, Groves walked into the office. The incumbents were pleasantly surprised by his appearance and a half bottle of scotch was recovered from Doreen's desk, poured into, and then proffered, in a tea cup.

Groves willingly accepted without quibble, and downed an inch of golden liquid in one shot, and accepted a top up. An hour passed as they discussed Murray and the case. Quite openly, Groves stated he hated being a DI and having to sit behind a desk every day, and hankered for his time when he was an active DS working the streets. He confided in them in no uncertain terms that whatever he did or said was bound to upset someone, and he had become what he always detested in ranking officers: a political animal. Then he apologised profusely to Prodow, who, to an extent acceded his comments.

They all went their different ways, and were back in the office well before 8am. John and Jimmy had breakfast together in the canteen, and Paul and Doreen had made sure they were fully sustained before they left home. All four were expecting a long day. Prodow entered the office with Groves and asked if there had been any change from overnight, and was thankful when told there had been none. Then after coffee for the majority, and a cup of tea for one taken in the office, they went to the briefing room walking in at 8.15am. All those assembled expected the 8.15am entrance and most were holding or drinking from polystyrene cups.

Prodow started the meeting off, and quickly let everyone know the Chief Constable would be in the office at about 11am and it would be best if all the enquiry teams were not in the station. They all took the flagrant hint. Updating all with Murray's condition in hospital, he handed over to Paul, then sat by a window adopting his 'praying' mode. It took a fairly long time for the full briefing: but everyone present was in no doubt as to what had already been discovered relating to the Armstrong enquiry and Masters. Paul allocated each team of two their first address and told them to get their copy video footage from Jimmy.

After the main meeting, the interviewers were given additional briefings by Paul and John, and it was just after ten when they both got back into the office. Prodow and Groves were talking to Jimmy who had handed out the first ten addresses' media. Groves requested that he stay in the office as liaison with Paul, the hospital and family of Murray. Prodow wasn't sure, but seeing a subtle nod by Paul, agreed. The phone on Paul's desk burst into life, and was answered by Doreen who hung up straight away.

"The Chief Constable is on his way from the car park. That was his driver."

"Good morning. Hardly any traffic today, so got here early. Hope I'm not inconveniencing you at all?"

"Not at all Sir" was the glib lie that Prodow uttered with no sincerity.

"Well now, hello Doreen, nice to see you are still sorting out everyone's hieroglyphics. Paul: you still running the place?" Paul mumbled some incoherent reply. "Groves: how are you finding work on a major enquiry? Prefer it to a station?" But before he could respond, the Chief continued, "Looking at that lot, you must be the exhibits officer."

Jimmy was quicker than Groves, "Yes Sir. My first major job."

The Chief cut across him, "Good man. You must be Oscar. Heard a lot about you. Not all good I must say, but you can't boil an egg without cracking a few shells."

John thought it best to say nothing.

Doreen cut in and said, "Still two sugars in your coffee?" and took the kettle out.

"You sure you don't want to come and work for me?"

"No thanks. Too far to travel. I always told you, your writing is the worst in Sussex."

103
Thursday 16th June 2011

They all sat round Paul's desk with Prodow in his chair, and the Chief was brought up to date with the minimum amount of information. Prodow was always impressed how much information the CC retained and recounted at later times practically verbatim. What they told him now did not seem to tax him at all. His priority, as they all expected, was concern for Murray and his condition and what he could do to help. Concern for his staff endeared him to them. Groves gave him the latest news, and what was arranged at Southampton. The Chief's attitude was that Murray; a Sussex Police Officer should be brought back to a Sussex hospital; preferably St Richard's in Chichester. It was agreed by Prodow, but Groves was starting to assert himself, and pointed out that until all the main operations had been conducted successfully that he should not be moved from the hospital in Southampton.

The Chief, who had heard unfavourable accounts about him, listened to his argument and saw it made sense. He didn't seem as inept as others had suggested, and was not afraid to challenge a senior officer if he disagreed with him. It made a pleasant change from all the 'Yes' men at headquarters. His driver had already told him it had been Groves who had brought the prisoner, Gary Simpson, under control with a simple threat. The bit about the iron bar having been conveniently missed out. Looking at Groves with new eyes, he was amazed that a near six-foot body builder, who withstood gas to the face and blows with asps who had seriously assaulted one officer and injured another, could be brought under control by an apparently unfit DI with a simple threat.

The Chief was drinking coffee and reminiscing with Doreen about long past jobs where he had been the Officer leading enquiries. As Bruce Springsteen put it so well, 'Glory Days.' Two officers from the enquiry team, one a sweating DS, burst into the office and suffered a harsh glare from Prodow.

"Sorry to interrupt, but we got back as soon as we found out. You have got to hear this."

Paul said, "Go on?"

The DS told them the address they had been given, was just North of Chichester in the village of Lavant. They had viewed the tapes given to them by Jimmy and had seen Sally Simpson visit the premises on eleven different days which, when checked, turned out to be on Tuesdays between 2.pm and 3.pm. On two separate days, three months apart, when she exited the house via a side door, she had given a 'thumbs up' sign in the direction of the camera. On the first day she did it, an ambulance arrived five hours later, and conveyed the elderly lady occupier to hospital in Chichester.

The second time she gave the signal, nothing happened until the following day after a visit from a neighbour. When the ambulance turned up, the crew went into the house and left an hour later, with an empty ambulance. The reason being, the coroners officer had arrived. When the DS checked, he discovered that the lady had died from an ongoing unknown stomach complaint being treated by her GP. She had been advised to visit him when discharged from the hospital. A post mortem was not called for as two Doctors signed the death certificate. She had no known relatives, and had died intestate, so the inquest had been a formality.

She had been cremated, as was the custom with people with no relatives or will, and her remaining monies had gone to Her Majesty's Treasury. There was one piece of good news that they had found: one of the doctors had taken some kind of biopsy from the lady the first time she had gone to hospital and it was still in the pathology lab at St Richard's Hospital. The Chief looked shocked.

Prodow said, "Shit."

Paul said, "This is just the start" as Jimmy started to arrange for a SOCO to get the specimen.

104

Thursday 16th June 2011

Groves, Paul and John went into a huddle and decided that the interviewing teams should be acquainted with the new information, and Paul set about phoning them. Prodow and the Chief wandered out of the office together, and to the waiting Jaguar with the Chief's driver sitting in the passenger seat reading the Sun newspaper. He saw them approaching and was out in a flash and holding the back door of the car open.

"How many do you think these two have done for?"

"There's two hundred and twelve different addresses. I hope to God it's nowhere near that."

"Are we dealing here with a pair of serial killers?"

"It's starting to look like it."

"What do you think, all poisoned?"

"Certainly looks like a possibility."

"What about Armstrong?"

"Poisoned with a weird concoction. Thing is: these two probably weren't responsible."

"For fuck's sake Trevor, find out quickly what these two were up to, and who did for Armstrong. When the press get wind of this, the shit will really hit the fan" and with that he got into his car and told his driver to get to Southampton hospital as fast as he could.

Paul spoke to the team at Worthing first and informed the DS leading it of the new information. The first interview of the morning had resulted in Sally Simpson sitting next to her lawyer examining the walls of the interview room as questions were put to her which she totally ignored and did not bother to grace with an answer. She had probably been told by her lawyer that without any evidence, the Police would have to let her go within thirty-six hours at the most unless they got an extension from a court. Prodow was told this and took the phone from Paul.

He told the DS to officially arrest Sally for the murder of the lady at Lavant and then ask her specific questions only on the new information. At the conclusion he was to let the lawyer know, if possible in her presence, that she would be charged with murder and Gary was not being charged at the present time. As an afterthought, Prodow told the DS to let the lawyer know that she was being investigated for in excess of two hundred offences.

"See what you get from that" and he slammed the phone down on its plastic cradle adding another crack to the growing number.

Prodow sat back down, and Doreen put a cup of coffee in front of him.

To no one in particular, he said, "The Chief has asked me to delay my retirement till this case is put to bed, and I agreed."

Groves said, "Thank God for that. Could you imagine what would happen if I was to take over?"

They all looked at him and there was silence for a clear five seconds before they all started to laugh.

The DS leading the team interviewing Gary was faring slightly better, and told Paul that he was coming over to see Prodow. It only took him a couple of minutes as Gary was being held in the custody suite next to the station, and he would have been even quicker if he hadn't had to wait to be let out of the secure building. He headed for an empty chair, and removed the telephone from Paul's desk with the toe of his right shoe followed by a swift expletive.

Prodow said, "What's the problem?"

The Sergeant told them that Gary was admitting the two assaults on the Police and accepted he would be charged with them. When he was asked about all the tapes and both Armstrong and Masters he ignored the questions. Then, after the morning's interview, the lawyer who was acting for him, had approached the DS and told him that Gary would only speak to Mr Groves.

Prodow looked at Groves and said, "Maybe your last words have no substance. It's down to you now."

105
Thursday 16th June 2011

Groves walked back to the custody suite with the DS who on the way gave him a brief resume of what had been put to Gary, and what he'd said. Basically: nothing. The lawyer was waiting for him, and they sat down together in an interview room. What the lawyer said surprised him as assurances were requested.

"My client realises that he must accept he is guilty of the two charges and will admit them at the very first opportunity, and, he believes that he will receive a reasonably long custodial sentence. What he asks via me is that you could arrange for it to be in a maximum security prison. I must say that this is something I have never requested on a client's behalf before and I could give him no guidance."

"I can't promise anything because I have not got that level of authority. It would more likely be something that would be arranged via the sentencing Judge or the prison authority. I will see what I can find out and will inform you as soon as I know."

"Thank you. I will inform Mr Simpson of that fact."

"I will speak to Gary, and explain or answer any questions that he may have. Providing of course that is acceptable to you. Then I need to formally ask him under caution, questions on tape about various other matters."

The old DS in him was starting to shine.

"I have the feeling then that what he may tell you will probably ensure without recourse to a presiding Judge or prison authorities that he serve any potential sentence in a maximum security facility."

When Gary was brought into the interview room, both Groves and the brief were already waiting for him, and Groves stood and shook his hand. Gary sat down in the seat next to his brief and the DS sat next to Groves.

"Before we start Gary, are you getting enough food? You're a big lad. It looks like you may need a bit more than most."

He confirmed he was being well catered for considering what he'd done, and asked that his apologies were passed on to the officers, and Groves agreed to do so.

"Do you want a tea or coffee?"

"I would like a tea if I could please."

Groves asked the DS to pop out and get one for all of them. The DS wasn't sure about leaving Groves by himself in the interview room but did as requested.

As the door closed behind him, Groves told Gary that he was going to be charged with the assaults which he was already aware of and accepted.

"Before we start, I have informed your learned solicitor that I will answer any question that you may have which are unrelated to this matter. Is there anything you wish to ask me?"

Gary asked a couple of questions that Groves answered as best he could.

The DS returned with a tray holding four polystyrene cups and various sachets of sugar and dried milk, and a packet of custard creams. Only the brief declined his cup, which looked to him like liquid mud; the other three didn't seem to object, and Gary had the majority of the biscuits.

Once the drinks and biscuits were out of the way. "OK. We have to interview you on tape. But just off hand, why did you ask for me?"

"You could have hit me, but you didn't, you gave me the chance. You were fair. I like that. I trust you."

Groves began the interview on tape by introducing those present and then cautioning Gary Simpson. He could not have believed what he was going to be told as Gary had remained silent during his previous interviews by the DS.

Before a question could be put, "I will give you the whole story which will save a lot of time. I know I will be going to prison, but I want you to know what has really been happening."

The interview ran for an hour and a half before they stopped it for a lunch, and comfort break. Gary was cooked two steaks and a mountain of vegetables by the cook who brought it over from the canteen, and the interview started again as more tea was drunk. By 6.30pm Groves was sure that Gary had told the whole story.

He was taken back to his cell, and at the door Groves said, "I'll come and see you tomorrow and I will be able to give you some information as to how this enquiry will proceed."

"Thanks" and he went into his cell as meek as a lamb and lay on the bed.

Prodow said, "We've got all this, and we're still no nearer who did for Armstrong."

John was sitting at his usual desk and Paul and Doreen were behind theirs. Jimmy had deserted his which had a wall of exhibits piled up high on top of it. Groves had bought a couple of fresh bottles of scotch before returning to the office, and the first half of one had been divvied up between them into mugs and cups. Even the semi teetotal Doreen was nursing a cup containing the liquid that was turning her face a slight crimson. A SOCO had been sent with the DS from the interview team to return to the house to pick up the jar from inside the cupboard.

The Chief walked back into the office, but no warning was received this time. He looked at all the mugs and cups.

"Hope there's some left for me" and was gratified when a bottle re-appeared from Doreen's desk and a generous portion was poured into a fresh mug and given to him by Paul.

"I think I am going to have to re-assess this policy of no coffee or tea in the offices" and then took a hefty swig.

"Wow. That's good. I needed that."

He let them know that Murray had successfully undergone all the operations, and would be staying in Southampton for probably two more days in order that they could confirm no further complications, and then he would be transferred to St Richard's.

"I hope that meets with your approval Mr Groves?"

"Thank you. Yes Sir."

"Right. Now how are you getting on here?"

They all looked at each other wondering who should speak before Prodow said, "Mr Groves has interviewed Gary Simpson during the day and he has admitted that they have killed: albeit some by accident, to his knowledge, fifty-nine people although not Armstrong. They may have killed more than he can remember and some that they don't know about."

The Chief looked shocked as the colour left his face: then draining his scotch he held the mug back towards Paul who half-filled it again.

106
Thursday 16th June 2011

Simon moved to the rear of the prison inside the barn, and then sat where Dimitri had met his demise. The gun was no longer on the wall, and there was nothing evident to show any misdeed having occurred there. He was wide awake and contemplating how the day was to evolve. Already, he had planned for the worst possible scenario. It was sunrise when Simon was finally settled down to wait having phoned Graham and told him: not asked him: that he would be taking Alison out during the day.

Calling John, *"She's not good John. She needs a doctor. I'm taking her out today. I've spoken to Graham and told him. He's not happy but it's got to be done. I've called Kent for transport."*

"I'll speak to my friendly doctor Carol and see if she's free. Take her to my place. I have a large spare bedroom. It would be better if she was nowhere near her flat."

"Yeah. Good idea."

At 8.30am Simon heard the engine of an approaching car, and then the door of a vehicle being closed. It was slammed more than closed, and he knew it was one of the Lithuanians from the BMW or the gorilla as the little Russian made hardly any noise when he shut doors. Remaining rock still, and blending into the dark recess of the wall, he watched as one of the Lithuanians moved towards the door of the prison to look through the spy hole. He'd obviously had his orders. For nearly a full ten minutes he kept his eye glued to the spy hole peering hard through it in order to observe the condition of Alison's thumb. Eventually satisfied that it was still in a dislocated state, he stood back from the door and rubbed his eye hard with the knuckle of his thumb. Then he opened the food hatch and rolled a bottle of water through it. Putting his eye back against the spy hole, he watched as Alison picked it up and struggled to open it without the use of her left thumb to hold the bottle as she turned the cap.

Shutting the hatch without leaving any food, he walked back to the car, and Simon heard the door slam and the engine start, but the car didn't move off. The Lithuanian was on the phone to his little Russian master as the car sat idling. Moving quickly and quietly from his observation position knowing any noise would be masked by the idling engine, he worked his way around the dilapidated wall. Simon could hear a muffled voice and was able to get close enough to make out that it was confirming she still had a dislocated thumb. He was within four yards of the vehicle when the passenger window was lowered and the ash flicked from a cigarette. The window stayed down.

The passenger who had supplied the information about Alison was becoming agitated and was gesticulating inside the car as though the little Russian could see him. It was becoming clear to Simon that Grigoriev was not coming back today. A bit of the lit cigarette he was holding in his waving hand caught the dashboard and dropped onto his trousers. The door flew open and he jumped out brushing the burning ember off. Leaning on the roof of the BMW, he smoked the remains of his cigarette while managing to continue his conversation on the phone. Simon could understand part of the conversation and it seemed that the little Russian who he called 'Greg' did not believe him.

As he snapped the phone shut, he bent down to speak to his brother through the open window.

"We are to stay here till he's spoken to the boss. Then he'll call back."

"What's the problem?"

"Doesn't look like it's worked."

"It's your turn to do it."

"We'll just leave her here. She'll be dead soon enough."

107

Thursday 16th June 2011

Simon didn't move. The slightest movement would have attracted attention. Both Lithuanian brothers stayed as they were, and the engine of the BMW died. Even the slightest noise would now attract attention. It was the start of another hot June day and the driver got out of the car. He lit a cigarette, and just walked slowly away from the car towards the track smoking it. As if a signal, his brother lit another and followed him. Sidling back along the wall to his observation post, he could barely hear the two men talking as he took out his phone, turned it on and sent a brief text to John.

'If you don't hear from me within the hour, send the cavalry.'

He checked that the message had gone and waited for the requested receipt before turning the phone off. Standing now as still as a living statue, he waited. It was nine minutes before he heard the phone in the Lithuanian's hand ring. Simon was too far away to hear what was being said and he needed to know. Casting prudence to the wind, he moved quickly back to the entrance of the barn and stopped behind a complete bit of the wall which concealed him from anyone outside. As soon as anyone entered, they could not fail to see him. It was a gamble he had to take.

The two men were walking back towards the entrance and the BMW parked directly outside. They stopped by the car and both lent on the roof facing each other as the passenger was speaking on the phone.

"What do you want us to do then?"

. . .

"Are you sure?"

. . .

"If we just leave her that will do it. Then if he changes his mind we could probably recover the situation."

...

"She'll be dead in five days. We did this a lot in Serbia."

...

"We cleaned the place before she went in. They won't find any marks from us."

...

"Nothing here can link us to Birmingham."

...

"He's well buried. The only animals that will get him are the worms."

...

"OK then. Bye."

"What does he want us to do?"

"Leave her where she is. We'll come back in a week and clear the place up."

"She might drink the water out of the sink."

"That'll speed it up then" and they both laughed.

"I'll turn the generator off" and the passenger walked off towards the out building. The driver watched him go to it and then walked into the barn. He wanted to try and see what she would do when the light went out.

As he entered the barn, he saw Simon. He was quick as he reached with his right hand pulling his favourite old service automatic, an MP-443 Grach that he'd had no trouble smuggling in to the country, from its trouser holster. Simon was quicker. The butterfly knife flashed as the blade first went through the back of the Lithuanians right hand and then out of the palm. Pain was immense and sudden and he dropped the gun. Before he even thought to call his brother, Simon had hit him hard with the flat heel of his now empty right hand driving it hard up through the point of his nose. It broke without a discernible sound as it was driven swiftly into his brain killing him outright before he even had time to fall to the ground.

Simon stood on the Lithuanian's wrist as he pulled his butterfly knife clear of his hand and casually wiped it clean on the dead man's shirt before closing it with a simple deft movement of his wrist and replacing it in his pocket. He had always preferred knives as they were quiet and efficient and their use came naturally to him. Now he picked up the fallen gun and checked it. It was fully loaded with eighteen rounds in the magazine and one in the breach ready to go with just the safety catch keeping it safe. Even if he had been able to bring it to bear on Simon, turning the safety off would have slowed him down much too much.

He was as good as dead with a useless weapon.

Flicking the safety off, Simon put the gun in his other pocket. Having no idea if it would fire or not would be a gamble so he preferred the dependability of his knife. Dragging the dead body to the back of the barn, he left it on the floor out of sight of the entrance. The small amount of blood that had seeped from the man's hand was lost in the mud of the floor. He resumed his position at the front of the barn and he heard the generator slowly shut down. There was a muted shout from Alison within her prison that had now become pitch dark as the light in the wall died. The Lithuanian came out of the outhouse and back towards the BMW and got into the passenger seat. He sat there waiting for his brother. Minutes passed and he got out of the car with his own gun a GSh-18 in his hand leading the way. Simon saw the gun enter the barn and the cautious Lithuanian following.

Simon was crouched down behind the wall which gave him a millisecond's advantage. He fired the recovered gun slightly upwards towards the man's stomach. As the Lithuanian had seen Simon, he began lowering his own weapon trying to bring it to bear, but it was too late. The strange heavy calibre of the bullet ripped into his stomach and broke into several pieces which all went their separate ways. It was as if they each had to find a certain organ inside the body.

By chance, the only one not found was the heart.

He had been lifted slightly into the air and then driven backwards by the impact and lay on the floor dying in horrendous agony. His gun had fallen way away from him and was beyond his reach. He knew it was only a matter of minutes, but the pain was excruciating. If he could have reached his weapon he would have put it to his head to stop the hurt.

"Shoot me."

"If you tell me who is behind this?"

"Grigoriev."

"Not him, the one in Birmingham."

"Richard Davies."

He heard the gun and died instantly as the bullet ripped his skull apart.

108

Thursday 16th June 2011

Alison heard both gunshots and was starting to panic. She was in unyielding pain. It was bad but nothing to what the Lithuanian had borne for just a few seconds. The light had slowly been extinguished in her prison just minutes prior to the first shot having sounded and within thirty seconds she heard the second. She couldn't see a thing. It was pitch dark. 'Surely someone must have heard the noise? Would they think it was a bird scarer? It sounded like a cannon! They must come.'

The flap at the bottom of the door dropped down and a little light found its way in to the gloom to give some respite against the darkness.

"You ok?"

In a rasping loud lisping shout, "Simon! What's happening?"

"I've just got to finish a few things off out here, and then we'll go."

"Let me out now!"

"No. You really do not want to see all this."

"Let me out now. I don't want to stay in here a second longer."

"I'll open the door, but please stay on the bed till the ambulance gets here. Movement could cause your ribs to puncture a lung or something."

Simon opened the door and wedged it wide. She looked longingly at the gaping hole.

As her eyes became accustomed slowly to the bright light, she caught sight past him of the body on the floor with very little head left. She fought the urge to puke.

"Jesus Simon. What have you done?"

"I had to stop him."

"Have you called the Police?"

"What? Of course not. I'm putting him with the others."

"What others?"

"The one from the other night and the one round the back."

"Simon, you can't just keep killing people."

"They were all for killing you."

"Oh."

"Is that all you can say?"

"Sorry." Then within seconds, "Thank you."

"Stay there and don't move till I get back" and with that, he jogged to the outbuilding and set the generator in motion.

Within minutes he was on the phone to John and told him everything was now in hand and that as soon as he could, he'd get Alison to his flat. John said he would be waiting with Carol who had already started to prepare the room. Searching both Lithuanian brothers, he found their mobiles and with their guns, left them all by the entrance to the barn. If Petrovski or Grigoriev should turn up he could get to them and start a gun battle if needed.

The next hour and a half was spent getting the two bodies to the drainage ditch and burying them as best he could and as close to the water line as possible where very few animals were likely to get at them. It was unlikely that the bodies would be found in the foreseeable future. When the team from Kent arrived, they would ensure the place was properly cleaned, and the bodies would be dealt with. Back on her prison bed, Alison was fast asleep.

Simon began cleaning the inside of the outbuilding by wiping every surface he'd touched with an old oily rag he found by the generator. Once he was satisfied, he moved to the barn and checked around the perimeter of the prison making sure nothing could be attributed to him. Lastly, he moved into the prison itself. Simon started wiping down every surface with his oily rag, trying not to wake Alison. There was no way he wanted any of Alison's or his fingerprints to be found. He'd rub the bed down once she was out.

He knew that a thorough search would reveal DNA, but it was a risk he could not eradicate. Rearranging one of the hoses from the generator and connecting it to the water supply, he hosed down the ground where the blood from the first man's hand had sprayed. Picking up the bits of the second man's head in his cloth, he took them twenty yards into the field and shook it out. The scattered remains he hoped would be picked clean by the birds and other animals and finally the insects would clean them up completely. Returning, he hosed down the whole area where the man had fallen. It didn't worry him so much if any DNA was found as long as it wasn't his or Alison's.

Sitting in the passenger seat of the BMW he phoned Bruce, a medic, who was bringing the Mercedes van from Kent which was fully kitted out as an unmarked ambulance. Bruce had been parked waiting for the call in a lay-by on the A27 at the Chichester by pass. The call from Simon spurred him into action. Tuning his Sat Nav, he located the signal from the 'trembler' and drove straight to it. Simon was standing by the wattle gate which he opened and signalled the van through. Jumping into the passenger seat, he directed him to the parking area at the front of the barn. Reversing the vehicle to the entrance, they both got out and the tailgate rose at the instigation of a pressed button. A black Gladstone bag sat conveniently in a holder by the door which Bruce grabbed before following Simon into the prison.

Gently waking Alison, Simon introduced her to, and told her Bruce was going to get her out.

"Hi. If I said you look rough, will you be offended?"

She looked at him, "Don't make me laugh, I know it will hurt."

"Wait till you see how we are going to get you out."

"Are you a doctor?"

"I was once. I won't bore you with when it all went wrong."

"Please. I don't care. Just get me out."

A quick check revealed Alison's broken ribs and Bruce indicated to Simon to go back to the van.

"She's going to have to come out carried on a stretcher. Anything with wheels would be problematic and I don't want to bounce her about. She can't weigh too much so we can easily manage between us."

"OK."

Alison was soon strapped into the ambulance.

Simon cleaned up the remainder of the prison and locked the door before turning the generator off. Collecting the stash from by the entrance to the barn, he put the items into his various pockets. He drove the BMW and soon caught the ambulance up as it neared the wattle gate. Bruce was going so slow that Alison could hardly detect any movement and did not feel one bump on the unmade track. Definitely preferable to her arrival. The two men held the gate for each other to leave and Simon left the BMW where he collected his Lexus. Calling Ian with its details and location, he knew it would never be seen again.

109
Thursday 16th June 2011

When the ambulance got to John's block of flats, Bruce found him walking about between the visitors parking area and the road. Simon had arrived at the same time but parked in West Street. Alison was fast asleep again and Bruce, at John's direction, parked directly outside the entrance to the foyer. No one noticed her being carried on a stretcher into the entrance and up to the spare bedroom in John's flat. After a quick chat to Carol, Bruce was soon gone again in the ambulance heading back to Kent where it was in use daily with the disabled veterans.

Carol took one look at her discoloured thumb and putting Alison's arm under hers gripped the thumb and gave it a sharp yank. Alison woke and yelped in pain as the thumb was returned to its normal position. The throbbing which had been getting progressively worse over the day seemed to stop directly. Soon Carol was using Alison as a pin cushion sticking a needle into the base of her thumb and then into each arm. She ordered John to fetch water and when he returned with it, she put a tablet into the glass that began effervescing. Alison gagged as the water was poured into her mouth as she lay flat on the bed.

"Hope you have a bucket handy, I reckon she'll throw up in about three minutes."

John ran from the room to find his cleaning bucket.

Simon, who was sitting on a side chair watching the goings on said to Carol, "She was punched in the side of her head, had a knee stamped on and kicked in her ribs."

"Why do they always kick people in their ribs?"

"Easiest place I suppose."

Carol checked Alison's ribs, "I think some are broken, but without an x-ray I can't be sure how many. I'll sort something out for that to happen."

She looked in Alison's mouth after telling Simon to hold it open while she had her fingers inside. Having been bitten before, she took precautions. Carol took hold of a very loose rear top molar and found it practically came out without any effort from her. The tooth next to it also followed. Alison's face was contorted in agony.

Carol saw Alison looking at her with hate in her eyes.

"Shan't be much longer, then you will feel much better."

Alison was desperate to speak but seemed unable to get anything out except some grunting.

"We'll sort out a dentist later."

Simon noticed Alison was now looking at him with vicious eyes.

"Don't look at me like that. I got you out didn't I?"

Another short burst of grunting.

"Let's see her knee" and she started to take off Alison's chinos.

"Better idea. Pass those big scissors." Simon handed the big scissors from the huge bag of Carol's that she was picking things out of. She cut up from the ankle just past the knee.

After a cursory examination, "That one's ok" and she cut up the second leg. "That feels ok. Next time she's awake and talking coherently, we need to know which knee it was."

John came puffing back into the room with a brown plastic bucket.

"Looks like she won't need that now."

He still put the bucket next to the head of the bed.

"Right gentlemen, please leave the room while I put this lady to bed."

Both John and Simon retired to the kitchen and Simon had the first decent hot drink he could remember in about three days. He briefed John as to 'Grigoriev' and Richard Davies but failed to mention the three bodies. John knew something had happened but did not want to know any details if Simon chose not to tell him. Carol joined them and informed John she would be spending a few nights there to make sure Alison was alright.

"I'll go to Alison's flat. I can stay there."

Carol looked astounded and said, "There's the other spare bedroom here. I'm in the master bedroom with the master."

John looked around for something to focus on.

"If that's alright."

"I would suggest you have a shower though as soon as possible, you actually smell quite strongly."

Simon stripped off his clothes which John took and threw all together into his washing machine. He didn't bother with the shower, he went straight for the bath. Letting the hot water lap over and around his body caused him to drift off a little and close his eyes. He was in there for nearly an hour topping up the water regularly and using up a whole new bottle of John's favourite Radox. Several times, he was on the verge of falling asleep. John provided him with an old but clean pair of jogging pants that were way too small for him and appeared never to have been used much, if at all. They were a little too big for Simon, but they sufficed. Once dry, he moved back to the kitchen where pleasant smells were being created. Carol was cooking a lasagne with additional vegetables and saw his torso as he entered.

Rhetorically she said, "Why can't John look after his body like that?"

As they ate, Simon, who had not been formally introduced to Carol, told her who he was as it was patently obvious John was going to say nothing. Between mouthfuls, he told her he was ex-military and had been looking after Alison and watching over her as she had been held prisoner. Mentioning nothing about the three corpses and their sudden departure from life, he explained that Alison could not be rescued until certain criteria could be established. Unfortunately, it appeared that it may all have been in vain.

She in turn explained that she had once been an army doctor and had worked in the field of various war zones. That was why she was quite happy looking after someone away from an actual hospital. Having met John originally in Ireland, she knew not to ask questions of him, and was happy to renew their acquaintance when she moved to Sussex.

John said absolutely nothing.

At the meal's conclusion, Simon asked, "How's Alison?"

"She'll sleep for at least a day or two. What I gave her would knock out an elephant. I will arrange for x-rays later and John can organise the dentist."

"There is one thing I need to do at Alison's flat before I can come back and sleep."

110

Thursday 16th June 2011

Parking his Lexus in the Nuffield hospital's car park, he jogged directly to Alison's flat meeting Hannibal as he climbed the stairs where they both evaded the cotton trap and went inside. Simon opened a tin of cat food dropping it directly into Hannibal's bowl which was still where he'd left it previously. The cat seemed indifferent to the food picking at it apparently not very hungry. 'Typical' thought Simon, 'Cat's find food anywhere and never go hungry.' He gathered some clothes that he selected from Alison's bedroom and put them into a rucksack he found at the bottom of her wardrobe. Then he settled down to wait.

Hannibal joined him on the settee. Simon had left the front door slightly ajar as he dozed waiting for the visitor. It was 11.30pm when he heard slight puffing and panting coming up the stairs. As it reached the top, the puffing and panting stopped.

"There is a gun pointing at your back and one at your chest. Please put your gun away and come into the lounge."

Petrovski stood at the open door with his gun in his hand. He knew that if true, he could already have been dead. He wasn't that stupid an oaf!

Standing at the door, he considered his options. All of them seemed to end up with him being dead. No choice. He put his gun back into his shoulder holster and pushing the door fully open, he walked towards the lounge. Simon was standing by the kitchen door.

"I'm just making a cup of tea. Do you want one?"

Petrovski was puzzled and heard himself say, "Yes."

He watched Simon put tea bags into two mugs, "Milk and sugar?"

"Yes," then "one."

Simon completed the tea and handing a mug to Petrovski and taking his own, turned his back as he walked into the lounge. Petrovski followed totally perplexed.

"Have a seat Petrovski we have some things to discuss."

They sat facing each other.

"The reason you aren't dead is because of a bottle of water."

"I don't understand?"

"I have been at the barn from the first day the two Lithuanians took the lady there. I have watched the comings and goings every day and visited her every night. I had to kill your night watcher Dimitri, and I saw you bury him. The two, who I presume were brothers, are now lying next to him in the same drainage ditch. I saw 'Grigoriev' go into her cell and heard her screams as did you. I watched the fruitless search that you all mounted looking for me. But you had compassion Petrovski, and left her a bottle of water."

Petrovski drank from his mug.

"Grigoriev should not have hit a defenceless woman."

"You gave her a chance, and that is what I am offering you."

Hannibal, who had slunk into the corner of the room when the two men had entered and had sat watching, now started to feel confident and walked back to the settee and jumped up to sit next to Simon who casually stroked him.

"Who are you?"

"I am your worst nightmare. I kill people" and Simon sipped his tea.

"You led me to Crawley. Why bother?"

"To try to convince Grigoriev that I was no one to worry about."

"You know he suspected you from the first day he saw you here?"

"Yes. I presume he was once with the KGB."

"He is not a very nice person."

"Down to business Petrovski. I know where and what I will be doing in the near future. If our paths cross again, I will not be so amicable. May I make a few suggestions? Do not go anywhere near Birmingham or Richard Davies. Do not bother contacting Grigoriev again; he will think you are dead. Leave your car with the keys in it where it is now and dump your phone. There is £5000 in this envelope. Go back home to Russia."

"Why are you doing this?"

"Like I said, a bottle of water."

"I could just shoot you."

"You would be dead as soon as you tried to leave. A friend is outside with clear line of sight on the front door and he has never missed."

Petrovski drained his tea.

"The tea tastes better in Russia."

"I will signal him before you leave."

Petrovski looked at the money in the envelope, and then put it in his pocket.

"No one will be looking for you Petrovski. Go home to your family."

Simon opened the front door, and waved to his imaginary friend.

"You're safe to go."

He watched from the front door as Petrovski strode back to the Audi, put the keys in the ignition and walked off out of sight with no backward glance. Shutting the front door, he returned to the settee where he found Hannibal sniffing Petrovski's discarded phone.

111

Thursday 16th June 2011
to
Friday 17th June 2011

Simon scrolled through the directory on the phone and saw various numbers for the unfortunate deceased. He had kept the mobile phones from the Lithuanian brothers, but neither had the numbers he wanted. They were cheap untraceable pay as you go phones which only had Grigoriev's, Petrovski's, Dimitri's and each other's numbers stored and that was all. No calls were recorded to any other number.

Petrovski's phone on the other hand was a gold mine for Simon. It had a few additional numbers which were what he needed. There was a number stored under 'RD PA' and one for 'Sol Yusuf'. Other numbers stored appeared to relate to personal contacts in Russia which Petrovski called infrequently.

Putting the phone into the rucksack, Simon looked for Hannibal. The cat seemed to know he was going to be ejected once again from the flat, and had taken refuge on Alison's bed. Picking him up, he opened the door and put him out, and then followed him down the stairs having shut and locked the front door firmly behind him. Petrovski had broken the cotton on his way out and it seemed pointless for Simon to replace it. He went to the Audi and got in. It was a basic hire car which was good enough for what he wanted.

Parking it in one of the visitor's bays by John's flat which always seemed to have spaces, he locked it and gained access to the foyer by pressing the tradesman's bell. Climbing the stairs, he tapped on the door. Carol let him in and he joined her and John in the lounge finishing off a vintage bottle of Bordeaux. The rucksack was unpacked by Carol who confirmed that Alison would probably be wide awake the following afternoon and craving food. She tossed Petrovski's phone to him which he caught one handed as he'd forgotten he'd left it in the bag. He still managed to be in bed by 2am and had no intention of getting up to go jogging in the morning.

It was just past seven and Simon was wide awake. He lay in bed scheming and plotting and considering his options until gone eight. Then he knew exactly what he was going to do. He needed to speak to Graham, John, and Ian but not on a mobile phone. John had already left for the Police Station and would not be about until the evening. After an apple and yogurt for breakfast, he spoke to Carol and then walked to the Post Office in Chichester and using a pay phone called his Dad.

Carol let him back into the flat about 9am, and he went in to see Alison who was now inexplicably wide awake, contrary to what Carol had expected. She was conscious twelve hours too early. All the clothes that he'd brought were laid out on the bed and she had been discussing them with Carol. Now she had the culprit before her she started.

"Why didn't you bring my black jacket, and these jeans are my oldest. I can't wear beige shoes with these. How could you get it so wrong?"

"Recovered now have you?"

"You are totally useless. I put my trust in you and you can't even find matching underwear in a girl's drawers."

Carol who had been standing behind Simon said, "She has a point. Beige shoes with jeans really should be a no no."

Simon retaliated by changing the subject and told Alison that her Father was likely to be visiting which did nothing to endear himself to her or improve her mood.

When Simon added that there was going to be a meeting in the flat that night, Carol said she'd have to go out for more food. Asking her when she was next at work, Carol told him she was off for the next week on compassionate grounds. She had not had to divulge any details which had been a blessing as she hated lying.

Alison chirruped in, "You weren't very compassionate pulling and prodding bits of me and sticking needles all over the place. Then trying to drown me by pouring water over me."

Simon smiling provocatively said, "Always moaning. No gratitude."

He left the room before she could form a cogent insulting reply. Instead she turned on Carol.

"Mix with these people at your peril. Your life gets ripped to shreds."

"You could be right there. One thing though: it's never dull."

Petrovski's phone rang. Simon looked at the display. He wanted quiet so went into the kitchen and pushed the door to before he answered.

"*Yes?*"

There was an imperceptible pause before Grigoriev said, "*So Petrovski has joined the others?*"

"*May have done.*"

"*Impressive. Where have you put them all?*"

"*The ditch. They won't be found in a hurry unless you want to dig them up.*"

"*No. I don't think I will.*"

"*You know I'm going to be coming for you?*"

"*If you can actually find me, I shall be waiting.*"

"*It won't be long.*"

The line went dead.

*

Vilf was walking along the prom towards his stolen car. It was unusually quiet for the time of day with the occasional cyclists riding furiously towards unknown destinations, or joggers with ear buds in looking at the pavement and seeing nothing as they ran nowhere and then back. About a hundred yards in front of him he noticed a small man throw something at the sea wall. It seemed to shatter and break into pieces. As he got closer, he saw the little man bend and pick up a small piece and drop it over the sea wall. The small man turned and jumped down and onto the road. Vilf knew then who it was. He wouldn't lose him this time.

*

Carol who had overheard nearly all Simon's end of the conversation as she was walking towards the kitchen to get a fresh glass of water and a yogurt for Alison said, "You certainly know how to make friends. Just off hand, how many are actually in the ditch?"

"Only three. I let Petrovski go back to Russia."

"I don't really need to ask what regiment you were with do I."

"No"

Carol had picked up two yogurts and they went back into the spare bedroom.

Carol asked of him quizzically, "Has John got any normal friends?"

"He's got you and Alison."

Practically in unison the women said, "Huh!"

112
Friday 17th June 2011

John had somehow managed to get into the canteen at 7.20am and found himself at the rear of a queue of eight people, yet still got his breakfast first. The cook, cum chef, gave him a big wink as she handed the full plate to him. Offering excessive gratitude, he tucked in. The previous night's meal now all but forgotten.

Subsequently, he was in the office in plenty of time to have a chat to Groves, Jimmy, Paul and Doreen. They came to what they believed to be the logical conclusion, having all watched the video from the bird box several times, that whoever had done for George knew the camera was there. All had ignored the premise that they should only accept as fact, what they knew for certain.

It was the wrong conclusion!

It was agreed that Groves should press Gary as to who else knew about the bird box, and the known fact, it was also his coat that the murderer was using as a disguise.

Prodow arrived in the office early and confused all of them except John when he said, "At least one problem seems to have been resolved."

At 7.55am he addressed those in the office.

"Let's get this meeting underway" and he practically marched out of the room with all the others in tow like a line of ducklings following their parent.

He arrived in the briefing room slightly prior to eight. People were sitting about chatting to each other, eating breakfast rolls of sausages and bacon and drinking coffee and tea. It was starting to look like a worrying habit of his to arrive on time. If people could no longer be sure of his quarter of an hour's leeway, they would also have to be spot on time. A couple of chatting detectives ambled into the room carrying their beverages, and were seriously glared at by Prodow.

"If I can get here on time, I do not expect to have to wait for you!"

Chairs were scraped on the floor as all those assembled scrambled to sit in an arc and recover some decorum.

He seemed to ignore the general shock he had generated, and launched into the medical progress of Murray. His entire family were being catered for by The Holiday Inn at vastly reduced rates as a favour to the Police. They knew that it was something to do with a major Police enquiry and they often assisted when they could. In return, the Police would always give them a large slice of publicity come the end of the day. Most of those gathered had heard there had been progress in the enquiry and were waiting to hear what.

Groves was the one to conduct the briefing and he held nothing back. Some in the room were visibly shocked at the scale of what had been disclosed. They all knew that the enquiries they were engaged in had taken a turn for the worse. Some were told that their addresses were where people had died by Sally's hand. Gary had stated that Sally had used the crushed and fermented substance from the fruit of a passion flower, which according to the laboratory contained cyanide. She mixed it with other substances she had obtained from her garden or else she got from a chemist. Unfortunately, Gary was not privy to what the full concoction actually comprised of.

The laboratory had been consulted and was conducting a full analysis of the liquid from the container under the sink trying to work out what it was.

Jimmy butted in, "The lab has provided one analysis in relation to Armstrong which gives three different ingredients and their origins. To speed up the identification of the liquid, they are going to confirm quite quickly whether it is the same or not."

Prodow said, "Thanks Jimmy. Keep on top of that and let us know as soon as possible what the conclusion is."

Groves continued. No longer constrained by office politics he was back as he used to be, a good Detective Sergeant.

Prodow was at ease with the briefing and at the culmination added, "The Chief Constable is going to conduct a full press conference in company with me and Mr Groves at mid-day to catch the main news."

He paused and looked slowly round the room.

"Any questions?" There was a stunned silence. "I'm sure when you have taken in what Mr Groves has said, there will be questions. Please feel free to speak to any of us in the office. The Chief will be spending the next few days in the vicinity and visiting Murray which will probably set his recovery back a few weeks." There was a muted titter of laughter.

A voice from near the front asked, "Why is she doing it? She can't mean to kill them. Can she?"

Paul said, "I can probably answer that. The poison, if the same as that used on Armstrong, causes severe stomach cramps and can destroy part of the lining rendering elderly people seriously ill. If the person doesn't get medical help reasonably quickly, that's it. If they survive, and are not firing on all cylinders, they take their eye off their finances and that's where she steps in. Gary told Mr Groves that she can get hundreds of pounds from some, and thousands from others. It all depends on how well off the person is. We have found an account that shows her taking up to nine thousand pounds from it. If she thinks she has been or is about to be rumbled. She finishes them off."

Groves cut in.

"Because they have been seen at a hospital and have probably visited their own GP afterwards, it's likely that they would not have had to undergo a PM. Two doctors could sign the death certificate although what they would show as cause of death, I'm not sure."

The voice persisted.

"So the bird box just let them know what the result of the poison was. If the person was in hospital or not. Then I suppose they went in and took what they wanted especially if they knew where the keys were kept as a carer would."

Paul considered that for a second and said, "We hadn't thought of that scenario."

John said, "They know from the camera when someone is likely to make a visit and would find the victim and get them to hospital. If she wanted to finish them off, she would know the best time to do it."

The voice continued.

"That must be then when they take the bird box down."

Prodow chipped in.

"This is the sort of thing that we need to hear."

He scribbled feverishly in his 'Murder Book' updating it with the details of the briefing and what was said. Prodow was fast. He wrote in a style that was clearly readable to him and just about readable to anyone else. Every day, he read up on what had been said at the previous meetings. Thoughts he had and ideas that would progress the enquiry were added and later gone through in minutiae with Groves. Then during the following briefing, they would be either discussed or acted upon. Today he was writing more than he was saying.

Paul was also scribbling down in his book ideas that were flooding his head and actions that he foresaw.

The voice as a denouement said, "So we still haven't got a clue who murdered George Armstrong?"

113
Friday 17th June 2011

Back in the office, John considered the facts they had established about the murder of George Armstrong. He reflected on what had been said in the meeting and now something was starting to irritate him. All the other victims were apparently poisoned to some degree by Sally without their knowledge. Gary had told Groves that she put small amounts in coffee or tea. In the majority of cases, it wasn't meant to kill anyone, just put them in hospital and away from their abode. The Armstrong case was different since he knew he had been poisoned because he wrote it down before shattering his pencil on the fire place as the murderer stood over him watching as he died. He was meant to die.

John started to talk rhetorically as Doreen listened to him.

"Why didn't the murderer take the diary unless they wanted it to be known he had been poisoned? Did they see him write the word poisoned? He wrote Pois. We have all presumed it was the start of poisoned. He was poisoned. The jar of poison was left where it would be found and likely moved. Did the murderer watch him die? Does the date in the diary where he wrote pois have a bearing?"

Speaking to Jimmy, as Doreen still listened in, he was told Paul had a photocopy of the relevant diary entry. Paul told him where it was in the file, and Doreen retrieved it and handed it to him. It was nothing like the writing on the gas bill and other correspondence, and had a slight reverse slant as opposed to a forward one. It was as though someone else may have written the word.

"Why?"

Doreen looked at the diary and the gas bill and understood his question.

"He was suffering. It was an effort for him. He may have even written it with his weak hand."

"Possible."

"Look at the date. 5th March 1974. Who keeps a diary that old?"

"I need to see the original."

Doreen called to Jimmy and requested the original diary. Jimmy was busy handing out tapes to various officers, but realised something was brewing. He practically dived into a pile of exhibits and reappeared with a clear plastic bag which he delivered to Doreen and John. There he stayed hoping to hear some kind of pronouncement.

Doreen looked at the original exhibit through the bag. It was open at the 5th March 1974. It was a small bog-standard pocket diary with a ring binding. John looked at it as Jimmy looked over his shoulder. Other officers waiting for tapes took a casual interest.

One officer said, "My kids like that sort of diary."

John scrutinised him and said, "Why?"

"Because you never lose the pencil."

Then it dawned on Jimmy how the diary was kept closed by the pencil slotting through the rings when it was closed and it kept it so. As it had been open when it had been seized, no one bothered to close it.

"Hang on," and Jimmy dove back into his exhibits and pulled out the plastic exhibit bag containing the pencil.

The officer saw the little broken pencil with a small plastic top.

"Yeah that's the pencil that would slot through the rings. The top stops it falling right through. When you take it out, the diary flips open."

Prodow who was now in the room and taking an interest said, "Open it up Jimmy."

At his words, Jimmy produced a lock knife, opened it and slit the bag open.

"You are really starting to worry me Jimmy. You shouldn't be carrying a thing like that."

Jimmy ignored the jibe and removed the diary.

"Has anyone got anything roughly the size of the pencil?"

An officer handed a lollipop forward and said, "The stick is about the same size."

Jimmy shut the diary and slid the stick through the bindings and it held closed. When he removed it, the diary flipped open to the 5th March 1974.

John said, "That's probably why he wrote on that page but why 1974?"

There was a palpable silence. No one could come up with any feasible answer.

John continued his deliberations.

"What was the gun doing in the hole? Why were the papers hidden in the fireplace? Why keep all the money in a dictionary? The bird box video illustrated the person knew about the camera. How?"

Doreen said, "How what?"

John answered, "How did they know about the camera?"

Both sat in contemplation. There was a general buzz from officers going in and out of the office talking to Paul and Jimmy, Groves having gone to see Gary. Jimmy tried to keep an eye on both John and Doreen as he was dealing with other officers because he anticipated something else boiling to the surface. He wanted to be involved. The two sat oblivious to it all considering the question.

Doreen broke the silence between them.

"The person knew because they had stumbled across either the poison in the jar in the kitchen or the tapes in the workshop. This means they have access to one, or more likely, both locations. A family member? A trusted friend?"

"They do not have children, and live alone. They would not tell anyone else as it could lead to blackmail or disclosure. The liquid does not lead one to automatically believe it to be poison: in fact, it looks like water. Somehow, they had to know about the poison to use it. Therefore, they would not necessarily know about the workshop as no poison was kept there."

"That's of course if we believe what Gary has said."

"We are now assuming the poison in the house is the same as what did for George."

"It's got to be family."

"I was coming to that same conclusion, but the fly in the ointment is why didn't either Gary or Sally identify them or the car when they watched the video?"

They sat again in silence.

Groves came back into the office with the news that Gary was adamant that no one else knew what they had been up to. Doreen offered to make the teas and coffees assuring everyone that the poison had all gone to the lab.

When she put a coffee in front of John who hadn't uttered a word for some time, she said, "Work on it and it'll all fall into place."

"Thanks for the confidence boost Doreen."

114

Friday 17th June 2011

Vilf saw the little man cross the road into the west arm of The Steyne. He was ready and got across the road himself. Following at a respectable distance on the opposite footpath he watched him walk up to a house with a board in the window showing 'Vacancies'. The little man climbed the three steps to the front door, pushed it open and walked in. Vilf had him. He didn't know what to do. Should he go for his car and sit in it and watch? That would make him vulnerable to any passing Policeman. Sitting on one of the bench seats in the garden would make him visible to anyone in a front room of the Bed and Breakfast. Why hadn't he found John?

Sod's law. A couple of uniform Policemen were in the gardens talking to some vagrants who were taking their first drink of the day. Now he knew what he had to do. It was a risk. His equaliser and stolen car were some way off and couldn't be attributed to him. He watched the little group. Eventually the Police moved off to the east arm of The Steyne. Vilf followed them until they reached the Esplanade.

"Officer."

The Policemen looked round as Vilf closed on them.

"I can't speak for too long. I need you to get hold of DC Whiles. Tell him there is a kidnapping going down. One of them is in The Gardens B&B in The Steyne. I'll be around here all day and should be able to find the others. He'll know what to do."

One of the PC's was an old sweat and was showing the young new PC the ropes.

"What's your name?"

Just tell him it's Vilf."

The youngster said, "Do I know you?"

"Possibly. I often pass information on. Look, I've got to go. I can't be seen talking to you" and with that Vilf jogged off.

The youngster said, "What do we do?"

"You find out where DC Whiles is and then pass it on to him."

"Did he look familiar to you?"

"No. That doesn't mean anything though. You'll meet millions of people over your career."

"I've seen his picture somewhere."

"We'll go back to the station and see what you come up with."

Both walked onto the prom and strolled back chatting to anyone passing who wanted to. Then they walked through the market at the Regis Centre gossiping to all the stall holders. Ambling through the Arcade and down London Road they were in and out of the shops. They finally made it back to Bognor Police Station at gone noon.

The youngster checked on the Sussex intranet database of employees for DC Whiles and drew a blank.

He said to his colleague, "There's no trace of any officer in Sussex called Whiles. Do you think he was just taking the mick?"

"Where else have you checked?"

"Well. Nowhere."

"Have a look on the CAD."

Instead, he looked in the 'wanted' book. That's where he found the picture of Vilf.

"I've found the picture. I knew I'd seen him somewhere before. That guy is an escapee."

"Just because he's an escapee doesn't devalue any information he may have. Think logically. He had to take a chance to approach us. Why would he do that?"

"Just a nut case. I'll circulate his details. Then he can go back to prison."

The old PC sat alone in an office at a computer terminal and tapped out DC Whiles in the search box of CAD. Reams of data started to scroll across the screen. Reading the latest reports, the PC picked up the phone and called the temporary incident room at Chichester.

"Incident room."

"Do you have a DC Whiles working there?"

"Yes. He is in the office now. I'll pass you over."

"Whiles."

"Hello. PC Brady from Bognor. I met a guy this morning who asked me to get in contact with you. Gave the name Vilf. He said there was a kidnapping going down and one of the perpetrators was at The Gardens B & B in The Steyne."

"Where's Vilf now?"

"Somewhere near the pier."

"Can you get into civvies and I'll pick you up as soon as I can get there."

"I'll be at the front of the nick waiting for you."

John's Vauxhall drew into the car park in front of the Police Station. Standing by the door was a man who looked about sixty years old, but was just hitting fifty.

"You PC Brady?"

"Yeah."

"John Whiles. Jump in."

They were off before he had his seat belt on.

"What's this all about?"

"This goes no further. A woman was kidnapped some days back. The people who did it may be about to run. If Vilf told you where one was, he would be spot on."

"Did you know he was an escapee?"

"No, but that does not invalidate his info."

"My attitude too."

"We need to find him and quickly."

They searched the roads around the pier.

"I hope he's not gone after him."

Vilf was walking in the gardens of The Steyne. Grigoriev had seen him earlier and was watching him from his first-floor bedroom window concealed behind a net curtain. He knew he wasn't the Police but it was positively time to move. It was someone paying him too much attention. His Saab was outside. Clearing his room, he took his bag to the reception desk and settled his bill. They could whistle for Petrovski's because he wasn't going to pay for it. When Vilf reached the southern end of the gardens, he went to his car. Vilf didn't see him because he saw John on the Esplanade and signalled him to stop.

"Vilf, get in. What the hell is happening?"

"Hi John. Long story short. I got moved to Ford open and was forced to share a cell with a Russian. He was a 'wheeler dealer' and had a mobile. When he wanted a private conversation on it, he spoke in Russian. I never told him I spoke it. He was in for molesting women. I heard him discussing kidnapping a woman and that someone called Petrovski was building a secure room to keep her in."

"What was his name?"

"Dimitri."

"Go on."

"You know that isn't my game, so I just listened. Then I heard him say it was a WPC here in Sussex. I couldn't let that happen."

PC Brady said, "Who was it?"

"Someone called Daines. Dimitri was looking forward to making her acquaintance if you get my meaning. John, I couldn't let that happen."

"What did you do?"

"I walked out and went back to London to find you, and I was told you were down here. I've been trying to find you in all the pubs."

"So it was you who has been looking for me. I thought it was someone else. Go on."

"I was on the prom when I heard a snatch of conversation by two people talking in Russian. They mentioned Dimitri. Both got away from me, I'm getting slower."

"PC Brady said wistfully, "Happens to us all."

"Today, I was back on the prom and I saw the little guy again. He lobbed something, I think a phone, at the wall and it smashed. Then he picked up a bit and tossed it over the wall. This time I followed him to the B & B."

"Show me where you first saw him today."

"Just over there. Level with the arm of The Steyne," and Vilf pointed.

"Have you got a phone Vilf?"

"A borrowed one if you get my drift."

John told him his mobile phone number and Vilf rang it to pair them.

"You know you're now shown as wanted for being an escapee?"

"I couldn't let it happen John. I had to go."

John turned to PC Brady.

"What he has just said is extremely valuable. As far as I am concerned, he's earnt a chance."

"Fine by me."

"Vilf. Go back to London and try and keep out of trouble."

As Vilf was getting out of the car, "Keep in touch John" and then he ran back to the prom.

John gave PC Brady a potted version of what had happened to Alison before dropping him back at Bognor.

Driving back to the seafront, John parked his car close to the pier and got out to walk along the promenade. He soon came across some of the fragments of the phone. He kicked the bits about and saw the battery but no sim card. He went to the sea wall and looked over. The shingle stretched some five yards out before hitting sand. It was a long shot. The tide had not been in. He found a ramp leading down to the beach and walked to the rough area of shingle. No trace of anything.

Strolling back towards the ramp he saw an old man walking towards him with a metal detector.

"How good is that thing?"

"Top of the range. Pick up a pin under a foot of sand."

John identified himself to the man and asked if it could pick up a sim card from within shingle.

"Show me roughly where and we'll see."

It took less than ten minutes.

115
Friday 17th June 2011

Grigoriev had found a phone box.

"I'm coming back."

"What's happened?"

"Everyone's dead."

"What? How?"

"I'll tell you when I get there."

"Is the girl dead?"

"No."

"Where is she?"

"Don't know."

"How did she get out?"

"She had help."

"Can any of this be traced back to me?"

"No."

"Come and see me before you go anywhere else."

"OK."

Grigoriev sat in his car and considered the alternatives. He was the best they had and could look after himself. Would they try to eliminate him? Unlikely. Should he run? They would definitely try then. He decided to go back, but would have some kind of insurance.

—
*

John called Simon.

"Just met a snout. He told me the little man is in a B & B called The Gardens in The Steyne. Can you get there?"

"On way."

---
*

The youngster said to PC Brady, "Where have you been?"

"I'm afraid I can't tell you. Had you checked the CAD as I said, you would have met DC Whiles and found out more about Police work in an hour than you could learn in several years."

Then he went to get his uniform back on. While he was in the locker room, the youngster searched the CAD as the old sweat knew he would. The whippersnapper's eyes widened as he read. Two offices along, a meeting of the finance group was disturbed by a clearly shouted expletive.

"Shit."

116
Friday 17th June 2011

Simon parked the Audi in Fitzleet car park, and jogged the couple of hundred yards to The Steyne. His butterfly knife held closed but ready within his hand. Running up the steps and into The Gardens B & B he arrived at the reception. No one was there and a note was beside a bell, 'Ring for Service.' By it was a registration book. He swivelled it round and looked at all the names. G Vasiliev and a passport number and below it, P Mikhailov and another number, caught his eye. Rooms three and four respectively. The signature of the first looked like Grigori. Simon noted the room number, and did not concern himself with Petrovski.

Behind the reception was a selection of keys hanging on hooks. The key for room three was there but not for room four. He was too late. Returning the book to its original position, he rang the bell. Mrs. Greenhugh came through from the small dining area.

"Hello dear. Do you want a room?"

"I'm looking for Grigori. Is he still here?"

"Who did you say dear?"

"Grigori."

"You mean Grigoriev. You've just missed him. Left a couple of hours ago. His friend hasn't come back yet."

"No, it's just Grigoriev I'm after. I'll see him later. Thanks."

"No problem dear."

She went back into the dining area as Simon went back to the Audi.

"I was too late John. The bird has flown."

"Any idea where to?"

"Yes. I'll see you later. I'm going back to your flat."
"OK."

*

Vilf had meandered off after the meeting with John and gone back to his own lodgings to collect his things. Dragging them all in a small stolen suitcase on wheels, he walked back onto the prom. The beach walk to where his car was had become an enjoyable daily stroll. He'd come to love Bognor. Understandably, he preferred the bustle of London, but Bognor had the sea. Arriving near his car he decided to have one last lunch in The Waverley pub. Sitting on a bench in the eating area by the front door, he savoured a pint while he waited for his food. The sea was a deep blue again today reflecting the sky.

A couple of cars drifted casually past on their way towards the yacht club.

The driver of one was the little man!

Beer sloshed onto the table from his glass as Vilf leapt to his feet and moved the two yards to the very edge of the pavement to try and get the index number. Going in the opposite direction was a scaffolding lorry with a couple of poles rolling about having broken loose from their tethers. About to pass The Waverley in the same direction as the little man's car was an old open top Southdown tourist bus. It swerved less than a foot to avoid one of the scaffolding poles poking over the side of the lorry. The bus's old, protruding, metal nearside mirror hit the side of Vilf's head.

He would never see London again.

The ambulance was there quick enough but not for Vilf. He was dead. The traffic Police turned up and closed the road while they investigated.

The old sweat said to the youngster, "You are going to have to get used to death" and took him to the scene.

Both saw and recognised Vilf immediately. An ambulance man walking past saw the colour drain from the faces of both of them. The youngster from nausea and Brady's from sorrow. He could only think that Vilf was just one of life's unlucky losers.

117
Friday 17th June 2011

By late afternoon, Graham, using his wife's car, had parked next to the Audi in the visitors' bay outside the block of flats. When he got to the foyer door, he pushed the buzzer to John's flat not knowing if it was working or not as there was no inside audible tone. Carol's voice answered on the speaker.

"Yes?"

"Graham."

"Come on up. The doors open."

He climbed the stairs with the effortlessness of a fit man and straight in through the door being held by Carol.

Graham acknowledged Carol with a kiss, and a handshake for Simon.

"Thanks for what you have done," and turning to Carol, "and thanks for what you're doing."

Carol responded, "She's in there" indicating the spare bedroom.

Graham walked straight in without a thought of knocking. The argument was on from the word go.

"Do you walk into every girl's room without knocking?"

"What's the problem? I've seen you naked since you were born."

"I'm bloody older now. It's not the done thing."

"Stop swearing. I presume Carol has sorted you out?"

"Thanks for the concern. Yes she has."

"Good. I have arranged for you to have a fortnight off work to recover."

"Stop organising my life. You're nothing to do with my force. I can arrange my own affairs."

"It's done now, so don't worry."

"I'm not worrying. Where's Mum?"

"She's gone to New Zealand to see her relatives. Safer for her there."

"Did she have a choice?"

"Of course. I'm not an ogre."

"Debateable."

There was a loud knocking on the door.

"What?" was the shouted retort.

Simon opened the door enough to put his head round, "Do you want a coffee Graham?"

"Jesus, it's like Piccadilly Circus in here. Do I get one? Fat chance. Stuck in this bed and told not to move. Brought clothes by someone with the fashion sense of a slug."

"I'd love one please Simon, milk and no sugar. Makes people tetchy sugar," and he nodded towards Alison.

Simon added, "I think she's recovered."

"Call yourself a minder" followed him as he closed the door.

Graham stooped forward as though he was about to hug his daughter.

"Was it worth it?"

"We are going to discuss it shortly, but I think so."

"It hurt Dad, it really hurt" and she burst out crying as they hugged each other.

118
Friday 17th June 2011

Ian had arrived and was in the lounge with Simon, Graham and Carol when John got back. Carol was back and forth to the kitchen looking after a large piece of venison that was cooking slowly. There were a couple of exceptionally good clarets that John produced from his small, but rather exclusively well stocked wine rack to go with it. All relaxed in the sumptuous surroundings cradling their wine glasses. As the discussion was getting under way, Alison, wearing her mismatched clothes walked gingerly into the room. Graham and Carol rose as one as if to go to her assistance which she refused with a slight wave of the flat of her hand.

Before anyone could say anything, "This concerns me as much as you all and I desperately want to eat some proper food."

They looked at the still standing Graham who was watching his daughter intently before saying, "Alright."

Alison lowered herself tentatively into a chair which Carol moved from as it was the most suitable for her. Carol sat in a low squashy armchair.

"About a year ago, the Home Secretary sprung a bombshell on the City of London Police Commissioner at short notice. She claimed she wanted to discuss the 'Ring of Steel' which has operated quite successfully in the City of London, and has been managed effectively for many years. As his deputy, the Commissioner took great pleasure in passing this request on to me. The Commissioner has never been a fan of hers and she was well aware of that, and also that he would pass the request downwards. That, she knew, would automatically filter down to me.

When I arrived at the Home Office, I was met by some hapless civil servant who told me that Catherine, the Home Secretary, had recently got a bee in her bonnet about the 'Ring of Steel'. Seemingly, she passed through it on her morning commute to the Home Office and was invariably delayed. Never more than a few minutes, but that was enough. Then I was rushed through corridors and upstairs to her office for what I presumed was going to be some form of rebuke.

It started off that way. In the room with us was some sycophantic, flunky Junior Minister, and a secretary who was taking notes. She asked Nicholas, the Junior Minister, if he had anything he would rather be doing, as he didn't need to stay unless he wanted. He was off like a longdog. Shortly after, she told Kathy, the secretary, that she had a frog in her throat, and would she mind fetching a cup of tea for her.

As soon as we were alone, the Home Secretary dove into her handbag and extracted a small mobile and handed it to me. She told me to conceal it. At the time, I was rather confused."

Alison said, "I could see that" before realizing that she was the only one to comment.

Graham continued unabated, "Catherine told me to keep it turned on every night between 10.pm and midnight. Then she disclosed there had been what she referred to as 'irrefutable intelligence' which showed the Chief Constable of the West Midlands was in bed with a top criminal who dealt in all crimes from murder to prostitution with impunity. If any Police Officer got close to obtaining any evidence, they were promptly moved by the CC to an obscure Station. As most of us here know, we have encountered previous problems in that Force area."

He allowed a short pause.

The image of his friend flitted across John's memory.

Then, "Catherine told me she had sent in undercover operatives from MI5 who were blown within days which implied to her that there was an acute leak in her department somewhere. That was her problem. That was what I was really there for."

His eyes rested briefly on Alison as if daring her to make an utterance. She preserved her muteness.

"She told me the Chief Constable was soon to be eligible for retirement or have his contract extended for a further five years. As she vehemently said, 'It will not be extended!'"

Graham went on to tell them that the Home Secretary wanted him to apply for the job when it became vacant. She had confidentially divulged to him he would be the successful candidate come what may because she wanted a trustworthy Chief Constable in place who could make a start of sorting out the major criminals who were trying to take over the cities in the county.

The Home Secretary added that included in the 'irrefutable evidence' was the fact that a Minister somewhere in the Government was also involved in some way, but the problem was, the people who had obtained the evidence did not know who. That was the reason no immediate action had been instigated against any person.

As a bonus to him being promoted, she wanted him to find out who the bent Minister was. She believed efforts would be made to prevent him taking up the position and the Minister would be involved in some way.

He informed the small assembly that Catherine did not beat about the bush when she told him, 'You have access to people who are not establishment figures and have more 'unorthodox' means of establishing the truth. Just try to keep it lawful. I will not be able to bail you out.'

Alison's gaze fell casually on Simon.

What apparently concerned the Minister most however, was due to his reputation of honesty; some action would be taken to stop him applying with the possibility of an attempt on his life. Alison listened agog at what her Father had been asked. The effort to remain mum was nearly too much for her. Graham took a full, mellow, mouthful of wine which he savoured before swallowing. He persisted by saying that he was to keep the details of what he was doing secret, and to trust no government agency in case the information got back to the bent Minister.

Graham had only just confirmed to the Home Secretary that he would take up the challenge as the harassed secretary returned with one cup of slopped tea. Then the Minister continued to lambast the City of London's Police for delaying her every morning.

119

Friday 17th June 2011

When it had come to applicants being sought for the post, Graham had applied. As a precautionary measure, his wife had taken a long planned trip to see relatives.

Alison was getting into combative mode. Now deciding she had been quiet for far too long. "So long planned, I never knew."

Graham said the wrong thing. "I never thought you would have been in danger working as a Police Officer down here. Otherwise I would have made provisions for you too."

"Still trying to sort out my life."

Ignoring her sneer, he went on to say that shortly after his application, he received a phone call from a foreign sounding person with a command of good English who categorically told him that unless he withdrew his application, there would be repercussions. In anticipation of any threats, Ian had previously positioned monitoring equipment on his phones and was able to trace and locate the mobile phone used to the Birmingham area. From numbers obtained recently by Simon, the phone user had been identified as 'Grigoriev.'

He received several other calls making threats from different mobiles, and the phones were all traced by Ian to the Birmingham area. Although he had not been informed as to where the 'irrefutable information' had come from, he had assumed it was from either GCHQ or MI5. They too were probably monitoring his phones on behalf of the Minister. Hence he was in possession of a 'pay as you go' untraceable mobile provided by Ian for any confidential information. Passing on the number to the others, they noted it in differing ways in the directories on their mobiles.

Alison said, "What about the phone from the Minister?"

"I have only been contacted twice so far by the Minister asking for any update. That phone must remain confidential."

Ian interjected saying, "I considered supplying everyone with encrypted phones, but the cost would have been exorbitant. PAYG untraceable throw away phones are nearly as good and a lot cheaper."

Graham savoured the last large mouthful of the wine as he drained his glass. Carol who had assumed the role of mine host swiftly refilled it. Then he continued. John had let it be known via Ginger that there had been several incidents of someone asking after him in Sussex. No one had seemed to understand why.

John butted in, "We do now. God rest your soul Vilf."

They all raised their glasses. Alison knew nothing of Vilf but decided the time was not right to ask. She would question one of them later as to who he was. Graham told them it had first alerted him to the possibility of Alison's safety. Then for his daughters' benefit, he told her he had arranged for her to be paired up with John on a convenient murder enquiry where she could be kept an eye on.

Sarcastically, she said, "Thanks" and then remembered the day wondering how as a uniform officer she had been seconded to the Armstrong enquiry.

Graham continued ignoring the blatant sarcasm, saying that when he and John realised she was being lined up for a kidnapping was when Simon was called in.

"I did actually appreciate that."

Simon said, "No problem."

"Just don't get cocky."

Graham asked Simon, "I understand you have had some success" which was his way of saying 'your turn to speak.'

Simon explained that he had been contacted by Barry who told him that he had been paid to conduct surveillance on Alison. Her gaze bore into him and he deliberately refrained from looking at her.

"Why didn't you tell me?"

"You may have acted differently to your normal routine and we didn't want that."

She crossed her arms which sent a pulse of pain through her chest as she just said, "Huh" and tried to stop herself going into a blatant sulk.

No one asked how he knew Barry, and he wasn't going to volunteer it.

Barry had told him he had been approached by a lawyer in Birmingham who had employed him in the past for 'off the books' work. The approach had been the same on every occasion. A phone call which gave instructions who to meet, where and when. No mention of what the work would entail and he never asked. It was understood that the contact, in this case, Grigoriev would be the person controlling the operation. He would also be the person who paid him and always in cash. It appeared to Barry that the lawyer, a man called Yusuf, was the conduit between his own employer and the operational controller. It was as if Yusuf did not want to know any details.

John said, "Typical brief. Able to plead ignorance and row for the shore if it all comes on top."

Simon continued telling the assembly that Barry had found it strange that the subject was so far distant from Birmingham and that his contacts in Sussex were Russian. Whenever he had worked for Yusuf previously, it had always been within the environs of Birmingham and his contacts had always been Asians.

Simon glossed over the incidents at the barn which Alison appreciated quietly. She had decided that she was going to keep quiet as to the fateful final hours of her captivity. Carol was a doctor and used to keeping confidences and would not say anything as to what she had heard said on the phone.

All he mentioned was hearing the name of Richard Davies used by one of the Lithuanian brothers as the person having ordered the kidnapping. Graham confirmed it to be the name of the alleged main criminal in Birmingham who was trying to take over the city. Simon continued telling the group that once he had found Petrovski's abandoned phone, he had retrieved from the directory the hard-line numbers of both Sol Yusuf and Davies PA. Other numbers were found including the one that identified Grigoriev's mobile phone.

John cut in again, "I think I may have Grigoriev's SIM card thanks to Vilf" and he passed it to Ian.

Ian who had not actually spoken during the meeting was checking a small hand held electronic 'personal assistant'.

Without looking up, he said, "I'll work on the phones and SIM tomorrow. We have an old soldier who has been through Kent and has a florists in Birmingham. He should be able to get the addresses of both Yusuf and Davies without trouble."

Graham said, "Only if he can be trusted. No Police involvement. I don't want anyone being alerted."

Carol said, "Let's go and eat because all the food should be ready."

Alison was still upset when she stopped Simon. "When did Barry contact you?"

"The first day when we got back from the run."

"How? I never saw him."

"He left my butterfly knife the wrong way round."

"You never told me. You let me stew."

"Sorry."

"No you're not."

"You're right. I'm not. It was for your own good."

"You rat" and she strode off with as much dignity as she could muster without causing herself too much pain into the dining room behind the others.

120

Friday 17th June 2011

They sat in the separate dining room around a table that could quite easily have accommodated ten, and as if to confirm the fact, had ten chairs. Graham quipped that the size of the flat led him to believe that Metropolitan Police detectives working in Sussex were either over paid or needed investigating. Alison, who had not been aware of John's flat in Chichester, was surprised by his obvious eye for style in furnishing which was belied by his usual dress code. She really liked Vettriano paintings and noticed what she assumed were three prints hanging against one wall in John's dining room. Had she examined them more closely she may have noticed that two were originals. Ian and Carol who had both spent some time in the flat, both for differing reasons, just ate.

Alison was struggling to chew the tender meat, and trying to keep it away from her tooth sockets that were still a little painful. Her jaw was starting to ache as it got more movement than of late and appeared to be remembering the hard punch it had received from Grigoriev. The clove oil that Carol had given her seemed to be slowly working on the raw gum. Her thumb was starting to feel normal and her bandaged ribs were recovering with the odd twinges just to let her know she was moving about too quickly.

She wasn't looking forward to the hospital visit for X-rays, although John insisted it was 'fun'.

Remembering the unexplained laughter, she scowled at him and said, "There's a bit of difference between the gentle tap you received and what I've suffered."

With sheer mockery in his voice, he said, "You may become a martyr," and they all burst out laughing as she turned her now familiar rubicund.

Overall: although she would not yet admit, she felt she was recovering thanks to Carol's ministrations.

Simon was enjoying his second decent meal in as many days as cooked by Carol and the wine provided by John. As his parents ran what some people called a 'gastro pub', he was accustomed to both good food and a choice of good wines. It had become a successful pub when his parents first took it on due to their perseverance and sheer hard work and as a result had gone from strength to strength. He'd sleep well again tonight because tomorrow he was going to be busy.

John did not normally have so much company in his own flat, and sat listening mainly to the general banter as he finished his meal. Ian and Graham who had to drive later that night limited their drinking to a couple of glasses of wine each. Alison was starting to appreciate the good quality wine which seemed to be have a pleasant numbing effect and knew that she'd sleep well. Carol didn't worry that Alison shouldn't have been drinking with some of the medication she had given her, and knew it would probably have proved fruitless to try and stop her. It was a convivial meal.

At the conclusion, they took their wine back to the lounge with John carrying a third bottle with due reverence.

With a backward glance at the empty plates and debris on the dining table, he said, "The cleaner will sort that lot out in the morning."

Carol replied indignantly, "Is that what I am now?" feigning hurt.

The men laughed as Alison said, "I'll help you."

"Thanks."

Once settled, Simon told them he intended to go to Birmingham and see if he could ascertain who the treacherous Minister was. No one asked him how he expected to achieve this as they all had their own ideas of his methods. He considered it his duty as Alison had suffered so much in an effort to discover the person's identity. She made no comment because she had fallen asleep in one of John's large Stressless recliners. Simon's main object, although not divulged, was to make the acquaintance of Grigoriev and educate him in the art of dealing with ladies.

Graham politely pointed out to him that he needed to be careful and aware that the Chief Constable, who he reiterated was highly likely in the pocket of Davies, could bring considerable resources to bear in trying to locate him. John also reminded Simon of the trouble a previous Chief Constable had caused him so many years previously. It seemed to be endemic in the Birmingham area that the top Police Officer was corrupt.

He accepted he had to tread carefully.

Graham commented ruefully, "I may be in a position to do something about it one day."

Turning to Ian, Simon enquired if he had brought the items he had requested of him. Ian went to the hall and came back in with a small sports type black holdall.

"You'll find everything is in here."

Asking how he was getting on at the barn, Ian told him that the generator and equipment from the outhouse had been completely dismantled and was now in a vehicle and on its way, or already at, his unit in Kent. The actual prison was to be demolished by a couple of disabled Royal Engineers who were desperate to keep their hand in and needed places to practice on.

"They want to start a demolition company."

No one bothered asking where the explosives were being sourced. It seemed rather bad manners.

He volunteered the fact that he had also arranged removal of both the BMW and Alison's Ford Fiesta on covered low loaders. Each would be dealt with separately.

By 1am, two had gone their respective ways, and the others were all in bed.

121
Saturday 18th June 2011

Doreen couldn't sleep. She kept mulling over in her mind what John had said. She knew the case now as well as anyone. Although she hadn't visited the bungalow personally, she had watched both the Police photographers video and Gary's recording. The new book, a biography by Conan Doyle, hadn't been out of its drawer for days. How many exactly had escaped her. That evening's book club meeting was the first she had missed in years. It hadn't been the fact that Sally had been arrested; she just hadn't actually read the book to be discussed.

With her insensitive Mother, she had watched the BBC's 10pm news which had featured as the main item the arrests of Gary and Sally and the incidents under investigation. Then the regional news which went into much more detail. Doreen's Mother was shocked and upset at the thought of all the people who had been killed or injured and then that her daughter was involved with the minutiae of it. The Chief Constable had appeared sufficiently grave as he gave the press conference with the air of a man who knew how to present news. Prodow and Groves who were fidgeting in the spotlight, were on the platform flanking him and all were in front of a large blue screen emblazoned with the Sussex insignia and marked 'Sussex Police'.

Doreen thought, 'Not the best advert for the county.'

Lavinia had retired to bed fretting that there were such nasty people about. She consoled herself with the knowledge she had Doreen to look after and care for her. Her anxiety didn't stop her getting straight off to sleep as opposed to Doreen. Lying in her bed staring at the ceiling, she considered every person who could possibly know about either the poison or the camera in the bird box.

She thought 'a plumber fixing a pipe in the kitchen' but then he would not know about the bird box. A 'grocery delivery being put in the cupboard by the delivery driver': he wouldn't know about the camera. A burglar? No. The poison was in a large unmarked jar anyway, and was a clear liquid. Even if someone saw it, they wouldn't know what it was. She considered the workshop: who would have access there? It had an alarm which would stop anyone going in without Gary's permission. Who would he take in there? 'A customer?' He had no need to take a customer there. 'A friend.' Highly unlikely. Gary had said no one knew.

Doreen struggled to go to sleep, but it was no good. She got up quietly so as not to disturb her truculent Mother and went downstairs turning on only the kitchen light, and made herself a cup of tea.

She sat in the dark in her usual chair in the sitting room and closed her eyes but didn't sleep. Sipping her tea with thoughts spilling around in her head she became annoyed with John for planting the seed in her mind. Maybe a hot milky drink would help her sleep. In the dark she bumped into the coffee table as she made her way into the kitchen. Opening the fridge, she found the milk and filled a mug. Then putting it into the temperamental six-year-old microwave her Mother refused to let her replace, she set it off for one minute. It whirred as the plate turned and then gave a loud 'ping' at the conclusion of the minute.

Doreen took the hot milk back into the dark sitting room and nearly dropped it at the unanticipated shadowy shape of her Mother sitting in her normal seat.

"You gave me the shock of my life. What are you doing up?"

"The noise you have been making would wake the Devil himself."

"I couldn't sleep."

"Nor could I with you clattering about."

And then it came to Doreen.

She gave her Mother the milk.

"I don't need this, I'm going to bed" and she was asleep in less time than it had taken the microwave to heat the milk.

122
Saturday 18th June 2011

John was back at his regular seat before 7.am and way before the queue formed. The chef had cleared the table in front of him and they'd engaged in their usual natter. He'd asked how her family was as he knew she had a slightly wayward son. She appreciated his concern and said that the school seemed to be sorting him out. The school's liaison officer that John had once mentioned to her had had a word with him which seemed to have made a difference to his indifferent attendance record.

His food soon appeared after the canteen officially opened at 7. It never hurt to be polite.

In the office, John found Paul and Doreen both working on their own enquiries in a silence broken only by the clacking of keyboard keys.

Paul said in just above a whisper, "She was in before me today, hasn't had a tea and hardly spoken."

"I'll have one now. I didn't realise what the time was."

Paul set about brewing drinks for all three of them.

John enquired, "What are you up to then?"

"Just an idea I had. I'll let you know if it works."

Paul looked at John and raised his eyebrows.

"That's all I've got from her all morning." He passed the tea to her which she took without acknowledging.

Jimmy burst boisterously into the office at 8.15am in company with one of the younger women detectives and was brought to a sudden halt.

"What's happening?"

"If you must make such a racket would you please go elsewhere."

"Sorry Doreen" and then to Paul in a stage type whisper, "What's happening?"

Paul just shrugged. Jimmy and his latest lady exaggeratingly tip toed noiselessly to his desk. Then they hid behind his biggest barricade of exhibits where they engaged inaudibly in co-ordinating their social calendar. Eventually they got round to a little Police work. From time to time one of them would glance out from cover and down the office towards the unusually aggressive Doreen.

She was busy going through the bundle of papers prepared by the arresting officers, and was glowering at them if they weren't showing her what she wanted. Corroborating as much as she could by visiting web sites and Police indices caused her to huff audibly at them when they disproved what she wanted. There were the pictures of both Gary and Sally, copies of Fingerprints, Antecedents, Social Service records going back years, school reports, copies of phone records (both hard line and mobiles), details of contact with Police going back the ten years that Sussex kept records. Even details of Sally's work record with Boots the Chemist and her qualifications and Gary's attendance record at Chichester College with his diplomas, copies of birth and marriage certificates, and the DVLA (Driver and Vehicle Licencing Authority) records of their driving licences and applications made when they applied for their Passports.

She even had all the Sussex Police confidential information reports relating to both. Hardly anything was on them. The fact that Gary was a burglar alarm engineer and also boarded up insecure premises. Sussex Police would not use him however as he had never been vetted or had a CRB (Criminal Records Bureau) check completed. Gary had his details taken once when he was in a pub that had been raided some six years earlier, but so had some off duty Police officers. Sally had been seen and interviewed when Boots received a visit by the chemists' officer as restricted substances were held on the premises and proof of security had to be confirmed. Applications made by both for visas to the American Embassy for an extended stay when they wanted to travel around the States. Another visa application for an extended stay in Australia, again to travel the country. Nothing detrimental.

Doreen was playing on the internet with details from the files that she thought were useful to her. Then when nothing was found she'd do what John thought was a female trait and just say, "Huh" and try something else. She picked up the phone and berated an officer at HQ for full details from their social media sites saying her authority was the Chief Constable himself. It was all e-mailed to her within thirty minutes. When it was printed, it ran to ninety-four pages. She was back on the phone to HQ,

"Are there any transactions on E-bay or anything with PayPal?" "Please. Within the next half hour" and she hung up.

She examined everything. John and Paul kept reasonably quiet although they found it hard not to chat. Groves came in after an hour and commented on the calm in the office, and was glared at by Doreen. The three men decided the safest place to go to was the canteen and leave Doreen by herself. Signalling for Jimmy to follow they all sat round a table as Groves got the tea and buns. The Polish pot washer saw the group and knew something was afoot. He had seen the previous evening news and recognised Groves.

Soon the Chef knew.

They were joined after half an hour by Prodow.

"I've just been kicked out of the office by Doreen. What's she up to?"

Paul said, "We've no idea, but we're safer down here."

Groves told them that Gary had been charged with the assaults on Murray and the other detective, but not with the murders as yet, and had resigned himself to a life in prison. Sally was still staying quiet, although her solicitor was 'making noises' that she would probably put her hands up to manslaughter.

"What! On the grounds of insanity more likely" came Jimmy's surprisingly cogent reply.

The canteen had gradually filled and was full of early lunch time visitors, and at 1pm the men agreed to go back into the office and Prodow, as senior officer present, was elected to ask Doreen what she was doing. When they walked in, Doreen was reading her book.

123

Saturday 18th June 2011

On arrival at the station and even before his morning canteen visit, John had completed a search on the PNC for the Audi. Telephoning his home phone, he told Simon that it had not been reported stolen. He knew Petrovski would not report it, but he could not be sure about Grigoriev or even the hire company. If questioned as to why he had done the search, he would say it had been seen near Birdham which was true. While he was on the terminal, he also put a marker on the PNC that if seen, not to stop the vehicle, but report its position to the murder team at Chichester. It had two effects: if it was reported stolen, he would be informed immediately and he could warn Simon. If it was seen in Birmingham, he again could warn Simon that it had been noted, and he could abandon it. Paul was made aware of the Audi as a suspect vehicle but knew it was not worth questioning John further.

The vehicle was actually registered to a local Chichester company that only had a portakabin as an office which was at the rear of a small forecourt for cheap second hand and hire vehicles. It had a reputation for sharp practices in the area as some of the hire cars were not in a good or even road worthy condition. It's owner had convictions for fraud and other motoring offences and was well known to, and often visited by Police. Most likely thought John, the vehicle was hired using false details which weren't verified, and a substantially large cash deposit paid, probably more than the vehicle's worth.

Simon had his new 'pay as you go' mobile provided by Ian with just one number stored which was another 'pay as you go' phone belonging to him. Both were untraceable. Contact from John and the others would be via Ian unless urgent. Ian had already been in touch with the florist and got the two addresses which were reasonably well known by people who liked to keep their fingers on the pulse. He had added the additional information that Davies was apparently not a nice person and definitely someone to be avoided unless you wanted to visit a hospital.

He was at the Audi by 9am and checked that it hadn't been tampered with. In the glove box, he found a screwed up hire agreement which he smoothed out and then folded twice before replacing after noting the name shown on it. From the bag supplied by Ian, he took out and connected a small Sat Nav into a power socket, stuck the screen to the dash board with the two rubber suckers and punched in the address of Davies. The Sat Nav took a while to locate satellites and identify its own location and then the location sought. Once the Sat Nav confirmed it had downloaded all fixed speed camera locations within the country, and had checked for traffic hold ups it played a few melodious notes.

Taking a spray can marked as 'glass cleaner' from the bag, he threw it into the glove box. The bag and its remaining contents were placed in the boot with a similar bag of his own containing personal items. He was wearing heavy soft soled shoes, jeans, a checked work shirt and an old worn leather jacket. Making sure no one was watching, he removed Petrovski's mobile from one of his inside jacket pockets and left it visible on the passenger seat, but turned off. Picking up his new phone, he made sure it was working with Wi Fi turned on and in silent mode before placing it in his now empty pocket.

Still verifying he wasn't being watched, he took the MP-443 automatic gun he had used to shoot the Lithuanian from his waistband and wedged it under the driving seat. The unfired gun from the shot man he stuffed under the passenger seat. Both guns had been cleaned and checked and Simon was confident that if needed, they would both perform well. He had established the ammunition to be a form of hollow point bullet which breaks up into fragments when they enter a body. Now they were out of his waistband, he felt lighter and took his jacket off and draped it over the back of the passenger seat as many workmen tend to do.

He set off for Birmingham. There was no hurry. As long as he arrived by early afternoon he would be happy. No point in drawing attention to one's self by speeding. ANPRs would be no problem as the vehicle was legitimate. Before leaving the flat, he'd said goodbye to Carol, but not Alison who was still fast asleep due to mixing excessive amounts of alcohol with medication. Simon knew when she found out he'd gone without saying goodbye, she'd be ratty.

It amused him for some reason.

124
Saturday 18th June 2011

The Sat Nav sent him across country to link up to the motorway network and he stopped when he judged he was nearly half way at a service station for a comfort break. Buying a pre-packed sandwich, he struggled at first to open it wishing he could use his butterfly knife which would have made short shrift of it. Then he encountered more difficulty trying to eat it. Not that it was wholly inedible (although close) it was tasteless. Giving up after just three bites of it, he discarded the rest, and continued his journey. It was a boring road as most motorways in England are, and the radio in the Audi did not work.

Simon was at the southern outskirts of Birmingham by 1pm and the Sat Nav was showing him the shortest route to Davies's address which was in an exclusive suburb well to the North of the city. He ignored the Sat Nav's preferred option and skirted the conurbation by keeping to the motorway on the east side passing the turnings for the international airport and the conference centre. The Sat Nav kept altering its instructions as the satellites in conjunction with the computer realised that the vehicle was ignoring the course proffered. Like all Sat Navs, it never quibbled but just got on with its job. As he travelled across the north of the city, he again took up the directions dictated to him and followed the Sat Nav route.

Turning off at the junction indicated, he soon found himself driving through a street of independent shops all slightly set back from the road and fronted with well-established trees. Expensive cars, some with chauffeurs were parked on faded double yellow lines ignoring the free car park indicated by unobtrusive but clear sign posts. There was no traffic warden or parking attendant to be seen. Simon pulled into the side of the road and stopped. Looking about, he could see no traffic cameras, but a few shops had CCTV cameras mounted high on their outside walls pointing down at front doors. People were scurrying about on the pavements darting in and out of shops, and some carrying bags bearing inscribed logos. The pedestrians were mainly Asian and all appeared affluent in their appearance.

Simon travelled on a few hundred yards and drove into the indicated car park. According to the sign there was room for only fifty cars, but it wasn't even a quarter full. The spaces marked were so big that they could quite happily have accommodated panel vans. No chance of getting a door hitting the side of an adjacently parked car. There was a large pole in the middle which had four downlighters resembling a strange mushroom. He hadn't been in a civic car park that was free for about the last five years and it was mainly empty. No security cameras were evident and he could not believe they were hidden. He locked the Audi leaving the mobile still on the passenger seat in clear view and his jacket on the back of the seat.

Walking back slowly along the street, he window shopped for nothing he wanted. Arriving at a small bakery he saw that there were two tables nestling close together on the pavement outside which were bathed in the afternoon sun.

Stepping inside, he saw three more small tables alongside the wall opposite the display counter. They were all unoccupied. Cakes of various colours, shapes and sizes filled the display. Against the wall behind the display were trays containing a huge range of breads. Choosing a simple, but rather expensive Danish pastry and a coffee, he was told to take a seat and await its delivery. Moving back outside, he sat with his back against the window and sipped his freshly ground coffee as he watched the world go by for half an hour. Numerous women rushed into the bakery and then rushed out again with cakes in boxes or bread in paper bags. No one else stopped to have afternoon tea and cake on the premises.

The only thing of note were two, newish and surprisingly clean, marked Police cars, which cruised slowly along the road with one uniformed occupant in each. No one in the street took a blind bit of notice of them. All the vehicles parked on the yellow lines which were restricting traffic flow were left by their drivers with impunity. Simon could only marvel at the temerity of the drivers and considered those in Sussex who were fined for stopping just long enough to let someone out of the passenger door.

Wandering into a small, empty independent bookshop, he engaged the owner in casual conversation and quickly established that the area was relatively crime free. Obtaining a map of the area and the local newspaper, he determined that there were a few local up market B & B's but no hotels.

He walked further along the road and went into a small 'tea rooms' where he was the only patron, ordered a coffee and sat by the window and skimmed the local paper. Prominent people were reported doing charitable things, and adverts of local up market establishments filled half of it. His attention was drawn to one of the original Police cars that cruised slowly along the road weaving to avoid illegally parked obstructive vehicles. Minor traffic collisions which would not have warranted a mention in a local Sussex paper were reported fully. The court reports were about the occasional drunk and minor offenders. Simon started to chat to the young lady who had served him and again established how crime free the area was.

She became more forthcoming than the bookshop owner and vociferously poisonous as she confided that the area housed some aggressively vicious criminals that did not 'shit on their own doorsteps' and took a very dim view if anyone else did. People like her had to live in a different part of Birmingham because they couldn't afford the local property prices. Her and her ilk commuted in to work only because it was worth it due to the wages in the locale being so very high. Whittling on, she claimed the local residents treated shop owners and staff like pariahs and second class citizens. Simon tried to lighten the mood and quipped he'd never seen such neat streets and clean Police cars.

Although she knew they were the only people in the place, she still patently glanced about the premises to check. Then quite freely, she told him the local Police and council were in the pocket of one of the resident villains.

"Who?"

For a few seconds, she became a little recalcitrant then "I don't know that I should say."

"Go on. It must be common knowledge round here."

"It is. He uses his initials. RD. Richard Davies."

"How are they in his pocket?"

"He tells the Police how often he wants them to cruise this area. Every fifteen minutes during the day and thirty minutes during the night. You could set your watch by them. He won't let the council put up any cameras anywhere, says it 'downgrades an area'. They'd probably see what he's up to."

"What's he up to?"

"Some say murders: bit of everything if you ask me. He runs most of the prostitutes in Birmingham and probably the drugs trade."

"Not good."

You're telling me. I work here."

125
Saturday 18th June 2011

Simon promenaded the local streets, and soon noticed that the Police only kept to the main road and streets off to one side of it. They seemed to have a set pattern which they adhered to doggedly. The uniformed officers in the cars looked bored witless as they drove past him oblivious to his presence. Not one of them took any notice of him or considered stopping him, and he was often the only pedestrian walking in a suburban street full of detached houses. Most Police officers would have been all over him wanting to know the ins and outs of his business in the area. The other side of the main road was where Yusuf and RD lived and Police seemed to be proscribed from that side which would prove extremely useful to him.

He strolled past Yusuf's house first. A tall undulating wall surrounded the property with two ornate iron gates protecting the short drive leading to the parking area and bank of three garages. There was a video system built into the offside pillar supporting one of the gates where visiting drivers could request entry. As he passed indifferently by, he observed a large well-kept two story Victorian styled mansion with out of place white plastic double glazed windows.

A CCTV security camera sat above, and pointing down towards the front doorstep of the house, and there was another over the middle of the three garages. Tucked up high under an arched gable was an alarm box and a couple of floodlights: one directed towards the parking area and the other to an area in front of the main door. It was obviously an expensive property due to its size, and Simon estimated at least five bedrooms. He soon spotted where the wall dipped low enough at one point where he could easily climb over to get into the garden later, unobserved by either camera.

Still walking on two streets further, he turned into a cul-de-sac where RD's house was the last and largest in the street of five. The road seemed to terminate at the entrance to his property. Within the first ten yards and before the entrance to the first house there was a little green sentry type box on the pavement big enough for one person to sit in, and it was occupied. Simon walked slowly on towards it taking out his local map and studying it as though searching for an address. As he approached the box, the man exited out of the door at the rear of it unbuttoning his jacket in the process. He was a good six feet three inches, slightly overweight, 'suited and booted' and looked reasonably smart and was carrying a large black Maglite torch in the bright daylight of a late afternoon of a beautiful summer's day. It was a blatant threat.

"You can't come down here."

"Why not? I'm looking for someone."

"I'm telling you. Turn round and go back."

"I didn't know this was a private road."

"You're not expected. There is no one in this road who wants to see you."

"Ok. Sorry."

"No problem" and the man stood and watched Simon leave the road before returning to his seat in the box having done up his jacket.

Simon had seen that there had been an old fashioned bakelite corded telephone on a small triangular shelf in one of the corners of the sentry box. The cord was twisted from use over time and no one had seen fit to untwist it. It did not impede the movement of the occupant in any way. As he'd spoken to the 'sentry' he'd noticed that he had his suit jacket undone which would not normally be unusual on such a hot day, but he'd undone it as he exited the box. 'Why would he have it done up while sitting down and undoing it when he got out? Only one obvious conclusion.'

Glancing past him as they'd spoken, he'd seen RD's house: more a palace than a mansion at the end of the cul-de-sac with large wide open inviting gates. It made Yusuf's place look like a cheap pile of bricks. In his snatched views, he'd not noticed any sign of a camera or alarm, but he could not rule out their absence. He had to assume that there was another 'sentry' of some type either stationed at the rear, or inside the house, or even maybe patrolling the grounds. So far, everything seemed as though it would be an easy couple of nights.

His mentor's words drifted back into his mind, 'Plan for the worst, hope for the best.'

He made his way back to the Audi, unlocked it and got in. Petrovski's mobile phone was still on the seat and his old jacket still over the back of it. Not a sign of anyone having tampered with the car. This truly was without a doubt a crime free area. Leisurely, he drove back to the motorway, and on to a service station with a Premier Inn hotel. The barrier lifted as he pulled up to the entrance of the hotel's car park, and he drove in and parked with the boot towards a hedge.

As he alighted from the car he wore a long peaked baseball cap pulled down low to obscure his face should there have been any CCTV cameras. He kept it on as he registered, aware that most hotel reception areas had a camera positioned to record a customer's identity as well as covering any cash drawers. Booking in using the false name from the hire agreement, he paid cash for four nights. Then to plant an informal notion, Simon remarked to the surly clerk behind the desk that his work should take no more than that. Then he asked if he could confirm that his car with his tools would be secure overnight in the hotel's car park.

Bordering on rudeness, the clerk verified that, "Of course it will be," and jabbed a pointed finger at a small TV screen below the reception counter which was split into four different views.

Accepting the unexpected offer to examine the images, Simon saw one was of the reception desk, one on the car park entrance, and two were on corridors. He looked hard at the pictures before he endorsed satisfaction with the security. The only one he could see that he needed to avoid was the one on the reception desk which was deliberately aimed to catch a full facial aspect. He did not bother looking up to see where the camera actually was, but it plainly didn't catch anyone entering or leaving via the main door. In reality, he noted it was a worthless system that had probably been installed as economically as possible.

Returning to the car, he fiddled about in the boot and confirmed that the only camera on the car park was at the entrance where it was positioned to record the index number plates of the arriving vehicles as they waited for the barrier to lift. Simon eyed the unobstructed exit which led no more than twenty yards straight towards a Shell garage with a forecourt littered with top of the range CCTV security cameras. The exit to the motorway itself if petrol was not sought, circuited via the nearside of the garage so avoiding its stringent detection system.

In order for him to avoid every camera on his return, Simon considered his options. He concluded that on leaving the motorway, he should drive towards the service station and then the wrong way along the twenty-yard short exit and back into the car park. No one should be any the wiser that the vehicle had moved.

Now already in the car park having passed the welcoming barrier camera, he manoeuvred the car to the end nearer the exit and backed up to a wall. People could see through the hedge as they passed by but they were unlikely to climb onto a wall to see what was happening on the other side. Taking his 'glass cleaner' from the glove box, he carefully sprayed both back and front number plates. Emitted was a very fine mist of a clear liquid that coated them with a thin film of plastic containing microscopic slivers of aluminium. Anyone looking at the plates would see nothing untoward, but no camera would be able to read them. An ANPR would still photograph the travelling Audi but it would display an illegible blurred image. Somehow the aluminium broke up radar beams and as a result the car was unidentifiable except to the human eye.

It was one of Ian's new discoveries of which he was extremely proud. He was in protracted negotiations with a section of the military to allow them to utilise the patent. They could envisage its potential use in the dryer regions of the world that they operated in. The only fly in the ointment was that water was what washed the substance off. Simon knew this and thought, 'Summer in England. No chance of rain then!' Taking his own bag from the boot, he stuffed Petrovski's phone and his jacket into it, and withdrew to his room. He liked Premier Inn hotels because they always seemed to have big comfy beds. This one was no exception, and Simon had a long early evening nap.

126

Saturday 18th June 2011

Prodow said, "Spill the beans Doreen. What have you got?"

She closed her book and put it nonchalantly into her top drawer. Giving a forced single cough, she rubbed her throat.

"It's such a long story. I think I'll need at least one cup of tea and some nice biscuits because I've had no lunch today."

Paul said, "On way" and pulled the kettle out of her large bottom drawer as she sat looking serenely into space.

She held her hands together and even imperturbably twiddled her thumbs. Jimmy being the fittest was dispatched to the canteen for packets of at least three different varieties of biscuits. Chairs were pulled to face her desk in a semi-circle as the door was slammed shut after Jimmy's arrival with an armful of biscuits and fudges which he let drop on her desk. Disdainfully, she glanced at them.

Then seeing a small packet, "Oh, Rich Teas, my favourites."

A couple of teams of detectives who had returned to the office to write their reports stopped and perched on desks waiting to see what was happening.

Within ten minutes, everyone had a drink in front of them and they were all assembled in front of Doreen's desk like a group of naughty children in front of their teacher awaiting chastisement.

Between biscuits she said, "I haven't total proof who did it or why, that's down to you. I can say unequivocally that I can point you in the right direction."

Prodow said, "Doreen. Stop talking in riddles."

"Yesterday, John was doing his usual talking rhetorically and for my sins, I listened to him. Thanks to him, I was unable to sleep last night because I couldn't stop thinking about what he had been saying. So, I got up and went downstairs to make myself a hot milk drink in the middle of the night. I had considered every possible person who may have had access to the house and the poison and the workshop and tapes. There was no one. Gary had said no one knew. But they did."

She paused and sipped her tea.

"Ah. Nectar."

Prodow said, "Doreen. Get on with it or by God I'll sack you here and now!"

"While I was in the kitchen using the microwave to heat my milk, my Mother had heard me and had come downstairs as well and sat in the darkness of the lounge listening to me. I hadn't heard her because of the noise the microwave made. That's when I realised without a shadow of a doubt: at some point, they had to have been overheard."

John said, "Who by Doreen?"

"Sally's daughter Deborah: Gary's step daughter."

Groves butted in.

"What daughter? There's no daughter shown anywhere on any of her antecedents."

As if in a faraway thought "Yes. I did notice that. Strange really" and she picked up a wrapped slice of fudge and looked at it longingly for a good ten seconds.

"No. I mustn't."

Paul in his loudest voice cried exasperatingly, "Doreen!"

"Well, you can imagine my surprise when I realised that. I don't think she has ever tried to hide the fact that she had a daughter, but I can't be sure. I think I may even have seen her once when Sally brought her along to a book club meeting six or seven years ago. She told our group she was a relative, but not which one."

She picked up the fudge.

"Why not" and started to unwrap it. Several detectives practically falling off desks shouted at her. Jimmy virtually screamed at her.

Prodow loudly above them all said, "Come on now everyone. Calm down. A little decorum please. Let her speak."

"Thank you sir. I came to the conclusion that the officer taking the antecedents had probably used a wrong word when he was questioning her. He may have said, 'Have you AND Gary got any children?' and she could honestly answer, No. The question should have been, 'Have either you OR Gary got any children' and then the answer would have been yes."

She took a bite of the fudge while everyone considered the hypothesis.

Prodow enquired, "Where's the proof they were overheard?"

"I'm coming to that" and she took a custard cream from the packet. "I think these must be my favourite biscuits now."

Prodow said, "So help me Doreen, I'll kill you now myself."

"Once I realised someone must have overheard them, I searched for a person who would be likely to stay at their house. It had to be someone at the house as Sally was unlikely ever to go to the workshop and the chance of someone being there to overhear was negligible. Also, the person would have to be acquainted with where the actual poison was in the unmarked bottle."

She paused and sipped her tea.

"I have gone through everything that I thought would be helpful. An old Passport application that Sally made showed Deborah as her next of kin with her old full address."

There was silence.

"Sally's birth certificate showed her Mother as Jean. I have searched the phone records, and I have located their telephone numbers, and from them I've confirmed their addresses. It had to be either Sally's Mother Jean, or her child by her previous marriage: Deborah. Jean is an older lady and would not have been as sprightly as the person on the video. The problem that arose was that neither owns a green Micra and that threw me for a while.

Gary has no relatives to speak of, a few cousins and that's it. There was no one close enough there."

She paused again.

"I do love custard creams. I think I've actually gone off Rich Teas today" and she took another from the packet.

Paul said, "Doreen. You are skating on very thin ice."

"It appears from all my enquiries that Sally did not get on too well with her Mother. Jean had, how can I put it, found God having been adopted and brought up in a religious environment by a priest and his wife. Sally was more a rebellious non-believer, and moved on at the age of fourteen or fifteen years. She was married at seventeen and divorced by nineteen. Most of this was buried rather deeply in the files. The rest I got from different agencies."

She slurped the remnants of her tea, and took a biscuit.

"Let's see if they are nicer than custard creams" and she bit into it. "Any chance of another cuppa? I'm getting parched with all this chat," and she forced a slight cough as if to embellish the fact.

Prodow, in his sternest voice said, "Doreen!"

"Well. Deborah was an unplanned and unwanted child and Jean being a devoutly nice sort of person kind of adopted her and has brought her up. As she has grown older, Sally has taken her back very occasionally. I really must have another drink."

Prodow said to one of the Detectives, "For God's sake make her a bloody cup of tea."

Groves said, "Doreen. Stop toying with us. What's the killer piece of information you have?"

"I pinned my hopes on Deborah having a Micra, and I nearly lost it then. When I got her Facebook information, she showed swapping dresses with her friends for nights out. Then it occurred to me she may have borrowed the car from one of them. None of them owned a green Micra, I checked all her friends thoroughly. I'd noticed on her Facebook page was a reference to a site called Flickr which is where some people post photographs. I was checking it and found an old photograph from a year ago where she was posing with a boyfriend. The photo was dated and timed and was titled with the location and her and his details."

She handed Prodow a coloured printed photograph as if to confirm what she'd discovered.

Grasping the produced cup of tea in both hands, she sipped it.

"That's really nice. Thank you."

Prodow said in pronouncement as he glared at Doreen, "I can now quite understand why some murders occur."

"It has taken me a while to locate him and get all his details. He has a green Micra that he bought from E-bay. He's still got it and shows Deborah on his own Facebook page as his current girlfriend."

She handed Prodow a PNC of the green Micra as nearly all those in the room crowded behind him to look over his shoulder as he viewed it.

"As you can see, he still owns it" and she took several gulps of her tea. Then as though an afterthought she added, "Oh, and by the way, do you notice some of the letters and numbers are identical and in the same position as the ones I spotted on the Micra in George's drive?"

Prodow exclaimed, "Doreen, I love you."

"You just threatened to kill me!"

"Never!"

127

Saturday 18th June 2011

It was very late in the evening when Simon left the hotel with his baseball cap pulled well down and headed for the car park. Another hour and total darkness was looming. The single camera that picked him up was in a corridor and then only for a couple of seconds. He hadn't had any warnings from Ian or John, so was confident the car was still not shown as stolen. Being cautious, however, he still checked the Audi for any tampering. He'd used two of his own security measures. A small piece of paper under the driver's door which would flutter unobtrusively to the ground when the door was opened and a sliver of wood by the hinge of the boot which would lodge in the rain channel should it have been disturbed. Both simple, and crude, but efficient indicators. Neither had been disturbed.

Joining the late night motorway traffic without passing through the garage or by any CCTV camera, he returned to the leafy suburb. Simon parked in a road where a few other vehicles were, and not far from Yusuf's house on the side the Police were disinclined to visit. He had dressed in black trousers and dark shirt under his black leather jacket. In one pocket was a dark woollen balaclava and his trusty butterfly knife in another. His shoes were dark tan leather with rubber soles and had never once so much as dared to utter a squeak. Walking to where he had decided to climb over the wall, he checked the street, put on a pair of latex gloves and was in Yusuf's garden with hardly any effort at all.

He remained crouched where he'd landed and surveyed the house. There was a light showing behind a drawn curtain in one downstairs room with a light flickering occasionally indicating a TV. No lights were evident in any upstairs windows. Scanning the building keenly, he spotted several of the first floor windows had not been closed having been opened to let air in during the day. It would suit him if he could get in through one of them in case Yusuf set a ground floor alarm system at night. Although there were a couple of drain pipes, they could not be relied upon to take the weight of even the lightest person. Slowly, he manoeuvred round the garden keeping in the shadows close to the boundary wall. He dropped his bag behind a bush where he could collect it later.

While he was looking for a way in, he noticed the land line telephone entry point connection attached to the wall at the rear of the house. It was as far from the lit window as was possible to get, and the opposite side of the premises. With his butterfly knife in hand, he crept forward and cut it by the connector knowing there was probably at least one mobile phone in the house. He knew that even if it was reported immediately to a phone company, it would not elicit a response for a day or two at best. Ian had told them, and Simon had seen, that there had been a mobile number shown on Petrovski's phone for Yusuf. He was about to move further round the house in his quest for entry when he noticed a rear window was no more than two inches ajar. Considering the risk and the fact he couldn't see a safe way to climb up to the first floor, he took a quick peek.

It was an office of some kind with a large desk in the middle of the room and a leather chair either side of it. On the desk was one main set cordless telephone which implied to Simon that there were other handsets dotted around the house which would now no longer work. Twelve mobile phones were aligned neatly next to it all connected to chargers. There were no passive alarm detectors in the two corners of the room that he could see. He eased the window slowly wider without a sound and then put his head very, very, slowly in to check the corners that were invisible to him whilst outside. None.

It looked like a main communications room, yet there was no alarm visible and the window had been left ajar. Even in a crime free area, Simon thought it was 'pushing one's luck'. He climbed in waiting for an audible alarm to activate. Still nothing. Moving to the shut door, he checked all round it for alarm connectors, yet found none. 'There must be a panic alarm in here somewhere' he thought and moved back to the desk. Searching for a foot operated one first, then he worked his way around the chairs and through the desk.

He opened the door just a fraction, and checked again for alarm contacts. It was starting to mystify him. There seemed to be no internal security alarm although there was an alarm box on the outside wall. A television was blasting out a one day cricket match direct from India in the room with the light on. Simon could see the light spilling from the open door which was illuminating part of the yawning hallway. Even in the dimly lit corners, there appeared to be no alarm control box anywhere. He crept silently to the closed door of the next room and slowly opened it. Still not a sound.

Stepping into the room he gently shut the door behind him and looked about. His little torch flashed on for a couple of seconds as he swept the beam around the room. It was some kind of store room with small step ladders, brooms, mops, buckets and shelves with cleaning products neatly lined up upon them. There were a couple of broken chairs and some old cushions that looked like they had been thrown in some time back and forgotten. A small single window was what attracted Simon. Just big enough to climb through. The crispy dried spider's webs disclosed it had probably never been opened. He unlocked it with the key that appeared to live constantly in the lock, but had seemingly never been turned. Pushing the window open no more than an inch, he was satisfied. From outside he would be able to get his fingers around it and fully open it.

Carefully, going back into the office, he left via the window and pushed it fully closed.

128

Sunday 19th June 2011

Simon collected his bag and left the grounds by the same part of wall that he'd originally climbed. There was no one about to witness it. He walked on towards RD's.

Dropping his bag on the ground just out of sight of the road's guard: he walked as if he was going to cross the entrance to the cul-de-sac. Just half way, he staggered and fell over in clear sight of the sentry sitting in his box. He writhed about for a second or two on the floor as though struggling to get up. When he managed it, he started stumbling towards the sentry box as though he was still pursuing his original course, but he kept his face well down.

The man in the box had watched with mounting amusement believing Simon were a drunk, and left his preserve to put him back on course. It was going to be a kind gesture which transpired to be a grievous mistake. Simon struck him hard twice in the face before he knew he'd been hit and it was too late for him to react. His eyes watered and blurred and started to glaze over. The third punch was the really hard one aimed at his jaw. He fell to the floor unconscious.

Simon pulled his balaclava from his jacket pocket and slipped it on. Had the guard been observant enough, he would have seen that he was already wearing latex gloves.

Retrieving his bag, he used two of Ian's supplied plasticuffs to first 'handcuff' the sentry's feet together and then handcuff his hands behind him and either side of the feet 'handcuffs'. It was a secure method tried and tested by various military units during active combat to incapacitate a combatant quickly. If a British Police Force used it there would be an almighty outcry.

Conducting a quick search of the sentinel, Simon found and removed the Glock 19 handgun from his shoulder holster and a modern mobile from his inside pocket. It was Simon's favourite make of handgun and he considered keeping it, but instead placed both items over the wall of the first house after turning the mobile off. Then dragging the unconscious man unceremoniously to the rear of the sentry box, he left him on the concrete pavement and out of sight to anyone passing the cul-de-sac's entrance. To make sure he didn't upset any of his plans, Simon put a strip of duct tape over his gaping mouth.

Simon bore the man no ill will as he was just a paid lackey doing a job, but to be carrying a firearm in an English street with no consequence as to Police action was perturbing. He probably had no idea what Richard Davies was up to and didn't care if he was being paid well enough. Being knocked unconscious was no real problem, but if someone did call the Police or an ambulance, he would struggle to explain what he had been doing. Simon relied on the premise that all five houses in the cul-de-sac were owned by people who did not want Police prying into their affairs: and he moved on to the wide open gates of Richard Davies.

He stood before the gates and regarded the drive with prudence. There was no obvious security. No one walking in the grounds, no CCTV and no alarm. Moving back to the sentry box he looked inside. Just a single telephone on a shelf in a corner with a tangled cord and no numbers to dial. It was a simple 'pick up to call' telephone, but to who and where? Not even a video system to contact anyone. Simon could not accept that a person of Richard Davies's reputation would rely solely on one person. He did not like the idea of ambling up the drive where he would be a sitting duck. Instead, he went a few yards to the right of the gates and found a tree that appeared to have been grown specifically to be climbed. Even carrying a bag posed him no additional problem as he shinned up it and then transferred to sit on top of the wall. Still nothing moved in the grounds so he lowered himself down into the front garden.

It was a very large house, modelled badly on a French chateau with turrets set at each corner and surrounded by what appeared to be several acres of well nurtured gardens. Simon felt confident to walk in them taking very few precautions. As he approached the back of the house, he soon concluded that it was square in structure. At the very rear and set a clear fifty yards away from the back door and directly in line with it, was a summer house. It looked big enough to accommodate a small family on its own. He heard soft music coming from a radio inside, and cautiously approached.

It was a two story structure, an open plan room upstairs and one down with a separate bathroom. There was a simple stable type wooden front door with a small square insert glass panel that faced the main building, and a large picture window downstairs that looked out further towards the rear of the garden. Upstairs, there was a single window to each side and another larger window that was above the front door and level with the back door of the 'chateau'. All the windows were devoid of curtains. Noiselessly approaching the rear, he glanced into the lit downstairs window and saw two men sitting at a wooden square table playing cards.

Clearly visible in one corner of the room was a small drop leaf table housing a kettle, a five-litre bottle of water, a collection of odd mugs, a jar of coffee and a bottle of milk: 'the essentials of life' reasoned Simon. On the floor, next to the table was a simple telephone which Simon concluded was obviously connected to the sentry box. He knew he could not surprise both and incapacitate them without probably a fair amount of noise and even gun play. It was nearly 2am and Simon was hoping that it was the time that the man in the sentry box would be changed.

Moving to observe the stable door, he sat with his back to a tree where he could just see into the room through the small glass pane and waited. One thing Simon could do with little effort was to watch and wait.

2am came and went and they still played cards. He thought he'd wait till after 3am and then reassess his plans if still no movement. If the three had started at 9pm they may be doing three hours each which would be a logical time. At 2.45am the cards were put onto the table, and one of the men climbed the open plan stairs to the upstairs room, a bedroom, for three hours sleep. The other started to make a cup of coffee and picked up the phone as he waited for the kettle to boil. It looked like 3am was the change over time. Simon waited for him to call the man from upstairs to go and check why the phone hadn't been answered.

He returned it to its cradle, and poured the water into the mug. No reaction at all when it hadn't been answered. He'd have been court martialled in the army for ignoring it.

129
Sunday 19th June 2011

Simon waited, and just prior to 3am the door opened, and the man came out. He made no more than two yards from the door before Simon touched him with an electronic Taser sending fifty thousand odd volts careering through his body. Shuddering involuntarily, he collapsed to the floor where he suffered the additional indignity of being struck on the side of his head with the sentry's large Maglite torch. His body had gone into mild convulsions, but was recovering quickly and the Maglite ensured the opposite. He was unconscious on the floor and Simon trussed him up in the same manner as the first sentry. Again, on a cursory search, Simon found him to be sporting a Glock 19 which he put to the side of the door under a shrub.

Waiting ten minutes more: which was the amount of time he estimated it would take for the man to reach the sentry box, have a quick chat and then for the other to return, Simon entered the summer house.

A voice called from upstairs, "Can't you ever stay awake just once. If Grigoriev came round, we'd all be for it."

Simon grunted in reply.

"Useless shit. Bring me a coffee when you come up."

Turning the kettle on, he boiled the water and when the kettle clicked off, he held the switch down forcing it to override and boil the water a little longer. Pouring the boiling water into the two biggest mugs he could see, he started up the stairs.

As he neared the top, he saw two basic single beds with no bedding, just bare mattresses, facing each other as there was no other way in the space available to place them. The one with the head closest to the stairs was occupied by a fully clothed man and he didn't see Simon coming. He heard him, and started to sit up expecting his coffee. As he turned and saw Simon, he took the full two mugs of boiling water in his face. From going for his gun, his hands involuntarily went to his face. He couldn't see and his eyes were streaming and his whole face was burning. Using the Maglite, with slightly less ferocity than previously, he struck the man knocking him unconscious and so relieving him of the searing pain the water had caused.

Retrieving the still holstered Glock 19, and a new type 'smartphone' from the man, Simon used plasticuffs to truss him up and some duct tape to keep him quiet should he come round too soon. If Richard Davies had supplied the guns, Simon conceded he had taste in weapons. They were not cheap guns if bought legally, and if illegal the price could be astronomical. Placing the gun and disabled phone with the others under the shrub he decided he would retain all three firearms if he had the chance later. He was still carrying the Lithuanians MP-443 gun which he knew worked fine and he needed to complete his plan. Time was now of the essence that he should get into the house.

While he had been in his hotel room, Simon had casually trawled the internet and discovered that Richard Davies was on his fourth wife and had a total of five children, but none with the latest. All the children had stayed with their respective Mothers who had all been made financially secure in non-acrimonious divorces. Yusuf had acted on behalf of all of them. Simon found out from 'Wikipedia' that there was a flat in an upmarket part of Manhattan and a boat moored in Puerto Banus. The web site claimed that his current wife, Jacqueline, preferred America, and it suited RD as he could search for wife number five with gusto. Simon knew most of what he had found out was rumour and ambiguity. He was just hoping that RD was alone.

He searched for an unlocked or open window, but couldn't find one. All the ground floor windows were secure and having seen all the upstairs windows were shut, he had no alternative but to break in which he really did not want to do. He recovered his bag and took out a glass cutter formed inside a set of four suction cups with a handle in the middle. Also in the bag was a large piece of mica which he thought he would try first. At the double-glazed back door, he put his hand on the handle with the intention of trying to place the mica between the door jamb and the door lock to prize it to open. The lock was a Yale type which was susceptible to mica.

The door opened: it wasn't even locked.

130

Sunday 19th June 2011

It was closing in fast on 3.30 in the morning when Alison awoke with a start. Whatever Carol had given her earlier had worked up until now. Normally, she slept undisturbed throughout the night without any assistance from any pills, but for some reason, she was wide awake and desperate for water. Her mouth was as dry as old sticks. She gingerly got out of bed and padded bare footed delicately towards the kitchen. A light was visible from beneath the door to the lounge and attracted her like a moth. Without thinking, she opened the door with the intention of turning it off. John was lying supine on one of his recliners with a book in his hands, and was also wide awake. On the side table next to him were a couple of mobiles, a glass and a bottle of wine.

Alison froze in the doorway.

"Either come in or go back to bed, but please shut the door. I don't want to disturb Carol."

She checked quickly that she was modestly attired, and walked in.

"What are you doing up at this time of night?" and lowered herself tentatively into an armchair.

"I'm waiting to see if Simon calls."

"Where is he?"

"Birmingham."

"What's he doing?"

"Making some enquiries."

"Why didn't he say goodbye to me before he went?"

"Not being too delicate about it, you were slightly drunk and dosed up on pills. He didn't fancy a fight."

She looked disdainfully at him for a few seconds, "I'm not really that bad" and then sullenly after a couple more seconds, "am I?"

The door opened, and Carol walked in wearing John's thick 'Guinness' dressing gown and carrying an unbranded one which she draped over Alison.

"You're not. The pair of you could wake Old Nick himself."

"I'm sorry I woke you."

"Any word yet from Simon?"

"Nothing."

"I'm going to make some tea. Do either of you want one?"

Both replied "Yes please" in unison.

*

Simon stepped inside and waited and listened. Then he went through the kitchen and into the hallway. He heard water splashing. Keeping close to the wall, he started along the hallway which was in effect a wide corridor. Listening at each door he passed, he soon arrived at the front of the house. The corridor turned into a large vestibule with two equally opposed slightly curved stairways facing the front door. It was a square building with a covered quadrangle in the middle. That's where the splashing noise was coming from. Having done a complete circuit and arriving back at the entrance to the kitchen he looked for a way into the 'central piazza.'

He hadn't seen it on his first lap. When he got back to the stairs he saw the door set into the wood panelling level with the ornate entrance. Unhurriedly he opened it a couple of inches and peered in. There was a paved plaza of sorts with a centralised swimming pool with subdued underwater blue lighting giving it a spectral aura. A naked woman was leisurely swimming up and down. She was in her early thirties and as Simon noted, was in perfect physical shape. A pile of clothes was on a poolside lounger. There was no sign of anyone else.

Simon pushed the door wide and went in. She didn't hear him and kept swimming. He went to the lounger and sat down feeling the clothes and the designer bag. Pulling his balaclava off, he stuffed it back into his pocket.

"Who the hell are you? The guards aren't allowed in the house."

She swam to the side of the pool in an effort to retain some decorum.

"I'm not a guard."

"Oh? Were you sent to check up on me. I know I shouldn't be in the pool. The old man's ok. I changed the drip at three."

402

"Where is he?"

"Upstairs. Do you want to see him?"

"Yes. Who else is in the house?"

"Only me. I swear it."

"Let's go and see him then."

"Do you mind turning round while I get out?"

"Afraid I do. Some people might hit me over the head when I'm not looking."

"I won't. I promise."

"Sorry."

She scowled at him, and then climbed out.

"You certainly keep in trim."

"You bastard."

"What's your name?"

"Mercedes. What's yours?"

"Simon. Mercedes is an interesting name."

"My dad was saving to buy a car when my mum fell pregnant with me. All the money they had went towards preparing for my birth, clothing and feeding me. Because the money should have gone towards a car, my dad didn't want me ever to forget."

"Seems fair."

"Depends on your point of view."

"Suppose so." Simon could see some bruising about her body. "How did you come by the bruises?"

"Some girls pleasure is other girls pain."

Simon could not think of an appropriate riposte.

Once she was dry and dressed, she led Simon to the stairs and went to the first floor. Then following the corridor which overlaid the ground floor, she walked to the back of the building and into a bedroom complex that spanned from one side of the house to the other. First, they passed by a dressing area that had a couple of chairs and some walk-in wardrobes and then next to a large en suite bathroom. Under a window in the bedroom itself, was a large divan bed with a sole occupant. Next to it was a drip stand and a strange looking pump which were connected via tubes to the wrinkled old man in the bed.

Mercedes checked that the pump was still operating and that there was still plenty of fluid left in the drip bag.

"See. He's ok. I know I should stay with him all night but what's the point. I'm here for twelve hours. A swim keeps me awake. He comes to no harm."

"What's your role?"

"What do you mean? I just change the drip and keep the pump working."

"How long has he been like this?"

"I've been doing the night work for two years and he had been like it for some time before I started."

"Do you know his name?"

"Who are you? Who sent you?"

"Grigoriev."

"Oh. Richard Davies."

"Thank you."

"Why did he send you? The old man's wife is due back today. She'll see for herself."

"Perhaps he wants to make sure everything is spot on for her arrival."

"Please don't tell him I was swimming. He'll beat me."

"Has he before?"

"Yes."

"Why don't you leave?"

"The money is exceptional."

"Do you swim nightly?"

"Yes. Please don't tell him, I'll make it worth your while."

"Nice offer, but I will decline. I won't tell him. What time do you finish this morning?"

"Nine o'clock."

Simon looked closely at the old man in the bed with the tube from the pump attached to a cannula. He was seriously wrinkled and had a deathly pallor. The infrequent whirring of the pump pushed the fluid into his body. To all intents and purposes, the man looked as good as dead. A different whirring started as an electric ripple mattress moved gently beneath him preventing bed sores. It appeared he was being kept alive by machines. It was obviously Richard Davies. The internet had several pictures which Simon had seen. 'So much for Wikipedia' When he turned back to where Mercedes had moved, he saw her pointing a small calibre gun at him.

"That's not very nice."

"Who are you?"

"I came here to ask him some questions. Perhaps you could answer them for me?"

"Why should I?"

"I was under the impression that he was trying to take over as the crime lord of Birmingham. Looking at him now, I can see that's patently wrong. So, who is running his empire for him?"

"As you are unlikely to leave here alive: I am."

131
Sunday 19th June 2011

"I don't understand. He is married, who are you?"

"I am his first-born daughter as I told you earlier. He hated me, but I watched his violent rise to power and knew one day I would get my revenge. He killed my mother when he tired of her and became more and more powerful. It was just a litany of women one after another. Then he met Jackie and I found a soul mate. She soon saw what he was like and got fed up with his constant philandering. It doesn't take long to find a compliant doctor if the money is right and you have a little dirt on them."

"Why not kill him and have done with it?"

"I was made to suffer as a child. Now it's his turn to suffer."

She indicated for Simon to sit.

"Put your hands on your head and don't move."

Backing away from him, she felt in her bag for her mobile. Holding it up in her line of vision so she didn't miss any movement from him, she tried to call a programmed number. Nothing happened. The mobile was off. Mercedes eyeballed the phone for a split second. That had never happened before. Hitting the power button, it burst back into life. Simon looked blithely about the room. This time the programmed number began to ring. He could faintly hear the acknowledgement.

"Yes?"

"Hi it's me."

"What do you want?"

"Can you come over? I have an intruder."

"How did he get past the security?"

"Don't know. He's under control now."

"I'll be there in fifteen minutes. Take care."

"Love you" and she blew a couple of kisses as the phone disconnected.

Simon said, "I hope that was Grigoriev."

"He will take pleasure in killing you."

"I really want to meet him again. He ran away from me the last time."

With that, he took his hands off his head, stretched and stood up.

"I'm warning you. I will kill you if I have to."

"Not with that pop gun. I unloaded it when I turned your phone off at the pool."

Mercedes pulled the trigger and heard a loud click.

"Now this gun is loaded," and he pulled out the Lithuanian's gun that he had fired before.

"If you are running the show now, you sent people to Sussex to kidnap a girl. Bad move. All bar the coward Grigoriev are dead. This is one of their guns. By the way, I just disabled the outside security and took all their weapons. They should all recover in time."

"Don't give me that. I know you must have had help."

"We will wait and see."

Within five minutes, Grigoriev arrived and saw the bound man by the security booth. Abandoning his car in the middle of the cul-de-sac, he jumped out of it with a rifle in his hands. He did not hesitate, nor did he walk down the drive. The same tree that Simon used saw him enter the grounds and he ran off in a crouch. He was sure he knew who the intruder was and he wasn't going to take any chances. At the rear of the building he kept to the perimeter. Arriving behind the summer house he could see the lights burning in the old man's upstairs bedroom. He needed to get higher for a better view. Stealing round to the front of the summer house he found another bound security man. It had to be Simon's handiwork. He should have killed him the first time he met him.

He couldn't afford to take any risks. All his men had died in Sussex: or so he thought. If he could kill him from a distance, all the better. Mercedes was no walk-over, but a trap may have been set for him. All his life he had been cautious. Ruthless: but cautious. It was a trait that had saved him before and made him one of the best. The only thing he would never do though was take on someone he wasn't sure he could beat either by fair means or foul. He believed Simon was on a par with himself and therefore a serious menace.

There was no time to release the lashed security man as he burst into the summer house itself and sprang up the stairs. The third man was tied up and softly moaning in pain on the bed. Grigoriev silenced him by hitting him hard with the rifle butt. He hated off-putting noise when he was going to take a shot. From the window, he could see he was a few feet lower than the lit room. It wasn't going to be a problem. Pushing the now unconscious guard callously from the bed, he dragged it to the window. Laying prone on the bed, he lined his rifle up on the lit window. He was ready.

Putting his mobile phone in front of him, he rang Mercedes number.

"Feel free to answer." She tossed her phone towards Simon.

Catching it left handed, he answered the call.

"Yes?"

"If you think I am going to stroll in there, you are not as good as I thought."

"I didn't think you would being a coward."

"You can't provoke me."

Mercedes was slowly backing away from Simon and moved in front of a lit standard lamp. The silhouette cast onto the window blind was all he needed. He didn't care who it was. If it was Simon, he would have a result. If it was Mercedes, it would shut her up and he could always find someone else. There were plenty of other people who would pay well for his services.

There was very little recoil as the gun fired. Mercedes was thrown forward with a gaping hole in her back and a larger one in her chest as the high velocity bullet ploughed on and lodged in the wall. All the lights in the room were dowsed.

"I presume you are still breathing."

"I'm coming for you."

132
Sunday 19th June 2011

Grigoriev was off the bed with his rifle in a trice. Running down the stairs and straight out of the summer house. He knew that Simon was alone because he was like him, a lone operator. Instead of running to the perimeter, he ran into the garden and towards the kitchen and dived into a flower bed full of tall ornamental grasses. He drew a bead on the back door. Simon hesitated as he ran into the kitchen. If he had been outside, he would have covered the back door. There was no way he would go through it. It was a portal to death. Grigoriev allowed a few seconds to pass. Then he knew Simon was not going to leave via the door. If he had been inside, there was no way he would come out through it.

The morning was becoming progressively lighter. There was still over an hour before dawn. Both men knew that movement would attract the other's attention and could prove fatal.

Grigoriev considered his options. He was not going to go anywhere near his abandoned car. If he was inside the house he would be watching for movement along the perimeter. A proficient person with the right handgun would have no trouble hitting him. He would have to move soon under the retreating cover of darkness, or become a sitting duck to anyone on the first floor of the building in even partial daylight.

Simon was searching for an exit from the building. He wanted to be outside where he would be on equal terms. The logic stated that Grigoriev would cover the back door, but he had not proved logical in the past. If he left by any back or side window, he could easily be picked off from the back garden. That left the front door. Simon wasn't sure. Grigoriev may have predicted that and moved position. He wouldn't have moved to the front door. Just because he wouldn't didn't mean Grigoriev wouldn't. It was a gamble with his life that he wasn't willing to take.

They both had life-threatening problems. Each considered the other their equivalent. Neither was going to take a risk with their own life. Grigoriev knew that he could not afford to wait for the nine o'clock security team's arrival which would solve all his problems. He would already be dead.

Simon knew he had to be out and gone quickly in case Grigoriev had called for help. The exiting from the building could result in his death. Using Mercedes mobile, Simon tapped the number and watched the garden from the darkness of the kitchen. It was a forlorn hope that he would spot a small mobile's light in the breaking mornings gloom, or hear one ringing. Feeling the phone vibrating against his torso, Grigoriev smiled. 'Clever.' The phone was tucked in a pocket and on mute.

Simon saw and heard nothing. Grigoriev waited for it to stop vibrating, and waited another couple of minutes for it to return to standby. Then he took it out of his pocket, pressed redial and stuffed it hastily back into his pocket before the screen lit up. He saw the small glow of the ringing phone in the kitchen and put one round slightly to the left of it and one to the right of it.

As the second round left his gun, he knew he had been duped. Simon was watching from a room away. He had expected the return call followed by gunshot. The muzzle flash had given his position away. Grigoriev cursed himself. 'Very clever.' Now Simon could get out of the front of the building. Time was of the essence for both of them yet again.

Grigoriev jumped up and ran to the rear of the summer house and the perimeter wall beyond. Fear drove him up and over the wall with little effort. Simon exited the front door after grabbing his bag and ran down the garden and out through the main gate and all the way back to the Audi. He sat in the driver's seat for ten minutes and let his adrenalin subside as he got his breath back.

133

Sunday 19th June 2011

"Hello John."

"Hi Simon. How are you doing?"

"Long story which I'll tell you when I get back. What I have found out is that RD has been bedridden for at least a couple of years and totally incapacitated. His empire has apparently been run by his present wife, and a lady called Mercedes. Unfortunately, Mercedes was killed by Grigoriev before I could have a proper chat with her. I had to make a swift exit but I'm going back to wait for RD's wife. I'll see what she has to say. Can you update Graham and Ian for me?"

"Yes, will do. Is there anything you need?"

"Not at the present, but I'll keep you or Ian apprised."

"OK."

Putting the phone back on the side table, John sat in silence adopting Prodow's praying mantis mode as he considered what had been said. Carol could hold a silence, Alison couldn't.

"Well? Come on."

John passed the call on as near to verbatim as damn it. Both women took it all in.

"If RD is a vegetable, who ordered my kidnapping?"

"He's still trying to clarify that."

＊

Simon looked around. It was still too early for most people, but a few were starting to move about. He left the Audi and cautiously made his way back to the cul-de-sac. Slipping his balaclava back on, he saw Grigoriev's car was still in the middle of the road but Simon was sure he had left via a different route. The Saab was no longer of use to Grigoriev and obviously abandoned. In his own hasty exit, he had left the front door ajar. The bound security guard by the box watched him curiously as he had watched the arrival of Grigoriev and then Simon's swift departure.

"I'll be back in a little while and I'll set you free then."

The guy on the ground managed a muffled grunt.

Simon was taking a chance, but he was sure that Grigoriev was well gone. He needed time and he hadn't got enough of it. With a precautionary gun in his hand, he sprinted to the summer house and sprang up the stairs and to the now fully conscious trussed guard who was lying on the floor, and ripped the tape from his mouth. The man's face had cooled marginally and was no longer burning.

"What time do you get relieved?"

"You know you're a dead man?"

"I'll ask you once more. If you do not answer, I may have to kill you."

Simon flipped open his butterfly knife and touched the man's throat with the point. A smidgen of blood appeared and ran onto the blade.

Showing it to him, Simon said, "When?"

"Nine o'clock."

"Who pays you?"

"It's a lawyer."

"Yusuf?"

"Yes. How did you know?"

"Wild guess. Who gives the orders on the ground? Grigoriev?"

"Yes" and then he realised he wanted to rub the fair size lump that was growing by the second on the side of his head.

"Who supplied the guns to you?"

"Yusuf."

"How do you get away with having them on a British street?"

"He said there was no problem with the Police and anyhow, some knew we had them."

"Have you been inside the house?"

"Never! We were told that was totally forbidden. Grigoriev would probably kill us. He's a psychopath. There's a mad woman who lives in there. She's his girlfriend."

"He killed her earlier."

"Shit. You reckon you're up to dealing with him?"

"We'll see soon enough as long as he stops running away from me."

Simon wanted to collect his booty.

"I'll be back in a couple of minutes then I will free you."

Simon ran around and collected all the guns and phones and stuffed them into a Tesco's jute bag that he had brought from his car. Ian would like the phones and the armourer in Kent would love the guns. He put the bag just inside the front door and out of sight. Running back to the summer house, his knife re appeared in his hand as he freed the guard outside.

"Follow me."

Going back upstairs, his knife flashed again, and the man was free. He stood up determined not to rub his face. His head was killing him thanks to Grigoriev but he was thinking fast.

"Here's the offer I'm making you. You go now and don't come back. I have no beef with any of you. Otherwise, I will have to incapacitate all of you."

"You think you could take all three of us together?"

"Effortlessly and without the gun. You are not who I want. It's Grigoriev."

"Now I know you're as mad as he is."

"Well. What's it to be?"

"I could say, ok and then we could come back for you."

"You would be three corpses. I'm letting you go. The choice is yours."

The two men looked at each other and nodded.

"OK. At nine there will be our three replacements. You think you could take six of us."

"I wouldn't be making the offer if I couldn't."

As a show of contempt for the two men, Simon turned his back on them. His bravado was enough for them to accept his word. Neither wanted to be the first to attack him even if his back was to them. If he was senseless enough to take on Grigoriev then Grigoriev could kill him.

"Pick up your colleague from the booth on your way out" and then he walked down the stairs and to the glass kitchen door with its two small bullet holes close together. 'Fair shooting in the dark.' He went in and then locked the door behind him. Not worth taking any needless chances of a surprise attack.

*

413

Carol said, "Alison. I know you won't like this. You should tell your Dad."

John reaffirmed he would update both Ginger and Ian as Alison slunk off back to her room. She was happily looking forward to waking her Father before 5.am. Picking up her new mobile phone, she rang Graham.

"Hello. It's me," slight pause, "Alison."

"I know who it is. I'm just surprised you are awake this early. What's happened?"

She nearly hung up. He was already up and about. The wind was taken right out of her sails. Then gritting her teeth and being as true to the narrative as she could remember, she brought her Father up to speed. At her conclusion, she waited for some kind of response.

"Thank you" and he hung up. Looking at the phone, she thought, 'Why me?'

Carol knocked and went into Alison's bedroom. She was going back to St Richard's Hospital and she told Alison she would make arrangements for her X-rays. It was accepted that John would transport her to the hospital at the appointed time. Carol sat at the foot of Alison's bed and they discussed how Simon was going to progress any enquiry.

134
Sunday 19th June 2011

Simon slammed shut the front door and went up to RD's room. The house was secure. Daylight was breaking, and he saw no point in advertising his presence by turning a light on. There was sufficient ambient light to see what he needed to. If the guards alerted anyone, so be it. Mercedes' body had been propelled to the side of the room as the bullet had hit her. It wasn't the prettiest of sights and Simon found a sheet and covered her. He pulled his phone from his pocket and called Bruce. He needed some medical advice.

"Hi Bruce. Sorry to wake you I need some help."

"Yeah. Go on?"

"I am next to a man who is unconscious in bed. He has apparently been kept in this state for a long time. There is a drip stand with a bag of clear liquid that is passing through some kind of a pump and going into his arm."

"That sounds like liquid to keep him hydrated. Can you see what is being used to keep him sedated?"

Simon looked about and found a larger than average syringe on a small wheelable trolley and a bag of brownish powder.

"There's a bag of brownish powder next to a large syringe."

"Nasty. That could be a concoction including Diamorphine. Heroin in other words. That would keep him unconscious. Too much though could kill him. Is there a pump where the syringe could be fitted?"

"It could probably be fitted on the bottom of the pump with the clear liquid."

"Simon, if I am right, taking him straight off it could also prove fatal. You need a qualified doctor to deal with him."

"I will probably be able to get him to a hospital some time tonight. Will that be too late?"

"You're pushing your luck."

"Thanks Bruce. This chat didn't happen."

"Obviously" and the line went dead.

*

The three guards stood by Grigoriev's Saab.

The one from the booth said, "What do you reckon?"

"He was happy to take three of us on. If he's after Greg he's got to be good or plain mad."

"I think I want to give this a miss. I'm going home and I ain't coming back."

The other two agreed.

"It looks like Greg has legged it and left his car."

"I'll park it and then I'm off."

"You going to tell the day team?"

"Yeah."

"What about Yusuf?"

"Fuck him. He's a slime ball."

"Jackie is meant to be coming back today."

"She'll find out then soon enough."

They all went their separate ways.

*

Simon busied himself checking the Glocks. They were all fully loaded and all looked well maintained. That wasn't a benchmark though that would prove they would fire if called upon to do so. He would rely on the Lithuanians' tried and trusted gun the MP-443, but preferably, his own butterfly knife. Sitting in one of the plusher chairs that he hauled from the middle of the room and put against the wall opposite the bedroom door, he dozed. He wanted to be awake for any of the 9am team arriving.

At 8.30am Simon roused himself. There had been no efforts by anyone to enter the building and search for him. He moved to the front of the house and watched and waited. Another beautiful June day was in its infancy. 9am was soon past. No one had turned up. Then at ten a lady in her senior years with a slight stoop, pulling a stainless steel wheeled trolley suitcase walked into the cul-de-sac and stopped by the booth. She looked about for a minute and then started to walk up the middle of the drive as though she owned it. Simon watched her approach the front door and then heard a key in the lock.

'Surely this old lady is not Jackie?'

135

Sunday 19th June 2011

John had updated Ian first who immediately set off for Birmingham. It had been agreed the sooner he could take possession of any phones the quicker he could work on them. The firearms were a bonus, and would join the arsenal in Kent after the armourer had checked them out and removed any identifying marks. Most of those working or living at the Kent base had skills taught them by the military and had honed them during their careers. That the majority were disabled was no bar to their knowledge.

Ian had taken a youngish woman who had served in the signals regiment with him who had become adept at recovering information from mobile phones. He knew she was better at it than him. Her only mistake in the army was that she was too close to someone who stepped on a land mine. She now sported a prosthetic leg.

Ginger was quickly updated as to Simon's situation. Although exhibiting a laissez faire attitude over the phone, he was quietly apprehensive. He didn't tell his long suffering wife as she had never wanted to know what Simon was up to because she was a serial worrier. Ginger knew his son's abilities and was confident he could deal with any situation, but he still became anxious. It was natural for a father to worry about his offspring.

Graham had phoned John with some details he had learnt about Richard Davies. They were sketchy. He had not wanted to utilise computerised Police indices for fear of alerting the wrong people. Mostly, the information had been given to him by word of mouth from some old acquaintances, both active and those retired, that he knew and trusted. Even so, he was extremely economical with the truth as to why he sought the information, and downright lied to some of them. None considered passing any information back to unsavoury characters, or even discussing the nature of the conversations let alone admit they had actually spoken to him.

At 7.15am, John was at his usual table with Jimmy. Both gave the impression, thanks to several uncleared plates, that they were working their way through the canteen's menu. They weren't in talking mode and other customers recognised the fact and gave them a wide berth. They were getting ready for a long day. The urgent quest for sustenance was due to the belief that this would be their only meal of the day and they were stocking up. Groves ordered his food at the servery and bought a tea for Jimmy and coffees for John and himself. He placed them on the table in front of each, and received a grunt of sorts from Jimmy and no sound from John. Sitting down he said nothing to either of them. The whole canteen seemed crowded, but hardly a susurration stirred in the room. Everyone knew it was going to be a long haul today and was likely to be very disquieting.

Chairs began to scrape the floor as their occupants pushed them about as they stood up. People were on the move, mainly going to the conference/briefing room. John and Jimmy waited for Groves to finish his meal and then went up to the office. Sitting behind Paul's desk was the Chief. Prodow was at a desk still piled high with exhibits. Doreen was at her desk looking disconsolately at a blank screen on her computer. Paul was leaning against the office door trying to look between slats in the blind at one of the windows and out towards the old playing field. Groves and co propped up the wall by Jimmy's desk. It was as quiet as the grave.

The clock crept slowly towards a quarter to eight.

The Chief said, "Listen people. We have got to get to grips with all this. I will conduct the briefing this am. I've read the original documents folder which is plainly bloody useless. That nurse is patently innocent and I will have it out with her brief as to why she has said nothing. It's her own bloody fault she's been locked up and charged. I will be in court and I'll make sure we fight costs tooth and nail."

Prodow said, "That's a bit strong you going to court guv'nor. You'll be right in the firing line for everyone to have a pop at you."

"Sod 'em. They will see what we're made of."

Doreen said, "Who's going after Haskland, the Micra man?" to no one in particular.

Prodow answered saying, "The surveillance team have been on the car since 5am. We want Deborah in it as well as him so we'll have them both together. Anyone goes near it, they're good as nicked."

As the clock hit 7.40am the CC snatched a phone from the desk and punched in some numbers.

"Hello. Southampton Hospital. Emsworth Ward. How can we help you?"

"Hello. I am Chief Constable Robertson from Sussex Police. I would like the update as to how one of my officers, Sergeant Murray is doing?"

"Good morning sir. Nice to hear from you again. Murray had a good night and is gaining strength. He is still being fed by tube and should be on solid food either later today or tomorrow."

"Thank you for that. I shall call again for an update about 1.pm."

"I'll look forward to that."

"Good bye."

The day sister on the ward said to a minion, "That is the personification of what a good manager should be. Thinking all the time about the wellbeing of his staff."

"Shame some of the managers at this hospital don't think about us."

The CC said, "Right. Let's get this briefing going" and they all followed him down and into the briefing room.

As one, all those seated rose as he strode purposefully into the room.

"Sit down please. No ceremony. This is going to be swift."

He updated the room as to Murray's continuing progress and said, "Today maybe the hardest day any of you have had with Sussex Police. Some things happened yesterday that have traumatised a lot of you. Today, you may learn even more that is going to be upsetting to some, and shocking to others. You are all experienced professional Police Officers and support staff. You can cope with this. However. I know that it helps to talk. In Murray's old office you will find the Force's counsellor. I want each team member to pop in and have a chat during the day. No exceptions!"

He scanned the room and looked at all the faces.

"Understood?"

Several minutes passed. No one moved a muscle. Some seemed to have stopped breathing. They were all staring back at him.

"These are dark times for us. We will prevail. Come the end of this, each one of you will have the satisfaction that you helped solve and prosecute the most complex criminal case this county has known." He looked about. "Where's Doreen?"

Paul said, "She's still upstairs manning the office."

"Could someone please fetch her."

A detective ran to get her.

As she walked into the room, the CC said, "Doreen. Please join me."

Doreen felt scared, but she didn't know why.

"Ladies and Gentlemen. You all know Doreen. It is entirely possible that she has provided evidence that may lead to the correct murderer of George Armstrong. She is not a trained detective, yet she has put together through her own pure dogged perseverance enough to give us a good starting point. As we are speaking, a surveillance team is watching a green Micra vehicle that may have been used by the killer. I believe we are close to catching the real culprit. By the end of the day, I expect a satisfactory result."

He turned directly towards Doreen.

"You sure you won't come and work for me?"

The ice was broken. Doreen exhaled loudly, and the room seemed to breathe a collective sigh as people started to fidget about in their seats.

136
Sunday 19th June 2011

A voice called out.

"Mercedes. Where are you? There's no one in the booth."

Simon stood out of sight. He heard the noise of the old lady wheezing as she started to drag her case up one of the staircases, one step at a time.

"Mercedes. For God's sake, come and help me."

Simon moved to the top of the stairs and started down towards the woman. She stopped dead in her tracks.

"Who are you?"

"Simon. And you are?"

"Doctor Bandell. Where's Mercedes?"

"Upstairs with the old man."

"There's no one in the security booth."

"I know. I sent them home."

The old lady looked incredulous.

"I hope you know what you're doing. Greg will go mad."

"I don't think he really cares now. After you. I'll bring your case."

The old lady struggled up the remaining stairs puffing loudly even without her burden, and straight to the old man's rooms.

She stopped when she had passed through the dressing area and got a few feet into the bedroom.

"What's happened in here?"

"Last night, Greg shot Mercedes. That's who is under the sheet."

The woman was totally unfazed by the corpse in the room of someone she evidently knew.

"How's RD?" and she went to his bedside. Checking his pulse and seeing the empty bag of liquid, she said, "Pass me a bag of fluid. It's under the trolley." Within seconds, the fluid was dripping back into RD's arm. "Do you know when he last had any heroin?"

"At a guess, about 3am. I think Mercedes probably gave him some about then."

Glancing indifferently at his hands clothed with his latex gloves she passed no comment.

The doctor opened her suitcase and took out a phial and a hypodermic syringe.

"Do you have to give him that?"

She looked at Simon. "Why do you ask?"

"I was hoping to speak to him today."

"Not a hope. He's been on 'H' for about five years to my knowledge. This is all that keeps him alive. If he came off it, he would probably die. His wife and Mercedes want him kept alive, so I give him this a couple of times a week."

"Mercedes won't be having any more input as to his treatment."

The comment spurred the doctor to go to where the sheet covered the corpse and she removed the shroud. Looking at the hole in Mercedes back, she knew without checking further that she was dead. It was clear to her that she had died instantly. Without rite, she threw the sheet back over her.

Sitting down in an easy chair, the doctor lit a cigarette.

After a couple of puffs, she said, "Alright. Tell me what happened last night?"

Simon lied as he kept the narrative simple. Saying he wanted to speak to RD and was permitted entry by the sentries, and was chatting to Mercedes when Greg phoned. Then Greg shot Mercedes and all the guards ran away. When the doctor had finished her cigarette, she looked hard at Simon for several seconds.

"I've heard some crap stories before, and that's right up there with them."

"The true bit is Greg shot Mercedes."

Doctor Bandell did not seem to worry about the ash that had fallen on the carpet, and even ground the end of her cigarette into it under her shoe. Simon supposed that the blood and entrails of Mercedes that were strewn across part of it were a lot worse. The doctor picked up her syringe and moved to RD's bedside.

"Can you give me a little help here? Mercedes used to hold his arm for me."

Simon moved beside the bed and as he stretched forward towards RD's arm, the doctor, with amazing speed, tried to stick the syringe into his exposed bare wrist. Simon's reactions were fast, but not quick enough. The needle went through the glove and grazed the back of his hand as some of the fluid found its way into his blood stream. Doctor Bandell let go of the syringe which just clung on limply to the back of Simon's glove and swung from it before dropping to the floor.

The doctor moved away swiftly from the bedside. Simon started to feel dizzy within seconds. He staggered to a chair and collapsed into it. The doctor stood by the light that had been Mercedes downfall and lit another cigarette.

"It doesn't take much and only a few seconds. It's got a sedative, Fentanyl, that is used to relax muscles ready for an anaesthetic and some of my own mixture, I don't know who you are, but I'm sure Greg will like to see you. I'll give you the proper dose in a minute."

Simon had seconds and he knew it. With great effort, he hutched slightly forward in his chair. Reaching around to the back of his trouser waistband he took out the Lithuanian's gun. He spoke in a sluggish far away voice.

"Sorry. I can't let you do that."

Doctor Bandell looked prudently towards the black shaking muzzle of the MP-443 automatic. It seemed to be dancing all over the place. It was apparent to her that enough sedative had got into him. She was sure he would pass out quickly but the shaking gun pointed in her direction was intimidating her. This was the first time she had had a gun pointed at her in her long life and she definitely didn't like it. Killing someone had always been easy for her with the use of a syringe and her victims had never fought back before.

With fading eyes and a quickly growing heavy arm, he raised the gun. It was shaking. He tried to steady it. There was only one thing for it. Simon pulled the trigger as the gun was pointed in the general direction of the doctor. He kept pulling the trigger which became more of an effort each time. The recoil helped keep the gun up. Five shots echoed around the room deafening both him and the doctor. He didn't care. He could no longer see. Three shots hit the ceiling and one lodged in the floor. The fourth in the sequence had gone through the doctor's right eye and out through the back of her head with part of her brain and most of her skull. She had fallen on top of Mercedes. Simon saw nothing, he was unconscious.

137
Sunday 19th June 2011

"Incident room."

"Is that you Paul?"

"No. It's Chief Constable Robertson."

"Sorry sir. It's Vince Casey. I'm team leader of the surveillance team."

"I know who you are Vince. Have you some good news?"

"Yes, and no sir. We watched a male, I believe Haskland, get into the Micra and drive to one of the grace and favour cottages in Fishbourne. Its occupied by an elderly lady called Jean. From this morning's briefing, it appears that she is possibly Sally's Mother and Deborah's Grandmother. At the moment, there has been no sighting of Deborah. Until I can confirm she is present, I intend to wait."

"Make sure you get confirmed sight of both before you nick them."

"Yes sir. I thought I should phone in case there was any update."

"Right thing to do. Don't lose him Vince. I want these bastards in the pokey tonight."

"We have a chase car running with us that could keep up with this Micra without getting into third gear!"

"Stick to it like glue, and Vince: see me when you get back."

"Yes sir."

Vince switched his covert radio back on and updated his team who all confirmed receipt in call sign order. There were three vehicles with drivers' eyes on the parked Micra. Several officers had left their cars and were on foot loitering in positions to keep the back and front of the premises clearly in view. A motorcyclist was fetching teas and coffee from a local café and supplying the team members surreptitiously as and when he could. The marked chase car, a BMW that was coloured yellow in a 'Battenberg' pattern was parked out of sight half a mile away with its two uniformed traffic officers desperate to be involved. Today was the first day Vince had ever had a full team of nine unmarked vehicles, a covert motorcyclist and twelve officers and a dedicated chase car. Everyone, it appeared, in Sussex Police wanted to be involved.

The clock ticked on. Every fifteen minutes, Vince called each person in turn and rotated his officers. Then out of sequence, the concealed miniscule radio receiver in the foot officer's ears and the receivers in the vehicles suddenly crackled. They all knew the crackle was usually prior to a message. Each one suddenly became more alert. The chase car crew started their engine ready for a quick take off.

"For information, the older woman, possibly Jean, has just put some rubbish in her dustbin."

All bar Vince relaxed.

"Was that genuine or was she looking?"

The officer thought for a couple of seconds, "She looked about, but I don't think she was looking for us."

Vince knew his team well and trusted the officer's judgement.

"Ok everyone. Relax."

Ten minutes later they were back on tenterhooks. The man they referred to as subject two, Haskland, jogged out of the front door and to his car. He had no idea that nine vehicles were soon following him and rotating every few junctions. It was a drive of just over twenty miles to Durrington using the main roads and then the Micra just stopped dead in the street outside the railway station. It didn't pull over or into a parking space, it just stopped. An irate business man in the vehicle directly behind lent on his horn which elicited a 'finger' out of the driver's window from Haskland.

The following surveillance officer in his vehicle that was three back in the traffic saw a young woman who he believed to be Deborah step off the kerb and get into the passenger seat. The whole team knew within five seconds. Subject one, Deborah, was now in play. Then the Micra pulled off back in the empty road in front of it.

Vince called up the chase car.

"It's all yours. Stop it."

At the conclusion of Vince's message, the team heard the sirens start. So did both subjects although none could see exactly where it was coming from they could all hear it was behind them and making ground. The Micra shot right into a side street nearly wiping out a couple of pedestrians. A surveillance vehicle followed now without clandestineness constantly updating the traffic car. It was no longer a wait and watch exercise, but an arrest scenario. The Micra dodged and weaved in the backstreets but was no match for the large marked BMW that soon caught up and practically latched onto its bumper as the surveillance vehicle well-nigh jumped out of the way.

It would not stop. The traffic officers reported to the Sussex Control Room they were now in pursuit of two suspects for murder. The Control Room Duty Inspector, official known as OPS 1, was already aware as he had been monitoring the radio transmissions from within his 'glass bubble' office. His four display monitors were all in use. One showed all the locations of the Police vehicles following the suspects' vehicle on a scrolling map. The surveillance vehicles appeared to be all overlapping each other as they followed the traffic car. Another showed an image from a forward pointing camera from the traffic car.

One was a relay from the fastest typist who was a member of the Control Room Staff in the main office spread out before his 'bubble'. It was lines of text which she was typing as radio transmissions were heard. A full transcript would be prepared by her later from the tapes that were recording everything. The last was displaying a still image of a patch of grass.

He had already been briefed earlier that morning personally by the CC of the potential arrests and what he expected from him. Sussex and Surrey's joint helicopter was 'resting' at Goodwood aerodrome but was off the ground and heading towards the Durrington area within seconds. The patch of grass grew smaller as the helicopter became airborne and the image showed the countryside and then buildings racing past some hundred feet below.

Marked traffic cars driven by advanced drivers started to converge on Durrington from all points of West Sussex as OPS 1 switched the text to show the image from the second traffic vehicle that was closing rapidly on the chase. The Control Room Duty Inspector continually stipulated over the radio only two vehicles to engage in the pursuit. He was the arbiter of how any pursuit was to be conducted. He knew today it was likely a lost cause.

The Micra was no match for any of the surveillance vehicles let alone the large traffic cars. It still was not stopping. No Police vehicle seemed to be able to anticipate where it was going or get in front of it to stop it. It dodged and weaved about both side roads and main thoroughfares. It reached Goring traversing more side roads in a vain effort to lose the following pack.

Eventually passing through Goring it entered Ferring and bounced over occasional 'sleeping policeman' dotted along private roads as it neared the sea. Local officers knew it was running out of options. The Duty Inspector was monitoring its progress on his map and watching the live feeds fed into his Control Room from the helicopter and traffic vehicles. He could see it was now only a matter of minutes until the subjects were apprehended.

There was only one way left for the Micra to travel. Between two six feet high brick walls towards the Bluebird Café's gravelled car park. One way in and the same way out, or so the pursuers thought. Without slowing down, the car did not turn to the right as expected, but accelerated hard straight on past the last beach hut and onto the shingle leading down to the sand. Its speed was just sufficient to allow it to clear the shingle without being dragged to a halt.

All the pursuers, bar the helicopter came to a standstill. The bigger traffic cars would have ground to a halt and sunk in the shingle. No one else was willing to risk it.

The Duty Inspector watched agog at the live feed as the Micra hurtled onto the beach with the helicopter no more than six feet above it. Under his breath he kept saying, "'Please don't crash." Everyone in the Control Room knew the pilot had been recruited from the Navy on his retirement. He had been a specialist low flyer, but he could still come unstuck.

All the operators in the Control Room had turned to watch the twenty large screens against the wall which showed various images from cameras around Sussex. They could see the four which OPS 1 was monitoring and were agape. Marked Police cars and surveillance vehicles were all trying to manoeuvre in the car park. Some officers were trying to check Sat Navs and others had paper maps. All searching for a way onto the beach.

Punters at the café had all rushed out to watch as the cacophony of sirens had arrived, and were now bemused at the antics of the car and the helicopter as they raced around the sands and then on towards Angmering and Littlehampton.

As soon as Vince had unleashed the chase car he phoned the incident room. Paul had answered and groups of detectives had rushed out of the building to crowd around cars that had radios. Passing uniform officers stopped to listen in. Groups of civilian workers left their offices to step outside and also listen. John sat in his car with his radio on high volume. Doreen was in the front seat and Paul in the back on a mobile to the CC. No one in Sussex had heard such a chase and word spread quickly as to who were in the vehicle.

The Duty Inspector had regained his composure and was directing vehicles to access points along the route. 'Under no circumstances' the CC had told him, 'are the two subjects to be allowed to escape.' The first 'four by four' marked Police vehicle got to the Angmering yacht club and weaved past some bemused sailors and onto the beach via their slip way. The crew could see the helicopter above the Micra racing towards them and the driver accelerated towards the sea and after it as it hurtled past. The Micra was rounding breakwaters by going into the shallow water pools which seemed to have formed around them as the tide was on the turn and coming in. Any further out and the sea water would have slowed it down or forced it to a halt if it infiltrated the engine. Several bathers were clipped and other beach users didn't know which way to run. The shallow water was no bar to the traffic car.

OPS 1 came off the phone to the CC and immediately called the pursuing traffic officers.

"You are authorised to use any means to stop the vehicle. Protection of the public is paramount. Do it now."

Nothing else was said. The officers knew what was meant. People on the beach were seriously at risk and the beach off Rustington was crowded with locals and holiday makers alike. At the next breakwater as the Micra started to go around, the large 'four by four' BMW rammed the rear offside of it at speed. On tarmac, the Micra would probably have spun to a halt which is what the advanced Police driver expected to happen.

It didn't.

The Micra was like paper and did not spin on the sand. It just crumpled and rolled over. The speed of the BMW carried it over the rolling car. Both subjects in the car were seriously injured as the BMW came to rest on top of the upside down Micra.

The helicopter landed higher up the beach on the dry sand and the crew ran back. The two officers climbed down out of their vehicle and looked in the crumpled cabin of the Micra. Deborah was hanging upside down held in place by her seatbelt. She was a mass of blood. Her boyfriend, Haskland, was crushed with his head on the roof which was now next to the sand, and it was slowly filling with water with each gently lapping wave. If he wasn't dead as a result of the ramming, he was likely to drown as the water seeped in. Neither could be got out without cutting equipment and it was likely to be too late coming.

The Control Room Duty Inspector had witnessed the crash via the helicopter's camera and was instantly aware of the situation. Fire brigade assistance was called for, but they were not sure if they could get an engine onto the beach. They stated they would try. Whatever had been asked of them before they had achieved and today the Duty Inspector had no doubts they would not fail. Emergency medical assistance was called and they dispatched ambulances and their own helicopter. Those on the ground believed it would be far too late for subject two.

138
Sunday 19th June 2011

Ian rang Simon's number for the second time. Simon could feel the little mobile vibrating in his pocket but could not move to get it. He was conscious and aware of his surroundings, but could not move and felt like a piece of lead. The house he knew was secure. How long he had been out was anyone's guess. At least he could see he was now alone, bar RD, and still alive. Slowly, he realised he could move a little. His strength seemed to be returning. Another five minutes made all the difference. His head was clearing, but he felt a little nauseous. There was no pain. Feeling for his phone, he rang Ian. He didn't quite trust himself to stand up just yet. His gun was on the floor where it had previously fallen. It could stay there for another ten minutes.

Just short of an hour later, he met Ian and his advanced apprentice Laura in the free car park. Handing the jute bag to him, the young woman snaffled the phones and with nimble fingers she soon confirmed Greg's new phone number and Jackie's two mobile numbers and a new number for Yusef. Nothing really of much use. It wouldn't have taxed Simon to have established the numbers if he had been firing on all cylinders. He asked Ian if he could stay in the area for a day as he expected more productive phones would be available. Then they left in different directions. Both with index numbers unobtainable to any camera. Simon left his car in the hotel's car park having entered via the exit. He was soon in bed and fast asleep.

When Simon awoke he was incensed. He knew 'action was quicker than reaction' but he was too slow to dodge an old lady, who, with no good reason, he had trusted. As a result, he had killed her which was something he hadn't wanted or expected to do. Now with his baseball cap pulled low, he walked out of his room and into the Beefeater restaurant next to the hotel which was a risk but a necessity as he desperately needed food. His throat was dry, and he believed it all to be a consequence of the drug the doctor had stuck in him. He needed to be on top form if he was to face any further challenges.

Thinking what Jackie would have done when she had discovered the bodies was troubling him. Would she call the Police or tell Greg? Unlikely she would tell the Police anything, and the chance of Greg returning to the house was negligible. Would she tell Yusef? Had the guards told Yusef? That was a strong probability. Would Yusef take precautions? If he knew, very likely. Was RD dead? He didn't really care one way or another.

He needn't have worried. She was still tucked up in New York with her current toy boy, a second rate model looking for a rich woman to ponce off. An extra day or two in bed with a fit young stud would make her feel so good. Then she could ditch him and fly home. Jackie was happy in the thought that Mercedes would still be running the show with Greg. No one other than her murderous blackmailed doctor was due to be visiting the house. She was so confident, she didn't even try to contact Mercedes.

Simon had checked his phone when he got up. No warnings from anyone. He would still be cautious. No Police activity yet in the cul-de-sac or he would have been made aware by Graham or John. That meant none of the occupants of the other houses in the cul-de-sac was making any fuss about the empty security box. They would not dare challenge RD removing the guards even though they had not clapped eyes on him for at least five years. His reputation was such that to question him was to die, or worse, a major beating first. Some had heard the gunshots during the night and in the morning, but what happened at RD's was not their concern.

To call the Police was another route to the cemetery.

He ate his fill and felt better for it. He drank several glasses of water and a cup of coffee. It just about lubricated the dryness in his throat. Such a small quantity of sedative should have such a large effect was new to him. Bombs, knives and guns he could deal with, but little needles were a new experience for Simon and he didn't like it. How he was caught by an old lady annoyed him even more. Her age and proclaimed profession had lulled him into a false sense of security which was nearly his downfall. Had his wild firing not killed her he knew he would never have woken. He shuddered.

Occasional heavy raindrops started to plop against the windows of the restaurant. They got steadily faster. Simon sat and supped a beer as he watched the water running off the glass. As quickly as it had started, it stopped. An April shower in June. He strolled back to the hotel, and checking his baseball cap, he pushed open the glass door. By the reception desk with his back towards him was a large man in a crumpled black suit. He only heard a few words.

"If you see anyone like that, it's a straight grand. You know who to call."

Simon recognised the voice. It was the man he had thrown the boiling water at.

Stopping by a drinks dispensing machine, he turned his back and started to fumble in his pocket for some loose change. He watched the poor reflection in the glass as the man turned away from the reception desk to exit the hotel. Putting money into the machine, he bought a small bottle of water. The man didn't leave the hotel, but stood by the dispenser waiting for Simon to complete his transaction. His face was blotched with red areas where the water had burnt him. Thinking quickly, Simon knew he had not been seen at either time because he had been wearing his balaclava. But why was he looking for him?

Walking back out of the hotel, Simon ambled towards the Audi in the car park. The voice came from the door.

"Hey you. Stop."

Simon stopped and turned around to see the man was approaching him fast.

"Police. What's your business here?"

Putting on an Irish twang, Simon said, "I'm a plumber. I've a contract in Birmingham."

The man stood face on to Simon.

"You look like someone I'm looking for."

"Can I see your ID?"

"No. What have you got in your pockets?"

With the unopened water bottle held in his fisted hand, he hit the man with an uppercut square on the jaw.

He went down in the middle of the car park. The bottle of water which had added impetus to the blow had burst on impact but had prevented any damage to Simon's hand. No one was about as Simon grasped the man's jacket and dragged him the remaining distance to the rear of the Audi. Placing his own bags onto the back seat, he contrived to put him in the boot. It was harder than he thought although finally managing it. Then using his plasticuffs, he disabled him completely with his hands wedged behind his back and each side of his plasticuffed legs. For good measure, a strip of duct tape across his mouth. Sitting in the driver's seat, Simon considered who was looking for him. It could only be one person, but he saw a golden opportunity arising.

139
Sunday 19th June 2011

The crowd was growing larger as they strained to see what was happening. Uniform officers were keeping them back and rolls of blue tape marked 'Police. Do not cross' in white were strewn about and ends were fluttering in the breeze. A small 'Mercedes' fire engine slightly bigger than a 'four by four' had made it onto the beach. The large engine was still on the slipway and firemen were running between the two with odd looking bits of kit. A portable pump was engaged trying to suck the water out of the Micra, but as quickly as it cleared it, another wave rolled in. The ambulances were next to the fire engine and the medical helicopter was on a large part of the promenade. Even some small boats had appeared slightly out at sea.

The Police BMW 'four by four' was brusquely dragged off the Micra by use of the winch on the small fire engine and was able to be driven back to the promenade. Sparks were flying as several cutters were being utilised by fireman at the same time. Standing in water to work didn't seem to fluster them one bit. The paramedics believed both would survive providing the tide could be slowed from pushing water into the vehicle.

King Canute had failed to stem the tide some fifteen miles along the coast and several centuries past. No one else had ever succeeded. The Police were not confident.

They had no need for concern. The fire brigade had the Micra in pieces in minutes. Then with paramedics, they got both occupants out and onto stretchers. Carrying them at walking pace, they took them to the ambulances. It was agreed that the medical helicopter was not needed and the male was taken to Worthing Hospital and Deborah to St Richard's. Each ambulance was accompanied by Police traffic cars back and front.

The young uniformed PC Robertson waded alone into the ever-rising water to look inside the remnants of the Micra. In the compacted glove box, he found a tea cup that miraculously had not broken. Next to it was the broken fragments of a small glass bottle. Sheets of soggy paper floated about the car. He grabbed as much of it as he could. The water lapped around his knees as he stuck to his self-appointed task. He stuffed the items into his pockets and kept looking.

The roof was completely submerged and was a few feet away from the main section of the Micra. Wading to it, he saw through the water something resting partly concealed by the shifting sand that had already got into it. Feeling about, he found a key. Putting it into a pocket in case a fireman or emergency worker had dropped it, he decided the time had come to retreat and let the rising tide swallow the car.

Come the next low tide would see the Police recover what they could of the wreck.

He squelched his way back up the beach and to the van that had been his transport. Water was dripping from him as he scrambled into the back and was taken to Chichester. Climbing the stairs, he left wet footprints all the way to the temporary incident room.

"Excuse me."

Paul saw him still dripping water from his sodden uniform trousers.

"What the hell has happened to you?"

"I thought someone should have searched the Micra, so I waded into the sea to do it."

"I'm impressed. That is remarkable."

"I found a couple of things that may be of use to you."

Doreen, John and Jimmy heard, and with Paul, they mustered around him. Jimmy said, "What have you got?"

He said, "In my top left jacket pocket are some broken fragments of glass that I found in the glove box. I don't want to touch them any more in case they need examining. I have kept them as dry as I could. The sea has only just touched some of them."

"Slip your tunic off."

He did. With a large exhibit bag held in place by Doreen, Jimmy shook the glass fragments out. Then to make sure, he turned the pocket inside out and shook it.

"We are going to have to keep your jacket for a couple of days."

"Ok. In the lower pocket is a tea cup I found."

Jimmy put on his gloves, and removed the tea cup."

John said, "Bingo. That matches the set in the kitchen cupboard at Georges bungalow. What else have you got?"

"A fist full of soggy paper that's in my right lower pocket."

Jimmy still with his gloves on pulled the bundle out.

"Doreen. We need blotting paper."

"We haven't used that for years."

Paul said, "We'll get someone to take you to Staples. They should have some."

"John asked, "Anything else."

"Oh. There's a key that I think someone dropped. I put it in my top right pocket."

Jimmy fished for it. When he pulled it out, he put it on the desk.

All bar the young officer saw the keys likeness to the bungalow's back door key.

Paul said, "John. Can you take this and see if it opens the back door?"

Picking it up, "On way." He left the office.

Paul addressed the young officer, "Well done mate. Do you need a lift home to get cleaned up and pick up a new uniform?"

"If it's at all possible, it would be helpful."

"Have a seat. I'll arrange it. Doreen, it must be tea time."

The young PC Robertson sat on a metal chair proffered and accepted a coffee. Twenty minutes later, the CID car was put at the officer's disposal. Even the driver knew he was chauffeuring the PC who had, by his own foresight, provided crucial evidence against Deborah. He was happy to do so.

John called Paul from the phone inside the bungalow of George Armstrong.

"Double Bingo."

140
Sunday 19th June 2011

Simon locked his car and went back to his room. He lay on his bed and thought things through. Slowly a plan formed in his head that seemed reasonable, and had enough leeway for adaptation should the need arise. 'Plan for the worst and hope for the best.' Always have a plan B. Going over time and time again what had happened at RD's was crucial. Timing was not so important to him now, but where he had walked and what he had touched were. By the time he had drifted off into a fitful nap he knew what he had to do.

At 8pm he checked his phone. There was nothing from John, Ian or Graham. That meant he still had use of the Audi.

Calling John, he said, *"Things are progressing here quite quickly. I expect to acquire a few mobiles later tonight and will give them to Ian as soon as I can. It's possible that we will be able to identify the person in question. Once I have them, I will be ruffling some feathers. There is still someone who is looking for me up here. May I suggest that everyone has a cast iron alibi tonight in case it all goes pear shaped."*

"I'll make sure we are all bullet proof. Take care."

The line dropped.

John spent some time in his car calling the others. Graham knew who his alibi would be. At 10.30pm he called the Home Secretary.

"I need to meet you tonight. Anywhere you like."

She was working late at the Home Office and they agreed to meet there. She often stayed the night on a put-u-up bed in her office. It was unlikely that prying eyes would be about. Graham called his official driver and arranged his transport. That would be one alibi. The doormen at the Home Office would also see him and be his second alibi. Then the Home Secretary would be his third. He knew he would be safe. Whatever Simon had planned was going to happen tonight and he was the one who needed the strongest alibi. There was only one person stronger than the Home Secretary.

Simon went to his car and got his spray can out of the glove box. He wiped his number plates dry before spraying them with the liquid. 'Caution' tonight was his watch word. As Graham entered the Home Office, Simon was climbing over the wall into RD's garden. No guard was on station at the sentry box. The house looked unoccupied, but he was ready for Jackie or Greg. He put his gloves and balaclava on and on the top of the wall he made sure there were no marks or fragments of caught clothing. Traversing the garden via his original route, he checked for any signs that he may have inadvertently left. Nothing. He had been chary. Entering the empty summer house, he found the mugs he had filled with water. When he had held them, he had been wearing gloves. He put them back on the small table.

In the bedroom of the summer house, he left the bed by the window. With luck, there would be some fingerprints of Greg's on the bedframe or even the window itself, and maybe some firearm residue on the bedding. He didn't believe Greg would have been wearing gloves. Even better, there would be fingerprints of all the guards scattered about the summer house. Having dealt with them all, he was certain their identities would be on Police data bases. Picking up all his cut plasticuffs from the floor, he added them to his collection of the ones he'd gathered from outside and by the sentry box.

He made his way to the kitchen door passing the flower bed that had been Greg's last firing point. It was obvious that someone had been lying in the middle of it by the shape of the flattened grasses. Simon's gaze fell to the glinting metal on the ground. Where it had been abandoned in his haste to escape, was Greg's rifle. Simon picked it up by the barrel, and took it with him to the door.

Struggling to open it with his lock pick set without leaving any tell-tale marks or make any noise was hard. A shrewd investigator, or SOCO would spot the new scratching. Simon hoped the two bullet holes would attract the undivided attention of any sleuth. Pausing once inside, he listened, the house seemed empty of other living souls. If RD was still breathing, he posed no threat to Simon. Jackie was not in the house, and if she had have been earlier, there would have been signs. Even the smell of a different perfume would have been hanging in the still air. The house seemed as he had left it.

In the plaza area around the swimming pool, Simon was sure there were no marks as he'd been wearing gloves. Glancing about, he saw the chair where he had sat and the one where Mercedes had left her clothes. There was no need for him to move anything, and he shut the door behind him before going upstairs.

Entering the bedroom of RD, he was extremely careful where he walked. The first thing he had to do was find the fallen syringe. It was crucial to his main plan. He knew he hadn't trodden on it when he had left the house to meet Ian, and he didn't want to tread on it now. Finding it entailed him turning the lights on. There was no one at the rear of the premises who would notice. It was lying in the middle of the floor. His plan was coming together more easily than he had anticipated.

Replacing the chairs that had been moved was not difficult. They had been in position for so long they had left indents in the carpet. He lifted them back as opposed to dragging them when they would leave flagrant marks. The bullet hole in the window was in line with the dead body of Mercedes. Very helpful. Where he had fired his five rounds at the murderous doctor he was going to cover later. Checking where his four unaccounted bullets had ended up shocked him.

Three were embedded in the plaster of the ceiling and one had gone through the carpet, and deep into the wooden flooring beneath. He assumed correctly that as he was weakening and his arm dropped, the fourth was the bullet that had done for her. Luck had been with him.

Everything was ready. He had sanitised as much as was possible but again knew that DNA might pick something of his up. It was to be expected.

His next visit was going to be interesting.

141

Monday 20th June 2011

Back at the car he unloaded the second Lithuanian's gun, and removed all the ammunition from the magazine. Taking two bullets, he put them back into the clip, and reloaded the gun. There was still a round in the chamber ready to fire as soon as the safety was disabled. Three bullets in total which he thought would be ample, providing the weapon worked. He slipped the gun back under the seat.

Taking the trusted MP-443 automatic out of his waistband, he released the magazine and leaving one round still chambered, emptied it. There were only five rounds left. He wanted them at the top of the clip, so filled the bottom up with ten of the bullets from the gun under the seat and topped it up with the five. There were still five rounds loose which he put in his pocket.

He was parked in a different side road to previously. Never be predictable was what he'd been taught and tonight it was imperative he wasn't. The occasional vehicle drove by as a late worker or reveller made their way home. Putting his balaclava on, Simon went to the boot and opened it. The man was without a doubt conscious and not well pleased. His back was hurting where he was twisted into the confined space, and he couldn't feel either leg or one arm. Snot had been forced down his nose when he had tried to sneeze and had congealed on his cheek and chin. He'd wet himself due to the length of time he'd been incarcerated. His eyes were bloodshot and it looked like he wanted to puke. If he did, he would probably have died choking in his own vomit.

Simon said, "I gave you the chance to walk away. Because you didn't, you suffer the consequences. I don't know who's looking for me and I don't really care. In another hour or two, I'll come and get you out" and with that, he slammed the boot shut.

Whipping off his balaclava, he stuffed it into his pocket with a new pair of latex gloves and walked to Yusef's house.

Wandering around the streets surrounding the house, he checked there hadn't been any additional security employed. Simon could see nothing to trouble him. It didn't mean there wasn't any one behind a twitching curtain in a neighbour's room watching out for him or if anyone else, like Greg, may be inside waiting for him. Tonight, he was going in come what may. It was part of his master plan. He was over the wall and crouched down in the garden in seconds. His gloves and balaclava on. No patrolling security. His trip to the store room's window avoided the CCTV cameras. He still did not know if they worked or not, but he saw no reason to place himself in their view to check.

Easing the window quietly open, he put his jute bag inside and climbed in after it. His small torch showed him nothing had changed in the room. The door was still unlocked. Opening it a few inches by standing to one side was just a precaution. Bullets could go clean through doors but not often walls. No gunfire. He peered into the hallway. It all appeared the same as when he was there previously. The light was shining in the same room as before, and there was a game of cricket reaching some kind of crescendo on the television. Tonight, there was an additional noise: someone was shouting encouragement to players on one of the teams. Simon never understood the logic of shouting at someone who would never hear.

He crept silently across the hall looking for a security alarm control box or a CCTV monitoring unit. There was nothing that he could see. It was strange that there were outward signs of security, but nothing inside to say they worked. Simon came to the conclusion that they were dummies, but he wasn't sure. A big house without working security was boarding on the reckless. Time was approaching 1am and he had a lot to do. Looking through the open door, he could see a man was sitting in a large leather armchair facing the TV. He was alone.

"Good evening. Yusuf, I presume?"

The man jumped out of his chair, "Who the hell are you?"

He was a casually dressed dumpy Asian man about mid-fifties and some five feet seven inches tall with slicked back greasy black hair.

"I've come to ask you a couple of questions. Please turn the TV off. I'd hate for you to mishear me."

The seventy-two-inch plasma TV was filling the wall it had been mounted on. Yusuf had regained his composure from his initial shock.

"You obviously do not know who I am. The Police will deal with you" and he moved to a phone next to his chair.

Simon picked up a half sized decorative bowling ball from a mounted stand on a side cabinet and threw it at the TV.

There was a strange noise as the screen smashed but remained within the confines of its frame and the TV stopped, holding a gradually fading stuttering image.

"Now perhaps you can hear me better. I don't want any misunderstandings."

Yusuf could not believe what he had just witnessed. The phone was in his hand and he had dialled the second of the three nines. He scrutinised Simon.

"You are new round here or you would not have done that."

"Put the phone down please, it won't work."

Yusuf pushed the third nine and placed it to his ear. There was no ringing tone.

"Now, I just want to ask you why you employed someone to conduct surveillance on a young lady in Chichester, which if you didn't know is in West Sussex?"

"What I do is up to me. I am a lawyer. I am not going to tell a burglar anything."

"That is your choice. I will tell you she suffered horrendously because of what you arranged. Therefore, it is only fair don't you think that you should suffer as well."

"What?"

Simon took out of his trouser waistband the gun that he'd used previously and taking a quick aim, shot Yusuf in his right thigh. It shattered immediately as the bullet broke into fragments destroying the bone and sending small chards out of the back of his leg through a gaping hole that had opened up. The explosion of the bullet from the gun made a blinding flash and a deafening noise in the enclosure of the room, matched within a second by a piecing scream. Yusuf was lying on the floor in a slowly growing pool of dark blood. He was breathing heavily and could feel the pulse in his leg which was a new experience for him.

At the front door of the house, Greg's index finger was inches away from pressing the doorbell when the retort of the gun sounded. Instinct caused him to dive to his right rolling as he pulled his own handgun. No bullet had passed him and he concluded instantly that he was not the target. His adversary had got to Yusef before he could warn him. His next thought was it had to be Simon shooting Yusef, but he didn't care who was killed as long as it wasn't him. Greg realised that Simon must have broken in as he didn't believe he would have gone to the front door, so he began to look for his point of entry.

"If that is treated in hospital, you may walk again with the aid of a stick. I'll ask again. Why? If you don't answer you will need a wheelchair for the rest of your pitiful life."

"You are a dead man. You don't know who you're dealing with" was the screamed reply.

Another explosion erupted as the gun recoiled and another scream.

"You are now probably a cripple no matter how good the NHS is. The next bullet will shatter your right arm and you will have to wipe your arse with your left hand as well as eat with it. Answer the question."

"I was told to arrange it by Richard Davies."

Greg had found the open window and believed he now had the advantage. Should he stay outside or go in. The sound of the second shot meant Simon was still with Yusef, so he climbed through into the store room. Simon had left the door wide open, and extraneous light from the TV room just penetrated the gloom like a weak night light. It was just enough for him to see objects to avoid. He could just make out Simon's muffled voice. At the door, he saw he had a clear view of anyone moving in the hall and they would probably be backlit slightly from the lit TV room. He pulled the door closed leaving a gap of a foot where he could aim through without leaving himself too vulnerable. Now all he needed to do was wait.

"I will tell you why you are lying. I have recently left his bedroom. He has not left his bed for years and is basically ga ga. Who told you?"

"Mercedes, his daughter."

"She is dead. Who?" and he started to take aim at Yusef.

He screamed, "Both her and Jackie told me to do it. I swear."

"On whose behalf was she acting?"

"Someone in London."

"Who?"

"I don't know. I swear it."

"Does one of the phones in the office out there connect to them?"

"Yes. Yes. The second from the left. For pity's sake call an ambulance."

"Is there a set time to call?"

"After five."

Yusef felt groggy. He knew he hadn't long.

"I hope you get to hospital" and Simon walked out of the room as Yusef screamed after him to call an ambulance. He fell unconscious and would never come round.

142

Monday 20th June 2011

As soon as Simon entered the hall, he noticed the store room door was not as he had left it. It hadn't swung freely when he had passed through it before, so why would it do it now? Someone had moved it. He dropped to the floor and rolled as he felt the bullet graze his side. It had been aimed directly at the centre of his chest and would have killed him instantly had he not reacted. Instead, as he dropped, Greg had tried to compensate and the bullet went through his clothing and scorched his ribs. Painful for Simon but not debilitating. He had replaced his gun into his waistband as he had left Yusef, but had it out and back ready in his hand.

Firing at the gap in the door, the noise was like a cannon in the cavernous hall. Simon's ears were still ringing from the noise it had made in the TV room. The bullet struck the edge of the door flinging it wide open. Greg stepped back for cover behind the wall. Simon took his chance and dived behind a solid looking wooden hall table. Greg cursed his luck. He didn't want to engage in a gun fight he might lose, and decided to run again. His problem was the open door would let Simon see him moving and he would present an easy target. He hated him. How he wanted to kill him.

As he flattened himself against the wall to consider how to move, he stood on a broom. At last some luck. With the broom, he pulled the door to and shut it. If Simon put a spray of bullets through the door, it was unlikely he would be hit if he kept to one side. Most professionals would not waste bullets by firing randomly in the hope of hitting somebody, and Greg considered Simon a professional of some standing. He confidently moved to the window and out of the house. No gunshots or bullets followed through the door. Then he ran a zig zag route through the garden and away.

Simon worked out swiftly what Greg was going to do and decided to let him go as he had more pressing matters. He ran into the office and ducked to the side of the window and watched the zig zagging runner. Making sure he'd left the grounds completely before running into the store room to collect his bag. Caution being his watchword tonight.

Back in the office cum communications room he took out of the bag a folded up piece of paper that he had picked up in his hotel. It was a sheet of twelve individual sticky labels that he had already written a sequential number on. He stuck the numbers on the phones starting from the left as seen from the seat behind the desk. Then disconnecting all the phones with their chargers, he put them into his bag. There were three, four gang extension leads that the phones' chargers had been connected to which Simon detached from the wall sockets and put into his bag. Without the extensions and phones, the room now looked like a simple home office.

There was a sudden short indecipherable noise from within the house. Simon with gun in hand moved to the door and peeked into the hallway. Nothing moving that he could see. He knew he would have to check. Opening the door wide he waited for a gunshot. Nothing. Running back to the hall table he ducked down. Still nothing. The house appeared to Simon's senses as being empty yet there had been a definite noise. He was apprehensive that Greg may have snuck back in and was laying in ambush for him. It was time he didn't have.

Running in a crouch, he went into the TV room. A contorted part image was flashing on the smashed TV. Yusef was lying in a pool of his own congealing blood which had stopped flowing as his heart had slowly wound down and stopped pumping it out. Then Simon heard it again, and it emanated from the TV. It was a short burst of distorted noise of the crowd cheering. Swearing under his breath he ran back to recover his bag and then exited via the store room window pushing it tightly closed before he jogged back to the Audi.

Jumping into the driver's seat, he flung his bag onto the back seat before driving to the cul-de-sac by the sentry box. Still empty. Manoeuvring past the Saab which was parked at an awkward angle, he entered RD's drive. Knowing the Saab was previously driven by Greg he would have been expecting trouble if it had only just appeared. He drove as close as he could get to the front door. Running around to the kitchen door, he found it open as he had left it and went inside. Then he stopped. His senses were kicking in and telling him someone else was in the house. 'Why tonight?' Everything was going haywire.

The gentle noise of very slow movement was coming from upstairs. He had to take a risk there was no one downstairs, so running up one of the staircases, he flattened himself against the wall. The noise was from the back of the house. Moving furtively, he arrived at the entrance to the bedroom and heard the noise from within. Simon knew Mercedes and the doctor were dead as dodos but that left RD. To all intents and purposes, he should also have been dead. It had to be him.

Simon went into the bedroom through the dressing area. RD was on the floor as was the drip stand and pump. He was trying to crawl to the dressing room and out to the hall and beyond. He'd only made about three feet and was dragging half his bedding as well as the medical bits behind him. RD was seeing nothing. His eyes were closed. How he'd made it three feet astounded Simon, but he didn't mind where he went or how far. It would only enhance his plans. Satisfied, he ran back downstairs to the front door and slipped his balaclava on as he stepped out to the Audi.

Now he had to get the man out of the boot. When he opened it, he saw the man was fast asleep and snoring intermittently through his stuffed up nose. He cut the plasticuff off his feet and the man woke with a start as his legs seemed to break free. His hands were still locked behind his back, but they weren't being pulled now and feeling was rapidly coming back to his limbs.

"Your choice, I can carry and drag you which will be very painful, or you can walk."

To get out of the boot, the man would do anything. He swung his legs over the lip and tried to stand but couldn't.

Simon pulled him up by his suit jacket and the man wobbled as he seemed to be learning again how to use his legs. He started to walk as guided through the front door and towards the stairs.

"I'll be right behind you and you won't fall back down."

The man climbed warily to the top hanging onto the banister with both bound hands for support and Simon directed him to RD's bedroom. They passed through the dressing area and fear drew across the man's face and sweat started to form below his hairline. He'd seen RD on the floor pulling all his paraphernalia first and then the dead doctor. The outline of a human form beneath the sheet did not bode well and he assumed correctly that it was another body.

"Sit anywhere you like."

The man tottered to the closest chair and dropped into it. Sweat was now dripping from all over his face and terror was etched across it.

"I'll tell you this. I am not going to kill you, so you do not need to panic."

If the man believed him it didn't seem to stop the sweat. Simon ripped the tape from the man's mouth and he gulped air as though mimicking a goldfish.

"Who sent you looking for me?"

"Greg."

"How were you to let him know if you found me?"

"The phone number in my top pocket."

Simon put two fingers into the suit jacket pocket and pulled out a small leather folder and a piece of paper with a phone number on.

The folder bore the crest of what Simon believed was Birmingham. Flipping it open, Simon saw the picture of the man on one side and a badge stating he was Detective Inspector Beadle from the West Midlands Police Force on the other.

"You really are a Policeman! What were you doing here? Moonlighting?"

After a pause.

"Yes."

Simon went behind Beadle who felt a sharp prick in his forearm.

"What's that?"

"It's a sedative. Nothing to fret about. I had a quarter of the mixture and it did me no real harm. Makes you dizzy and feel a bit sick and knocks you scatty for a while."

Beadle's head lolled forward as he became numb and started to lapse into unconsciousness.

143

Monday 20th June 2011

Simon ran to the kitchen and outside the door to where he had left Greg's rifle. Holding it by the barrel, he scampered back upstairs and into the bedroom. Opening a window, he went to Beadle and cut the plasticuffs off freeing his hands. He pulled his right arm forward and placed the rifle stock against his chest and put his right index finger on the trigger. Making sure the gun was aimed through the open window, Simon pulled the trigger over Beadle's finger. That would put some residue on his crumpled suit and a fingerprint or two on the gun. Within a minute, Simon had laid the rifle on the bed in the summer house pointing directly towards the hole in the window of RD's bedroom.

Then it was his faithful liberated Lithuanian's gun. Same procedure as before but a couple of shots through the open window. Then the gun discarded on the floor directly from where Simon had killed the doctor. Pulling Beadle forward out of his chair, he dropped him on the floor just by the gun. He put the spare five rounds into one of Beadle's side pockets. Simon was satisfied with his handiwork and picked up the plasticuffs and the empty syringe and did a check of the room for any signs of his presence. He saw RD was now laying still and had stopped moving completely. Closing the window, he left the bedroom. and went out of the front door and to his appropriated Audi.

He drove to the car park where he joined three other vehicles. Picking one of the mobile phones out of the bag, he put a handkerchief over the phone and dialled nine, nine, nine.

"Emergency. Which service do you require?"

"Police."

"Connecting you now."

"There's been a lot of shooting of guns over the last couple of nights round here. I saw a Policeman I know called Beadle go into a lawyer's house tonight. I think his name is Yusef Benozin. Then there was some shooting. I am so scared. The Policeman ran out about an hour ago with a rifle and I watched him go to RD's house. There was a lot more shooting. I think he may be dead. You need to get there quickly to help him. Get an ambulance."

Simon hung up and took the battery out of the phone.

Picking out another mobile, he phoned the Birmingham Gazette. The midnight receptionist who was half asleep with his feet on a desk reluctantly set the recorder before answering the ringing phone.

"Hello. Birmingham Gazette news desk. How can I help you?"

"A Policeman, Detective Inspector Beadle has shot and killed a lawyer called Yusef Benozin and has killed a couple of people at the criminal Richard Davies' house. Now the Chief Constable and his force are trying to cover it all up. They are going to move dead bodies trying to hide them before the press get wind of anything. You need to get people there now with cameras."

The receptionist's feet shot off the desk.

"Who are you, how do you know all this?"

"My name is not important. Consider me a whistle blower. I'm in the know, and don't like what is happening."

Then Simon hung up and again took the battery out of the phone.

The receptionist was efficient when he had something of note to get stuck into. Within minutes he had spoken to his roaming night team and they were dispatched to Richard Davies's house. They knew who he was and had been desperate for several years to get something on him or his organisation. Their editor had always seemed to have had a reason not to publish though. The driver took a chance and broke every speed limit. Several Police vehicles overtook him on blue lights which only made him drive faster. The receptionist was busy waking the two best journalists and harrying them to get up and out. Photo journalists were mobilised and knew a good picture would increase their standing with the paper and may mean a large bonus.

The roaming team arrived at the entrance to the cul-de-sac and found a Police car blocking the road. Tape was being strung across it and uniform officers were running about in RD's drive. Jumping out of their van, the photographer was taking pictures before his feet had hit the tarmac. A uniform officer told the driver to move the van and the journalist stuck a tape recorder in the officer's face.

"We have information that there may be dead bodies here and a Detective Inspector Beadle has killed them. Also, you are trying to cover it up. Have you any comment?"

"Just move along."

"So you are trying to cover it up. You don't want us to see anything."

The officer did not like being misquoted.

"Turn that contraption off."

The journalist obliged, because he had another recorder working in his pocket.

Looking around to make sure he was not being overheard, the officer said, "I can't say on the record, but you are right. Detective Inspector Beadle is in the house and there are two dead bodies. They have found a gun that may be the murder weapon. Davies is close to death and the ambulance is on way. That's all I know at the moment."

"What about Yusef Benozin? Is he dead or alive?"

"I haven't heard."

Then the officer was called away. The journalist saw promotion looming on the horizon and called the BBC news room in Birmingham.

A photo journalist who lived close by was the first press man to arrive at Yusef's house. He photographed the Police from the road trying to get into the premises. Seeing where the wall dipped, he climbed onto the top to get a better shot. Then realising he could get into the garden, he dropped down. Creeping forward, he took some great pictures. He photographed the Police ringing the doorbell then breaking a window and climbing in. His best shots were of two officers exiting the front door to throw up. Staying where he was, he continued to get ameliorating shots of the ambulance arriving and then leaving empty.

The road in front of Yusef's house was cordoned off by the Police and all the others from the press pack were kept at a distance. From his premier position in the garden he watched the window of the TV room being flung open wide and an officer lean out to gulp fresh air. When he had withdrawn inside leaving the window wide and the lights still on, the photographer knew this was his Pulitzer moment. There were no Police in the gardens, so he ran forward to the window and peered in. He caught the vomit as it rose in his throat and forced it back down. His camera clicked and clicked as he took one digital image after another. Then he turned his camera onto video record.

Between the Police moving about inside the houses and the photographer in the garden, anything left inadvertently by Simon was destroyed.

144

Monday 20th June 2011

By the time the whole palaver was playing out, Simon was entrenched in his room at the Premier Inn fast asleep. He had only waited five minutes in the hotel carpark for Ian and his apprentice to arrive via the exit. The handover of the jute bag and all the phones was swift, and Simon told them which ones he had used to call the Police and press. He explained that the one marked number two was the one likely to contact the home office mole. Laura asserted that the one he had used to call Police would be the last one she checked in case there had been a trace put on it by the Police Control Room.

Greg answered the phone.

"Hello."

"Do you know what has happened?"

"I have a rough idea."

"The shit has hit the fan. I can't stop it now. Too many of my officers have been all over both houses. I can't vouch for more than one of them. I've been told there are three dead and my right-hand man may have done it and RD may be on his way out."

"No he didn't."

"What do you know?"

"Someone who uses the name Simon. I don't know if that's his real name or not. He's done it."

"I've been told Yusef's office is empty. He's got all the phones."

"Do you know everyone's numbers?"

"No. I don't know anyone or their numbers except yours. What do you think he will do?"

"I think we will have to wait and see."

"I can't do anything to jeopardise my position. Somehow the press has got wind of all this. They will be watching like hawks. It's got to be straight down the line. I don't know what Beadle is going to say. He might drop us all in it when he comes round."

"Where is he?"

"In Birmingham General."

"Anyone with him?"

"Just a uniform PC."

"Can you call him off for an hour?"

"Yes. Are you going to do what I think?"

"Yes. Better safe than sorry."

"I don't want to know. Just do it."

"Bye."

The Chief Constable put his head in his hands. He had envisaged this happening one day but it had still been a shock when he had received the phone call from the City Control Room. It was worse than he thought. If Greg dealt with Beadle that would close that avenue. Then the thought crossed his mind that Greg might consider him a weak link. Would he try and silence him? Once he got to the office in the morning, he would arrange some personal security. He couldn't get back to sleep. What was going to happen? Every sound made him jump nervously.

Ian connected all the phones up to the extensions except the one that Simon had used to call the Police. If he put the battery in that one, it didn't matter if it was turned on or not, it would show its position to the closest mobile phone mast. The Police could then trace its location without much difficulty within a few hours. Ian sat back to let his apprentice do her work. It had actually occurred to him that he had relinquished the mantel of tutor to her and he had assumed her role as the apprentice. Laura soon found that each phone only had one number stored in its memory and only had calls to and from that other phone shown in its logs. It was the easiest work she had been asked to do. The only exception was the phone that Simon had used to call the press.

Phoning Graham, Ian filled him in regarding the phones. He had recently arrived home and had released his driver. It was agreed that Ian and Laura should get back to London as soon as they could and meet Graham in Snow Hill Police Station. They anticipated no more than two hours hence and no later than 6am.

Turning the TV on in his lounge, Graham searched the rolling news channels. They were starting to report a serious incident in Birmingham but with sketchy reports. Some claiming many dead at the hands of a deranged Police Inspector.

Graham called John. For twenty minutes, they chatted. Tossing scenarios about as to how to proceed, they played devil's advocate even for their own ideas. Sluggishly, a plan was formulated. It seemed a reasonable idea but Graham needed to speak to the Home Secretary for her agreement. John was watching Sky rolling news and Graham was watching the BBC. They were relying on the mole seeing the footage when they woke up in the morning.

The PC who was sitting on a borrowed chair outside the single room occupied by Beadle took a phone call. Ordered to stop the press entering the hospital via the main door he left his post. Greg strode passed him in the corridor. When he walked into the room, Beadle was starting to rouse. It didn't take much. Greg gripped Beadle by the throat and squeezed. Beadle's eyes were wide and staring with pure hate. He couldn't defend himself. His arms and hands wouldn't do what his brain was telling them. Trying to shout for help was lower than a whimper. It was the end and he knew it.

At the nurse's station, a machine burst into life beeping stridently and the steady rhythmic dance of the moving graph changed step. By chance, there were three male nurses having a break from their services to the sick, injured and dying of Birmingham. They ran to Beadle's room and saw Greg with his hand gripping Beadle's throat. One dived at him knocking him clear and the other two challenged him. A gun appeared in Greg's hand and all three nurses backed off. Greg had wanted to eliminate Beadle with minimum fuss and not be observed. It had all gone awry because of some wires that he had not seen under Beadle's arm. He had come to kill him and decided that was now imperative. He put the gun to Beadle's head and pulled the trigger. He was no longer being surreptitious and didn't care. The nurses were petrified. They were witnesses to a cold-blooded murder. Were they to be next?

All three ran from the room shouting for help. Greg followed. He knew his image would be plastered all over the place as honest Police sought him. No one would be able to protect him however high they were in the establishment. He cursed Simon. How he wanted to kill him. He would give a king's ransom for the chance. Running down the stairs, he passed the PC running up them. His time in England was up. He had to get out of the country fast.

His escape plan had been in place for several years. Within four hours, he was on his way to New York.

145

Monday 20th June 2011

Alison awoke again with a raging thirst. Whatever the tablets were that Carol was feeding her were having some strange effects on her. She wriggled about to sit up in bed without too much pain, then downed the glass of water on the bedside table. In the quiet of the night, she heard faint voices. Checking her watch, she saw it had just passed four. 'Am I the only one to try to sleep in this house?' She got out of bed and wrapped John's dressing gown around her before stealing out into the hall and then into the lounge.

John was laid flat on his favourite chair watching the television. She sat gingerly down in the chair she had found most comfortable previously.

"Why pray are you watching TV at this time of night?"

"Your dad asked me to."

"It's like getting blood from a stone with you two. Why?"

"Just watch and see if anything springs to mind."

Alison watched as the news scrolled round and then to an incident in Birmingham. Her eyes widened as the reporter stated that a rogue Police Inspector had shot and killed at least three people and was under guard in hospital.

Alison whined. "Please. Don't tell me Simon was involved."

"Did they say anyone else was involved? The person who did it is in hospital. Simon is in his hotel probably asleep."

"Why do I worry then?"

"Maybe you are very fond of him?"

She chose not to answer and continued to watch the news. A ticker tape running constantly across the bottom of the screen added a new item. *Breaking*

News: A shooting in Birmingham Hospital. Believed Detective Inspector Beadle has been shot dead whilst under Police guard as a suspect for murder. Alison looked at John who seemed non plussed.

"Tell me what is happening. I'm going mad. Is Simon in trouble?"

Carol strode into the room.

"For goodness sake. When you two are up, everyone is up. Just tell her, then we can all get back to bed."

John looked at Alison and said, "No. He has just picked up some phones. He'll be back tomorrow: or rather later today."

She glared at him. She knew there was so much more. She knew he was not going to tell her just yet.

"Alright. I want the full story in the morning" and she stomped sullenly back to bed.

Carol sat in Alison's vacated chair.

"Is he ok?"

"Yes. I think so. We'll know soon enough. He should be back by midday."

Carol watched the repeated rolling news.

"Looks like he's caused mayhem."

"The murder in the hospital is strange. I can't work that one out."

"I'm going back to bed. I presume you're staying up for a reason?"

"Yes. I'll grab a nap sometime later."

John phoned Graham who was in a different car with a fresh driver.

"The DI they have attributed all the murders to has been shot in his hospital bed. I can't work that out."

"Maybe to stop him talking."

"It's the only answer, but he was under Police guard and they never saw a thing."

"We need to know why? I'll get the Home Secretary to find out. She can ask questions without raising suspicion."

"There's no way Simon could have been involved. I would hope he's bullet proof."

"It means there is a killer up there that we don't know about. Let Simon have a few hours then fill him in."

"Ok. Do you think I should tell Ginger?"

"No. Not yet. We don't want to worry him unnecessarily."

They hung up without acrimony that neither said goodbye or exchanged accepted pleasantries to end the conversation.

Graham phoned the Home Secretary who was still at the Ministry in her office watching the rolling news with foreboding. She'd been up all night and was getting crotchety. The more she watched, the grouchier she got.

"Good morning Minister."

"No it bloody isn't. What the hell has been happening up there?"

"I don't know yet, but will in an hour or two. My man was able to get hold of some phones which are now on their way back to London. He believes one is a direct link to the mole. As soon as I can, I will come and see you. I would ask though if you could find the time, could you contact the Chief Constable up there and find out how the killer got past the Police guard in the hospital?"

"I'll ask him a damn sight more than that."

"Thank you."

"Make sure you get to me before ten o'clock. Preferably before nine."

"I certainly will."

"Goodbye" and she slammed the phone down on its cradle.

Within minutes she was on the phone to the Birmingham Police Control Room Night Duty Inspector insistent on speaking to the CC. When told he was at his home address and not contactable, she exploded.

Demanding to know, "Why hasn't he attended to take control of the situation?"

The Inspector tried to placate her. "I have been able to keep him fully briefed as to the situation as it has developed."

"I am in my office because it is a serious incident. It's all over the TV. Tell him I expect him to be in his office."

"Yes Madam. I shall pass on your observation."

"It's not a bloody observation, it's an order."

The Inspector realised the mistake of his words and compulsorily stood up. "Yes Ma'am."

She changed tack and launched into an attack on him in the absence of the CC.

"You have dead bodies all over the place and the potential killer in hospital. Why the hell did you only have one PC guarding him? An apparent proficient killer?"

"The instruction came directly from the Chief Constable."

Steaming straight on she challenged him.

"Then how did another murderer get past him? Three medics were able to witness it all according to the TV so why couldn't he? Why didn't he try to prevent it?"

The Inspector had already spoken to the PC.

"He was at the front of the hospital to make sure the press didn't get in."

"What!" Sarcastically asking the Inspector before he could reply *"Was he the only officer working in Birmingham tonight that is capable of doing everything?"*

"The officer was instructed personally by the Chief Constable to leave his post without my knowledge."

She practically took off.

"How?"

"He phoned the officer directly from his home."

As he spoke, he realised what he was saying. The Home Secretary realised what he had said. Neither spoke as both came to the same conclusion. She became rational.

"Inspector. I want you personally to take a full statement from the PC and I want a copy on my desk within the hour. I shall be sending in the IPCC (Independent Police Complaints Commission). As far as I am concerned, they will be investigating your CC for complicity to murder. When you have the statement, and not before, I want him made aware of this fact. Do you understand?"

"Yes ma'am."

"Get on with it then" and she hung up.

146
Monday 20th June 2011

Graham was in Snow Hill eating a 'plastic' sandwich with an expiry date three days previous that he had picked up from a small twenty-four hour convenience store on the way in. At least the coffee was hot. He hadn't had time to get anything decent. There were three men sitting with him saying nothing. They had been summoned from their beds, as far as they could tell, in the middle of the night to meet him. None had been up this early for years. All accepted that what they were going to do was of national importance. The officer manning the front counter had been instructed to conduct the expected two people directly to him.

Ian and Laura arrived and were ushered into the small, now crowded, office. They handed the single mobile phone marked 'Two' to Graham. He passed it on to one of the three men.

"I need to know the address where the phone bearing the number that is stored in this one is located. Urgently. The minute you know, call me."

The three left the office and went to a small building a couple of hundred yards away and within minutes had located the mast nearest the phone as Harrow on the Hill.

They went to three identical VW vans in an underground car park and all drove to Harrow on the Hill. Arriving at pre-determined points, they all climbed into the back of their vans. Electronic instruments were turned on and all coordinated and triangulated with each other. The signal was from an area to the East of the mast. Driving to new agreed points, they parked and climbed into the back of their vans again. Now they were getting closer. One of the vans repositioned two streets further North. The instruments were delicate but exceedingly accurate at short range.

They pinpointed a tree lined road and the vans were again repositioned. One went to a junction and when the equipment was turned on, it indicated a gated group of four houses about midpoint of the road. The vans' instruments could see the phone was in one of the two houses to the East side. It was the best they could do. They couldn't get through the secured gates. One van using different equipment sat outside in the tree lined road and listened for any transmissions to or from the phone. As the unelected leader of the three was starting to call Graham, one of the others called him on their unique radio band to let him know a government car had arrived at the gate entrance.

Recording the index number was simple enough. These were not Policeman but they knew it would prove useful. A smartly dressed fit looking man of about five feet ten inches left one of the houses carrying a red box briefcase. It was a giveaway that he was a Minister. His face was buried in concentration as he watched the news on his new government issued smart phone. The chauffeur hurried to meet him and take the case from him.

The technicians concluded from their instrumentation that it was not the phone in question although they could see that the phone was on the move. It was clear to all three that he had to have it somewhere on his person, or in the case. From their access to the unabridged electoral roll, they had the man's name. Graham was given the full details within the hour of the three leaving the little office.

His car was brought to the front of the station. Ian and Laura would meet him later. He had good news, or so he thought, for the Home Secretary.

147

Monday 20th June 2011

John stood with a mug of coffee in his hand as he looked out of the kitchen window across the fields surrounding the university buildings. Birds were on the move searching for food. There were swifts or swallows, he wasn't sure, flying high in the sky. Marvelling at their acrobatic aerial antics, he didn't hear Alison walk in.

"Hello."

The liquid sloshed all over the counter as the mug left his grasp and he spun round with hands coming up in a defensive posture.

"Wo. It's me. You are edgy this morning."

"Sorry. I didn't hear you coming."

"Any news?"

"The press have got hold of a CCTV image from the hospital of the person who killed the Policeman. You'll be glad to know it's not Simon. Check it out on the TV. You never know, you might recognise him."

Alison looked at him dubiously.

"What you are saying is: I should recognise him?"

"Possibly."

Alison went into the lounge and sat down in front of the TV. It wasn't long before a clear frozen image was shown, and the voice over claimed it to be that of the murderer. She didn't recognise the man. Having cleared up his mess, John joined her.

"Well? Do you recognise him?"

"No. You think I should though. Tell me: who is he?"

"His name is Grigoriev. Greg for short. He was the leader of the group who kidnapped you."

Alison scowled as she examined the image watching it until it was replaced by a reporter.

"Is Simon alright?"

"Yes. I spoke to him just before you made me spill my coffee. He was asleep when the murder happened in the hospital. He told me Greg had tried to kill him."

"What's happened to Greg? Has he been arrested?"

"No. Not yet. He's disappeared."

The thought flitted through her brain that Simon may have dealt with him. She really hoped so.

"There's a meeting tonight at your dad's house. Do you want to come?"

"Course I do."

"Well. I'm off to work now. By the way, have I told you how we have solved George Armstrong's murder?"

A plaintive cry. "No!"

"What about all the serial killings?"

Louder now, "No! What serial killings?"

"Remind me to tell you sometime" and he walked to the front door.

"You bastard."

"Bye. See you tonight" and he left.

John needed breakfast and was in the canteen earlier than normal. Doreen walked in to John's amazement. He had never once seen her in the canteen.

"Hello Doreen. What brings you here so early?"

"I wanted to have a private chat."

"What about?"

"Deborah and Haskland."

"Go on."

"I feel it's my fault they are in hospital."

John thought he could see slight reddening of her eyes.

"Not at all. What you did was what lots of detectives throughout this country do each day. You used your brain to work out a problem. They have committed at least one serious crime. It was their choice. The way she and her boyfriend reacted was their choice. It was nothing to do with you how they would react. The result was of their own making Doreen."

The lady from the canteen had seen Doreen: assessed that she had a problem and made a quick pot of tea.

"Here you are dear. I have found that he does have words of wisdom. They have worked for me in the past."

John didn't know which way to look.

Doreen said, "Thanks. I suppose now I'm here, I should have some breakfast."

"What do you want? Healthy or coronary inducing?"

Doreen was slightly shocked and amused.

"Healthy please."

"Ok. One of each coming up."

She darted back to her kitchen.

As other early visitors to the canteen arrived, they were surprised to see both John and Doreen already half way through their breakfasts and deep in conversation. Jimmy and Groves were the only two that appeared confident enough to sit with them. Doreen was soon put totally at ease mainly by Groves who could empathise with her. The pair seemed to have a lot in common and were quickly laughing at each other's problems. John and Jimmy sat quietly listening. Eventually, all four made their way up to the office.

Talk in the canteen and the office revolved around the reported incidents in Birmingham and how it appeared they were apparently incompetent up there. Sussex Police had a guard outside the wards containing Deborah and her boyfriend. No one other than medical staff and identifiable Police Officers were permitted entry. Standard procedure. Every Police Force complies with it: or should do.

There was no briefing scheduled this morning. All the officers had their allotted addresses and had viewed either the video cassettes, CDs or DVDs. It was likely to be another long hard day's slog for a lot of them who were going to establish harrowing facts. Paul had arranged for two officers from the Littlehampton MIT with knowledge of the Armstrong murder to be available to interview Deborah who was fully compos mentis. She was expected to remain in hospital for some time, so it had been agreed with her lawyer for an interview later in the day.

Paul said to John, "Looks like everything is slotting into place now. All we need to know is why did Deborah do it?"

"She may tell us later."

"I hope so. Is the CC still insistent on going to court today?"

"Yes. Both him and Prodow. It's going to be right fun and games. The press will be there en masse. I think they are going to try and upstage Birmingham."

Both laughed.

Then Paul confided, "Prodow spoke to both PCs guarding Deborah and her boyfriend this morning and told them if they left their posts even to go to the loo, they had to have someone take their place. He threatened to skin them alive if they moved. I think he's really scared that the murderer from Birmingham might come and do for them."

John made no comment.

148
Monday 20th June 2011

"Bloody dirty" and she paused, abstaining from using the first word that had come to mind, "rat!"

Graham said, "They located him just before his Ministerial car turned up."

She interrupted him again.

"Dirty no good rat. I've looked after Nicholas for over six years. I dragged him out of the Foreign Office where he seemed to live whenever we have been in power and got him made a Junior Minister and that's how he repays me. Bastard."

"What do you intend to do?"

"I'm going to have to tell the PM. He'll probably go mad. He'll sack him straightaway."

"That just sends him to the back benches. He hasn't been doing this for love. He must have been getting well paid. Can't you put some investigators on to him? If they could trace the money, he could go to prison."

The Home Secretary said, "Talking of prison. Read this" and she handed a faxed statement to Graham.

"My God!"

"That's why he wasn't going to get a second term as CC."

"This practically proves him complicit in the murder of one of his own officers."

"I've sent the IPCC in already. I know he will be expecting them. It will be interesting to see what he does."

Graham looked hard at her.

She said, "It's up to him what he does."

Graham didn't pursue it. Any Police Officer would not fare well in prison, and such a high ranking one would be a feather in the cap of any prisoner.

"Getting back to Nicholas, what time does he normally arrive?"

"Any time before nine."

"He should be here by now. The car left Harrow nearly an hour and a half ago."

Picking up a phone, she asked if Nicholas had arrived in the building. Slamming it down, she thought for a second or two.

"He got into the building and was coming to see me as he does every morning for a briefing."

She paused, still fighting to regain her temper. "Kathy told him I was in conference with you and not to be disturbed."

Graham enquired, "Yes?" as a question.

"He told her he was feeling ill and said he would go home to recover."

"Damage limitation. He must have something there he needs to get rid of."

"What the hell am I going to do?"

"He's got to be stopped. Has his car got a radio?"

"Yes."

"Call it and find out where he is. He won't be at home yet with the traffic about at this time of day. Try and delay it. I'll get some Police there and arrest him for conspiracy to murder."

"You'd never prove that!"

"I don't intend to. It will keep him away from his house until we can search it."

The Home Secretary nearly broke into a run as she dashed to the communications room. The PM was her second call.

Graham called the City of London Police Control Room. Two city cars were dispatched and the Metropolitan Police Information Room was briefed that units were passing through their area at speed. A local car from Harrow was sent to stop anyone entering or leaving the gated houses. All eventualities were covered in minutes.

The Ministerial car was only two miles away when the driver, a retired marine, took the call.

"Home Secretary here. Could you please pop into the constituency office in Harrow as a matter of urgency and pick up a parcel for me. If you could do it on your way to where you are going."

"Yes. Certainly Minister."

Nicholas had heard every word and knew that something was afoot. Catherine, to his knowledge, had never once used a radio to pass any message. As Home Secretary, she would have arranged for the radio controller to have sent it. He was fully up to speed via the scrolling news channels on his mobile as to the occurrences in Birmingham. A senior Police Officer was already in her office before he got in to work. There had been no way he was going to wait and find out if he had been rumbled. He needed time to think.

When the call finished, he told the driver that he would be sick in the car if he diverted. It posed the driver a dilemma. The Home Secretary was technically his boss. If Nicholas was ill in the car, he would have to clear up the mess. He decided to continue to Harrow on the Hill and collect the package on the way back.

As the vehicle turned into the road with the ornate gates to one side, both Nicholas and the driver saw the local Met Police car pull into the road from the opposite end. They would both arrive at the gates simultaneously. Nicholas pointed his remote control at the gates and kept jabbing the button willing them to open. When they were in range, an orange light started to flash on one of the pillars and they began to swing leisurely open. The Police vehicle was speeding up to prevent the Ministerial car from entering.

Nicholas flung the door open of the moving vehicle and fell onto the road. As the driver saw him go, he did an emergency stop. He was bruised and his suit was torn, but it was of no consequence. Getting up, he ran through the still sluggishly opening gates leaving his red box in the car. The retired marine could not believe his eyes. The Police Officer jumped out of his car and chased Nicholas towards his house. Weighed down with a 'utility belt' laden with odd objects and wearing a stab proof vest, the driver was amazed the PC could stand, let alone run. It was no contest. Nicholas Boon was through his front door and safe.

Once inside, he went into his reception room and sat down. He was shaking from head to toe. The Police would not get in. His house had been adapted when he had been made a Minister. The glass windows could withstand bullets and minor explosions. The doors had been strengthened with steel inserts and metal rods into the jambs. There was even a panic room which could withstand more. As he assessed his situation, he realised that the object of the security was to keep him safe until Police could arrive and rescue him.

Now it was keeping them out. What could he do?

149

Monday 20th June 2011

John, Paul and Doreen sat by Paul's desk drinking tea and coffee as they awaited news. Jimmy was still running around supplying officers with exhibits and details of where they could view media. All the rooms where the kit was available were being utilised. Copies of death certificates were being obtained and funeral directors were being asked for details of any next of kin. Doctors were being solicited to supply urgent statements. Hospital pathology labs were being harassed to find any specimens of relevance they may have kept. It was organised chaos.

Paul was feeding the press who kept calling as to why the CC and Prodow were both at Chichester Crown Court where the case had been transferred to from Lewes to accommodate all parties. TV crews had been scrambled and journalists were jostling for the best positions. Some managed to get into the public gallery and totally illegally, set tape recorders in motion. Photographers were setting up step ladders behind the journalists still outside to get unobstructed shots of anyone of note entering or leaving the court.

Chris had got to court early and had seen nothing of the press. Sam had bemoaned the fact he had never been called for jury service. He was secretly jealous of his wife who had never shown any interest in having been selected. It would have given him 'bragging rights' for a whole year at work or his local pub, whatever the cases he heard. She had so far just heard one which was a case of dangerous driving.

Now she was waiting with fourteen others for the jury bailiff to collect them and take them to the court room where they were to hear their next trial. They had all been relaxing in a large room where they sat about and chatted amicably between themselves. Eventually, they were all told that they were to deliberate in a case of murder. Only twelve were to be selected and each hoped they were not one of the three rejected.

The Judge and court personnel were all gathered as the fifteen selected random members of the public stood in the well of the court. Chris had her name called first by the court clerk, and she was shown into the jury box. Eleven other people followed her and all had to swear an oath to 'try the defendant faithfully and give a verdict in accordance with the evidence given'. The three who had not been called left the court dejected.

Then the lawyers fired up.

Chris was fascinated as to the workings of the court. It was all new to her and she listened intently. The Judge told the jury he was the arbiter of the law and it would be him alone that they would defer to for such guidance. Lawyers for the Defence and Prosecution would put the 'facts' of the case according to their instructions. However, today there was going to be submissions by the Prosecution that the jury would hear. It didn't take long.

The Prosecution Counsel stated that they no longer wished to proceed with the case as it transpired that the accused, Olivia Munroe, was innocent of the charge of murder. Facts of the matter being that the Police had arrested another person where the evidence appeared overwhelming. The Defence were fully aware and had insisted on the case being heard in open court so their client could be publicly acquitted.

The Judge asked Chris to stand and instructed that she should speak on behalf of the twelve. He then directed that she should say that Munroe was innocent of murder. Chris was bemused and did what was requested. Munroe watched and listened impassively. She knew that the Police were going to ask her some questions later which she would answer truthfully.

Then the expected bombshell. Munroe had been incarcerated for over six weeks and the Defence Counsel asked for costs.

The Prosecution barrister defended the claim by calling the Chief Constable. From below his wig, the Judge raised his eyes. He'd never seen a CC in a witness box before and believed it to be a first in the Sussex Courts. The CC launched into a verbose and lengthy argument as to why costs should be refused even quoting previous stated cases from memory. The Prosecution Counsel let him speak uninterrupted. He held the court spellbound. The Judge enjoyed it. Even the Defence Counsel was impressed. Chris really enjoyed it, thinking, 'If this is the calibre of Sussex Police, we can all sleep safely in our beds.'

At the conclusion, some in the court even felt like applauding. The press had never heard such eloquence from a Police Officer in a court room. They would report it verbatim. Leaning back in his chair, the Judge glowered at the Defence Counsel as if challenging him to rise and argue his case. He rose, not to argue, but to capitulate. It was a lost cause and he knew it. Chris and the others in the jury box all sided with the prosecution and could not understand why Munroe had not spoken to the Police when she had the opportunity. It was her own stupid fault she had been locked up: 'so tough!'

The press ambushed the CC and Prodow as they left court. It was a major scrum as they all jostled for position. Other people leaving the building were knocked over and Chris was sent flying. The CC saw her as she fell and pushed past journalists with tape recorders and helped her to her feet. Cameras clicked and videos whirred. Ensuring she was ok he offered her a lift to wherever she wanted to go.

Embarrassed, she said, "Home."

A minute later, the CC's driver was by her side shepherding her to a sleek new jaguar.

After talking to the press for half an hour about Munroe, the incident on the beach with Deborah and the investigation into the serial murders, both the CC and Prodow walked the quarter of a mile back to the Police Station.

The jaguar arrived outside the small house lived in by Chris and Sam. It did not go unnoticed by local residents as the driver assisted her to her front door. Chris could not believe the CC's kindness and would write a letter of appreciation.

The press had begrudgingly started to admire the frankness and co-operation the Police were providing. The CC had raised the profile of Sussex Police a hundred-fold in just one day.

150

Monday 20th June 2011

Nicholas was a fast thinker. As a Minister of the government, he had to be. Unfortunately, he did not always make the right decision. Outside was one weighted down PC who he could outrun. The chauffeur would not get involved so posed no threat. He knew others must already have been dispatched and would be on their way. Once they arrived he knew the game would be up. Trapped inside his fortress, he could survive no more than two or three days before running out of food. There was nothing for it, he had to get out and promptly.

Running through the connecting door into his garage, he donned a crash helmet and a large motorcycle jacket. Grabbing one of his skeet shotguns from the unlocked gun cabinet, he stuffed a handful of spare cartridges in his pocket, dropping more than he kept. His motorbike was a hybrid road and trail machine and was one of his passions. He ran it once a week and kept it in pristine condition and fully fuelled. When outside he would head up to an old friend in Scotland while he decided what to do. It was all going to rely on timing to get away.

He pressed the gate release and the electric release for his garage door together. The PC heard the gate opening but had his vehicle parked across it. No car could get past. He hadn't catered for a motorcycle. The noise the motorbike made starting up in the garage was deafening but Nicholas was focused and hardly heard it. With the shotgun wedged in front of him, he roared out once the garage door had lifted sufficiently. The PC saw him coming and realised he was not able to stop him.

The two city Police cars were entering the road with blue lights and sirens screaming as they approached the gates. The PC saw the shotgun and dived for cover behind his vehicle as Nicholas hurtled past him out of the gates and away from the advancing cars. He breathed a long sigh of relief as he knew he had only just made it in time. The city cars had no chance of catching him and were updating their Control Room. Now sitting on the cold floor, the PC updated the Metropolitan Police Information Room. The retired marine was updating his supervisor in the Home Office.

*

The Home Secretary was drinking a cup of tea in her office while chatting off the record to Graham as they awaited news. Kathy burst in without knocking as Graham's mobile started to ring. Kathy updated the Home Secretary as to what had occurred according to the chauffeur and Graham listened as he was brought up to speed by the City Control Room. Both sat in silence as they took in the events relayed. The Home Secretary was the first to speak.

"Kathy. Find out if we have Nicholas's red box and if so, I want it here asap."

Kathy swiftly left the room.

Graham called his technicians.

"Where is the phone?"

"At the address. We saw him leave but the phone is still here."

"Can you get hold of it?"

"We'll try. We think it is in the Ministerial car."

"Can you pass your phone to one of the City PCs?"

"Give me a second."

"Hello sir. PC Tiverton."

"I'd like you to check if the garage is still open."

PC Tiverton cut in, *"I can confirm the door is up and still open."*

"Good. Please have a discreet look inside. The suspect had to have accessed it from the house. Therefore, I need to know if the adjoining door is still open."

PC Tiverton said, *"Please give me a few seconds sir."*

Graham heard the PC moving and voices in the background. After a short time.

"The door is ajar."

"That is the only way inside the house. It must not be shut. Can you wedge it?"

"I think I can smell gas sir. Should I go in to check? I would have to open the front door and open some windows to let any fumes escape."

"I'd hate to delay you averting any explosion. Get on with it and see me when you get back to the city."

"Yes sir" and the line went dead.

The Home Secretary said to Graham, "How the hell are we going to find him now?"

"The Met has put his number plate as a priority suspect vehicle on the ANPR system. We will know where he is soon enough and the Met has sent up one of its helicopters. Once they latch onto him it will not take long to catch him."

"Why has he run?"

"There must be something damning in his house. I've already asked my deputy to put details together in order that a search warrant can be acquired. Then we can go in and search."

Kathy knocked, waited, and then entered on command. "The red box is still in the car and the driver is bringing it back here now."

"Bring it straight to me."

"We have seen on the news that something has happened to the Chief Constable in Birmingham."

The Home Secretary turned her TV on with the sound on mute. She often found the rolling news channels had information before she did.

"Thanks Kathy. Any chance of some sandwiches?"

"On way" and she left.

It didn't take long. The scrolling 'tic a tape' reported, *Breaking News: The Chief Constable of Birmingham Police has been found dead at his home.*

"You may not agree with me Graham, but I think that's the best bit of news I've heard today. I just hope it was a clear case of suicide."

"I'm sure it was."

"I don't intend to ask how you came into possession of all the phones and any involvement you may have had directly or indirectly. I sincerely hope you and any of your colleagues and associates are not going to feature in any enquiry up there."

"I'm as much in the dark about it as you Minister."

"Let's keep it that way. I think we should let any investigation run its course. Then I want you in post and sorting that Constabulary out."

Kathy was beckoned in after a short rap on the door. "Here's Nicholas's red box Minister" and she placed it on the desk.

The Home Secretary opened it.

"He didn't even lock it."

All three peered inside. There was a mobile phone. Graham put on a pair of latex gloves and picked it up. It was the one linked to Birmingham with several calls recorded as being made to the singular number.

"That links Nicholas to the lawyer Yusef."

The Minister saw at least five manila envelopes beneath a few sheaves of Ministerial minutes.

"While you've got your gloves on, can you take those envelopes out?"

Graham took the five envelopes out and saw none were sealed.

"Come on Graham, let's see what's in them. Don't dally."

He shook the papers from the first envelope and the Minister sat back startled in her chair.

"Jesus."

Kathy said, "Oh dear God."

Graham said, "What?"

The Home Secretary said, "These are top secret papers that were for the PM's information in relation to anti-British activities by various hostile embassies and their clandestine employees. Spies if you like. This is information gathered by our security agencies. It's highly classified. Kathy typed this report at my dictation. Nicholas should not even have been aware of it."

"How did he get it then?"

They checked the contents of each envelope and they were all the same. Graham watched the two women going paler and then a small mark in the corner of one of the envelopes caught his eye. He picked up the envelope and saw in light pencil a name.

"Excuse me Minister, there is a name here."

"Let me see."

She took the envelope using a tissue and the colour drained further from her face. Kathy was looking over her shoulder. She wobbled and held the back of the Minister's chair.

"Who is he?"

Kathy said, "He is the top spy chief for the Russian Federation. If he got his hands on this, it would set us back decades."

Graham found a faint name written on each envelope. As he read them out, Kathy sat down. The Home Secretary looked as though she was about to be sick. If each envelope was passed to the named person, the potential damage to the British Government was horrendous. If Nicholas intended to sell them, he could have commanded an exorbitant fee.

Graham found himself asking again, "How did he get a copy?"

151
Monday 20th June 2011

As soon as he was on the street outside the Ministry building, Graham called his technicians who were already back at their base. They confirmed that the Met helicopter had picked up Nicholas travelling on main roads parallel to the M1. It was obvious to all that he could easily have been stopped if he had used the motorway. He was already approaching Rutland and the constabulary units being directed by the helicopter were having trouble either catching up or intercepting him. None wanted to be responsible for causing him to crash at the speed he was travelling as death would be inevitable.

The Home Secretary phoned the PM. Both set their phones to scramble the conversation.

"I don't know how he's done it, but he has a complete copy of my report to you and it looks like he was going to sell it to all our main protagonists. It would have been disastrous for us as a party and more importantly, the country as a whole. In addition, all our efforts to clean up the Midlands have been scuppered by him. When the press gets hold of this: and they will sooner or later, we will be crucified."

"Can you find out how he got a copy of that report?"

"If we get our people in to run security checks, someone will let the cat out of the bag and the press will be on us like a swarm of locusts."

"Something must be done, we can't have any potential leaks."

"Daines seems to have access to various experts who get things done and keep their mouths shut."

"If you think he can be trusted, have a word with him."

"He's just left. I'll get him back."

The PM put his scrambler phone back on its cradle. He was thoughtful. In his six years as PM he had not considered the option that was now foremost in his mind. It was something that he had been told by a security officer shortly after his elevation to the highest office. Once every three months, he was contacted by the same security officer who checked the phone lines were still working. Now he knew that the time had eventually arrived when he was going to utilise the facility.

Pulling a thin gel pad towards him he put a sheet of paper on top of it. On the paper, he wrote down his dead dog's name and the year it died followed by his daughter's two Christian names and date of birth. Whatever he wrote could not be ascertained by forensic examination of the gel pad. The paper would be destroyed later via a special shredder. Unlocking one of his top drawers, he took out a small black book. On the second page, he found the number he wanted. Using an unscrambled phone, he dialled the number.

"Yes?"

"My reference is" and he then read the numbers and letters off in reverse order.

"Call third number on scrambler" and the line cut off.

Checking his black book, he rang the third number from a list of ten on his scrambler phone.

"Password."

The PM was ready.

"Churchill1066."

"Yes Sir. What can I do for you?"

"Nicholas Boon is on the move somewhere North of London. Can you identify if he is wearing a lapel pin?"

"Wait one moment please."

There was silence for over thirty seconds.

"He has two lapel pins. His Government one and a Home Office one. The Government one is stationary at his HA (home address). The Home Office one is approaching Leicester."

"Please activate the Home Office pin urgently."

"Yes Sir. Is that all?"

"Yes."

The line cut off.

Nicholas was aware of the helicopter and believed that if he could avoid being followed by mobile units, it was only a matter of time before the helicopter would need refuelling. One thing he knew nothing about was ANPR cameras and their capabilities. He'd fired his shotgun once at the helicopter which ensured it kept at a respectful distance. It also alerted other officers to the fact he was willing to shoot if they got too close to him. They in turn were waiting for him to run short of fuel. The excessive speed he was maintaining on his machine good as guaranteed no one in a car could keep up, and the dangerous manner of his riding reinforced it.

In an office at MI5 a senior officer who had replied to the PM's call, manipulated a strange keyboard below a standalone terminal connected to an individual roof top aerial. He double checked the code number of the lapel pin. He was one hundred percent certain it was correct before he triggered the enter key followed within an obligatory five seconds by a key marked 'Confirm'. Nicholas was still wearing his tatty suit jacket under his motorcycle coat with the lapel pin in situ. A small cloud of gas escaped from it and drifted upwards towards his crash helmet. Some stuck temporarily to his clothes and a miniscule amount crept under his helmet and into his nostrils.

Within ten seconds, Nicholas's eyes watered and then his vision blurred through to blindness. His lungs were heaving and his breathing started to speed up and then he felt as though they were failing through lack of air. At ninety plus miles an hour, he had little chance. He took both hands from the handlebars and tried to rip his helmet off to get air into his lungs and clear his eyes. The machine started to wobble violently. It was impossible for him to stop it as it careered across the road into the front of a delivery van which propelled him into the air and across the small pavement and face down into a stream.

Nicholas was dead before he hit the van. The gas had dissipated completely from his lungs but left an insignificant trace in the corner of each eye. A pathologist would never spot it unless he knew what to look for. Unfortunately, Nicholas was the proud owner of so many broken bones, smashed internal organs and a shattered brain that no pathologists would bother to look any further. The helicopter crew reported they saw Nicholas lose control of the motor cycle and crash. Having videoed the whole time they had been in pursuit, the images confirmed that fact.

The gas was colourless and odourless and was invisible to the helicopter crew or their cameras.

Graham was sitting in the Home Secretary's office when Kathy walked straight in without knocking.

"The Metropolitan Police have just informed me that Nicholas has crashed. He's dead."

The Home Secretary looked furious.

"The bastard has got away from us again. Now we don't have any chance to find out what else he's been up to or how he got hold of my report."

Graham didn't care either way about his death. Thoughtfully he commented, "The advantage if there is one, is that he won't be able to tell anyone else what he's been up to."

Both the Minister and Kathy looked quizzically at Graham but neither tried validating what he meant.

The Home Secretary asked both Kathy and Graham to wait in the anti-room while she phoned the PM.

"Hello Prime Minister. I have some news about Nicholas."

"Go on?"

"Apparently he has had a fatal crash near Leicester. The helicopter crew that was following him reports he lost control of his motor bike at speed and hit a van."

"That is unfortunate. Now we shall never know the full extent of his corruption. I suppose the only silver lining in this sorry saga is that he can't tell anyone else."

"That's what Daines said."

"We need to tell the press something. May I advocate that you say he has had some sort of mental breakdown and the Police were trying to stop him for his own safety?"

"That was what I was thinking. The Police were alerted as he had documents in his possession of a secret nature. They will say that because it is true."

"Has a search warrant of his home been executed yet?"

"No, I don't believe it has."

"That needs to be furthered as a matter of urgency. Can you get Daines to expedite the matter?"

"I shall."

"Is it likely that Nicholas was working with anyone else?"

"Please: Prime Minister: I can't take the thought of that."

"It's something that must be considered. I will instruct that security in all Ministries be updated and all personnel be re-vetted. That way, nothing can be specifically attributed to your department."

"Thankyou."

"By the by Catherine, I still have confidence in the way you are running your department, and your tenure there is safe."

"Thank you, Prime Minister."

"I'll see you tomorrow after the cabinet briefing."

152
Monday 20th June 2011

The two officers who had interviewed Deborah walked into the office. It was crowded. The CC and Prodow had featured already on the news and some had seen it on the TV in the conference room and others on their smart phones.

Their entrance was spotted by Paul who shouted, "Quiet folks. We need to hear this."

Doreen was making teas and coffees for all and had dispatched a young woman PC to collect some extra cups. She tottered in carrying a chinking tray full of cups and a carton of milk supplied by the lady in the canteen.

The CC sitting behind Paul's desk saw her enter and said, "Put them on here."

The sergeant who led the interview started speaking. Everyone was listening.

"I'll precis as best I can. The tapes we have can be transcribed later. Deborah was Sally's unexpected daughter from a brief first marriage. She was not wanted nor loved as she curtailed Sally's carousing and general good time attitude. Jean, Sally's Mother, took it upon herself to raise the child who lived with her and her husband from birth till about fourteen years old. Gradually, Deborah became recalcitrant, belligerent and confrontational and Jean asked her to leave."

Prodow said, "What about Jean's husband?"

"He died when Deborah was eleven."

"Right."

"Then Deborah moved from one man to another and from place to place. Occasionally she would stay with Sally at the house in Birdham. Apparently, one night when she was there, she wanted a glass of water and went downstairs to get it. She overheard Sally and Gary talking about an old lady and saw them filling a small jar with the poison. They were talking about putting her out of her misery as they had got enough money from her."

Prodow interrupted again.

"Did she hear how they got the money?"

"Yes. Sally had managed to get the woman to sign some cheques and she had stolen her bank card."

"Simple enough. Gary has told us that was one method."

"Deborah didn't know what to do and decided to keep quiet. Time moved on and she met her current boyfriend, Haskland, in a squat in Brighton. Then she saw an article in a paper about Armstrong winning the chess competition and a picture of him. She told us he was the spitting image of Jean."

A slight murmur grew and faded just as quickly. The sergeant waited for silence.

"Jean had told her that during the war, she had been with her Father, Archie, on a train that got bombed. Her memory was clear with one fact, she had been told at the time he had been killed. She did not know where she had been going or where she had come from, other than London. Then Jean was fostered by a local clergyman and his wife here in Chichester. When Deborah showed Jean the picture, she dismissed it as her Father out of hand. The article referred to Armstrong having survived being on a train during the war which had been bombed. Deborah got it into her head it was Jean's Father using an alias for whatever reason he may have had."

The murmuring stuttered again for a few seconds.

"With her boyfriend, they hatched a plan. Deborah wanted him to suffer for deserting Jean. It was easy for her to locate him and easy to get the poison. Deborah got Gary's coat out of his van and used it as a disguise in case she was seen."

John said, "Did she know about the camera in the birdbox?"

"No. We asked that directly and she was shocked."

"So, it was just a precautionary disguise."

"Yes. So was the mud that they stuck over the number plates. It was part of their plan. The car being the same make and model as Munroe's was also a lucky coincidence for them."

Prodow said, "I'll say."

"Deborah left her boyfriend at the Murrell and drove to the bungalow. She found a key that hung on a nail at the back of the garage for the nurses to get in when the back door was locked. Apparently, it was in full view to anyone walking round the garage and it wasn't hidden or concealed in any way."

Prodow interrupted again.

"What was she going to do if there was no key?"

"Knock on the door or break in."

Sarcastically, he retorted, "Obviously!"

"Once inside she told Armstrong she was the nurse's supervisor and wanted a few words but asked if she could have a cup of tea first. She made two cups of tea and dropped the poison into Armstrong's cup. He drained his cup and then Deborah badgered him as to his identity. She became annoyed because he would not admit to her that he was Archie."

As he began to be overcome by the effects of the poison, he tried to reach the lifeline button or the phone, so she lifted his chair and pulled him out onto the floor. He was shaking about so much that Deborah put her foot on his neck until she thought he had died. Then she washed her cup and saucer in the sink with Armstrong's saucer. Back in the room, she picked up his cup and thought she saw movement in the drive so put it in a pocket. Running to the back door, she grabbed her jam jar which she had used to carry the poison from the windowsill before leaving. She locked the door and put the jam jar on the floor because it was very slippery to hold."

Jimmy piped up. "It wasn't mentioned by the lab that it was slippery."

Paul said, "I don't think it really matters now. What did she say about the diary and broken pencil?"

The sergeant continued. "That was something else we pointedly asked a couple of times. She was adamant she never saw the diary or pencil. She could not give an account for them."

"Right. Sorry. Carry on."

"When she was out she went back to the Murrell and they both had a drink and took the mud off the index plates. They stayed there till the first emergency vehicles went past."

John said, "So she knew nothing of the camera in the bird box or that Sally was getting ready to rip him off. Nor that Gary had disabled the alarm. She was one lucky killer."

The Sergeant said, "She expressed joy at his death and is confident that he was Archie."

The CC who had been sitting listening intently to the narration said, "Am I missing something here? Is it George Armstrong or Archie who has been murdered?"

Deathly silence. No one could say. Then John piped up.

"There is a simple way to find out."

"Which is?"

"Take a DNA sample from Jean and compare it to our corpse. The scientists can tell us if they are related or not. If they are: it's Archie. If not: it's George."

"Jimmy. This is your domain. Sort it."

"Yes sir."

153

Monday 20th June 2011

Simon arrived at Graham's and was permitted entry by Ian. Laura was in the kitchen with Carol creating some culinary delight. Alison had badgered John for information during the journey from Sussex which he had made her force out of him. Carol had drifted off to sleep in the car as the two Police Officers sparred with each other. Now the two were in the lounge still going hammer and tongs at each other. John was enjoying himself. Alison was getting more and more crabby.

Graham arrived in his chauffeured car and joined the company after releasing his driver at his front door. Everything settled down and they all gathered in the lounge. John had brought three good bottles of wine and Carol had assumed her normal role as mine host. It was for Simon to let the others know of any problems that may have arisen in Birmingham. Alison frowned constantly as he spoke, still harbouring a grievance he'd left without saying goodbye to her.

Simon was less than candid. He omitted more than he included. They could all see that there was obviously more to his narration, but deemed it superfluous to ask. He told them he had disabled the three guards and broken into RD's house and was talking to Mercedes when she was shot by Greg. Then he decamped believing Greg was trying to kill him. After some time, he returned to the house and found one of the guards, the DCI, had got free and was in RD's bedroom unconscious with a syringe stuck in his arm. A gun was at his feet and the woman doctor was shot through the eye. RD was on the floor, so he called for an ambulance. Grabbing the guards' guns, he ran for it. He thought it best to leave the apparent murder weapon on the floor for the Police to find.

At Yusef's, he found a window ajar and broke in to find him dying on the floor. Yusef was just able to tell him which phone was the one used to call the contact in London. He did a quick search and recovered all the phones. In the process of marking them as he put them into his bag, he heard someone else moving in the house so he bolted from there as well. Naturally he thought it was Greg who was still after him, and did not want to get entangled with him in case the Police were on their way.

Laura butted in and said, "It didn't take long to ascertain the numbers that each phone called. We have been able to identify one to the CC of the West Midlands and one to his deputy, one to the Leader of Birmingham council, one to the Clerk to the Magistrates, one to the deputy prosecutor, one to the editor of the Birmingham Newspaper, and some people running brothels in both Manchester and Birmingham. Then of course, Nicholas Boon. A couple I can't identify: two unknowns who must have disabled the phones at their ends."

Graham said, "The CC of the West Mids has committed suicide. Nicholas has died in a major road accident. Tomorrow, with the Home Secretary's authority, I shall be speaking to all these other people. I expect they will all be resigning their positions and departing the UK. A week will be ample time in my opinion, otherwise they will likely be arrested. I have been contacted by Heathrow Special Branch who have identified Greg from his TV still, as leaving under a false name for New York. The Americans are already looking for him."

John said, "That'll be some arrest if they find him."

Simon said, "He'll shoot it out, I have no doubt."

Alison couldn't help herself. "I hope they kill him and he dies in pain." Everyone in the room looked at her.

Graham recognised Simon's silence as the end of his story.

Addressing Ian, he said, "Is there anyone you know in Kent who could do a discreet security sweep of an office?"

"There is one guy but he only has one arm. Someone would have to carry his gear and set it up for him."

"Could you act as that person?"

"Yes. When would you want to do it?"

"Tomorrow night, about two ish."

"Ok. I'll arrange it with him. Where do you want to meet?"

"At the Home Office front door."

"You know there are cameras all over the place inside and outside of that building."

"I know. Can't be helped."

"Unless anyone else has anything to add, I would like to eat. Having survived on cardboard sandwiches for a couple of days, I'm likely to start losing unnecessary weight."

Simon chipped in, "Same with me" ignoring his meal at the Beefeater.

They all started to drift towards the dining room. Graham caught Alison.

"I know you suffered at Greg's hand, but please make sure you do not let your emotions get the better of you."

"Sorry Dad" but she wasn't.

After the meal, Simon who had been deliberately keeping a slight distance from Alison surrendered. With a large glass of red wine, he ambled out of the kitchen door into the freshening air of the late evening. Alison saw him go and made no pretence. She went after him. Everyone saw him leave followed swiftly by her. Graham didn't know who to pity. He knew Simon could look after himself physically but would be no match for his daughter in a full frontal verbal assault.

All the remaining group assembled in the lounge with their drinks and engaged in pleasant conversation. Simon had reached the bottom of the garden and sat on a rickety old wooden bench. He knew she was coming and was ready. She stood in front of him and launched into a tirade of abuse about him leaving without saying goodbye. He tried to butt in with his reasons, but she wasn't having any of it. When he took a sip of his wine, it seemed to spur her on. She was tiring as her body had not completely recovered and he could see that. Alison realised that she had been worried that something untoward may have happened to him and she wanted to be with him.

In her anger, she blurted it out. Tears started dripping down her cheeks. Simon was a gentleman, and rising to his feet he guided her to the bench and then sat back down next to her. It was too much. The seat had been there for twenty odd years. It collapsed under their combined weight. Simon caught her as she was falling, and she landed heavily on top of him. His wine had shot out of the glass and covered his shirt, but it was of no corollary.

"You OK?"

"No. My ribs!"

"Don't move."

"I can't. Don't make me move."

They stayed there, lying together with her on top of him. She was no longer crying. The closeness was much too much. Her lips met his. The pain in her ribs forgotten. Time passed.

"Can you move yet? They'll be wondering where we are, and I'm getting cramp down here."

"Always complaining. You implying I'm heavy?"

"Sorry."

"Stop saying you're bloody sorry. Now help me up."

"How? I'm underneath you for God's sake."

"Well I can't move. I'll try and roll off you. Just don't push me."

"I'll just lie here."

She slowly rolled off him to lie on the floor next to him. He stood up and stretched his body to get it working again.

"Don't just stand there. Help me up."

Slowly they managed to get her to her feet.

When they walked back in, no one had the temerity to ask how he came to be wearing a glass full of red wine on the front of his white shirt. Carol just handed both a fresh glass of wine and left it at that.

154

Tuesday 21st June 2011

Come the bewitching hour, all bar Graham had left. John and Carol together in the old Vauxhall and Alison and Simon in the still unreported Audi, were heading for Chichester. Ian and Laura, his young apprentice, were heading for Kent. Each had sprayed their number plates as a matter of security. Having been told by Alison that she wanted to go home to renew her acquaintance with her erstwhile feline Hannibal, John was grateful he was in for a relatively peaceful night. What she and Simon got up to was a matter for them.

Seven in the morning saw John in his usual seat stuffing himself with his regular choice of breakfast. Jimmy joined him and put a large manila envelope on the table before going to the servery. Sitting opposite John, he slid a coffee towards him and then slurped his own beverage noisily.

John emptied his mouth. "You have my undivided attention Jimmy. What is in it?"

"The result."

"I thought so."

"I haven't opened it yet."

"Did the scientist tell you the result?"

"No."

"I am extremely impressed that you have not looked."

"I want to give it to the Chief for him to see first."

"He's due in the office soon. Shall we go upstairs."

Both made their way to the office and spoke with Paul. The office was packed with people writing reports and filling forms. All the phones were being utilised by detectives seeking information. Then Prodow and the CC strode in. A hush descended and Jimmy, with a flourish before either had a chance to speak or sit down, produced the envelope.

"Good morning sir. I have here the result from the scientist. I have not looked, I believe that you should be the one to open it."

The CC took the proffered envelope and put it on Paul's desk. If Jimmy thought he could milk an occasion, he was a rank amateur compared with the Chief.

"Doreen. I am desperate for a cuppa. As keeper of the accoutrements, what's the chances?"

"I think I can manage that" and she set about boiling the kettle.

Those that had worked with the CC before knew he wouldn't open the envelope until he was ready. Others were impatient to know. They were all going to have to wait. Doreen took her time and a few stragglers managed to force their way into the crowded room. Supping his tea, the CC picked up the envelope. Turning it over with his free hand, he put it back on the desk.

It was like a football match where the crowd surged forward in anticipation of their team scoring and then settled back down again when their side was frustrated. He put his cup down and picked up the envelope. This time, he stuck his finger under the flap and prised it open and removed the single sheet of paper. Looking at it, he slowly shook his head.

"Well I'll be."

Then he put the paper back into the envelope. The silence was deeper than space.

"While everyone is here, I would like to thank you all for your work in relation to our two serial killers. I know you are working flat out to find out how many they have murdered. It must be traumatic for some of you." He picked up his tea. "I have been told that Murray will be transferred today to St Richard's hospital, and our traffic department will facilitate his journey." Looking at Groves, "I presume you agree?"

"Yes sir."

"For information of you all," and he sipped his tea as they all inched slightly forward, "the statement of Munroe came in last night. She has said that she had been promised £5000 to assist our victim to die and the final £1000 was awaiting her at the bungalow. One presumes that was the £1000 found during the search. Apparently, he was in so much pain, he was desperate. She was going to supply him a concoction of barbiturates, that were also delivered with this statement: which taken altogether with alcohol would have achieved his goal. Therefore, she has admitted an offence of preparing to assist a suicide. I, with Mr Prodow, have consulted the CPS and it has been agreed that it would not be in the public interest to prosecute." He sipped his tea again as the gathered officers considered the decision.

"Good. I think that's all. If there's anything else?"

The harshness of the noise was nearly deafening.

"What? Oh, the result?"

Various officers could take no more. Discipline and self-restraint flew out of the window. The CC didn't mind. In fact, he quite enjoyed it. He picked the envelope back up and removed the paper.

Like a TV host, "The result is in. Our corpse was not related to Jean. Therefore, we must assume it was George Armstrong."

A slow hum developed as more and more started to talk to each other. They all now knew that Deborah had without doubt killed the wrong man.

Paul took the paper and envelope from the CC.

Doreen, who was standing by her desk and next to Prodow and the CC said to him, "You can still command an audience."

He just winked at her and smiled. His appointment later with the Police Authority was going to be just as much fun. Everything had started to come together well.

Sussex Police seemed to be riding on the crest of a wave and he was the top surfer.

155

Wednesday 22nd June 2011

At 1.55am, Graham walked up to the main entrance of the Home Office carrying his briefcase. Then at 1.58am he was joined by Ian and Victor who were carrying three cases between them. The two security officers sitting at the reception desk just inside had watched them all arrive via their CCTV screens and became instantly worried. At exactly 2am, the Home Secretary entered the foyer from within the building and spoke briefly to them. It had a calming effect and they opened the door. All three entered and were logged into the building under pseudonyms before following the Minister to her office.

Once in her sanctum, Ian placed a twelve-inch square silver box just three inches deep on her desk and turned it on. Nothing lit it up. There were no listening devices active within her office. Graham introduced both Ian and Victor to her. With little pre-amble, Victor asked if he could place one of the cases on her desk and she cleared some room to allow it. When he clipped the lid up, she saw it was filled by a stainless steel unit with various lights, dials and switches. They all burst into life as Victor put a long round key with angled teeth into a hole and turned. The Home Secretary sat behind her desk watching. She and Graham were mere onlookers as Ian and Victor spoke in technical gobbledegook to each other. Ian had opened both other cases that were on the floor with their lids resting against the desk.

Victor only had one arm and hence one hand. It was all he seemed to need. Ian, at his request, passed him what looked like an old fashioned microphone on the end of a wire. He plugged it into a socket in the main case and hit a switch. A couple of dials twitched before returning to their resting position.

"Interesting."

Being handed an A5 size box he turned another switch on and walked the perimeter of the room.

"Very interesting."

He spoke directly to the Home Secretary. "Whose office is on the other side of that wall?"

"My personal secretary. Kathy."

"Can I have a look in there?"

"Yes. Is there a problem?"

"I'm not sure yet."

The Home Secretary handed Victor a couple of keys on a fob from a desk drawer.

"These are master keys. Please don't disturb anything."

"I won't need to."

"Be aware the security men walk this floor when they know I am still here."

He left the room as the Home Secretary, Ian and Graham indulged in general chit chat about Nicholas and his antics.

Graham confirmed that Nicholas's house had been searched under the auspices of a search warrant, and took from his briefcase a bundle of papers.

"I attended the search myself with two colleagues who are beyond reproach. We recovered these papers which we believed may be of interest to you. As yet, we have not recorded the fact we removed them. Should you want me to, I will."

The Home Secretary flipped through them checking the titles or headings.

"Have you taken copies of these?"

"No. A silly oversight on my part."

"Nicholas should not have had these. In fact, they should never have left this building."

"Well as they are no longer in my possession, and in their rightful place, there is nothing I need to record."

"Thank you" and the Home Secretary put them into a drawer and locked it pocketing the key.

Ian said, "I happened to be in the area when the search was taking place, and was able to have a look at his phone. There were no calls of note. They seemed to be all personal friends. I am still going through a couple of his old bills which show the numbers he called. If any transpire to be of interest, you will be the first to know."

"Thank you."

A noise came to them from the hall. It wasn't Victor. The Home Secretary said, "Damn. I'll go and fend him off." She was up quickly, and left the room. After a short conversation, she returned to her office. The security guard left.

A couple of minutes later, Victor walked back into the office and put a very small chip onto the desk next to his case. They all looked at it. He was passed a little metal box from a case on the floor which Ian opened up for him. Connecting the one wire to his desk case, he put the chip into a slot. The machine in the main case started to whirr. Dials started to move.

"I thought so."

The Home Secretary said, "What?"

"I took this chip out of the computer next door."

"What, Kathy's computer?"

"Yes. Don't worry. It shouldn't have been there. Someone had planted it there, and I think I heard you talking to the culprit."

"I only spoke to the guard."

"Yes. I know. This chip records some sound and which keys are pushed on the keyboard. It's called 'key logging'. Then it uses the host computer's wi fi to send its signal. Kathy had left her computer switched on."

"Yes. She always does so any e-mails go straight to her inbox whatever the time of day or night. Her computer and mine are linked, so I can see what has been sent. Oh no. Tell me they can't get into my computer through hers?"

"'Fraid they can, and they have."

"So anything I type or Kathy types can be seen?"

"No. Only what she types. I knocked the computer when I was unscrewing it which probably alerted the guard. As he arrived, I was able to get the mobile phone number that the chip sent the sound alert to. It was within five yards so could only have been the guard or you. I'll have to work on this chip to find where the main signal is sent. It shouldn't take more than an hour or so."

The Home Secretary slumped back in her chair.

"If that was in her computer. Why didn't the security scan find it?"

"Probably because it was turned off and did not have any output that could be detected. The guard could always let the main receiver know when there was to be a scan and they would disable it."

Ian said, "Yes. Logical."

Victor continued, "The guards phone will have an app on it which is connected to the bug. Get hold of the phone and Ian could find it and prove it in seconds."

The Home Secretary said, "How do you propose that we do that?"

Victor said, "That's out of my remit."

All in the room turned to Graham.

"I don't know. Other than by arresting him."

The Home Secretary said to Victor, "Is that the only problem?"

"I need to get into your printer room."

"One of those keys will do it. It's the room next to Kathy's."

Victor stepped out into the corridor. The hair on the back of his neck stood up to attention. He knew he was being watched and moved back into the office.

"The guard is watching. I need an excuse to go into the room."

The Home Secretary said, "I 'll print something for you to go and collect" and she tapped a few keys on her keyboard.

In the stillness of the night, the noise the printer made as it woke up and disgorged a few sheets of paper echoed about the corridor.

Both she and Victor stepped into the corridor.

"The printer is the second door on the right and the loo is further along round the corridor. It's marked."

Victor thanked her and started towards the toilet. He knew the guard would have to back a lot further off to prevent detection. The guard had other ideas and was already in the toilet when Victor arrived.

"Hello. Unusual for the Home Secretary working so late."

"Yes. We were meant to have arrived earlier but got delayed. She wanted to see us before tomorrow's disabled servicemen's lunch. She's the main speaker."

"I see. Without being rude, what happened to you?"

"Afghanistan."

"Not good."

"Were you military?"

"No. I worked in prisons."

"Just as bad. Anyway. Got to pick up her speech. See you" and Victor walked out.

The guard wasn't sure. His phone had let him know there had been a noise in Kathy's office. It had been a slight noise. He couldn't say if it had been verbal because the chip wasn't that good. Could have been the cat that frequented the building. How would it have got in? The door was locked. When he checked it: it had been. Maybe a mouse. He'd often seen them scuttling away when he did his rounds. Checking his watch, he realised he'd been too long. His fellow guard would be getting anxious. A mouse. Definitely. Running back to the foyer, he made the excuse he'd been caught short. An excuse that nearly always worked.

His colleague who was as straight as the day was long, said, "I'll have a wander round. I need to stretch my legs. Is everything ok with the Minister?"

"Yeah. They are talking about some do for ex-military personnel tomorrow. You were a squaddie, weren't you?"

"I was. I haven't heard of any do. Then again, I'm not disabled." Then with his shoulders back, stomach in, he marched towards the lift to imaginary marshal music. The guard watched him go. As soon as he was out of sight, he rang a memorised number on his mobile.

All he said was "I think we have a problem at the Home Office. Three people will be leaving shortly."

It was enough.

In the Minister's office, Ian was casually watching a screen on a piece of kit that he had brought. The oscilloscope oscillated. It attracted his thorough attention. A line flew across and then returned to normal. Within a matter of seconds, a number scrolled onto an LED screen.

"Now what?"

"Someone within fifty metres, ie: in this building, has just made a call lasting less than seven seconds. I'll have the number and what was said in a few more."

A paper printout scrolled from his machine. Just three inches long and an inch wide. He read out the line. The Minister was nearly apoplectic. Graham and Ian were not in the least bit daunted even though the message concerned them. When Ian confirmed it was a phone line listed as belonging to the South African Consulate, she let more expletives fly than they had heard for years.

156
Wednesday 22nd June 2011

Victor was soon to dispense more bad news. He walked back into the office and placed another chip on the desk. It was too much for the Home Secretary.

"Where the fuck was that?"

"In your printer. Everything that was printed was sent via wi fi. Basically, whoever has done this had no need to bug your office. They had access to everything they wanted. The only thing they hadn't got was what was said in here."

Ian added, "A security sweep of this office would probably find any listening devices whether turned on or off. It wasn't worth the risk. Although Kathy's office would be swept, it would not attract as much scrutiny as yours."

"It will in future."

The guard did not know what to do. He sat behind the reception desk. Within easy access close to his knees on a shelf was a Sig Sauer P226 semi-automatic handgun. It was a standard issue military firearm and he had been trained how to use it. There was no way he was going to shoot anyone in cold blood. Having been a prison officer, he knew what the inside of a prison was like and if caught he was going to become an inmate. He could probably survive a short prison term, but murder meant life.

Outside, two patrolling Policemen laden down with body armour, MP5 machine guns and side arms as well as tasers, handcuffs and radios ambled past. The gun under the desk was in case some idiot actually got past them and into the building. It was like the last line of defence.

The clock had crept unstoppably to just prior to 4am. Scotland Yard was within half a mile and the two officers decided they had time to walk the complete length of the building just one more time before they were relieved. Engrossed in conversation, only one of them noticed a black cab pull up against the pavement some fifty yards short of the building in Marsham Street. Sodium street lights lit wisps of smoke as they twirled into the early morning's air from the exhaust. Casually, he informed his fellow officer. They were both getting on in service and instinctively knew when something was wrong.

One of them spoke to the Yard's protection team's Control Room on his 'Airwave' radio. There were more armed officers within a mile's circumference than the rest of London put together, and they all heard the transmission. Three vehicles which were managing the reliefs and had four similarly armed officers in each drifted towards the Home Office. In the back of the taxi, the hit man waited for three people to leave the building. His driver, who was also armed, told him they would attract attention if they stayed too long in the same place. They could afford to move by going around the block as a car with another hit man in slowly cruised by. The officers heightened senses quickly ensured they spotted the car.

Inside the office, Graham phoned the City Police Control Room and asked them to arrange with the Met for protection officers to see the group out of the building. He was quickly phoned back and brought up to date with what was happening outside. Speaking to the senior officer at Scotland Yard, it was agreed that a 'hard stop' be invoked by the protection officer's red marked vehicles. Graham had a thought, and bounded along to the lift and down to the foyer. He stood looking out of the front door. Both security guards approached him.

"I think my driver should be here shortly."

The disreputable guard walked off. Upstairs, Ian noticed another short burst on his machine.

"They will be leaving any minute now."

Outside both the taxi and the car quickly made their way to the front entrance. Not one other vehicle was in the street, parked or moving. The taxi stopped directly outside the front door with the rear window wide open and the car a few yards further behind. There was not an ounce of subtlety.

Stepping back to stand next to Graham the guard said, "Is this your car?"

The Police vehicles suddenly swept round from the side roads. Two came out of Romney Street against the one-way system and one pulled up sharply behind the car as the other slithered to a halt alongside both the car and the taxi. The third, at speed, screeched into Marsham Street from Great Peter

Street and swerved across the road and bonnet on to the front of the taxi a few seconds later. Neither vehicle could move. Officers decamped from the vehicles brandishing their weapons.

Graham sprang onto the guard knocking him off his feet shouting, "They are going to start shooting. Get down."

The man in the back of the taxi raised a fully automatic machine gun. He pointed it in the general direction of the officers from the front facing lead Police vehicle and pulled the trigger. Twenty bullets were gone in less than two seconds. Three pairs of shots slammed into him from three different officers. Each of the individual rounds would have proved fatal.

Four officers were on the floor having collected a bullet apiece. Not one had a life threatening, or serious injury. The driver was pulled unceremoniously from his seat in the taxi and thrown brutally on the floor. An irate officer pushed his head hard against the road knocking him out.

The officers surrounding the car had less trouble. Both the driver and his backseat passenger sat in the vehicle with their hands on the top of their heads. Having heard the shooting at the taxi, officers approached the vehicle with extreme caution. Not one lowered his weapon. They carefully opened the back door of the car and saw a machine gun resting across the man's legs. One officer removed the gun and the man was searched in situ. An automatic handgun was found in a shoulder holster.

"Before we go any further officers, I must inform you that we have diplomatic immunity."

An officer replied, "That's as may be. First you are going to get out of the vehicle and lie face down on the ground with your fingers interlocked above your head. Or of course, you can object and make a sudden movement and I will shoot you. Your choice."

The man complied and was thoroughly searched. His driver was even more complicit. Graham seemed to struggle up and helped the guard to his feet.

"That was close. We must step forward as witnesses."

He opened the door and called to an officer who seemed to be in charge.

Identifying himself, he spoke quickly to him.

The officer said, "The ambulances will be here soon so I will arrange for a statement to be taken immediately."

A uniform protection officer sat at the reception desk and started the longest, most pointless statement he had ever taken. Outside was pandemonium. Graham bounded up the stairs, too much in a hurry to wait for the lift. Inside the Home Secretary's office, he found Ian and Victor packing up their kit.

"Ian, I've got the guard's phone but he doesn't know so I've got to get it back to him pronto" and passed a new type smartphone to him.

Grabbing a piece of kit back out of his case, Ian connected a wire to the phone and hit a button.

Three minutes dragged slowly by, then Ian disconnected the wire and tossed the phone back to Graham.

"I've cloned it so I can see what he's been up to at my leisure."

Graham was off again back down the stairs. Arriving in the foyer, he slowed to a walk. As he passed the reception desk where the guard was going through what he saw, "What's that" loud enough to be heard. He walked towards the door and bent down. Standing back up he showed the phone and said, "It's a phone. It's not mine. Someone must have dropped it."

The guard patted his inside jacket pocket and knew instantly it was his.

"It's mine."

Graham handed it to him.

The prisoners, as they currently were, were taken to Paddington Green Police Station. Senior officers at Scotland Yard began searching the diplomatic register for the names given by the three remaining assassins and finally found them in the list pertaining to South Africa. They all had to be released. Whatever the Police thought, they had no choice. Due to the fact there was a corpse lying in the mortuary at St Thomas's Hospital, a Chief Superintendent spoke to all three before they left.

"He is a colleague of yours. You can collect the body later today, or we will arrange for it to be disposed of. I am sure the Prime Minister will be having words later with your Ambassador. Now get out!"

Graham, Ian and Victor left the building as the Home Secretary woke the Prime Minister.

157

Friday 1st July 2011

Every officer from the Armstrong enquiry and those engaged with the Simpsons were seated in the conference room. There were uniform officers who had played minor parts and PCSOs and some civilian staff who had inputted information at one time or another. They were all facing three empty chairs. Some were chatting excitedly about the cases as others were holding their own opinions. One had his eyes closed and appeared to anyone who noticed, to be asleep. The temporary incident room above them was deserted and the answerphone was active.

Alison was there. She had explained her injuries to those inquisitive enough to ask as having been sustained falling down some stairs while suffering from food poisoning. It was a sufficiently adequate explanation.

Murray was sitting to one side in a wheelchair with Doreen acting as his carer. He had been carried up the one flight of stairs in his wheelchair by a team of four laughing male detectives. They had wobbled about so much, he had become more frightened than at any time in his entire career.

As the hands of the wall clock moved to 6pm with a slightly louder tick, the CC, followed by Prodow and Groves, marched into the room. Everyone except Whiles jumped up.

Groves called loudly to him. "Oscar. Just for once, do you think you could make an exception."

His eyes flipped opened. Smiling, "Sorry Sir. I was miles away," and he struggled to his feet. Prodow, Paul and Jimmy began to applaud and were joined by many others. Alison was amazed to see him turning a slight shade of red through embarrassment.

The CC was amused. "That Mr Groves is an effective way of dealing with the obdurate. Something you have picked up lately I notice."

John went redder still.

"Now please be seated. I have called this extraordinary meeting at the request of Mr Prodow and Mr Groves. I want first to bring you all up to date with where we are at the moment. In conjunction with the CPS, numerous charges have already been laid. For those that don't know, I shall summarise the main ones in chronological order. Deborah, who has taken to using her great grandfather's last name of Andrews, has been charged with the murder of George Armstrong. When he is fit enough Maurice Haskland, her boyfriend, will also be charged with murder. That will likely as not be dropped to accessory if he pleads to it in court. Both have a nice little additional charge of conspiracy to murder. One of my favourite charges. Shame it will probably be dropped as well.

Deborah has been shown the DNA results that proved it was Armstrong who had been murdered rather than Andrews. She is still refusing to accept the fact.

Coming on now to the Simpsons. As a result of the assistance given to Mr Groves by Gary, there are at the present time fifty plus charges against him of accessory to murder, various fraud offences and the main one, grievous bodily harm to Murray."

Looking directly at Murray, "Nice to see you back in the land of the living Murray. Welcome to the world of murder enquiries."

Carrying on, "Sally Simpson has been charged with fifty plus murders and there will be more to come. She is also facing numerous fraud charges. It seems she has started to accept the inevitable and is beginning to assist. There are various other minor offences I won't bore you all with. Now you are all up to speed on the main charges, I understand Mr Groves requires you all to put your thinking caps on."

"The floor's yours Mr Groves" and the CC sat down.

Groves stood up as Prodow was scribbling feverishly in his collection of murder books.

"Ladies and gentlemen. We have some unresolved problems with regards to the murder of George Armstrong. In the past, we have found that consulting team members have resulted in successful conclusions. I appreciate we are no longer in school, but it may assist to see and hear individuals if they raise their hands as opposed to calling out. We are willing to consider any response, no matter how outlandish, providing it does not involve the supernatural."

A small titter ran around the room.

"You all know the small diary which was found by George's body had nothing written inside it except the word 'Pois' which we believe was the start of the word 'Poisoned'. If anyone has any other thought, now is the time to put it forward." He looked about the room.

No hands rose.

"Right. It looks like we are all happy with that. How about the broken pencil?"

John looked towards Alison and nodded to her. She raised her hand.

"Yes?"

"The pencil was broken by it being smashed onto the stone slab. A lead mark is clearly seen in the original video footage by the photographer. In the cavity beneath were the papers about Archie Andrews. Maybe in his death throws, George was trying to give us a clue as to who had done it. i.e. Deborah Andrews"

Prodow cut in. "That's a fair assumption. How would you explain Deborah letting him write the word and then break the pencil?"

"I'm struggling with that."

Several hands shot up. One of the scientists was amongst them.

Groves pointed to him and said, "Yes. What do you think?"

"She wasn't there. In some cases, it is possible that a person would take some time to die. Deborah has stated that she put him on the floor and kept her foot on his back until she believed him to have died. He may have passed out and she believed him dead and left. Then he came round and wrote in the diary and broke the pencil. She is adamant that she did not even see the diary."

Groves looked at Prodow and said, "I like that. That then beggars the thought: where and how did he get such an old and out of date diary?"

No hands. Groves was about to move on when he noticed a young uniform officer towards the back of the room with his hand hovering about level with his shoulder. It hadn't gone right up, but nor had it gone down. He obviously wasn't sure.

"I'm sorry, I don't know your name. Do you have an idea?" Groves pointed directly at him.

"PC Abrahams sir. I don't know really if it's relevant or not."

"Go for it," came the reply from the CC.

"I was one of the original PoLSA team. I was the officer who bagged the diary. When I put it in the exhibit bag, I noticed the cover was coated in dust.

As I was searching under the electric fire in the fire place, I saw loads of dust. I have a feeling that there was a little square with no dust in. Maybe the diary was under the fire?"

Prodow was scribbling for all he was worth.

"Did you disturb the dust?"

"I don't think so."

Groves looked about the room for a SOCO and the photographer. "Gents your services are required. Jimmy. Where are you?"

"Here gov. I'll arrange it ASAP" and he sat back down next to a pretty WPC.

"Don't be shy people. That is the sort of thing we need to hear."

"Good work Abrahams" from the CC was praise indeed.

"Anyone else got any thoughts about it?"

No one else twitched.

Groves asked, "Our next problem PC Abrahams is why did he have Andrews documents and the firearm?"

"I'm sorry sir. I don't know."

"Shame. You were doing so well."

Paul said, "Doreen, Murray and I had a vague idea about that." He was above raising his hand.

"Yes?"

"We know Andrews died during the war when he had been on a train going to Pompy. Armstrong had made it known at sometime that he had been on a train that had been bombed. The media found that out. If they had been on the same train, in the confusion George may have picked up Andrews things. Overall, we have come to the conclusion it is something that will remain unsolved."

"Anyone want to add their thoughts?" Groves looked about the room.

No one responded.

"Another niggling little problem is the matter of the key found in the Micra of Haskland by PC Robertson. Deborah has told us it was on the hook at the rear of the garage. Yet Jimmy has a key also. Anyone know where it came from?"

A hand shot up.

"Go on?"

"PC Britlan sir. I was the first officer at the scene. Mr Chaplain had gone into the bungalow using his key. He was a keyholder for Mr Armstrong in cases of emergency."

"Thank you. That clears that up."

Groves looked at Prodow. "I think that covers our main problems."

Prodow nodded, but kept writing.

"Now I would appreciate your indulgence in this matter. Please chat amongst yourselves for a few minutes and see if you can come up with any ideas. While you are at it, please also consider the Simpsons and anything you would like to bring up."

There was a general hubbub for some five minutes before Groves brought the room back to order.

Various ideas were proffered by officers mainly relating to the Simpsons which were duly noted by Prodow who was developing writer's cramp. Paul jotted a few notes to jog his memory later.

The CC stood up. "Doreen, can you pass my bag please."

Doreen passed a large bag forward that clinked loudly.

"If anyone of you is teetotal, I recommend you leave now."

Not one person moved.

Bottles of spirits were placed on a desk and all the glasses that the canteen had were recovered from a cupboard where Doreen and Jimmy had previously stored them.

"Help yourselves people. You all deserve it. I think PC Abrahams gets first look in with a young PC Robertson closely behind. May even follow in his Father's footsteps one day if he puts his bloody mind to it."

PC Robertson whispered under his breath, "Thanks Dad" which elicited a few laughs from those immediately seated around him.

"One word of caution. Do not get nicked for drink driving. I won't bail you out."

158
Sunday 3rd July 2011

John listened intently to what Graham said. It was a satisfactory result all round. The CC of the West Midlands was dead as was Nicholas. No more leaks going North to Birmingham from London. Graham was to take control of the West Midlands Constabulary with due haste on 11th July.

"I'm looking forward to it John. I've been up to see how things are going. I have told them I will be making changes. The IPCC have been investigating the murders committed by the rogue DCI and have good as finalised their conclusions. It looks like they are saying he had some sort of mental problems."

"What about his murder?"

"They have solved that. They know it was Grigoriev from the three main witnesses and the hospital CCTV. His photo has been plastered in every newspaper up there and on all the TV channels. They have issued a warrant for his arrest. Mind: it looks like he's legged it to America. The only thing they haven't got clear is a motive. They know, or should I say believe, that he was acting on behalf of the CC. That does not seem to be troubling them though."

"Do you think Simon will feature at all in any of the investigations in Birmingham?"

"From what I've been told so far, he hasn't featured anywhere. It looks like they concluded rather quickly that the killer was without doubt the DCI and his killer Greg. They seem to be trying to wrap the case up asap."

"That would be a good result."

"I think so."

"What happened to RD?"

"Last I heard, he was at death's door in hospital. One of the uniform PCs who

found him on the floor, untangled all his bedding and accidentally pulled out the drip which was keeping him alive."

"He won't be missed."

"I'm sure there will be someone ready to step into his shoes. There invariably is."

"What about his wife?"

"Jacqueline. She's staying put in New York. IPCC is trying to have her extradited. Doubt whether they will get too far with that."

Alison would like to see her come back. She has decided that she was the person responsible for her kidnapping."

"She may well be right. I think the only person alive who knows the complete truth is Simon. He may choose to tell her one day. He may even tell us, but I think it unlikely."

"You know they are seeing a lot of each other?"

"She's told me. I like the idea. So does Ginger and his missus. I think he might actually be able to keep her under control."

"Two hopes!" John quipped.

"You are probably right there. What's happening with the two serial killers you've unearthed?"

"I've lost track of how many they have killed. It's about fifty at the last count and loads of others seriously injured. The enquiry will run for months."

"You going to stay in Sussex or head back to the Yard?"

"I don't know yet. I miss the Yard."

Graham understood what he meant. When he had left the Met for the City, he often thought of all the good times he had there.

"How has the incident at the Home Office gone down?"

"The PM went ballistic and threatened to expel the whole South African consulate staff. I think when he calmed down it ended up as a rebuke for the Ambassador and the three remaining killers kicked out of the country. The security service will be dealing with the guard."

"How did the Home Secretary take it?"

"Overall, not badly. She has promised that she will try and arrange some additional funds for Kent in recognition for what they have done."

"That would make a lot of people happy."

159

Sunday 3rd July 2011

As they were speaking, RD was sitting up in his hospital bed in Birmingham's main hospital. He should have died, and he knew it. There was a nurse straightening his bedding.

"Whenever I have needed hospital treatment in the past, I always went private. What the doctors and you nurses have done for me will be well rewarded. I won't forget it."

The nurse paused her ministrations.

"Mr Davies. When you can get out of that bed and walk unaided, that will be reward enough."

She left his side room. He watched her go. As she shut the door, he picked up a mobile phone that one had purchased for him.

He dialled an American number from memory. It was one he had occasionally used in the distant past. There was the usual delay before he heard the tell-tale single buzz every other second in his ear of the phone ringing over a thousand miles away. It was the middle of the night and the person was disturbed during some scarce, unusual and energetic bedroom pleasures. He checked his caller display and saw an unknown English phone number. Less than a dozen people throughout the world knew his number but when it rang he knew it was lucrative to answer.

Cursing under his breath, he said, "Hold your horses Jackie, I've got to answer this. I'll be back in a minute. Keep it warm."

Totally naked, he tiptoed out of his bedroom sweating slightly from his exertions, and into his lounge. Collapsing into an easy chair, he pushed the button to answer.

"Mike. It's Richard. RD."

"Jesus. I thought you were dead."

"I've been laid low for five years, but I'm back now."

"Good to hear from you man. What can I do for you?"

"Are you still in the extermination business?"

"Sure am. Might be getting older, but still keep my hand in."

"I've got two for you. One definitely your side of the pond, and the other could be anywhere."

"Should tell you, the price is a lot higher now from last time. Ten K straight job. Anything else, negotiable."

"Won't be a problem. Money to same place?"

"Yep. No change there."

"It'll be in your account within the week."

"Ok. Who's the first?"

"Jacqueline. Jackie. My traitorous wife."

Mike glanced towards the bedroom door.

"How do you want it done?"

"I want her to suffer. The longer the better. She'll be at my pad in Manhattan or screwing some poor sap."

Mike looked back towards the bedroom.

"Extra Five K and I'll film it if you want?"

"Sure. You know where to send it."

Mimicking RD. *"Won't be a problem."*

"The next is a guy in the same profession as yourself, so be careful."

"Go on?"

"I don't know him. He was working for Jackie. His name is Greg or Grigoriev. Get hold of some English newspapers. They have pictures of him and full description. Just waste him."

"Once I find him. It will be done."

"Cheers Mike."

"Great to be back doing business with you."